D0660806

SON of a BITCH

Jason B. Sheffield

**Michael Terence
Publishing**

First published in paperback by
Michael Terence Publishing in 2017
www.mtp.agency

This book is inspired by actual events but is a
fictionalized account of them. Neither the words spoken
by the characters nor the actions taken by them should
be attributed to any real-life persons, living or dead. Any
resemblance is purely coincidental.

www.jasonbsheffield.com

ISBN 978-1-9998366-1-0

To my mother, whom I love with all my heart.

SON of a BITCH

Jason B. Sheffield

One:
St. Benjamin And The Dragon Lady

I liked it when people lied to me. I saw it as an opportunity. And they saw it in me. The way my head would tilt down and cause my eyes to glare out from beneath my heavy brows. The way my lips parted and moistened. I became adept at extracting the twisted, contorted truth and laying it on the table in all its beautiful, bloody glory. Such was the life of a criminal defense trial lawyer.

Clients were the worst. When it came to admitting their guilt, they always said they didn't do it. It was many a day I thought to myself, Holy shit, I must be the only lawyer on the planet who represents only innocent people.

It was quite silly really, to act as if they were unaware of the direct question I asked them: Did you do it or not? They would work the "poor me" angle and convince themselves that in order to get out of trouble they had to convince me to believe they were innocent before I would actually work hard to "get them off."

Can you imagine? A criminal defense attorney needing to *believe* their client was innocent before they would represent them? The Founding Fathers would just die... again.

I did not appreciate the charade. I had traded on promises of innocence entirely too many times before, when a client later confessed of their "misstatement." Even as a new lawyer – which I was at thirty-two-years-old – I quickly developed a keen way of bypassing the "innocence" charade. I would not be made a fool of.

My latest client, who happened to be an attorney, was a bit different. She was the famed Mafia lawyer, Carter "The Dragon Lady" Scales, who was facing an excruciating professional embarrassment and possible disbarment after being caught *in flagrante delicto a la fellatio* with one of her clients, a reputed crime boss named Antonio De Silva. Said encounter between attorney and client took place at the mobster's residence at the time – a federal penitentiary – where he was serving two life sentences for racketeering and conspiracy. She was caught in the act.

With Ms. Scales, the truth had come out before I even asked. It was more like a blurted confessional that needed to be heaved from the body like vomitus after a night of heavy drinking. Instead of total *mea culpa*, though, she filled the room with hot air and excuses. It was when she said she didn't plan it, that I saw an opening to have a little fun. I was not about to let her get away with it.

"I see," I said, folding my arms in my lap. "Let's break that down, shall we?"

"I don't understand," she said. At fifty-six, Carter Scales had exacting blue eyes.

"How far in advance did you set up your visit with your client, Mr. De Silva?" I asked her.

"About a month," she said. "Why?"

"You had been to the prison before, I assume."

"Yes, several times. And why?" She had a new irritation in her voice.

"I'm sure you were escorted to see your client?"

"Yes."

"And there was a guard nearby, right?"

"Yes. Sitting outside the door."

"You knew you couldn't lock the door and that he could come in at any moment," I said.

She got a sense of where I was going and crossed her arms. "What's your point?" she deadpanned.

I ignored her question and asked my next one. "In fact, you actually knew this particular guard, didn't you?" I said.

"I did, yes. So."

"He trusted you?"

"As much as any officer trusts any attorney, I guess," she said.

"You knew he would give you a private room - not relegate you to some community station with other visitors, right? 'Come on in, Ms. Scales. Your room is waiting,' right?"

"Yes, I knew all of those things! So what!" she said.

"But you say that this wasn't planned – that it just happened!" My voice raised a little. "You *knew* before you made your reservations to fly out there you were going to do it! It *had* to be planned!"

Ms. Scales worked fast to gain her composure. "I mean, I knew it was not something I should do and, actually, I had decided that it was wrong for any lawyer to manipulate the system like that but-"

Her words irritated me and I snapped: "Was this revelation *before or after* you put your client's penis in your mouth?"

She stopped and threw daggers at me. "Benjamin Jacob Scales!" she exclaimed.

I paused on her use of my middle name. Historically,

it meant I was in big trouble. I grimaced. "Sorry, mother."

How I got to this point is a long, strange saga. Fifteen years ago, before I was a lawyer, before college even, my mother and I had a huge blowout, and I'd been estranged from her ever since. But now, over the course of our attorney-client meetings and strategy sessions, I'd come to understand her better - her feelings and motivations - something I, as a self-absorbed teenager, wasn't capable of back then.

My mother had spent three decades crafting her practice to cater to one of the most enviable clientele in the nation. With tenacity, she became the famed hired gun for some of the nation's most notorious gangsters – not the ones who yell "bitch" and "ho" as they rap the latest number-one hip-hop single; rather, her clients were consistently featured on the front page of *The Wall Street Journal* or *The New York Times* for cutting out a man's tongue or sticking a fork through a guy's neck for not paying his dinner tab – The Mafia. While I despised my mother's career choice, I despised her clients even that much more.

Her current predicament was the culmination of splintering life circumstances and bad logic that congealed into a rather feeble walking stick. With every other bridge burned she turned back to the only crutch she knew of - the little boy she left behind who wanted absolutely nothing to do with her.

Two:

Pu Pu Platter

Four months earlier, I was sitting outside at a patio restaurant having lunch with my girlfriend, Ayla. I quickly brushed my fingers across the thinning patch of salt and pepper and put on my fedora. I glowered at a young man with iron-like blades of coarse black hair and settled on reality: the improbable was, without a doubt, the impossible. I would never look that young again.

Scalding summer sun and frigid winter days forced practical headwear. My once tight abs had reached a long hibernating winter, sprouting a bit of a tummy. My shoulders were still broad but shaded by a bit of back hair, which had settled there after a southerly migration from the crown of my head. People said I was handsome now, but I felt compelled to show them pictures of me when I was shirtless and sixteen just to prove them wrong. Thankfully, being a lawyer did not entail time at a pool.

Ayla and I had been snorting and chortling, howling really, over bathroom humor – peeing and pooping and the like. Over the course of our relationship, we discovered no matter how fashionable our clothes were or how elite our professional circles had become, poop humor made us giggle like four-year-olds. It was a quality we shared that unequivocally confirmed that our love had reached its zenith.

It was really Ayla's game, although she would forever blame it on me and deny it like a skilled politician denies staining an interns dress or groping a woman's vagina. We referred to the act of pooping as making a "phone call."

"I really need to make a *call*," Ayla would emphasize. Ayla was from London and had a chiseled British accent that sounded eloquently formal no matter her choice of words. It was fun to make her say all sorts of dirty stuff.

"Well, let's get you to a *phone booth*," I'd reply.

When one returned from "making a call," the other would ask a series of questions about the "conversation." "Short and brief" for constipation; "talked on and on" for diarrhea and the like; and "left a message" if one experienced gas only. It always embarrassed the hell out of Ayla, but she always played along. Creativity was key.

When Ayla returned to the table, she had a smirk on her face. I asked, "So did you get them on the *phone*?"

"Uh... yes," she said, somewhat self-conscious by the venue but willing to play along a bit.

"And?"

"And what?"

"Did you have a *conversation*?"

"As a matter of fact, I did," she said proudly. Ayla was strictly beautiful when she smiled. It was the equivalent of putting the shine on the diamond. When I first met her, she was a dessert on display. Tight-fitting designer jeans. Polished leather shoes with large gold designer emblems on the toes. Accessories galore. And full-figured and tanned with jet-black hair that shimmied down to her firm shoulders. She wore a black scoop neck top that revealed ample breasts. She was a double chocolate cheesecake with caramel accents and two double-D cookies. I would forever keep the image in my mind.

I re-focused on the joke at hand. "When you were on this call, did you get some good information, or were they rude and short with you?"

"Oh, no," she said, very excited. "They talked. And talked. And talked! I couldn't get them to shut up. I thought, *When are these people just going to let me be and let me get off the phone?*" I laughed with her. "And then, finally, there was this one last thing they wanted to tell me – one *very big* last thing. Then, following a very short goodbye, they hung up." She smiled, beaming.

I covered my mouth like I was going to throw up. "Okay, now you've gone too far."

"Oh, stop it! You put me up to it."

"No, now you're just disgusting."

"No, *you* stop it!" she said, pulling my arm. "They did tell me to give you a message, though."

"Here?" I asked, sniffing the air. "Now?"

"No!" she said. "They said they'd be looking forward to hearing from you later."

"Oh," I said, grabbing my stomach. "Well, I'm working on it right now."

She laughed. "You're the disgusting one, and I'm ashamed that I enjoy playing this game with you."

My cell phone rang.

"Excuse me," I told Ayla. "I have a *real* phone call to answer."

On the other end, there was a gay man named Bobby-Charles who insisted that I meet with his employer – some woman named Lynn Turner – who wanted to speak to me about a sensitive legal matter. Apparently, her office was the only appropriate venue for our conversation.

"What times does Ms. Turner have available at the end of the week?" I asked.

"Lynn Turner is a *mister*," the gay secretary insisted. "And he's available on Friday at two p.m."

"And what area of law did you say *Mr.* Turner practices in?"

"Legal malpractice," Bobby-Charles said.

"If this is a solicitation, I'm not interested."

"I can assure you it's not. And I can assure you, you are." Legal assistants loved to be vague, and Bobby-Charles was especially good at it. I would soon discover Bobby-Charles was Mr. Turner's love and life partner. Thus, despite my pressing cross-examination of Bobby-Charles, I was no match Mr. Turner's instructions, which apparently were, "Don't say a goddamn word to the kid, or you'll be sleeping in the pool house with the maid." I bit and agreed to be at Lynn's office by 2 p.m.

Three:

Repeat That Again

When two o'clock on Friday rolled around, I pulled my car between a glorious set of marble lions frozen in time licking their paws and walked past a fountain of a cherub boy peeing on a lily pad. I entered the front door of Lynn Turner's office. It was a museum to various objet d'art – porcelain ladies, brass dishes, oil paintings, oriental rugs – and one King Charles Spaniel, who watched me enter from behind the antique leather top receptionist's desk where Bobby-Charles – I assumed – sat on the phone. Bobby-Charles waived me over to a gold velour couch. After I sat down, the dog leaped up onto the couch next to me and laid across my lap, tits up. It was a grand, yet submissive perversion. I immediately loved her.

Bobby-Charles gasped.

"Deidre, you slut!" he said, hanging up the phone.

I rubbed her belly, which caused her hind leg to twitch like it was on fire.

"I've never seen her do that with a stranger," Bobby-Charles said.

"I'm good with the ladies," I told him.

I heard another man's voice on the other side of a door a few feet away from the reception desk. His voice was deep. He was talking to a woman. Suddenly, Bobby-Charles's phone beeped and the speaker echoed.

"Would you ask Mr. Scales to come in, please?"

"You can go in now."

"Sure," I said, trying to push Deirdre off my lap. She

wouldn't budge.

"Deirdre! Get off him." Bobby-Charles got up and tried to pick her up, but she growled at him, protecting her new man-property, apparently. "Don't make me get my water bottle, missy."

I slid my way around the two sassing ladies and focused my attention on the second voice on the other side of the door. I didn't realize I was meeting two people. When I entered, I saw Lynn, who was a large guy with white hair and tan skin. Then I saw my mother. Lynn reached out to shake my hand but I didn't see it. The joy from the other room disintegrated like flash paper on fire.

"What the hell is going on?" I asked. "What are you doing here?" I said to my mother. My forehead tensed.

"Well, Ben," Lynn inserted, "come on in and have a seat. Please."

I didn't. I was confused. "What's this all about?

"Truthfully... your mother's in a bit of a pickle," Lynn said. "And, we, uh, need to... bring you up to speed."

My speech thickened and slowed as I spoke through a cloud of confusion. "I... thought this was about me... or something."

Lynn saw the pained expression on my face. His face opened. "Uh, it is. It is, in a way." He was trying to be delicate, because he could tell I was blindsided. It all overwhelmed me, and my need to think completely shut down every other bodily function, which left me there frozen like an idiot. Lynn stepped closer and placed his hand on my shoulder. "Why don't you come in and sit down here next to your mom?" He pointed to the couch. I sat in a chair instead - my arms crossed, my legs crossed, but my mouth gaping. Again, like an idiot.

She looked thin in a navy pantsuit and white blouse. As always, she wore large diamond stud earrings. Her gold Rolex dangled on her wrist as she wrung her hands nervously. Her hair was dyed reddish blonde and shorter than I had seen before. It gave her youth. Her pained face and furrowed expression were the only things that showed her age.

"Benjamin," my mother began slowly, "I've done something wrong, and I need your help."

It was odd to hear her voice. It had been so long. More odd, even, to be on a new subject with her without first addressing all the past subjects. Together, my mother and I were like a car that hadn't been driven in years, parked in a locked garage beneath a pile of boxes and blankets, with no gas and four flat tires. We might even agree that if you'd cleared the room, inflated the tires and filled it with gas, you'd sooner find a cat habitat under the hood than a working engine.

"Okay," I said, doing my best to adopt their apparent comfort.

She searched for words. "I don't know how to say this," she said then looked at Lynn. She gave up trying: "Lynn?"

"Sure," he said. Lynn sat in a chair next to me – at my eye level. He leaned back a bit to give me headspace. "Your mother has committed an ethical violation by becoming involved with a client." Lynn waited for a second to let the news sink in. I raised an eyebrow.

"This is a man who she happened to love," he continued, "who she fell in love with – and still loves dearly. And on a visit–"

I interrupted him. "Antonio?" I asked. She nodded.

"Yes, Mr. De Silva," Lynn said.

"Yes," my mother repeated.

"It figures," I huffed. "So you haven't killed anybody?" I asked.

"No," she said.

"Okay, go ahead." I let out a sigh and tried to shake off my stupor and somehow get involved in the reality unfolding.

"Well, your mother–"

I interrupted again. "Did you have sex with him?"

"No," she said, but her eyes dropped and avoided any further contact with me.

"Did you go down on him or something?" I asked.

She paused, not liking my choice of descriptive phrase but said, "Yes" nonetheless. Although she still didn't look at me, I could see her eyes welled up.

"Where? At the prison?" I asked.

"Yes."

"Okay," I said. I waved for Lynn to continue, who was a bit taken aback by my sixth sense.

"Your mother contacted me because the prison caught them in the act, and one of the DAs out there has filed a bar complaint."

I looked at him and nodded. "And that's where you come in, I assume?" I asked Lynn and looked to my mother for confirmation.

"Actually, that's where... *you* come in," he corrected.

"Excuse me?"

"Benjamin, I want you to represent me," my mother

said.

"Represent you for what?" I said in disgust.

Lynn began by backing up a bit; maybe a less direct approach was better. "Well, we've thought long and hard about this and–"

My mom interrupted, getting right to it. "My disbarment proceeding."

"Are you joking?"

"No," she said.

I laughed and rubbed my face. Clearly, I was dreaming. "My mother comes to you to represent her on her little blowjob case, and you," I said, pointing to Lynn, "with your thirty-something years of practice – I looked you up, just so you know – and your thousands of cases, want me to represent my mommy for sucking some guy's *dick*?"

My voice echoed into the front lobby where Bobby-Charles, with Deirdre in his lap, sat sipping tea. I heard Bobby-Charles gag and Deirdre yelp.

"Well–" Lynn began.

I interrupted again, "Talk about being a laughing stock! Yes, thank you. I've been a lawyer for eighteen months – this is just the legal boost I've been looking for!"

I rubbed my head. "This is my thing," I told her. "MY THING!" I screamed.

Her face paled.

"I did not do this to be like you and I certainly didn't do it so I could *REPRESENT* you!"

I stood up and paced the room. "This is fucked-up – I'm leaving."

I moved to Lynn's closed office door and turned the knob to open it. It nearly knocked me backward due to the weight of the person on the other side who had apparently been leaning up against it.

Bobby-Charles screamed like a teenage girl as he stumbled into the room. Lynn pinched his forehead, embarrassed. Bobby-Charles straightened his tie and jacket.

I got up and walked out the front door, stopping at a bench. I sat down and looked up to the sky, trying to take in some perspective.

A minute went by and I heard the front door open. Lynn walked outside and sat next to me on the bench. We both sat there staring off into space, shaking our heads.

"I'm so sorry about that," he said. "There's no excuse – he's just a child, I guess."

I ignored it. I had bigger problems than a nosy office assistant.

"Look, Ben, your mom is going to be tried before the Ethics Committee for doing this, and depending on their ruling, it will either be very, very public and she'll be disbarred forever, and everybody will know about it and that it was your mother who did that embarrassing act - maybe, as you may experience one day from a prosecutor or client, 'Hey, didn't your mom suck some client's dick?' - or it will remain private and be sealed, and no one will ever know." He softened his voice. "All we're here to do today is talk with you about what's going on and hopefully get you involved."

"Not *involved*. You mean *take over*," I said. "I mean, whatever happened to fucking introductions? Like a cup of coffee or a shot of Patrón before you kick my feet out from underneath me? I don't even know you, man. My mother and I haven't had any semblance of a relationship for years! I don't even do this kind of law. I don't know anything about it."

"I'll help you," Lynn said.

"Let me be very clear," I said. I was pissed but controlled my anger. "For whatever reason – and for my entire life, I might add – I've been making excuses for her, in my own mind, as to why she does the shit she does. My whole life, I've been covering for her – been on the hook for her – trying to make her decisions easier to swallow and seem somewhat remotely grounded within the boundaries of rational behavior." I glared at Lynn. "And you, sir, are my replacement. I'm not coming back on the hook. You can have that role, Mr. Turner."

"But I'm your mother," my mother said behind me. I turned and found her standing in the doorway, a Kleenex gripped in one hand, the other hand holding another tissue that she dabbed on her eyes. Her words weren't a statement of a right due to her, as in the past. This time she said them as a suggestion of mercy.

"Mom, I can't. It's ridiculous."

Four:
Quiet Before The Storm

Later that night, I went home to Ayla. Although we were not married, we'd been living together for about a year. She had a way about her that warmed my soul like a blanket and a crackling fire. I needed to see her eyes and find the love that seemed to refuel my tanks. I entered the foyer of our apartment and took off my jacket. It was dark outside, and our place glowed like a Japanese lantern. I heard her in the kitchen, frying onions, which filled the hallway and lifted my attention off my mother and into the air. I loosened my tie and pulled it off.

When I came into the kitchen, Ayla was partially dressed, wearing my oversize Miami football sweatshirt and her black tights with no shoes. She never fully undressed from work until bed; her post-work outfits were a combination of comfort and temporary laziness. The black fabric stretched up her slender thighs and disappeared under the tattered cotton edges of my sweatshirt.

"Are you hungry yet?" she asked.

"Not really. Just tired," I told her. "You?"

"Not really hungry either. Just thought you might be. This can wait. I was gonna make taco salad."

"I'm sorry," I said. "Maybe later?"

"It's only onions," she said, shutting off the stove. "I do have this, though." Ayla pulled a wine glass filled with red from the countertop.

"Wow," I said. "You read my mind." I took a long drink and held the wine in my mouth for a minute then swallowed.

"Did it not go okay?" she asked.

"No."

"You look exhausted," she said, as she came over to me and kissed me on the mouth and then the temple. "Is everything okay with you? Is something terribly wrong?" Her voice was heavy with concern.

"Yes," I said.

"Yes – which one?" she asked.

"Something is terribly wrong."

Seeing the pain on my face, Ayla took her hand to my neck and pulled me toward her. I leaned against her, between her legs, as she stood with her back to the counter. My body was pressed tightly to hers; warmth hovered between us. I lowered my head toward her shoulder and into her hair and let the strands cover my face. She stroked the nape of my neck and kissed me on the other side, her warm breath in my ear.

She moved her head to look me in the eyes – to see my expression again – and, upon seeing the stress, she kissed me again, longer this time.

Our lips spread into a deeper, softer, slower kiss. A welcome distraction.

She lowered her hands down to my shirt and untucked it from my pants. She pushed her fingers beneath the surface edge of my trousers and held my sides. I lowered my hands too, down to her hips, and pressed them against her tights. I wrapped my neck around her and moved my face into her thick black hair.

"So, what is it?" she asked.

I closed my eyes in the dark strands. I was so happy to be with her – more so than anyone in the world.

"I have to make a decision," I told her.

"Do you want to talk about it?"

I exhaled slowly. "No," I said.

When I left my mother at 18 years old, I dedicated my life to sealing the door between our two worlds. I fueled my anger rocket and left stormy skies behind for colder, darker space. I forced myself not to think about her – not to care.

What I didn't share with Lynn or my mother was that my mother had already been on my mind, way before I got Lynn's call. It had been a steady progression of thought that began years earlier, at a time I did the one thing I swore I would never do: go to law school and become a goddamn lawyer like my mother.

Five:
The Kotex Counselor

Law school was an institution founded on one's inherent need not only to know the truth but also to learn how to reveal it. It was a place for postulating. Theorizing. A place to shape modern skyscrapers from two-hundred-year-old bricks and mortar. An Age of Enlightenment. And while focus and initiative were never my forte – unless my adoring friends were cheering me on to chug a beer in under five seconds – law school deserved my full attention. I was, therefore, prepared to invest heavily in Dunkin' Donuts coffee.

I was twenty-nine and still three years away from meeting Ayla. It had been eight years since I had graduated from college in Miami and moved back to Atlanta. Eight years since I had forced myself to endure late nights of studying and early classes. Eight years since I had actually needed a cup of coffee to wake up. Back in college, I had made up for late nights by sleeping through many of my early-morning classes, but they were for a liberal arts degree, necessary only if one wanted to excel at Jeopardy.

In preparation for my first day of classes, I hadn't gone to bed until four a.m. due to the immeasurable number of pages I had to read. Actually, I knew exactly how many pages I had to read. Approximately sixty per class, two hundred and fifty total – two hundred and fifty of the most mundane yet apparently legally significant cases to come down from the high courts. My mother often bragged to me about the sheer volume of reading she similarly endured. And I, too, had read two hundred-and-fifty-page books before, some even in one sitting. But now I understood her vanity.

Legal reading was like reading Braille for the first time. A morning nap had been on my mind since I'd awakened and nearly fallen asleep on the toilet.

On my first day of law school, I took a commuter train into downtown Atlanta and leaped down an escalator to the street and hightailed it over to the college. I walked briskly only because I couldn't run, due to the fifty-pound briefcase bludgeoning the back of my knee. It contained all of my law books and various pens, highlighters, and legal aids and swung like a wrecking ball, causing me to walk like a cripple. Once up the steps of the school, I tried to squeeze the briefcase and myself through the rotating door and banged the bag against the glass.

Other students snapped their heads to the sound of the idiot. Most of them carted their morning workouts along in handy rolling backpacks via a pinky or pointer finger only, leaving their free hand for more important 8 a.m. tasks such as cells and cigarettes and, yes, coffee cups, too.

The College of Law was functional – one building, three floors, lockers, some seats, a library with soda-soaked carpet and gum stains, and a lunging elevator even the fire department feared.

I wandered the hallways like a lost tourist in a Paris subway station and wiped my forehead with a tissue. While I didn't mind being watched, I abhorred the idea of being embarrassed and sweated profusely at receiving unwanted attention. It gave me indigestion and gas so much so that one could poke me on my belly and make me fart. Other physical reactions included becoming dizzy, disoriented, and/or throwing up. Plus, I hadn't needed to remember a locker combination in years. The idea kept me up nights worrying I'd forget. Depending on who you asked – the Jewish community, of which I was a member, or the clinical one – I might be considered normal or a compulsive hypochondriac.

Truthfully, it was odd to be back in school, mixing with kids who weren't old enough to rent a car yet. I had more life experience than 90 percent of the class. I was also six years behind the current fashions. No one wore button-down shirts or slacks. You'd sooner find a garden hose around someone's neck than a tie. Instead, faded denim skinny jeans and Converse All-Stars were back from the 80's, along with various shirts portraying Homer Simpson and The Cure and slogans like, "Rehab is for Quitters." I think one kid was actually wearing *my* Members Only jacket complete with a Duran Duran button pin I had donated to the Salvation Army twelve years earlier.

Girls pulled at their curls while looking at boys who stood with their hands in their pockets. I felt like I was going to school on the set of a Disney television show.

I loosened my tie, slipped off my sports coat, and folded my fedora into my jacket.

I swung by my first class and saw that it was filling up slowly. I eyed the front row and saw that it was empty. Despite all the professors insisting that where you sit in the classroom doesn't matter, I knew better. Sitting in the front row was critical, and there were no takers, as I had assumed. With plenty of seats still available and my hair feeling a bit frayed, I lugged my briefcase back into the hallway and toward the restroom.

Once inside, I looked in the mirror and criticized my

hair and myself. If I had looked like this in college, dating would have been an observation, not a practice. I spiked my hair, trying to add life to the top of my head – something hip, fashionable.

I took a moment to size myself up and just breathe. The rush of the morning and the cardiac stress test down the street had me a bit frazzled, and I needed to settle down. I didn't want to underestimate my first class and my first professor. The law school experience was crafted to be harsh and unforgiving. They called it teaching by the Socratic Method. I recalled that my mother spoke of it often, although she referred to it as the asshole method.

Law school professors loved to question their students in such a way that forced the student to pontificate on and on and then attempt to deliver an awe-inspired, throat-clearing answer meant to impress. The professor would then seemingly accept the answer as correct but then add another layer to the question and prompt the student to further commit to his or her answer under the expanding set of facts, until ultimately the student would be forced to look back on their original answer with contempt and embarrassment on his or her failed interpretation of hundred-year-old cases and, thus, feel like an asshole.

For this very reason, professors knew that students didn't like to be called on. The professors also knew that the students who feared such an interaction ignorantly believed that sitting farther away from the front would decrease their chances of being chosen. I knew better.

Professors practically ignored the students who sat in the front row and placed their attention into the higher rows in contemplation of ousting ill-prepared first-year idiots. That and the fact that front row students, if any, were usually highly annoying intellectual types who loved to get called upon.

I tried to smile at myself and thought about not fucking anything up. Today was an important day for me. It was the first day of my first impression. I certainly didn't want to say anything stupid in class if I were forced to answer any questions. I had prepared obsessively. I'd made more notes in the margins of the reading material than there were actual words in the material itself.

In the restroom, I warmed up the water and washed my hands. I felt myself slow down a bit and find a calmer rhythm. I took care to dry the spaces between my fingers and used the moistened paper towel to wipe my eyes. *Better*, I thought.

I pulled one paper towel to finish the job but stopped at the sight of a second dispenser. I reached in curiously and pulled out a plastic tube. It was sleek and about four inches long. It read, "Tampons by Kotex."

"Oh, shit," I said.

My eyes opened wide. I looked around. No wall urinals.

"*Oooh, shiiit.*"

Suddenly the door swung open, announcing the arrival of two young women.

I looked for a trash can but had to jam the tube in my pocket.

They rounded the corner and froze on me – and me on them – the only movement being my cheeks blushing from white to red. I suddenly felt the expression on my face of a dog caught taking a shit on the rug.

"Well, *this* is funny," I said to their wide eyes. They blinked and said nothing. "Right," I said, agreeing with their disgust, and grabbed my briefcase and ducked my head. Their giggles followed me out the door, tampon in pocket. *Goddamn it*, I thought.

I slinked away, hugging the wall, trying to disappear into anonymity by humming and inspecting the concrete between the bricks. A duck, a spin, and a slide later, I moved back to my classroom like a shadow. A fat, balding shadow.

"Jesus Christ," I muttered, as I entered the classroom, keeping one eye on the door to see whether the two girls from the bathroom were going to be in my class. They entered, and I ducked again as other students flooded into the room at the pace of rushing water. I moved toward the front, but the rows had filled up suddenly.

The two girls sat down and spotted me. They giggled again and confirmed to each other that I was in the fact the boob in the bathroom. Stuck between sitting too close to them and too far back from the front, I turned my attention to residual seating and muffled the plastic in my pocket.

My plans were breaking down. Defeated by time, I looked instead for a seat near someone respectable looking – an organized, brainy type who didn't have a pierced eyebrow or pink streak in his or her hair or a brief history with me in the ladies' room. I noted a fair-skinned redhead who looked as uptight as the shell-shaped bun in her hair. She had the look of a know-it-all; I felt pretty good about the probability of her sacrificing herself to the teacher for a few extra brownie points. And since she was the only other student who dared to wear a suit on the first day of classes, I thought it fitting that we sit next to each other. With eight rows still behind me, I was close enough to the front. I slid in beside her.

"Finally," I said, as I sat down and smiled. "It's nice to see someone else who cared enough to dress up."

She forced a halfhearted smile but got distracted when she spotted my balding head. Her eyes enlarged then looked away, as if she were looking at my bare ass.

This isn't high school, I thought.

I looked at the cover of my law book, *Understanding Criminal Law*, and opened it to the pages I had marked with highlighters and penned notes. The sixty-five pages assigned had taken me six hours, two pots of coffee, and two naps to get through, and that was just one reading assignment for one class. I had five others that week. After one week of reading, my eyeglass prescription would be useless. The most annoying part was that the teacher would sum up the reading assignment in sixty minutes.

"The grind," my mother called it. She often reminded me about her being number one in her class, despite it. "And I was the only woman doing trial work," she added.

"I'm gonna be a doctor like grandfather," I told her when I was ten. "You help the crooks, and I'll save people's lives." Big cheeky smile.

"Medical school is about memorization," she responded. "Law school is about learning how to think."

To her, law school was always more elite than medical school.

Fortunately, I didn't find criminal law very difficult. It was in my blood – literally and figuratively. But *practicing* criminal law was another experience entirely. Defenders of the Constitution, yes. Protectors of our individual rights, absolutely. Upstanding members of society? Not that I had seen. Most criminal defense attorneys I had met were street lawyers, shtick operators.

Street lawyering was the worst. No skyscraper offices, no thirty floors up overlooking God's green earth, no high-profile clients, no extended lunches on grand expense accounts – just plain ol' dollar-day hustle and bustle. Five-dollar all-day parking, three-dollar early-bird specials.

Street lawyers keep their offices in their cars and jacket pockets – papers, receipts, parking vouchers. Notes scattered about on an infinite number of legal pads. Coffee stains on their suits, mustard on their sleeves. Street lawyers barely have time to be in the office to meet with clients and families. They're filing, making motions, meeting with prosecutors, meeting with judges, making arguments, doing arraignments and suppression hearings and bond hearings and trials – all at the same time for any number of clients.

"If I ever do become a lawyer," I once conceded to my mother, "I'd never practice criminal defense." The thought echoed into a visible ripple. I stored it in my mind in the Total Disbelief Bin... right next to the tampon in my pocket.

At six-foot-two and 210 pounds, I had size. I wasn't scared of much. I had been hit in the ribs. Had my nose broken once playing basketball and my heart on a couple of occasions. I had survived two decades in the trenches of psychological warfare waged by my mother. So when the redheaded doo-dah sitting next to me explained to her neighbor that our criminal law teacher was rumored to be a superb asshole, I didn't flinch. *So what!* I thought. I had a lifetime of experience with a brutal, cross-examining criminal defense attorney mother. That was my pre-law school training. My secret weapon. I already was way ahead.

I wondered whether I could win over my professors or whether, despite my being twenty-nine and mature, they'd cut me at the ankles like the rest of the babies in the class. Put a pacifier in my mouth and send me off for naptime.

Five minutes late, my criminal law professor burst through the back door. He was already halfway through his first sentence. Students began to write and type feverishly. Mass confusion and panic filled the air as he rattled off a combination of rhetorical anecdotes and questions. He continued, "Any time a government agent – federal, state, local, or otherwise – purposefully enters into your life, stops you on your way, or begins to question you outside of 'It's a nice day, isn't it?' it triggers a set of rights upon which you can mount a return charge. The US Supreme Court, at least for the purposes of this class, concluded that a person's rights are absolute and undeniable, placing emphasis on due process in an effort to ensure that violations of the Bill of Rights, specifically search and seizure, right to an attorney, and the right against self-incrimination, among others – i.e., the Fourth, Fifth, and Sixth Amendments – are maintained and upheld in such a way..."

I whispered to the girl next to me, "What the hell is he talking about?"

"The *reading* assignment," she said.

"Yeah, I read it, too, but... never mind," I said. I was suddenly pouty. My eyes glazed over, and the professor's voice trailed off like a bee zooming to a distant flower. After ten minutes of eye-glazing rhetoric, the professor stopped and scanned his classroom; everyone seemed lost.

"All right, let's liven things up and make us an example, okay? Volunteer? Is there anyone here named 'Volunteer'? If you're present, I need you to come up here, please," the professor ribbed.

He was a tall, gangly man whose suit draped across his shoulders like a sheet across a wire hanger. His peanut-shaped nose separated two protruding cheekbones that sank into gaunt cheeks. *Ichabod Crane*, I thought.

I joshed to Carrot Top, "Ichabod Crane is teaching us criminal law."

"Shhh," she said.

"Yes, you heard me correctly – a vo-lun-teer," Ichabod said, stretching out each syllable. The class didn't move. Even the air paused. The only movement came from all the eyes darting to their textbooks and Ichabod's tapping foot. Such a silly game.

I looked around the room; clearly, I was the most mature person here. The teacher grew impatient. "People," he said, exasperated, "we are adults here in this building. We do not pretend to be busy with other work while the legal scholar searches for an assistant," he hummed.

Insert five minutes of silence here.

I looked around again. The girl next to me turned backward and fished through her backpack, as if she suddenly remembered a peanut butter sandwich she had to eat.

Then the feeling hit. The one that comes as you're standing on a rocky ledge looking down forty feet at the river below – the one where you realize, *I climbed up here to jump, didn't I?*

My mind began, *Well, I am the oldest, probably, in the class. And everybody's just being pathetic. Come on. Somebody.*

Even the dorks in the front row didn't raise their hands. I let out a sigh and began to move my hand. *Put your hand down*, I thought. But I couldn't just sit there anymore.

"Yes, you. Thank you! You are?"

"Scales. Ben Scales."

"Ah, Mr. Scales Ben Scales!" He stopped suddenly. "Wait, any chance you're related to another very well known Atlanta-based criminal defense attorney, Carter-"

I froze on the words "another very well known" and began to think the jig was up. I tried to speak but my tongue went lame. Finally, I got the message.

"No!" I said, interrupting. My face flashed red. "No relation – I mean, my family – there aren't any other lawyers, so no."

"Ah," he said, "well, then congratulations on being the only one to bring shame onto your family. Come on up here and help an old man cross the street!"

As I rose, he directed the class to applaud, which they did, as if I had just successfully performed the absolutely daring task of tying my shoelaces. I obliged them with a nod. I was the hero who had spared the others.

"You find what you were looking for, chicken shit?" I whispered to the girl as I passed her.

As I approached the board, Ichabod continued on about the Constitution and some other rules and stuff that I was suddenly oblivious to. I couldn't hear much due to my ears ringing and my becoming very aware of my entire body.

He was saying something about P.O.S.T. certified officer and working the streets to fight crime. I thought about my junior-size gut and whether the overhead spotlights created one of those doughnut-looking shadows around my belly.

Ichabod said my name and pulled me out of my reverie. "Mr. Scales?"

"Sorry... Yes."

"I need you to step back a bit for the Terry frisk."

"Frisk?" I asked. The class laughed, and so did Ichabod.
"Okay, all right. Come on now. There's nothing to fear. You have your constitutional rights after all."

I turned back, milking the attention, and spread my arms open. "Okay," I told him. They laughed again, but this time at my apparent charm.

As the class sat forward, I imagined them liking me for volunteering. I suddenly enjoyed having all eyes on me. *Already considered cool*, I thought.

"Very good," he said. "Now... I've just approached you and told you that I have reason to suspect that you're involved with drugs."

"Drugs?" I asked with staged surprise. The class laughed again. Two for two!

He assisted me in milking attention and nodded. "Yeah, you know... Afghan?"

"What?" I said, honestly confused.

"Afghan. You know. Bhang."

"Bang?" I asked.

"Yeah, bhang. Black rock. Bobby Brown, broccoli, Buddha grass, bush, chronic, dope, draw, dry high, dubby, gage, ganja, gangster, giggleweed, grass, hemp, herb, Jane, jive, joint, kabizzle, kiff, loco weed, mary, Mexican green, nug, Otis, Panama red, pineapple express, pot, puff, reefer, resin, roach, sativa, smoke, spliff, tea, Texas tea, Thai sticks. You know. Weed, baby!"

The class exploded in laughter and applauded. Suddenly, Ichabod was totally rad. It was probably his one cool moment a year.

"Ah, yes. Drugs," I said.

The kids were rolling. We were having fun.

"Yes. I'm sure you've at least heard of them at some point in your life."

"Perhaps."

Ichabod moved to my right side. "Sir, do you have any drugs, weapons, or contraband on your person?" he asked with suddenly inflated authority. His smile vanished.

"My person?"

"Yeah, on your person. Your clothes. Your pockets," he said. "I have reason to believe you have drugs on your person."

"Uh, no," I said, as I reached down and patted my pocket. It crinkled and crunched. "Oh, shit," I said. My neck and face started to pump sweat.

The class laughed again, comfortably participating in my sudden agony.

"All right, everybody," he said, motioning for quiet. "What we have here is a very legally technical principle called... a lie." He dragged out the word "lie," as if explaining it to a five-year-old. More giggles.

Ichabod went on and explained some actual legal principle of law about "articulable suspicion of criminal activity" and the "scope of his investigation" and the Fourth Amendment and blah, blah, blah. The class burst into laughter again. I couldn't hear it. A nine iron had just struck my heart, and it was ringing like an alarm.

Before I knew it, he laid his hand over my pocket. I nearly fell limp. I scanned the audience and saw all of my favorite people. The two girls from the bathroom. The evil redhead next to my seat who was probably hoping no one had seen us sitting together.

I thought about the various speeches my mother had made about rising to the occasion and meeting challenges. I wasn't sure if they even had tampons back in my mother's day, but if they did, I could guarantee you that her professors didn't pull any off her person.

"I don't feel good," I whispered.

The class laughed again.

"Spontaneous utterances are not suppressible, Mr. Scales," he told me. "Sounds like a plastic baggie, perhaps containing contraband?"

Their laughter appeared malevolent as they took pleasure in experiencing this exercise from a distance.

"It's... It's just, uh, a candy bar and, uh... uh... uh... a wrapper!" I defended, as Ichabod felt around my pants pocket and goaded the class to encourage his intrusion.

Reading the panic on my face, one kid whispered to another, "What if he's really got a joint in his pocket?"

I'd settle for a bag of cocaine at this point.

A swift move in and right back out. All eyes followed Ichabod's hand like a line drive to center field. His bony fingers were raised high, as if they had just drawn Excalibur from the stone. "Aha!" he said. And then room-deafening silence, as all eyes freezing on the four-inch vaginal tube.

"Is this a tampon?" he asked.

I squeaked, "It's not mine?"

Ichabod jolted, as if grasping a cockroach, and hurled the tampon wildly into the room. The class fell apart.

A black girl fanned her face. Other kids wiped their eyes. One loser had to use his inhaler. My first day in law school had burned to ashes all around me, and all I had was a squirt gun.

After class, I contemplated using my law school student loans to relocate to Jamaica to braid hair for rum. I actually looked online for an apartment.

By late afternoon, my new moniker had already surfaced. The story had penetrated every student and faculty member's tympanic membrane. There was no spin control. Only the dizzying realization that I was in fact caught in an unforgettable whirlwind of tragedy and comedy. A "tramedy."

The Kotex Counselor was born.

Six:
The High Road And The Low One

Unlike my mother's generation, my generation struggled with our identity. We didn't have a great war or a great movement. We had MTV and Cosmo and Entertainment television. Even without Facebook, society was busy constantly thrusting other peoples' dreams, success stories, and happiness into our faces. I, like many of my friends, didn't get practical with my future and sign on to a particular career or trade simply because my parents had done it or because it was the opportunity presented to me. I had big plans that involved my heart and not my head. It is one of the reasons why I knew I would never be a lawyer.

As a child, I had set my sights on becoming a surgeon like my grandfather. I would rather deal with all of the gross and nasty issues that surgeons dealt with than become a lawyer like my mother. My grandfather had been a great surgeon, and I had his hands. I also had my grandfather's Dumbo ears, but that only gave me character. Constipation, intestinal blockage, vomiting, diarrhea – all preferable over having to try to save a client from the very place he needed to be. It was a bonus that my mother couldn't stand her father and thus couldn't stand the idea of me doing anything like him.

I had been accepted to the University of Miami – a university known nationwide for its coup in the world of great trifectas: gorgeous girls with great breasts and perfect butts. It also had a pre-med program and a medical school.

During my four years there, I took a job as an EMT at a level-one trauma center for children in Miami in order to beef up my resume. I hoped the experience would make up for my lack of A's and average intelligence. It would ensure my crossing the medical school finish line in an ever-expanding and competitive race to get in.

Level one meant that the hospital had surgical specialists and diagnostic abilities available twenty-four hours a day. It also meant that every horrific thing that happened to anyone under fourteen-years-old came to us. As most kids had a healthy disrespect for consequences on any day, nights with full moons were especially witchy.

During my first shift, I stood under such a moon on the roof of the emergency department, waiting at the boundary line of the helipad, wearing an oversize pair of goggles and a yellow gown meant to protect my scrubs from spurting blood. My spirits soared at the idea of having to fend off a runaway artery.

There had been a late-afternoon lawn mower accident in an orange orchard far away. A five-year-old boy was riding with his father on their tractor mower and had fallen off the front. The mower had driven over him until the blade had jammed on some part of his body.

The Life Flight helicopter made a rapid descent and opened its side doors the moment it touched down – a "hot" unload. Two paramedics jumped out under the pounding blades and hurried to a back hatch under the tail and whirling rudder. Usually, they waited for the blades to slow, but not this time. I waited alongside an ER doctor and a trauma nurse for the pilot to signal so that we could run out and pull the patient from the chopper. Despite my worry over the dying child, I felt more alive than ever.

I remember the wind from the helicopter blades

created a dizzying swirl of thoughts that caused me to become introspective. I considered my professional progress that had brought me to that moment. It was *my* idea to work at the emergency department – to work first as a technician, a position I knew without a doubt would give me more practical medical experience than anywhere else. All the different medical disciplines converged in the emergency department. It was truly the best decision I had ever made for myself.

I snapped out of my thoughts and turned my attention to the boy who had experienced the closest thing to a full-body Cuisinart. We ran up to the rear of the helicopter and pulled out the gurney. The kid was wrapped in a silver bag, much like a ballpark frank, to keep him warm, and had two IVs open full throttle. His blood pressure was dropping exponentially – a sign of internal or external bleeding, among other problems.

The pilot handed us various items: clothing, bags, medical equipment, all of which we set on the gurney next to the kid. I grabbed what I could and one of the IVs and lofted it into the air, using gravity to push the fluid through the tubes and into the kid. Suddenly, we were off, running away from the pad and into an elevator that swallowed us the moment we entered. Once in the elevator and away from the sounds of the roaring engine, the doctor ordered everyone to be quiet. He listened for chest sounds while the nurse listened to the boy's heart. The doctor and nurse worked as dancers in a ballet, reading and finding each other at precious moments in a grand exchange of observation and information.

"Weak on the lower left lobe," the doctor said.

"Heart's tachy," the nurse added.

"Plus three breathing – rails on the right."

The nurse moved to check the boy's circulation. She felt for radial pulses on the wrists, femoral pulses near his groin, then pedal pulses or pulses on top of his feet. Unable to do much myself, I decided to look through the bags we previously had set on the gurney. One was cold and collecting moisture on the outside. It was a Kroger grocery bag. I untied the knot and opened the plastic. It contained the kid's right foot, chopped off at the ankle, covered in shaved ice.

"Holy shit," I said, totally enthralled. They both looked up. "Don't bother checking for a pulse on the right foot," I said, as I nodded to the bag.

"You're kidding me," the nurse said, turning her attention to the stretcher, as she pulled back the silver wrapping. My wide eyes and her discovery confirmed that I was, in fact, not kidding.

Once we were down in the ER, a team of eight additional staffers swarmed around us in perfectly timed harmony: a second ER doctor; a respiratory therapist; a radiology technician; two other nurses, one to pull meds and another at bedside to help start IVs and such; another technician to pull supplies; a laboratory phlebotomist; and a priest. Like a volleyball team, some moved up while others moved back – constant motion around us.

The mower blades surprisingly hadn't killed the boy. He was, for all medical purposes, fucked, though. Really fucked. The medical community had shorthand ways of noting these types of nonmedical diagnoses. For example, a kid who looked kind of weird but didn't have one of the many genetic or systemic disorders that usually was the culprit was labeled "FLK" or "funny looking kid"; that way the staff would be forewarned not to ask the family if the kid had some type of genetic disorder – a question they were most assuredly asked all the time. The lawnmower boy was labeled a bit more severely as "FUBAR" or "fucked-up beyond all recognition." Lovely, right?

One of our docs, after removing a bandage that covered the boy's shoulder and neck, discovered that the blade had sliced down his neck, not across, but vertically through the collarbone, nicking his carotid artery. A geyser of red shot up like a solar flare. "Whoa!" I yelled.

This made the boy a thoracic surgical candidate, which meant he needed to be transported to the cardiac hospital. Oops. Once he was shipped out to the next hospital, I was moving on to a hot cup of coffee and my next case. And that's how it went. For twelve hours a day, three days a week, I saw a side of life most people never would imagine.

An obese teenager with "abdominal pain" proved tricky to diagnose.

"It's comin' out her anus!" the girl's grandmother declared, as the girl hovered over a toilet.

"It's. Comin'. Out. Her. Anus!"

We all, of course, turned to the opened bathroom door to see exactly what was coming out of the girl's anus. It was a baby's head.

"That ain't her anus," I said.

Ten minutes later, the lady's great granddaughter was born. Reflecting later to a nurse friend, I noted that the girl had told me in triage that she was abstinent.

Her all-knowing eyebrows compressed. "*Shiiiit,*" she said, drawing out the I's. "That's the *fifth* immaculate conception I seen this week," she said.

I made a mental note never to trust a teen girl with abdominal pain.

As my college years progressed and as I continued to work at the ER, I wondered what in the hell I was doing. I mean, the stuff I was seeing was fascinating – near-death dehydration, tumors, car accident victims, lawn darts in the forehead, bugs up the nose kind of stuff – but most of the doctors I worked with and many of the specialists who visited the ER to see patients seemed very stressed and unhappy. It didn't look promising.

Dealing with the emotional aspects of the business wasn't any big deal and it wasn't particularly difficult for me to do it. Perhaps it was genetic. I just treated my emotions like my mother treated me – they were objects to be used or forgotten. I cared at that ER because I was getting paid to care. When my shift was over, I took off my emotions along with my nametag and stethoscope and put it in my locker with the rest of my shit until the next time they would serve me well. It was the one quality I really loved about myself.

"So, what's the real downside?" I asked a general surgeon who was a lot like me. He held up a stack of papers. "All this. Four to five hours a day of this crap – and that's apart from just charting for patients."

Medicine was becoming a business overwrought with red tape and regulations and automated phone calls and electronic answering services that instructed physicians on which procedures would and would not be covered. "Medicaid" and "Medicare" had become curse words. For those doctors who were accustomed to implementing their decisions without interference, like my grandfather, the intrusion was inexcusable. As a bonus, for those doctors and practices who could not keep up with the proper insurance billing codes associated with those Medicaid and Medicare regulations, the prosecutorial arm of the Federal Government acted as a bill collector, seeking both fines and imprisonment for those recklessly ignorant physicians who chose to rely on their office managers and billing departments.

Every time a doctor asked me what I was going to do with my life after college and I replied, "medical school," they actually scoffed, rolled their eyes, and told me it wasn't worth it.

I also realized I had made the decision to become a doctor when I was twelve and that while I may have said I wanted to be a doctor like my grandfather, I was really more passionate about not becoming a lawyer like my mother. I suddenly felt the blinders. Irritation swirled around the glowing coals in my gut and lit a new fire.

With only one year left in undergraduate and nothing but pre-med classes to show for it, I couldn't for the life of me figure out what I would do if not medicine. Then, in the second half of my senior year, I got a clue.

Seven:
March Madness

It was spring semester in college and basketball playoff season was a high priority. I traveled to an out-of-state basketball game with my twenty-one-year-old best friend Phil and two other pre-med friends: Wayne, a Miami Hurricane's football player and biology major, and Carl, a bioengineering major. Wayne was driving and trying to make up for lost time through the southerly portion of my home state by daring to drive five miles an hour over the speed limit. My face was painted hunter green and orange and I had on a Hurricane's basketball jersey.

We were joking about racial profiling and stereotypes, having a little fun at our expense. Wayne and Carl agreed that they had to always mind themselves as there was no mistaking them as black because they were "Wesley Snipes black," as they put it. "There is no chance that anyone would be confused about both my parents being from Africa!" Wayne quipped while driving.

"Amen, brother," Carl said, giving Wayne a fist to pound.

I was sharing with them the hurtful experiences of my past growing up Jewish in an all Southern Baptist town when Carl made a rather astute stereotypical point.

"But see, black is for everyone to see. It's not like the people in your town could tell you were Jewish, Scales," he said. "I mean, you're six feet, two inches tall and you don't have a huge fucking nose." He gave me a wide smile. Wayne started coughing and laughing, his body jerking uncontrollably, and he covered his mouth with his fist.

The car was jerking a bit too, weaving in the lane.

"You could've just said I was six foot two," I told him. "Which by the way *is* the ultimate perk."

"How's that?" he asked, snickering.

"When I go to temple, it doesn't matter where I sit, I can see over everybody." The idea of a room full of short Jews made us all laugh even harder until we saw the nose of the silver cop car poke out of the woods and fishtail onto the highway. Within seconds the car was behind us. Wayne eased off the gas and pulled into the right lane. The car's blue lights weren't on, and the siren was silent.

It sped up next to us on the left, and the passenger, another officer, looked out the window and eyed each one of us. I could see him rise up in his seat and look over the window's edge and down into our car. His laser-focused eyes traced the contours of the car's interior, searching for something illegal, perhaps an open container or a kilo of cocaine. Suddenly, the cruiser faded back and then tucked behind us, igniting all sirens and lights.

"Fuck, man," Wayne said. "My father is going to kill me if I get another speeding ticket."

"How fast were you going?" Carl asked.

"Like five over... maybe."

The driver cop stepped out while his partner grabbed the radio. The driver sauntered to the back of our car and stopped. He straddled the air as if he had mounted an invisible bull and rested his hand on top of his firearm.

"Driver, step out!"

"What'd he say?" Wayne asked.

"He said, get out, man," Carl said.

"What do I do?"

"Driver! Step out of the vehicle and walk backward to me!" the cop said again.

Now the passenger cop got out of the car and unsnapped the safety strap on his gun holster.

"Scales, man, your mom's a lawyer, right? What the fuck, man?" Suddenly, I was the expert. Every complaint my mother ever said to me about an asshole cop came rushing in. I considered for a second that I was actually supposed to know what to do.

"I don't know – I guess, just get out. Just do what he says," I said.

"This is South Georgia, man," Wayne said. "I ain't from here, man."

"It's nineteen ninety-four," I told him. I was calm. "Okay? Just get out. We're all here together."

Wayne exited and faced the officer.

"Turn around and lace your fingers behind your neck!" Wayne was further commanded to walk a tightrope line backward to the rear of the car, where the other officer was waiting to shoot him dead if he varied from his choreography. As soon as he reached the back of his car, he felt a rod thrust into the back of his knee.

"Get down. On your knees, partner. Do it!" Wayne was a large guy. He liquefied and hit the ground.

"What the hell, man?" Carl asked us.

I saw the whites of Wayne's eyes flash with fear.

"What did I do?" Wayne asked, his voice cracking.

"This is bullshit," I said from the backseat. I pushed

the driver seat forward and got out.

"What are you doing?" Carl exclaimed.

I ignored him. "Officer, what is going on? Why are you putting him on the ground?"

"Sir, get back in the vehicle."

"But what did we do?"

"Sir, in the vehicle, or I'll have you arrested for obstruction!"

The officer reached for Wayne and cuffed his hands. He patted his clothing and reached into his pockets and lifted Wayne to the bumper. I sat down on the driver's seat.

"Nineteen ninety-four, huh?" Carl said to me.

I watched Wayne and the officer. "Wayne's straight, man. I know he is," I said.

"I know I'm cool," Carl said. He looked at Phil, whose scraggly goatee looked more like laziness associated with marijuana smoking than ever before. "Phil?"

"Phil, man, you cool?" Carl insisted.

"Yes, I'm cool," Phil said. We both sighed in relief. "Unless," Phil continued, "they ask me to piss in a cup."

"Shit, man," Carl said. "Shit, shit, shit, dude."

"What?" I asked.

"We're busted, man. Phil's got weed in him!" he said, sharply.

"They're not gonna have Phillip *piss* in a fuckin' cup, Carl," I said.

"It's too windy outside," Phil added.

"No, dipshit, we're on the side of the road," I said. "Look, if nobody has anything illegal, and all we've done

is speed, then everything is going to be fine. It's just...
Let's just relax."

"Says the white kid," Carl said.

The officer yelled out again. "Passenger! Step out of
the vehicle and walk backward to the rear of the car."
Carl's turn.

Carl complied, and the officer patted him down, too.

"Put your hands on the car like your *homeboy* here,"
the officer said to Carl. Phil and I stayed put.

It was at that moment, from the awkward safety of
Wayne's vehicle, while Wayne and Carl hunched
together as two black kids on the side of the road, that I
shared a host of unspoken words with them that seemed
to plant a seed of new purpose in me. The only attention
Phil or I received as the two white passengers occurred
when the officer came to the passenger window, looked
inside, and shook his head.

For forty-five minutes, we waited on the side of the
road – Phil and I in the back of the car, while Wayne and
Carl sat Indian-style in the grass just off the shoulder of
the highway. Finally, another cop car arrived.

I expected that it was some kind of a supervisor who
had come to browbeat two officers who dared waste their
shift time on a carload of law-abiding college kids. The
third officer retrieved a leashed German Shepherd from
his backseat, which gave me a different answer. The
three cops huddled for a moment while "Daisy" paced in
a tight circle.

"Passengers, step out of the vehicle," the third officer
instructed.

We did as instructed. It felt good to be near Wayne
and Carl.

In the comfort of four, I spoke up. "Officer, you have no right to keep us here."

"Shut up, Scales," Wayne said.

I ignored him and stood up. It felt good to be on my feet. I was slimmer, buffer and had better hair – a triple threat under any circumstance and one that always gave me added attitude. "Officer, why are you doing this to us? Why are they on the ground? Why haven't you searched *my* pockets? I don't look like a drug dealer to you?" The officer ignored me as he wrote a citation, using only a fleeting second to smirk at me.

"This is bullshit," I said. "You guys are racists."

It wasn't until I saw the look on the officer's face that I realized I had gone too far.

"What did you call me?" the officer asked.

"I think he called you a racist," the other officer said.

"Turn around," the officer told me. "Hands behind your back."

"What?" I cried.

"You're under arrest for obstruction. Turn around, hands behind your back, and if you don't fucking comply, I'm gonna take out my goddamn stick."

As the third officer took the drug dog around the car and the dog ran its nose up and down the sides, the front, the back, the tires, and the windows, I was placed under arrest and into the back of the cop's vehicle. All anger left, and the unknown impaled me. At that moment, I thought of my mother. As much as I despised her, I wished to hear her calm, strong voice. The one I liked. The one she used to restore me like a warm cloth over dry crackling skin. *Don't you worry*, I heard her say. *They are wrong, and you are right. And right will always win.*

I remembered my mother talking to me about her clients. I seemed to remember something about her telling a cop to go fuck himself, and she didn't get arrested. I was still handcuffed, though, and sitting in the back of a police car.

I heard Wayne yell, "Goddamn!" as they drove off with me.

I stared intermittently between the back of the officer's shaved neck and the dense forests of pines that flew in between the bars on the cruiser's window.

"I don't understand what I did wrong," I said to him.

"You're not very smart then, are ya?" he asked.

I felt my nerves unraveling like the discomfiting sound of a bow drawing back against the strings of a violin. I was headed to jail.

I walked in like it was pitch black, my eyes peeled, desperately seeking safety. My painted face got lots of laughs. Like being in a haunted funhouse, I was afraid of what was around the next corner.

They banded me with a bar coded bracelet – my tracking number. "Do not remove this band," the intake deputy said. "It has all your information." She scanned it and my name popped up on her computer screen. "See?" she asked. I nodded, as I wanted to cry.

She nodded back at me, satisfied. "Go with him," she said, now nodding to a black guard who must have weighed 300 pounds. He towered over me and was dressed in SWAT regalia, which included a gun, a baton, mace, two sets of handcuffs and a Taser. It was a cornucopia of beat-downs waiting to happen.

I waited to be fingerprinted and photographed in a glass tank with fifteen other men. A few of them were passed out drunk – the end game of many people I had seen out at bars before. A few talked about how their arrests would never hold up in a court of law. Some were career criminals who spun yarns about friends who had been sitting in jail for over a year waiting for their case to go to trial or "plea out" because they couldn't afford a bond. I wasn't sure how I would survive in here for more than an hour.

After two hours, a guard came in, barked my last name and told me to "kiss the wall." I didn't understand where he wanted me to go. Then one of the guys in the room with me spoke up and decoded the officer's meaning. "He wants you to go out in the hallway and put your nose against the wall."

"Oh, okay, thanks," I said and got up. As I walked away, I heard the same guy quip that "that motha-fucker gonna get his ass beat *in general*." I learned quickly that by 'in general' he didn't mean that I would get my ass beat in the broadest sense of the colloquialism. He meant that if I had to stay overnight and go into "general population" that I would surely get killed. I considered that I might have to fight somebody or take on a pretend identity. My thoughts of surviving ranged from pretending I was a medic who had to stab a crazy patient, to me picking my nose, eating my boogers and acting like I was the insane one. I said a silent prayer that my buddies would get me out because *in general* I was scared fucking shitless.

After two hours, I was taken to "intake." I held my bracelet up, showing the intake officer I was not willing to be lost in their system. She asked me about medical issues, including gonorrhea, lice, and AIDS. I told her I was innocent and that I didn't do anything wrong.

She put down her pen and closed her eyes slowly. "Well, while we wait here for the ghost of Johnny Cochran, can I assume that you have some mental problems?"

"I'm not suicidal if that's what you're asking."

"Well, that makes one of us."

By 1:30 a.m. – six hours later – a different guard retrieved me, scanned my bracelet, and handed me a blanket and an orange jumpsuit. I suddenly felt doomed.

He took me to a room, did not take the time to explain why we were there, and told me to take my clothes off. "Do it now," he said. I looked around for a camera. There was one in the hallway but not pointing into the room. The worst part was having to bend over and show him my asshole. I closed my eyes because I didn't want to have a visual of what I was looking at while he was looking inside my rectum.

He shuffled me in my orange jumpsuit down a cinderblock-lined hallway. Every sound echoed against the cold white walls. I heard the sound of men shouting. It was coming from the end of the hallway behind a door that read: Dorm A. It was hard to decipher what was going on but it sounded like a riot. One voice louder than the next – all competing to be heard. There were no sirens though. No guards racing to relieve the tension. No tear gas being thrown. I looked at my guide and he didn't seem to care. I didn't know what could be going on at nearly 2 o'clock in the morning, but my imagination filled in the gaps. I saw myself being strangled and no one being able to get to me before I died an untimely death at the hands of someone trying to "keep his rep."

Then the guard turned a corner and pulled me with him, shoving me toward another hall that read: Bonding.

"*Jesus!*" I gasped. I had seemingly been lifted from the mouth of a shark. My nerves were fried. A hundred yards later, the shouts and screams dissipated, as he walked me through a door and sat me near an elderly lady, who was most assuredly someone's grandmother. She informed me that my bond had been posted. I drew in a breath and clasped my hands together.

I asked when the bond posted and she said, "You'll just have to forgive us. We're running behind tonight, baby. I'm sorry to have kept you waiting."

"When did it post?" I asked her again.

"We loaded it in the system for you several hours ago. I guess they've been backed up."

I held up my band – the same one the asshole inspector just scanned ten minutes ago. "Onto this?" I asked her. "My release notice was scanned into the system and my ID?"

"Yeah, every-thang goes onto that bracelet."

I lost it and pointed to the guard. "That guy searched my asshole!" I was so upset. I knew that granny would be as incensed as me.

Her face opened and she titled her head. "Baby, that's jail."

Insert audible gasp here. I was ready to light the match that burned the entire fucking institution down.

I thought about my mother and the nights she cursed about crooked cops. I got it.

It wasn't good enough just to feel anger. I needed to feel connected to someone who could help me interpret the thoughts I was having. A week later, it caused me to go to a part of campus I had not been to before.

Eight:
A Secret Among Strangers

Back at Miami, word had spread rather quickly – probably because Wayne was an athlete – that I had taken on the good-old-boy establishment of Georgia State Patrol officers. Riding the wave of applause, I moved across campus to a part I had never visited and walked into a cramped office with a tall slender window that overlooked beautiful green space and a fountain. Flanked by a bookshelf strewn with textbooks, novels, and stacks of paper on one side, and a wall filled with certificates on the other, Professor Mark Cohen reclined in a palatial high-back leather chair and spoke on the phone while his bare heels rested on a crumpled pile of newspapers. The chair was meant for a Supreme Court Justice, not a cramped professor's office.

Professor Cohen wore a Hawaiian shirt adorned with hula girls, linen shorts, and flip-flops and looked as if he had just missed the tour bus back to his cruise ship. His skin was tan, which served as a stark backdrop to thick gray chest hair and a gold Star of David.

Immediately upon seeing me, he pulled his feet down, shoved the old papers into a wastebasket, and moved around the desk, stretching the phone cord while he motioned me in and cleared a seat, which was covered in more newspapers.

"Look," he said, interrupting the person he was speaking with. "The program is fine. I'm not concerned. Judge Rubin is a friend, and I doubt seriously that he's gonna make waves – or that the waves he makes will do anything more than get us a little wet. Yeah... don't worry." He rolled his eyes to me and puppeted a mouth with his hand that wouldn't stop talking.

"John! John!" he insisted. "He appointed me on a death penalty case that I tried in his courtroom for *three months*. We're like brothers. It's going to be fine!"

"One second," he mouthed to me.

"Okay," he said into the phone. "Now go drink some of that thirty-year-old scotch I got you last year for Christmas – yeah, the one your wife doesn't know about!" He hung up. "Mr. Scales, I presume?"

"Yes, sir."

He continued to clean up the space, pulling an old cup of coffee off the shelf and into the trash and a half-eaten bagel into his mouth. "I know your mother. Very well. We tried a case together in the Southern District of Florida here for three weeks."

Hearing her name made me nervous. It was the first time I had spoken with anyone at Miami who seemed to know my mother at all. For a moment, it was all a little claustrophobic. *This was a bad idea*, I thought. *Fuck, this guy is going to call her and rat me out!*

He sensed it on my face. "Don't worry, Scales. I read the memo – I won't say a word."

I breathed. "Thank you."

"And it's my knowing your mother that helps me understand – or at least it leaves room for my understanding. She's a real pit bull, yeah?"

"That's her."

Cohen smiled suddenly. His eye turned up and he chuckled. "I'll never forget something your mother taught me. I haven't thought about it in years." He chuckled again.

I felt a wall go up. My blood thickened and my face grew tight. I crossed my arms and froze into an impermeable stare. Cohen didn't notice.

"It was probably the most important lesson in my entire career. True as God, I'll never forget her for this. Changed my career." His face was beaming.

"And what was that?" I asked him. "Learning how to castrate someone without getting blood on your loafers?"

Cohen finally picked up my shift. He settled his excitement and narrowed his eyes at me. "No, that was something I already knew how to do. She taught me how to quote a fee."

I snuffed at the idea. "Learning how to quote a fee *changed* your life."

Cohen smiled big. "You have *no* idea."

My mother took great pains to outwardly demonstrate her financial success. It made her an equal among her male contemporaries. Everybody in criminal defense lost cases – nearly all the time. Winning wasn't the litmus test for success. Rather, it was winning the right cases – the ones that went public. A large public win could carry an attorney for five years or more just on the public perception alone. My mother was very good at grandstanding on her prior victories and raking in big fees.

"You have time for a little story, don't you?"

I started to shake my head. "Well, actually–"

"Good," he said, interrupting. "We were at a law conference in Key West, Florida. We met over a piña colada at a beach bonfire meet 'n' greet. We were both speakers but I was just a baby lawyer – in my first five years of practice. Somehow we got onto charging fees and

I was complaining about taking a nickel ninety-eight wanting to hit the payload. She asked me what I did to quote the fee and I told her that I didn't take much time with the client in the beginning. I just found out the charge and told my client the fee," he said. "Then she says, 'That's it?' and I'm like 'Yeah, that's it.'"

Cohen started laughing. "Your mother looks at me and says, 'You're a craftsman, Counselor, not a goddamn checkout clerk!'"

He straightened his face at me. "And she was right. She told me, 'If you want people to think you own this fucking thing we call the practice of law, then you've got to inspire them. You've got to reach them on a level that'll make them fear for their lives and at the right moment see that you're their only salvation. You've got to be the dying question and the life-saving answer all in one breath.'"

Truthfully, I really liked the story. And if I was going to do this, I definitely needed to know how to do it and couldn't ask my mother. But I was confused. "I don't get it," I said. "I don't get what you're supposed to do, though. I mean, connect with them, inspire them, make big money, and do good work, but how?"

Cohen swirled his coffee in his mug and sensed that I was eager to know.

"Quoting a fee to a client is like a closing argument," he said. "It's the first thing you think about when you learn about a case. It's also the first real test. The way you handle a client in those first few minutes can set your reputation for the rest of your life. Because, even if they don't hire you, they'll never forget you."

He explained to me it was a simple three step process. "First," he said, "you need to be very clear that they're in the most trouble of their lives."

"Like saying to them, 'you're in a lot of trouble?'" I asked.

"You're in a lot of fucking trouble," he corrected.

"A lot of fucking trouble?" I asked.

"Absolutely. Whether it's a theft case or a murder case, you want them to understand their life as they know it is about to end."

"What about the presumption of innocence and their side of the story?"

"All important, but just not at that moment. This moment is about getting fifty thousand for a case and not five," he said. "And truthfully, Benjamin, their life is over. An arrest is life changing. Going to jail and waiting for a bond is life changing for most people. It's a horrifying experience. You want to capitalize on that experience. And when you tell them that they're in a lot of fucking trouble, you show them the code section and the maximum possible sentence of ten or twenty or thirty years or whatever. Take them from, 'I can beat this shit' to 'I'm going to die in jail.'"

"Got it," I said.

"Then and only then do you extend them a rope, okay? So, the next step is..."

"Extend them a rope," I said.

"Exactly. Just after they've all but shit their pants, you tell them you think you can fix the problem. You see? Because now they can beat the rap but only with you and your help."

I was getting really excited. "Simple and concise."

"Right. No frills. Just order. And the way you do it is

you close your books and your folders and lean forward on your desk, and you look at them and say amidst stillness and silence, 'I think I can fix this.' Because by that time, you hope, they're crying or panicking or about to have a heart attack. Right? You see? Then, at the moment, when they're somewhat relieved at their unbelievable luck of getting you as their attorney – at the moment when they're able to take a breath for the first time – that's when you quote your fee. And make it goddamn good! If you quote the right amount, most clients find themselves breathless once again but grabbing for their goddamn checkbooks, hoping that passing the money to you will instantly grant them oxygen."

"Ha!" I exclaimed. I looked at him in awe. Actually, I was looking at him but I was in awe of my mother. That was a new feeling I wasn't sure whether I should accept or discard.

"One last little thing. Don't ever look away from their eyes when quoting your fee," he told me. "If you look away, they'll think you don't believe you're worth the fee and they'll walk out. Hold them in a stare and quote the fee like you're actually looking forward to seeing them writhe in pain."

Cohen looked invigorated too. "God, I miss having clients," he said. I could see how my mother had the balls to go toe to toe with the Mob.

Cohen watched me carefully. He was so excited to tell me this story.

"I saw your mother quote a mobster once."

"Really," I said.

Cohen stood up. He was making his hands look like

claws and he started raking the air. "Your mother ravaged him. Ate him raw like a goddamn lion! He walked in there like he was some goddamn body and by the time she was done with him he was fucking putty. Your mother didn't just act like she enjoyed seeing them writhe in pain; she actually did. Forget about the blood on her lips. She wore it like it was the latest shade of red from Chanel."

"Yeah, I've met *her*, too," I said. We both smiled and shared a laugh this time.

"Well, let's talk about you, shall we?"

Back to me. I let out a sigh.

"I was looking for you in the college registry, but you're pre-med, not pre-law."

"Right, well, I've been on that course for a long time, but – I've kind of got this wild hair, and I was hoping that you might be able to... talk me out of it."

He took a bite of bagel as I was talking but then he paused and spoke through the bread. "Talk you out of it? How would I do that?"

"Well, I've never wanted to be a lawyer. Mostly, for the reasons that caused you to be so impressed with my mother, but now... I don't know. Maybe I'm putting the car before the horse?"

He swallowed. "You mean the *cart* before the horse."

"Cart?" I asked. "Car."

"How would that make sense? If you had a car, why would you need a horse?"

"I thought if you put the car before the horse..." I pondered it for another second. "Jesus, I've been saying that my whole life. It *is* the cart before the horse."

"I'm glad I could help."

I dropped my face in my hands. "Oh, man. What the fuck am I doing?"

Cohen came around the desk and sat next to me. "You're Jewish, right?"

I nodded.

"It's either medicine or law, brother. Medicine's not working out, so..."

"That wouldn't be funny if it weren't true."

"Most stereotypes work that way."

I took a minute and shook my head at myself. "My whole life I've wanted to be a doctor, like my grandfather – to do something for other people, something dignified. The law is dignified too, right?"

"Not even close."

"I was worried it might not be."

"Consider this," he said, and motioned to his wardrobe. "I'm a lawyer, too."

"The University must be so pleased."

"Tenure's a bitch."

I immediately laughed and began to consider that I could be myself around him.

Without warning, Cohen got up from his desk and walked into the hallway, then popped his head back in the office. "Follow me," he said. *Kooky.*

We walked down a sterile white hallway and stopped at a double door encased by grand wood paneling and trim. He looked at me wryly and "crossed" himself as though we were about to enter the Pope's chambers.

I followed him into a richly decorated courtroom,

which felt more like a chapel than any courtroom I had ever seen. The walls were wrapped in honey-oak paneling and wainscoting. There were rows of burgundy-padded pews for visitors. As I thought back on the rather vanilla hallway, the room seemingly had materialized like an oasis.

Visitors to the room were able to watch the festivities on two high-definition monitors. It had a witness stand and the aforementioned judge's bench, wired with microphones and monitors, for ease of use during mock trials. The finishing touch was in the marble that covered the front of the bench and witness stand.

"Wow," I said.

"Right? I had it built when I designed the trial advocacy program at the law school. That's genuine imported marble from Tate, Georgia."

"As in my home state of *Georgia*?"

"Yes," he said, as he sat in the jury box.

"You know, 'imported' implies that it at least spent part of its journey on a boat."

"This same marble was used in the US Capitol."

"Next to the wall urinals, maybe."

"You know, Scales, something tells me you'll be the perfect lawyer."

I sat in the pews and got sidetracked by a serious thought. "I think maybe I have to be a lawyer."

He left me to my thoughts for a minute until I looked back at him. Then he picked up my cue and became the professor. "You came to me for advice. So here it is. A law degree is, hands down, the best degree you could ever have. Period. Because it has two features – it's the fish and the pole. It not only immediately provides sustenance to your life but also gives you the tools to rely on, which in turn gives you power."

"My mother likes the power."

"Your mother's helped a lot of people. She deserves it."

"I'm not in it for power – although I would love to have that cop's badge. And that fucking guard's at the jail."

"You take him through a lawsuit for three years and you will."

"That's what's also frustrating about the law."

"In what way?"

"They get to commit an assault on me, and in return, I get to throw paper at them for three years."

"Hey, man, I got into this business to tell people to go fuck themselves, but I never do."

"That's not fair," I demanded.

"It's not always the squeaky wheel that gets the oil."

"Tell that to my mother."

"What do you want to do, hit him?"

"Worse," I said.

"You've just stood in the shoes of every one of your future clients, assuming you go into criminal law – or insurance defense, for that matter." His humor went over my head, but I got the gist.

"My entire life, I swore to my mother that I would never be a lawyer. And if I ever decided that being scum was the right move for me, I would never stoop so low to become a criminal defense attorney." Cohen smiled at me. "But then I was arrested for mouthing off and–"

"You were arrested because you were standing up for your friends."

"I knew I was right."

"That's what being a lawyer is about. It's about being right and standing up against tyranny."

"And losing, apparently." My gut tightened, and the taste of Wayne's, Carl's, and my harassment returned.

Cohen stood and walked into the main space. "This courtroom is the ring, the battleground between good and evil. Overzealous DAs, crooked cops, lying witnesses, and the regular Joes like you and me who are willing to stand in front of a petrified defendant and say to the awesome power of the government, 'You gotta get through me before you take my client.'"

My eyes widened at the professor's sudden declaration.

The professor leaned in: "You can beat those bastards. Right here. Every time." I smiled at the idea. "To hold the trembling hand of the accused – someone like you that's been through hell – is the greatest honor on this earth. But you win by convincing others. By doing the impossible – by rising above bias and prejudice and stereotypes and anger and hatred – and bringing strangers together in an attempt to unite them in one voice.

"You wanna kick ass? The degree gets you in the ring – to the main event where the truth spews like blood from the mouths of the witnesses you destroy and the fanatical jury returns your verdict to back you, the warrior, in the form of a bone-chilling chant: *not* guilty, *not* guilty, *not* guilty. You do this because you believe you're right. In your heart of hearts, you truly believe you're right.

"But being right doesn't guarantee victory. It's why they call it the *practice* of law. You have to know that. You need to know that before you embark on this journey. Sometimes the crowd exalts you and acquits your client or throws you a multi-million-dollar verdict." Cohen looked himself up and down once again. "That's right. Multi-million-dollar verdict." I was impressed, and he saw it on my face. "This stupid Hawaiian shirt doesn't look so stupid now, does it?"

I readily agreed.

We both sat back in our chairs and thought about it.

"A damn criminal defense lawyer, huh?" I asked myself.

"Well, you still have to get in."

I scoffed.

"What? You think I'm gonna help you?" he asked.

"You forget, I don't need you. I'm Jewish. Acceptance to law school is practically guaranteed with a circumcision." We both laughed. "There is one thing I need you to promise me," I said. My tone reflected my urgent need to be understood.

"Okay."

"My mother can never know."

"You're serious about this? You know, I think she'd die and go to heaven."

I shook my head. "Never."

Cohen's eyes stayed with mine. "Consider it attorney-client privilege."

Nine:

Dinner Rush

I struggled with the idea of working in the same field as my mother, despite Cohen's swelling oration to me. While I would be doing it because of what I felt – again following *my heart* – and what I thought I could do to protect others, I couldn't overcome the immediate reality of eating my fucking words and satisfying her. For that reason and that reason alone, I wrote it off for another *five* years. My act on that day with the police would remain a non-starter. It was just another example of my mouth getting me in trouble, nothing more. *Having balls does not a legal career make.*

I moved back to Atlanta and got a position at Scottish Rite Children's Hospital in their emergency room, which remained exhilarating. We worked hard. Tried to suppress our emotions. And partied like our lives depended on it. Truthfully, in that environment, it oftentimes did.

I got a call from my college buddy Wayne, who said he was in Atlanta for a concert with his fiancée, Tanya, and wanted to get together. The three of us met at Zocalo's Mexican restaurant in the heart of midtown for frozen margaritas and tableside guacamole and the best chicken mole and hanger steak you could eat.

Wayne was just finishing up medical school and was deciding about whether to move to Atlanta to do his fellowship in the orthopedic surgery program at Emory University. I was thrilled. Wayne was still bruised about his police encounter in Georgia. We reunited like long lost brothers. He hugged me and then held me out to meet his girl.

"This is Ben," he said. His voice was filled with pride. I felt awkward, yet honored.

"I've heard so much about you," Tanya said. She had white teeth and short-cropped hair. She looked like a runner. "It's so nice to meet Wayne's hero," she said, holding my hand and squeezing it earnestly.

"Hero?" I asked him.

"Hey, man – you know that you're the man."

I shook my head at him and chose to divert us away from the serious tone. "So, he must have told you about diaper day," I said to Tanya, who snapped her face back. "Adult diapers, of course," I said.

Wayne looked at Tanya who was somewhat horrified, then back to me. His face paled, which was hard with his dark complexion. "See – you are wrong for that, man. I bring a nice lady out to meet my best friend from college and you're just all about gettin' crazy with the cheese wiz." That was a quote from Beck that Wayne and I loved.

"What in the hell is diaper day?" Tanya asked. "And did you just quote *Beck*?"

"She knows Beck?" I asked, totally surprised.

"I told you, man, she's cool. This girl is for real, dog," he said.

Tanya interrupted our bonding moment. "Listen up, fellas, I need to know about diaper day *right now* because either you spent the day at the children's hospital doing charity work or I need to find another man to marry," she said. Tanya was very funny.

I smiled like I just ate the canary. "It's hard to resist wanting to know about diaper day, isn't it?" I asked her.

Wayne put his hands in a praying position. "Please don't tell my smart, beautiful fiancé, whose father is a *district court judge in Chicago*, about diaper day."

I looked at Wayne and then at Tanya. "Oh, this is going to be a fun evening."

We carried on like that for an hour. When the laughter subsided because of stuffed bellies, Wayne finally asked me about law school.

I let out a sigh. "I'm struggling with it. It's such a drastic change in direction. I mean, I probably can't even get in."

"Have you applied?" he asked.

"No, but-"

"Scales, you're a fool if you don't." He turned to Tanya. "His mother is like a famous Mafia attorney and he spent his life swearing that he would never do what she does but, I'm telling you, babe, it's in his blood."

There was that saying again. I was growing to dislike it because I couldn't tell if "it" being in my blood was a compliment or an insult. If it was a compliment, did it mean that my ability to be an attorney was predetermined by my mother or her success?

Sensing my hesitation to discuss it, Tanya spoke up. "He tells everyone that story about your road trip," she said. "Even my father was impressed with it. And it takes a lot to impress my dad."

"I didn't do anything that anyone else wouldn't do," I said.

"No," Wayne demanded. "You are wrong." He leaned in and locked eyes with me. "You are very, very wrong."

I looked at Tanya. She raised her eyebrows as if to

say, he's right. I was suddenly feeling the pressure. "Oh, see, okay, babe – you see that look in his eyes?" Wayne asked Tanya, wryly. She nodded. "Yeah, that's called panic, babe – you see it?"

"Oh, yeah, babe. I see it," she chimed in quickly. I rolled my eyes, feeling the bullshit coming.

"Yeah, that's his look when he gets like, 'this shit is gettin' too real' and he just needs to bug out."

"Can't handle the heat, stay out of the kitchen," she said to me.

I started to smirk and shake my head. "Stop," I said.

"It's real man," Wayne said. "You can't turn this shit off like you do, man."

"I'm trying to figure it out."

"No, you're trying to walk away, like you do. You've walked away from it. You know how you do it. It's like one day it's there and the next it's like boom – cut off."

"Is that what he does?" Tanya asked. Her tone was teasing but I was starting to feel that Wayne was not teasing.

"I hear you, partner," I told him, trying to find something else to look at.

He dropped his smile and reached across the table and clasped my hand, forcing my eyes to join his. "Do you?" he probed. Tanya sensed the change as well and sat quietly, watching our private moment.

I locked eyes with him. "I do," I said. He pointed to my heart and then to my mouth. "Between this and this, you can change the world, brother."

Ten:

Last Stop: The Beginning

A dark train ride. Numb. On my way home from my first day in law school and my own worst nightmare. If Wayne could see me now. The memories of my life before law school streamed by with the power lines. I watched the tract homes pass. I was starring in my own worst nightmare. I had undermined the person I had hoped to be.

From "hero" to "zero." My misfortune, two hundred and fifty more pages to deal with, and a lovable nickname referencing a consumer device women jammed in their vaginas.

The legal learning establishment was exalted because of its historical ideologies and the good it created for the world. The honor of being selected by the admission committee belonged to the students alone. Our promise was to uphold their belief in us. The best of the best. The most promising talents. The next generation of greats. A coup even my mother had claimed. And then me. Mr. Tampon.

There was no conversation on the train, just people riding out their long days. Headphones. Books. Cold French fries. Rhythmic metal.

Going from stop to stop, I watched dozens come and go.

It was nice to be among people who didn't know me.

At last, there were only two others – a woman and a little boy. Her long red hair covered her face as she read. Her posture showed her exhaustion. The boy looked bored, wanting an action figure, or something to color.

They stared in opposite directions, she into her book and he at a moth stuck in a fluorescent bulb above. He giggled then caught me watching him. I smiled at his amusement.

The woman's clothes weren't high-end, but it seemed she was trying to impress. Inexpensive, yet professional enough. Purposeful. Functional. Shoes flat. Closed pointy toes. A woman not interested in compliments. No wedding ring.

She moved her hair and looked up at me. We locked eyes for a split second, then she turned hers down to the boy. I recognized her immediately. It was the girl from my class.

She pulled the boy's shoulders into her lap, turning his head to rest it, and stilled his movement. I stared directly at their private moment. She caught me watching, so I had to say something.

"Awesome time today, huh?"

She nodded slowly, biting her upper lip.

"I've also been trained to hold lipstick and driver's licenses."

"If I'm ever out at a club," she said, nodding at the boy, "I'll be sure to employ your services."

"Is that your little brother or...?"

"Son," she said.

I smiled. "How old is he?"

"Four."

"I'm Ben," I said.

"Paige," she said. "And this is Colby."

I put my fist out to Colby. "Sup, dude," I said. He barely extended his. We connected briefly.

"You have him in a day care near the school, I assume."

She nodded.

"You a good boy for your mom, Colby?" I asked him. He peeked back at me using her arm as cover.

"It's okay," she said. "You can answer the man."

The boy nodded then buried himself in Paige's arm again.

I looked away but kept the image. I felt for the kid immediately.

"It's tough trying to balance everything, huh?" I said to the kid. She thought I was being funny, treating him like an adult. I wasn't being funny. She chose to answer for him.

"It's okay. It's worth it. Right, kiddo?" She shook her son's shoulder.

"I'm hungry," he said.

"Me too," I told him.

I was done talking to her. I was suddenly in a different place now. Seeing her and the little boy reminded me of my mother and me. I knew her experience as well as she – but his even better. I looked at the boy in disbelief that I was ever that small, that dependent. But there I was. Tiny hands. Spider-Man shoes. Eyes as deep as space and time. I had spent a lifetime strapped to the waist of a woman like that. The title of that particular story hadn't changed despite two-and-a-half decades between my experience with my mother and this little boy's current experience with his. Two souls lost at sea – one totally unaware, the other terrified of death and survival.

I did not think about my mother in a good way. It wasn't like me. Quick retorts to questioning friends that she was "same old" or even more, accentuated with a grunt and eye roll. I chose to shut down emotional engines such as compassion and understanding and fueled my anger rocket, which made it easier to fly away.

Seeing the boy and his mother, I was suddenly aware of my total emotional separation from my own – that at one point, I loved her deeply like this little boy loved his. Unconditionally. And now? Nothing.

Paige was probably around twenty-seven, just like my mother at the time of her quest into single motherhood and law school. Such a heavy load. A child. Bills. Eggs and bread for dinner and eighty pages for dessert. Midnight hours, stirring coffee, digesting reality, standing in the doorway of my room, pulling up my blanket, answering my cries with hugs and strokes in my hair. Then back to the books that would make her or break her and a hundred more pages by 2 a.m. Law school is formidable under any circumstance. Virtually impossible now.

Observing the two of them suddenly gave color, texture, and form to the idea that my mother – a single mother like this woman – probably had it the same. And suddenly it hinted at a possible explanation for my mother's intolerable personality. My thought seemed like forgiveness, though, and I wasn't there, tough times or not. It still was no excuse. I looked back at the boy and felt sorry for him.

The train stopped, and the girl and her son exited. I left the train behind them and watched her drag him along. I guess I could have offered to carry her bag but she might as well do it herself. There was no room for weakness where she was going.

Then she looked back at me. "You look like *you* could use some help," she told me, eyeing my bag, and offering a hand.

"I forgot the combination to my locker. I got it though."

She smiled softly. "I'll see you tomorrow?"

"Still open for debate," I said. I saluted them off and watched her and the boy walk to their car.

Alone again, feeling my regret of ever going to law school. I didn't want to think about any of it, especially details concerning my mother. Empathy began to creep in once more. She didn't deserve it and never exercised it for me. But there I was, minutes ago on that train, just ten feet away from my past.

A single mother in law school was an oddity, clearly. But doing it three decades ago was suicide.

In my current law school class, half of the students were women. In Atlanta in 1975, my mother was the only woman. When she dared to practice in the trial courts, judges often thought she was a hooker waiting on her lawyer or a proud housewife come to see her husband at work. Prosecutors grabbed her ass. Prison guards laughed as she attempted to walk in high heels on gravel roads. Clients begged her to curry favors with the same judges and prosecutors who belittled and harassed her.

She was more out of place than a handbag at a duck hunt.

Despite the inequalities, my mother truly believed that, if she worked the hardest, she would rise to the top. It was much like basic physics. She simply refused to accept that there ever would be a force equal to her.

My mother tackled everything like a Great White on a seal. Control was key, and she was better than most at grabbing the tail and flinging it back into the murky depths where massacre and murder were assured.

But her ruthless ambition was a tricky business. Our life became a perfect storm of all of life's brutal elements. From the time of my parents' divorce when I was three years old up until I left for college, I often became entangled in her experiences, her vulnerabilities and jealousies, and her inability to maintain her emotions. Outside our house, men made fun of her; inside she demanded respect from the only man in her life she actually could control – me.

Paige buckled Colby into his car seat and gave him a kiss.

"You wanna chicken sandwich or a cheeseburger for dinner?"

"I wanna milkshake!"

"Done deal," she said. "But you have to eat a..." She paused with great significance.

"...a chicken sandwich," he groaned.

"A chicken sandwich first – you betcha!" she said, encouraging him with a smile. She gave him another kiss.

"Can I have French fries, too?"

"Oh, yummy!" she said.

When I entered my apartment, I did not turn on the lights. I shied away from the mirror over the table at the entrance. I looked down as I passed the hallway bathroom and the mirror over the sink. I was afraid to look at myself. I was afraid to confirm just how much time had passed to carry me away from that little boy.

I had just seen my past before my very eyes – an apparition that called into question years of brutal judgment by me against my mother. Ebenezer Scrooge and I could share a whiskey and relate.

I dropped my books. Tonight, there would be no reading. My keys missed the counter and landed on the floor. I didn't know if I would even go to class tomorrow.

I sat on the edge of my couch but slid to the floor. I needed to put my head between my knees to overcome the feelings of nausea.

I let out a sigh – the kind that empties the bottom of your lungs and hangs like a fog until you realize that if you don't take a breath you might never take another one.

I blended into the darkness of the room and didn't move.

It had been a decade since my mother and I had had a real conversation. Me and the Dragon Lady. Our break wasn't clean; it was filled with a lifetime of smaller fractures that when summed up as a whole translated into an inability to reset the bone and my subsequent decision to amputate the leg.

It was a trait I incorporated into most relationships. Relationship amputation. It was simply too hard to care about shit. Call me callous. Literal. Wry. Whatever you like. I invested heavily in my defense mechanisms and didn't do feelings anymore.

But now I was suddenly *feeling* for her. Not as an

outsider, but again as her son.

Moments like this had come and gone over the years – with my feeling nostalgic for some ideal that never existed – but they were more infrequent now. I didn't want to think good thoughts about her or have hope about her. I had worked so hard to get her to understand me, for her to understand herself better, and then, when she didn't, I had worked so hard to just get away from her. This was a time in my life where I was finally convinced that I had outrun my guilt over my decision to cut the strings. The distance between it and me could never have been closed.

But here I was, suddenly knocked off course, reeling back toward her and back into the name that she had given me. I wasn't the twenty-nine-year-old future lawyer, Ben Scales, who didn't need his mother anymore. Rather I was suddenly back to feeling those emotions I'd felt as a boy. Back to me in the time of being bathed. Being bottle-fed. Being wrapped in blankets.

The small me.

The nervous me.

The then me before the now me, back in the time of the queen.

I closed my eyes to the feeling of old emotions. I tried to remember whether we had sweet moments like the boy and his mother or whether it was the hell I clearly remembered.

A tsunami of images streamed. A rush of blood to my head, overtaking the set pieces.

Little Benny Scales, I thought.

Son of Carter Scales.

Son of the famed Mafia attorney.

Son of the Dragon Lady.

"Son of a bitch."

Eleven:
Pissin' With The Boys

I was Colby's age when the course of my life changed. My mother didn't have it easy. A domineering father. A failed marriage to a man who was pushy like her father. Both men underestimated her. It was defining until she had the strength to turn the lead page and start a new chapter for herself – for us.

It was just before my fourth birthday when my mother laced a handful of spaghetti between her fingers and hurled it into my father's face. She wanted a divorce.

Like a heroin addict running away from her past, she stuffed under one arm as much clothing, cash, and jewelry as she could fit, and me under the other and headed for the door. It was as if the Quarter-Life Crisis Police were storming the back door of her failed marriage and she wanted a clean getaway. The spaghetti stains on her blouse made that a bit tricky.

My dad, Ray, thought he had acquired the small-town-wife model, which featured, among other things, grand servitude to thy husband. He failed to read the small print, though, which read, "This wife may experience catastrophic breakdowns and lead to choking hazards."

My mother entered her first courthouse in 1974 when she testified about her "irreconcilable differences" with my dad. He kept his face in his hands, disappointed over the failure of his promise to love eternally. Afterward, my mom stuck around and studied the lawyers.

Those legal scholars, at that time all men, had great presence. With all eyes and ears on them at all times, they told their clients what to do, what to say, how to do it, and when to do it. Even the judges had to listen. They spoke with great measure and authority about people, events, and the laws that built the houses of truth within which they practiced. They were experts, often respected for their degrees alone. It was at that moment that she realized that she too could find her own kind of power in the law.

My mother always had been smart. Driven. The law was, at a minimum, a scholastic pursuit. At most, though, with persistence and a good sense for business, it was a ticket to independence and riches. A Juris Doctorate, or JD, was a surefire step up from working the makeup counter at Saks or becoming a bank teller. She called it her "Just Don't" degree. "*Just don't* touch me. *Just don't* fuck with me. *Just don't...*"

While my mother fought tooth and nail to rise into the number-one spot of her law school class, I spent each day at a local daycare with other four-year-olds. The strip mall establishment was run by a husky collection of social misfits who spread flesh-tone base makeup like mud over sheetrock. They reeked of coffee breath and wore sunglasses until noon and hacked while they laughed, covering their mouths with their yellow-stained fingertips. A lovely bunch really.

Six months after I started there, police arrested the day-shift manager for child molestation. With my dad on hiatus and my mother having sole custody and night school classes, my mother kept me there to walk in between the landmines to the best of my ability. She told me just to let her know if anyone touched me.

By the time she graduated from law school in 1977, she no longer needed permission from anybody to do anything. For the first time in her life, she wasn't someone's wife or someone's daughter. She was an equal among men – at least on paper.

As one of the first female criminal defense attorneys in Atlanta, Georgia – no small task back then – my mother was asking for entrance into one of the city's oldest boys' clubs. A city known for cultural riots and segregation, Atlanta had its share of upheaval. And it wasn't just about blacks and whites. Women were considered second-class citizens too. For my mother's sake, the Atlanta of the 1970s was nearly the same place it had been in '60s, and not all that far from the place it had been in '50s.

Men still wore cowboy boots under the bellbottom flair of their slacks and publicly picked the crotch of their pants when the inseam rode into their balls. The world was their men's room. Some of them deliberately wore pants that were so tight their balls would just sort of bulge to the side. "Crotch biscuits," my mother called them.

Judges and attorneys alike reclined back in their oversize leather chairs and paid special mind to keep their legs open just wide enough to give her a clue as to the immediate heaven awaiting her on the other side of their Levi's Action Slacks. The Southern cuisine of "biscuits and gravy" gave her a new appreciation for cold cereal. When she tried to dissuade them by hiding her femininity under pants, suits and wide-framed glasses, they mentally masturbated to the increased demand on their imagination. What you call sexual harassment today was business as usual then.

My mother's thick chestnut hair and pooling blue eyes didn't gain her any favors. In the early years, she would have gladly opted for breast reduction surgery and legs that weren't so long and thin.

On one particular morning, she had a meeting with a state judge in his chambers regarding a misdemeanor matter. She was there to educate him on the injustices being done to her client. He led her back into his cave-like, oak-walled office and closed the door so they might have some privacy. She found some comfort in his oversize office windows and the bright morning sun that streamed past the heavy wool curtains until he pulled the curtain edges together, leaving the room dusted in the dim light of a single desk lamp.

"Now," he said, turning his attention to her, "why don't we take a moment to get to know each other a little better?" The wrinkles on his forehead and face circled his widening eyes like the rings on a bull's-eye. In the darkened space, the age spots on his skin made him look like a dying vampire desperate for that last drop of blood.

Every time she spoke about the law, he slammed his fist on his desk and interrupted her. "Got-damn, those legs are purty!"

"Your honor," my mother said, hoping the two words used together would jerk his honor by the collar and slap him back to reality, "my client has been in jail for eighty days on a misdemeanor criminal trespass charge. He needs a bond he can afford."

The judge's reply was short and unfortunately persistent. "Lemme see what you got under that skirt."

"Don't, okay? *Just don't.*" Her standing response. Often it was accompanied with a red face and watery eyes from fear and adrenalin.

"Aw, darlin'," he said. "It's all right. I'd never do anything to hurt chew."

After a few rounds of this, she ran out. Her client didn't get his bond reduced, and she got no more respect than the little she had started with.

Clients were no better. As one of the only female criminal defense attorneys, she was an oddity. She took whatever came in the door, mostly hookers and drug dealers – the real heroin addicts. The drug dealers liked her because she was attractive and confident. They thought she might be able to bat her eyelashes and move them through the legal system – give a judge a blowjob to help them out. The hookers liked her because she bought them pancakes at IHOP and didn't try to fuck them.

"Everybody be tryin' to touch my pussy," one of her client's complained over a Rooty Tooty special.

She looked at the woman and smiled empathetically; it was amazing how similar their lives really were. She never felt more comfortable than in the presence of prostitutes.

By the time my mother learned her way, she had threatened nearly every judge in town with the promise of a very public sexual harassment lawsuit. The growing women's movement finally had made it down South, and my mother reveled in it. She joined the local criminal bar association and worked her way up to be its president. She lobbied the state legislature and got support for bills that eventually evened the playing field for criminal defense attorneys when battling against the awesome power of the state. She found joy in the feeling of having all eyes on her. She grew comfortable in uncomfortable situations – like looking at her naked reflection in her bedroom window then opening the shutters for the whole neighborhood to see. Only when she had nothing to lose did she have everything to gain. Eventually, they all knew not to fuck with – or try to fuck – Carter Scales. They were too afraid of what she might do.

She was also brilliant. Controlling yet polite. My mother stretched the seams of her confinement and grew into the newly created space. She was a performer, graceful in her ability to play a subtle smile across her face as she unzipped your fly and systematically removed your manhood.

She learned it all on her own. Having a mentor wasn't an option. There weren't any other female attorneys to show her the ropes. All the men she came across only wanted one thing in exchange for their services – *her* services. She refused. She drove down dirt roads and fought with overweight prison guards and militant Baptist wardens, sheriffs, and police officers. Just after they'd recite some verse from the Bible, they'd close their office doors and slide in next to her.

My mother's high heels and stretched nylon hose didn't gain her any favors. It was a boys' network, and none of them respected her. When she finally accepted that reality, she realized she could at least take pleasure in how much they wanted her and maybe even make it somewhat painful... for them. When dressing down didn't discourage unwanted attention, she swung the pendulum the other way. She dressed to be noticed, to be desired. She never left a room without at least one man making the "mmm" noise, as if he'd just bitten into the best damn pork rib sandwich of his life.

Despite her growing strength, she often relapsed. I never knew which version would come home. The sound of pots and pans crashing was usually an indication. If a hammering sound followed it, I had my answer for sure.

My mother called it 'anger chicken'.

A pack of chicken breasts that she would beat with a clawed mallet. Raw meat would fly all over the walls and countertop. She would release whatever tension she had on the pounding and then soak the devastated meat in egg and Jason breadcrumbs.

Then she'd fry it in hot oil and break open pepperoncini peppers and drizzle the juice on the crispy fried cutlets and drop the husks in the hot oil. I would eat it out of the pan off the stove. I *loved* anger chicken.

Some weeks, my mother cried almost every night. She'd look at herself in the mirror and watch her tears fall then wipe them away and call herself weak or worthless.

"What are you going to do, cry in front of the judge? Come on, Carter, you're better than that, damn it!"

I sat at the edge of my bed just down the hall as her self-deprecating curse words echoed through vents that linked our rooms. On those nights where she only got four hours of sleep, I only got three.

Then one day, an idea struck my mother. It came on the day that one of the secretaries at the Clerk's office brought her daughter to work.

The most important function of the Clerk's office was to maintain all the legal filings that made up the thousands of cases at the courthouse by the precise date and time they were filed. The Clerk was an elected official and had always been a man. The Clerk had a lot of power in the courthouse. He set the grand jury schedules, told the prosecutors when they could have trials, and knew the inner workings of every deal being made.

He couldn't do it all, though. Under the Clerk were a few dozen associate clerks and filing secretaries who were always women. The office looked more like a harem. Everyone got their shoulders rubbed, hair touched, and occasionally a gentle hand slid down their side and onto their rump. Except on the one day a year the courthouse held their annual "bring your kid to work day."

Thus, my mother devised her first partnership as an attorney. For me, it meant a day of skipping school. Together we would be stronger. As it turned out, most grown men felt a bit uneasy attempting to grope a woman in front of her child.

"My son," my mother would say. She patted my shoulder like I was a loaded firearm on her hip. I would shake the grown men's oversize hands and look them in the eyes. They'd put their hands on my shoulders and try to usher me out to the lobby. They'd call their secretaries to come and get me to go color while they spoke with "mommy." My mother, however, wouldn't let go of my hand. "No, no," she'd say. "You stay right here with momma."

"Why don't we not bore the little guy and just talk in private?" they'd say.

"He's fine. Aren't you, son?"

The first time I said I'd rather go play than listen to her talk about the Constitution, my mother sank her diamond-studded pinky nail into the soft underside of my arm. "You understand where I'm comin' from?" she asked me.

Even at eight, I understood her quite clearly.

My mother grew tougher in those times. Unlike a snake that sheds its skin, hers grew thicker. The scholastic pursuit of law didn't end once she graduated from law school; it continued and would do so as long as the Court of Appeals and Supreme Court of the United States was open for business and gave her ammunition for her next battle.

She romanced her law books, studying even harder than she had in law school, mastering her understanding of the law and what rights and recourse the law afforded her. The key to survival was in the fine print – the details – and the more she knew, the more powerful she became.

"You don't have a case, and you know it!" she blasted at a prosecutor. "Consider this a refresher course in something called the Bill of Rights and the Fourth Amendment, you sniveling little prick. Have you even read the footnotes in *Terry v. Ohio*? Even the goddamn dicta are law!"

She stood in hallways and outside the doorways of investigators, prosecutors, and judges, and she waited. They couldn't stay in their offices forever, though; eventually, their pissed-off housewives would call and demand they come home and relieve them from raising their perfect little brats. Once they came out, they couldn't dodge her. And once she opened her mouth, they knew – even better than I did – that they didn't have a balloon's chance in a room full of needles.

Even so, the beleaguered boys' club had one failsafe – the one place into which she never could gain entrance. Just as she'd raise her voice or lay the foundational framework of her argument, her male contemporaries would sidestep her masterful conclusions and excuse themselves... to take a piss. It was the bane of her gender-specific existence. As the door closed, she'd hear the laughter and the sounds of muffled talk. Whatever point she was trying to make was as lost as the urine swirling down the drain.

"God, I wish I could go in there," she once said. "Just to piss with the boys – just once."

Twelve:

Get A Grip

My mother took two cases that changed her life. The first led to the second, and the second led to hundreds. It all began on the palm of her hand.

Confused and terrified in the early phases of her career, she visited a psychic. She needed guidance and a stranger's opinion. Mary Rivers was a psychic who had assisted the Atlanta Police Department in their missing persons division for many years – without pay. She also had a private practice – a hopeful group of individuals who somehow "found their way" to her door. At this point, my mother felt more lost than most.

Mary asked her what she did for a living and, upon hearing the answer, declared unequivocally that my mother was going to get Mary's boyfriend out of jail. Mary's boyfriend was a charming criminal who had stolen the Six Flags Amusement Park payroll and ultimately got caught at a bus stop in Tulsa. He was a small fish by any prosecutor's measuring stick, but it was my mother's first federal case and the first time she got a taste of federal prosecutors and federal judges and the awesome power of the federal government.

Each state in the United States had a federal trial court system. Just as the state police and state prosecutors arrested and charged people with state crimes, federal police – the FBI, CIA, Secret Service, ATF – and federal prosecutors arrested and charged people with federal crimes. Luckily, practicing in federal court was as easy as applying. As long as you didn't have any strikes against you in the state where you were licensed to practice, you could practice in any federal court in the country. If you could master the rules and ways of the federal court, you literally had a license to kick ass all across the country.

State court was true "government" – lazy employees who reveled in the nine-to-five, no holidays, weekends, late nights, or early mornings to work, and plenty of cheap carpet. The Feds were a cut above. The finest. The smartest. Brilliant strategists. They weren't about reelection and local politics. They were about the FBI, the CIA, task force agents, wiretaps, surveillance, and a 95-percent win ratio. They were also *not* about, as it turned out, trying to touch my mother's ass.

After a two-week stay in New York City and a hearing in the Second Circuit Court of Appeals, my mother came through on Mary's prediction and got the evidence tossed out and the man a new trial. With no evidence, however, the government declined to prosecute.

When my mother returned to Atlanta, she knew she had done something big. She walked into our condo and looked through the small galley kitchen and imagined the future. "Do you know what I could do if we had twice the cabinet space?" she asked me.

Her feelings of grandeur were dead on.

Apparently, Mary's boyfriend told his good news to a colleague housed in a large federal penitentiary – a New York Mafia wise guy named Vincent Brusio who was "blood." Vin was a bit hesitant at first at the idea of a woman from Georgia leading his appeal.

"Don't worry," the guy told Vin. "She's a snowbird and a Jew."

Everybody in New York wanted a Jewish attorney.

The Mafia was no exception.

My mother read Vin's trial transcript and found a host of errors made by his trial attorney. In total, the trial attorney not only placed his client at the scene of the crime but also allowed, without objection, evidence of other previous crimes to come in at his trial, all in an effort to be cordial with the government – a sure sign in my mother's eyes that the guy's attorney was a giant wimp. The judge gave that poor bastard a new trial, and Carter Scales became an underworld hero. Although the Mafia never spoke about their business, this goodfella couldn't stop talking about the woman who singlehandedly had turned the government's best prosecutors on their heads.

It just so happened that the federal penitentiary he'd been held in was crowded due to increased federal funding for the FBI to make racketeering and conspiracy arrests against as many people as possible. Ultimately, the penitentiary closed due to unsanitary conditions, and the inmates were shipped all over the country – but not before they had a chance to hear from Vin himself about Carter Scales – the snowbird, Jew, magic maker, and Dragon Lady who was unafraid of anything or anyone. Vin was released on a new pretrial bond, and Carter was an overnight success, delivered nationwide on the lips of the country's worst criminals, courtesy of the United States Government. Not to mention, that one very happy Mafia higher-up whose son had just returned home adored her.

Mary's confidence in my mother made her a permanent fixture in our lives. Even though they were close in age, she became like a mother to her. She even made special appearances for me as a fortune teller at our annual Halloween party. She was quite a hoot.

Within months, my mother was working appeals for two of the five major New York crime families and rapidly leaving the state court system behind. Every wise guy from every street in the Northeastern tri-state area had her home number. The phone rang off the hook. My mother quickly instructed me how to answer the phone, which resembled a secretarial-type introduction.

"Hello. Scales' residence. This is Benjamin."

"You have a collect call from a federal penitentiary. Will you accept?"

"I'll accept."

Soon all the voices on the other end would respond in similar fashion. "Hey, Benji. How ya doin'? How old are you now?"

"Eight."

"Wow, you're gettin' big, you little basta'd, you."

"Yep. I sure am!"

I knew them all by name: Carmine, Vinni, Georgi, Pauli, Saul, Tony, Tony, and Tony. And they knew us, intimately.

"How's ya mom doin'? Still bustin' your balls?"

"Yes, sir."

They'd laugh then explain to me how I needed to stay in school and listen to my teachers. I would laugh, too. My mother would watch me on the phone and smile. I saw something in her too. It was pride, although I didn't know it then. The way she smiled at me enjoying her clients. I felt the return of happiness.

My mother would instruct me to say goodbye and

then dash upstairs to grab the phone in her bedroom. She'd spend the rest of the night on the phone with her new family – her clients. Whenever she got pissed off at one of them – which happened fairly regularly – she would remind herself that she didn't have to represent such high profile and high maintenance clients. The truth was it became her lifeblood. She told a colleague once: "All I've ever wanted was to be the one they called when the shit hit the fan."

As far as my mother was concerned, no one needed her like her clients. They were far from home, stationed in a dirty cell with no window, no one to talk with, and no one to discuss personal problems with. Worldly men, well-traveled men, savvy businessmen who had nothing but a cement wall and their cigarettes. The fact that I might need her beyond dinner never crossed her mind.

She was privy to intimate conversations with the nation's most feared gangsters. But these same men would sob to her like small children about premature ejaculation, sexual inadequacies, and fears of rejection and disappointment. They'd ask her how to deal with their inability to communicate with their children or how to show affection to their fathers. She had all the answers and worked her ass off for their legal issues twenty-four hours a day. She even sent them dirty magazines and books to cheer them up.

Plus, they were gorgeous Italian men. Muscular and tan. And wealthy beyond anything she had ever seen before. Even locked up, they were powerful. Money was no object, and they could influence people with it even from behind bars.

They were all determined to win her affection. Aside from being in her early 30's and looking better than ever, she was sensitive and smarter than any woman they'd ever met and a willing participant in their mind games. Their wives got fat and slaved over their fat kids. My mother wore tailored suits and understood the nuances of adding a hint of sexual suggestion to her professionalism. It was her body language. The glances. The way she held her mouth. She purposefully constructed her conversations like a tug-o-war – playful teasing; give a little, take a little.

She got purses, watches, jewelry, diamonds, and fur coats. I got birthday presents and checks and a whole lot of advice from "one man to another." She had relationships with them – non-sexual, long distance, collect call, phone love. She laughed with them; she cried with them. In a legal system where most women walked two steps behind their boss, as the attorney, she was the lead. Her career and her adoring clients were the only things that made her happy, and in the long run, I convinced myself to be happy for her. It was better than her crying and cursing. I even admired her clients. They got the best of her and always seemed to bring a smile to her face, something I felt I couldn't do. The mob brought laughter back into our home.

As news spread from the federal circuits back to the state courthouse and finally down the dirt roads about my mother's new clientele, jaws dropped. Attorneys and judges alike loosened their pants and the pressure around their crotch biscuits long enough to allow blood flow to return to their tiny brains. How did *this* woman do it? A woman once mistaken by a judge as a hooker dressed in a skirt suit. How did she rise above petty criminals and ass-grabbing state court judges and gain entrance into the Mafia, one of the most lucrative but frightening boys' clubs in the world? She had gone from skirts to pant suits, and once she had them by the balls, she wore skirts again.

Few were privileged enough to be in such company, and the few who had entrée were pursued by just about every media organization in the country. Calls streamed in like a heavy rain. Neither my mother nor I knew what to expect.

We each had our own interpretation. While I saw a tornado, my mother saw a yellow brick road that led right out of the City of Atlanta and the state court system, which suddenly seemed like a faded stop sign in the middle of nowhere town. And although she never got to piss with Feds, it didn't matter. Carter Scales had her hands down the pants of the country's most infamous criminal clientele, and she rather liked how it felt.

Thirteen:
Check Please

By the time I entered middle school, my mother's business was bustling. Turning the corners and racing for the Rat Pack, making sure the small-town train station platform retreated as quickly as she had leaped from it. She was too afraid to slow down, worrying that her success was just a fluke and that failure would overcome her and smother her like gravy. Her diamond Rolex watch sparkled as she ran; as the ultimate symbol of success in the early 1980's, it was enough to keep her motivated.

We moved from a 1,000 square-foot condo into a 3,500-square-foot house with a bonus room and a pool. A classically curved silver Jaguar sedan stretched catty-cornered in our three-car garage. Any and all of her feelings of inadequacy should have been left at the signing tables. But still, subconsciously, they remained.

She focused on the known – that she had a great chest and fabulous legs, which in particular emergencies could and would cause a professional traffic jam, resulting in all eyes on her; that she was loud, and her particular use of volume in and of itself was a weapon more powerful than flesh; and that her opinion, whether right, partially right, or even dead wrong, was best used as a wrecking ball. These, paired with her gifted ability to pinpoint and recall the minutiae of facts and law, made her irreproachable. No one knew the law like my mother. And no one knew how to stretch facts to fit the needs of her clients like she did. She argued as if she actually believed the square peg belonged in the round hole.

Internally, however, she felt a growing panic that she wasn't the star she imagined; rather, she was merely being tolerated. It was an insecurity she forced herself to ignore. With one eye so focused on the tasks ahead and the other on the obstacles now behind her, she was oblivious to the drama unfolding within. Her work had brought about a change in her.

Unfortunately, she never had a great ability or even a desire to do an internal self-check. If she had, she would have seen and felt the disturbance brewing inside. That her law practice was overwhelming and emotionally unrelenting. That her patience shortened as her hours lengthened. And that these irritations had become a drain on her soul; they slowly ate away at her small-town innocence and left behind a brute force – an expanding, highly charged, emotional weather system that was gaining speed. Hurricane Carter.

She wasn't the first, though, being preceded by another before her – the "B" to her "C." And as much as she refused to recognize that she could be the product of another person's personality flaws, she couldn't shake the original storm, her father, who was a Category 5 to her Category 3.

Jacob Silver slicked his hair back, the way successful, edgier men did. He had a broad smile that dominated his face. Full eyebrows shaded his hawk-like brown eyes, which were set nearly six feet off the ground. He was physically imposing for a Jewish man. He had few enemies, which was also surprising for a Jewish man – especially in their small Catholic town. He sang like an opera star without any training. Just had the ear for it. He served as the cantor at his temple. He went to medical school because doctors didn't have to earn anyone's respect and because he liked to tell people what to do. He started out as a general practitioner and became a dynamic surgeon. He was beloved by all the people in their small midwestern town. He had birthed practically all the children. Every household within thirty miles of their one-stop-sign main street had opened their front door to Doc Silver.

It was easy for Jacob to believe his daughter cared. Every time he left the house, someone wanted to shake his hand and remind him what a gem he was to all. Buy him dinner. Pay for his groceries. Women looked for him in public so they could thank him with a pie or pay a compliment to his worldly mind and compassionate bedside manner. He was a star. He was Bill Clinton before Bill Clinton became the Bill Clinton that became President Clinton.

My mother's relationship with her father was less than affectionate. It consisted of a phone call every Sunday so he could berate her on a wide array of subjects: "You need to grow your business. You're not late on bills, are you? You're always in money trouble – what's the matter with you?" It was all she could take. Although she played the part of the queen in our little parish, she remained a servant girl in the eyes of her father, the emperor.

The Sunday calls were a screen for the one important call of the year – the real reason she tolerated his evil ridicule. Every year just before April 15, she'd pull the phone onto her lap, pick up the handset, and hold the receiver down.

"I'm just going to tell him that we had some unexpected house expenses and that I thought I'd bring in some more business to cover it, but times are tough," she said to me.

I sat next to her on the bed while she lied to her father. While Jacob Silver heard praise, I saw pretend laughter, pretend care, and pretend interest in everything he had to say. Her words meant nothing.

In 1969, as per legend, grandfather wrote my mother and father a check for $10,000 just after they were first married – something to ease the transition. Jacob had an ass the size of a Cadillac bumper and it always took effort to remove his checkbook from his back pocket. He would extract it like a gold coin from behind your ear but without the smile and then would mumble over the math. With abrupt, exaggerated flicks, he penned his signature then ripped the check from the book, stopping it just inches from your face.

"Do you know what time I had to get up in the morning to earn this money?" he'd say.

Even before my mother and father's marriage began to fail, grandfather promised it would not last. "Divorce that asshole!" he told her. She obeyed him, and did so quickly. Delay or scrutiny weren't options. If he told Carter to jump, she'd say, "...and I'll do a Herkie!"

My grandmother was different. She had wrinkles and green eyes, and very soft skin and hair that smelled like honeysuckle warming in the sun. She hummed while she cooked and liked to ruin birthday cakes on purpose so I could eat them with my fingers. She loved her teal bangles and her chunky gold Star of David with triangle diamonds and her monthly *Reader's Digest*. She never raised her voice. Everyone adored her. Grandmother, on the other hand, adored me. She'd smile at me and kiss both of my cheeks. Grandfather was desperately jealous of me. Even my mother found that amusing.

She liked to see her father pushed into second place for a change. It was payback for the all times he had berated her.

When grandmother died, my grandfather flew her body back to the small midwestern town where it all started. We flew up. People came out of the woodwork: old friends, townspeople who remembered her, grandfather's old patients. The people who bought their house still lived there and hosted the wake.

When my mother's oldest and best high school friend, Dalia Wyatt, came to the door, my mother burst into tears. She and Dalia embraced and spoke about old times when grandmother would cook and what a lovely woman she was. They laughed about the way they used to copy each other at everything. The boys they dated. Prom. The overwhelming sadness that had brought them back together.

My grandfather braced himself against grief. Remembered for being a rock, he dared not publicly lament the passing of grandmother's ghost. But seeing the townspeople, specifically Dalia, became too much for him. Dalia Wyatt, it turned out, was one "ghost" that would not pass – well, more like a skeleton really.

Just as the guests finished their appetizers and my mother finally had stopped crying, grandfather pulled her aside and confessed that he had cheated on my grandmother. It turned out that my mother's best friend, Dalia, was really her half-sister. That was interesting.

A few days after grandmother's funeral, Dalia called her.

"Can you believe it?" she asked.

My mother coolly told her, "Don't ever call me again," and hung up the phone. Just like the day she left my father; the switch had been flipped again.

When grandfather remarried at eighty-five, Carter's inheritance was suddenly in jeopardy. She flew to Florida to use some of her newly acquired ball-busting abilities on her father and his new bride, Belinda. Hurricane Carter struck again. At his age, he was no longer a match for my mother's vindictive precision. Grandfather had blown himself out. By the time she left, there wasn't a lawn ornament left standing in the entire retirement park.

"I'll put you in an old folks' home so fast your fucking head will spin," she told him. "No golden years for you. No more nice meals, no cozy La-Z-Boy, just you and a one-room prison."

Finally gaining an upper hand over her father, the dictator, further proved that her newfound ability to be cruel was a useful tool. His waning fortitude and softer persona didn't forgive his acts. And my mother despised her "father's wife."

"Stepmother, my ass," she barked at me. "The woman's a goddamn babysitter."

Jacob's second wife, Belinda, was a nice woman who had an odd fascination with unicorns. Unicorn earrings. Unicorn calendars. Unicorn snow globes. Grandpa expected us to give Belinda gifts. Thankfully, when it came time to make the purchase, we always knew the theme; the trick was just finding a new spin. The unicorn-shaped toilet paper holder was the crème.

Belinda had met Jacob about a month after

grandmother had died - at a community hoedown during a do-si-do. She continued the move around his elbow, right into his house a few days after that. She fed him, gave him his pills, cleaned him. Their honeymoon consisted of a 4:30 supper followed by a BM.

By the time grandfather died, my mother's inheritance had held to about half-a-million in stocks and half-a-million in property. The last check penned out of grandfather's account that didn't get written to my mother was made out to Belinda for fifty thousand dollars. "For seven years of maid service," my mother told me.

Fourteen:
Shake, Rattle, And Roll With It

When I was in the 3rd grade, my mother turned to me while I was watching TV in the kitchen and asked me to come to her on the nearby sofa. I did, as always. She opened her checkbook register and pointed at a number.

"What's that say? Can you read that? How much it is?" she asked me.

"One six thirty-six."

"That's right. Sixteen dollars and thirty-six cents."

"Wow," I said.

"Get your father on the phone."

"Okay." I picked up the phone and dialed his number. It rang.

"Hi, Dad," I said.

My mom lit up a cigarette. "Is that him?" she asked.

I nodded proudly, with a big smile.

"You tell that prick he's late with my child support. I want his money."

I looked at her curiously. She took a drag from her cigarette again and spat snide remarks through a smoke cloud. "Cheap son-of-a-bitch," she said. "You hear me, Ray? Send my *goddamned* child support!"

I was nine. I thought child support was some kind of seat or highchair. I didn't understand why my dad had to send over a highchair; I was plenty big enough to sit in an adult chair, and I was very careful not to dirty my pants or the white suede cushions of our dining room chairs.

My dad's silence, followed by the soft tone of his voice, told me something was wrong. "Don't worry," he said. "This isn't something you should be doing. Put your mother on the phone." I held it out to her. She shook her head. When my mother didn't come to the phone, Dad assured me the "child support" was coming. He hung up.

My mother crushed her cigarette and straightened her blouse. "What did he say?" she asked, even though it seemed like she really didn't care.

"He's gonna call you later."

"Pathetic," she said, lighting up another cig. "Hey, how about a nice cold milkshake for dinner?"

I was already frozen. The juxtaposition of my mother's voice and my father's saddened me. It was the first time I'd been directly involved in one of my parents' fights. The fact that she had made me call made it feel like I had started it. I felt awkward. Tricked.

"Come here," she said, noticing I was a bit too still. "Give momma a hug."

Her demand didn't sit right with me. I didn't want to. I didn't feel like I had a choice, though.

She hugged me tight and gave me kisses all over my face forcing me to laugh. Then she tickled me, and I laughed harder. The sensation overwhelmed my sadness, and I let it continue.

The same night my mother made me call my dad she took me out to Steak 'n Shake but not before she put on her fancy watch and her fox-fur coat.

I'll never forget the look on the hostess's face. Even the cook came out to see. They looked at my mother as if she were the most famous person ever to enter the restaurant. The place was empty, save one couple. My mother stared at them as they sat in silence. Not having a romantic relationship herself, she loved to watch couples and imagine their lives. Nothing ever resembling a fairytale story came across – only that their lives were totally messed up. She particularly loved the cheating husband scenario. Not because my father cheated on her, just because that's what men did, including her father.

I was hurt by what she made me do earlier and commented on the people to conceal my hurt feelings. "The lady isn't eating at all," I said. I was very good at stating the obvious.

My mom ate the cherry off the top of her strawberry milkshake. "That's probably 'cause her husband is fucking his secretary like your father, I'm sure."

I looked at her with my eyebrows raised. That was the first time I'd heard the word "fuck." She read my confusion and giggled to herself at how innocent I still was.

"You're so cute."

Her tone told me she was again picking on my dad, although I didn't know what about. I knew my dad had a lady who worked with him. Did fucking her mean he was stealing her money? Of course, I figured it out later.

My mother reached into her purse when the waiter brought the check. She thumbed through a wad of hundreds, passing thirty or forty of them until she arrived at a twenty. My eyes grew big. That looked like a lot more money than what I had read in her checkbook.

She pulled it out and gave it to the waiter. "Keep the change," she told him.

I couldn't help but wonder why she needed money from my dad if she had so much already.

There was another moment that night that changed things a bit for me. It started with Kool & The Gang and their hit, *Celebration*. I was dipping my fries in catsup when it came on the jukebox. I got up on my knees and started bobbing in the seat. It was subconscious but it caught my mother's attention. She started to giggle. I turned and saw the gleam in her eye and made my movements a bit bigger, rotating my hips like I was humping the air. My mother covered her mouth and her bite of food because she started to laugh so hard. It seemed at that moment my shyness went away. I got out of the booth for a larger stage and started doing hula-hoop moves. I added a spin.

The cook, an enormous black man, saw it too and he turned up the volume. With no customers to serve, he came around the counter and joined me in the middle of the restaurant. He slipped, I slid. He bumped, I grinded. Carter fell out. It was the first time I saw my humor affect her and how she treated me. I cherished that moment.

Even at a young age, I couldn't leave her to her own misery – especially once I knew that grandfather was the mad scientist behind her monster. She was like a country in need – an entire country like Sudan or Ethiopia. I was going to stick with her – even if it meant I'd continually be on the losing end – just to receive the ray or two of the sunshine I was trying to spread.

On a particular morning, when the moment felt right, I tried my hand at cross-border reparations.

"I don't like it when you talk about my dad like you do," I told her one time on the way to school. "It's mean."

She snapped her finger and pointed it in my face, looking back and forth from me to the road. "Do not talk to me like that. I am your mother, and you'll treat me with respect!"

I chose to speak my mind anyway. "Dad told me he wasn't late. He told me he doesn't know why you keep making me call."

"Oh, please. Here we go again. Talking up for your perfect father. Why doesn't anybody defend me? I'm your *mother*!"

She placed explosive measure on the word mother. It was her badge.

Her voice turned hoarse, and she began to cry as we pulled into the elementary school parking lot.

I put down my Honey Bun breakfast on the car's console and watched my mother's eyeliner puddle on the tops of her cheekbones; her hands smothered her voice as they covered her mouth and wiped the black lines off her face. I couldn't bear to see her cry. I turned toward her quickly, suddenly concerned. I was the cause of these tears. I pulled at her shirtsleeve.

"Mom?"

She wept louder. People heard as they walked past our car.

"Momma?" I tugged.

"No. You don't care about me. You just care about your son-of-a-bitch father!"

"No, I don't." I pushed my way over the console and touched her shoulder with my hand, the psychiatrist in Underoos. She looked into my oversize brown eyes and rested her head on my shoulder. I tried to rock her back and forth like she had done to me when he was scared or sleepy. I patted her back with my little hands. Her blackened tears stained my t-shirt. I smelled her makeup as she buried her face deep in my neck. She crawled into me and rocked, breathing as if she were on life support; each breath was short and followed by a very uncomfortable nasal moan. It was almost sensual.

"Do you love me? Tell me you love me," she solicited.

"Yes, of course. I do love you, mommy."

Anytime my mother felt she was losing, we repeated this routine. She was a dynamic performer, accustomed to being challenged on all levels. She used every maneuver in the manual – anything to win. At those moments, she simply forgot she was a mother.

The problem was my mother's work and the stress associated with it. She didn't have extra time to develop parenting strategies and follow through with methodical parenting techniques. Nor the patience to do so. She needed to divide and conquer and was accustomed to quick results based on her demands. And because she did it so well, she wholeheartedly believed she could perform her mothering duties using the same skills proven useful to demolish her opponents in criminal litigation.

In translation, she imagined herself playing the role of a mother more than she just did it. She bought so heavily into the idea that her pedigree and professional fabulousness would produce such a great mother that she simply forgot the reality of just being a mother. And although she practiced the role in the comfort of her mind, she never quite performed under pressure as she imagined. When the curtain was raised and my mother's "mothering skills" were revealed, the audience gasped; a young girl cried and a dog howled somewhere off in the distance. Her Act One was a total failure.

Much like those who can't perform, she decided to

direct. I was her star and taking center stage. She was much more skilled at her ability to run my life than to battle against the difficulties of her own. I became a nice diversion for her away from her problems – a story she could write and rewrite, stage and restage, until it was perfect. Unfortunately, for me, she was erratic, a director with a growing history of emotional overacting and anger. Thus, taking center stage wasn't really the issue; rather, it was the lack of any direction in a very glaring and hot spotlight. And I was working without a script.

Fifteen:
Pound Of Flesh

I woke up from the floor where I had slumped into sleep and moved to the pantry door to look for "dinner" – most likely a bowl of cereal or a handful of granola bars. I loosened my tie and threw it over to the countertop and passed the entrance hallway where my house keys were still on the floor.

I rubbed my beard and dug my fingers in my eyes to clear the cobwebs. I scanned the space and stopped on a round tube of Progresso breadcrumbs.

"Breadcrumbs?" I asked out loud. Then I remembered one of my friends had left them at my apartment after he and several girls came over to cook meatballs and spaghetti before heading out to party. One girl was kind of flirty and kept dipping her finger in her spaghetti sauce and licking it at me. I thought, I didn't know it was going to be this kind of a night.

She scooped a bit of sauce and thrust her finger toward me. I wasn't sure if I should have taken it from her finger with my own or did she actually want me to suck her finger? She cornered me and brought it to my lips. Not wanting to suck her finger – I mean, I didn't really know her - I wound up playing goalie with my tongue, licking at the air until she fully inserted it into my mouth. I assumed sex was on the agenda.

Ultimately, we all got stuck watching an episode of ER. Of course, something tragic happened, everyone died and George Clooney found it difficult to speak about the tragedy through his tilted head and several oratory pauses. We all teared sufficiently to the point that partying until 4 a.m. didn't seem very appealing. Everyone went home to go to bed except the flirty girl who stayed to help "clean up"... in my shower.

At one point, it got so rambunctious and hot that she passed out. Literally slipped through my hands and dropped to the floor of the tub. I hoisted her body over the edge, knocking shampoo and conditioner bottles everywhere, and slid her across the bathroom floor into my bedroom. I raised her legs to return the blood to her head and thought to myself, as I was squatting over her, tapping her face, my testicles dangling, that there was no fucking way in hell I was calling 911.

"Come on..." I started to say, but forgot her name. "um, um... sweetie. Come on, *baby!*" I said, tap, tap, tapping her face. All of a sudden I was Dr. Doug Ross, Clooney's character from ER – just I as pictured he would be after bringing one of his patient's home and knocking her out from hot sex.

"Jesus Christ!" I yelled at her. "DON'T YOU DIE ON ME!"

She finally came to. "What happened?" she asked in a haze.

"George *Fuckin'* Clooney, that's what," I said to her smiling.

For those who heard about how I *rocked her sexual world* – I may have said something to a few friends - my reputation got quite the boost.

I took the breadcrumbs out and opened the top. Half full. I smelled them. Amazing. Suddenly, my mind exploded into an inescapable thought: anger chicken.

I opened the fridge and found an egg carton with two

eggs left. Perfect. I moved up to the freezer and spotted a pack of frozen chicken, dated a year ago. I spoke the recipe out loud.

"A pack of chicken breasts. Trim the extra fat. Tenderize each-" I stopped. I immediately went for the utensil drawer and fished through several metal spoons, tongs, bottle openers. No clawed mallet.

"Wait just a minute," I declared.

Remembering an old metal toolbox in the pantry, I found it and lifted the lid. Inside, I found an old rusted hammer. I settled on the image and smiled. In my best Scottish accent, I said, "That'll do, Pig. That'll do."

I wrapped the hammer in cellophane and began hitting the meat with it. Slowly at first, but then it felt good. I continued with a growing rhythm. The metal was heavy and each strike caused the dishes in the cabinets to rattle.

I had never done this myself, but I had watched my mother do it a thousand times. I remember seeing meat fly around the room. She would destroy the chicken, pulverize it.

In my kitchen, pink meat started to fly into the air too. I knew I was doing it correctly. I hit it harder. And harder still.

Bang, bang, bang. *Fucking tampon!* I thought. Bang, bang, bang. "Ha!" I yelled, over and over again. "HA, HA, HA – very funny!" I was breathless after having gone through four breasts. I felt like the killer in *American Psycho*! I wouldn't be surprised if the neighbors called the police.

Ten minutes later, breathless and exhausted, I gently placed the meat in hot oil. The egg and breadcrumbs immediately sizzled and began to brown.

The smell filled the air. I felt myself take a deep breath and release. As I cooked, the outside layer of the meat got crispy, while the inside stayed tender and juicy. I was able to break off little pieces. I closed my lips around my fingers, sucked on the soft chicken and felt something deep, something very real. *Anger chicken*, I thought and smiled to myself.

I sat on the kitchen counter and ate pieces from the pan. I didn't require a table setting or need to feel like I was part of a nice dinner. As I sat there licking my fingers, I accepted again that I would never understand my mother and confirmed in my mind that she deserved no part of me or my life. I dropped my piece of anger chicken back into the oil-laden pan and pushed the pan away.

Fuck her, I thought.

In my opinion, my mother had not endured any greater tragedies than I had. But my experiences of tragedies were worse because I was a child. I had hurt as much as she did. I had lost as much as she did. At least, that's how I felt after beating the daylights out of a chicken breast.

Sixteen:
Denver

Ayla and I stood in our bathroom and addressed one another in the mirror. We wore matching white robes. I was shaving and she was combing a piping hot flat iron through her hair. The morning rush was on.

I loved to watch Ayla straighten her hair. Her breasts would jiggle when she did it. Every now and then she would catch me watching and would shake her head in disbelief. "You're an infant, you know that?" she would ask. I would readily admit the same.

That morning, though, I was agitated. I had already nicked my chin with the blade and then my upper lip. Ayla watched me curse at myself.

"I would tell you to go back and get the spot on the side of your neck but I'm afraid you're going to *kill* yourself!" she joked.

"I know, right?" I said.

"Are you nervous about today?" she asked me.

"I don't know what to call it," I said as I struggled to shave.

Ayla put down her flat iron and came over to me. "Here, let me," she said. She took the razor, rinsed it and brought it to my neck. She used her thumb to make my neck skin tense and she shaved the spot I missed. She inspected the rest, trimmed a stray hair or two and then nodded. She grabbed a washcloth, held it under warm water and wiped my face. She kissed my clean cheek.

"Now that's love," she said.

I let out a sigh. She noticed concern on my face.

"My parents got divorced when I was three," I said, trying to think. "I don't remember them ever being together... like this."

"Hmmm," she said, feeling sorry for them both. "And after that, your mother never met anyone?"

I didn't speak for a second. "No," I said, "she did." I was suddenly lost in reverie. "Someone really special."

By 1983, Carter's professional and personal life had reached near perfection. Professionally speaking, she was in total control of her career. Her business was steady and growing; year six was poised to be the best, she said. She knew the bumps and dips. Carter hadn't just been around the block; she owned it. As a result of her increased comfort and knowledge, she expanded her clientele to a certain lucky few, who, in tougher times, she wouldn't even waste a phone call on – a handful of pro bono dregs with whom she rediscovered a bit of her own conscience.

She would never turn away her big-ticket Mafia clientele, but she became motivated to reinvent some karma for herself by helping a tangled mess of drug-addicted and mentally misdiagnosed petty criminals who just needed a break – a sentence to a mental health facility rather than a prison where they would go untreated for their illnesses. Despite her not making any money for these efforts, it helped her sleep better at night – something that traditionally had cost her a prescription or a nice bottle of wine.

"They're just a burning plane tumbling out of the sky..." she would say. "All I'm doing is giving them a safe place to land, away from society."

Ultimately, the reason why Carter put her monetary aspirations on the back burner and started to help the truly needy, aside of course from all the cosmic benefits, was that she met a man – her one true love, Denver Forester.

Denver sat as a judge on the criminal and civil trial calendar in Fulton County outside in the heart of Atlanta. He adored Carter's belligerent ways. He was a country boy who had come up. The son of an auctioneer, Denver spoke surprisingly slowly and without much flare. He was an artful speaker, though, who crafted his thoughts.

Their first semi-personal encounter occurred after she had lost a trial in his court. Denver called her back to his chambers to congratulate her on a well-handled and diligently prepared trial despite the fact that she had lost. Losing was inevitable in criminal defense, but Carter had put up one hell of a fight. Denver was impressed and wanted to shake her hand – or hold it, as it were. When she sat down before him and watched him light up a cigarette, she could barely breathe – and it wasn't the smoke.

"Tricky son of a gun, huh?" Denver said.

Carter had never heard a judge talk badly about a district attorney before. "Who? The DA?"

Denver nodded politely. "Don't care for him much. He's a real shark, but you handled yourself nicely."

"Thank you."

"It was a loser anyway."

"Well," she said with a smile, "if the jury had been able to hear Catherine's testimony, I don't think there's any way in hell they would have convicted."

"Colonel, the trial's over."

'Colonel' was a title many of the old judges called attorneys back in those days to place a name on their fighting spirit.

"You could have let that testimony in," Carter told him.

"Not if I was following the law."

"It's relevant."

"It's a sideshow with nothing to do with the trial and the issues before the jury."

"She knew that asshole," she said. "She could have educated the jury."

Denver frowned at the use of the word "asshole."

"Her testimony would have been entirely based on hearsay. I know the case, Ms. Scales. The state has the right to a fair trial, too."

She huffed. "You gotta be kiddin' me."

Denver laughed. "You are somethin' else." Clearly, he'd never seen a woman with that much spark. It was due to the years of confidence building she'd endured and her trained ability to be fearless no matter the audience.

She gave him a questioning look, and he offered her a cigarette. She held it as he extended his lighter, and she exhaled deeply. As she took another drag, she caught Denver watching her.

Carter tapped her ashes and cocked her head. They held each other in an age-old stare. Neither ever recovered. She kept her crushed cigarette as a memento of the smoke that changed her life. She loved to collect little symbolic things.

Denver was twenty-two years older than Carter who

was now in her mid-thirties. He had soft facial features and the kindest Basset Hound brown eyes she had ever seen. Under his robe, Denver was a cowboy. He collected pocket-knives and guns and wore giant belt buckles, cowboy boots, and Levi's plaids with pearl snap buttons encased in silver. Their age difference didn't matter to either of them. She was young and feisty. Denver was a warm hand over Carter's high-strung personality. Like a summer rain, Denver washed a calm over her, and for the first time in her life, she felt settled and safe and deeply in love.

His confidence complemented her insecurity, and she marveled at his ability to let things lie – to float on the rolling tides and just enjoy the ride. Life was more than just a series of events divided in time by the twenty-four-hour clock; it was rolling hills, deep valleys, and brilliant pinnacles, and when looked at from outer space, it remained the loveliest shade of green. Carter, however, didn't buy it. She worked better on high octane and lighter fluid.

They had their share of arguments, but Denver's status as a judge continually kept Carter in check. She placed a lot of emphasis on her career. Her career was her life, and she respected all aspects of it. Denver was both smart and witty, and she respected his knowledge and life experience. Denver knew exactly how to handle her irrational temper and misguided insecurities. When she got madder than hell, he'd simply laugh at her, which of course pissed her off even more. It also convinced her that Denver was the man of her dreams. He took her just as she was. He never tried to push her like Ray did. He never tried to change her like her father did.

Denver was also a kinder, gentler entrée into the Atlanta boys' club. On Denver's arm, Carter got smiles and handshakes instead of double talk and sexual harassment. She went to barbecues, lake parties, wore cutoff jeans, and cowboy boots and hats. They skinny-dipped and drank moonshine and howled at the moon and laughed at the sunrise. He even made her being Jewish more acceptable to others.

Normally, when Southerners heard that she was Jewish, they'd twinge. "Jewish, huh? Didn't y'all kill Jesus?"

She would just stare blankly and say, "Yes, that was my parents who did that."

With Denver by her side, though, people said, "Oh, how interesting," or "Neat," as if being Jewish were some new type of vacuum cleaner that also polished silver. The subterfuge was palpable. She knew what they meant. They meant; Oh, look, dear, the murderer who killed our Lord and Savior has arrived. Carter liked it better when all the cards were on the table. That's why Denver loved her. She wasn't the traditional Southern cuisine of homegrown reserved politeness. She was out in the open – shocking. It made him laugh.

Carter had fallen in love with Denver immediately. She knew they would spend the rest of their lives together. She just had to get me to bite.

Seventeen:
Judgie

I got my first real taste of Denver the fall after my eleventh birthday. It was 1984. The city of Atlanta's population was still under a million people. And thirty minutes outside of Atlanta was the "cun-tree."

My mother dressed me for a day of rumble and tumble in an outfit she had purchased at Saks Fifth Avenue for $500: a pair of corduroy overalls, a cashmere cap and sweater, suede boots, and a pair of leather gloves. "You'll need those gloves for later," she told me.

"Where are we goin'?"

"There is somebody momma wants you to spend some time with," she said, as she put me in the car and drove us out of the city. "He's a very special person, and I think you two are going to be very good friends. As a matter of fact, I know it."

She tried to explain Denver to me. How he was a very accomplished attorney like she was, how he could whittle any issue down to a grain of sand and then erect a skyscraper of an argument on its foundation. How he was a judge and respected by everyone he knew, and how he lived in the greatest house in the world. I didn't really understand talk about accomplishments and skyscrapers, but "greatest house in the world" - that sounded appealing.

When we pulled into the driveway, my mother looked at me with Disney World eyes. All I saw was red brick and a front yard of dirt.

"Isn't it great?" she marveled. I was rather unimpressed. "You see those trees over there?" she asked, referring to a lengthy row of green and red trees. "Those are apple trees. We're gonna make apple jelly."

"Strawberry's my favorite," I said, refusing to acknowledge any potential for fun.

As we stepped out of the car, my mother maintained her smile as a promise of good things to come. And then I heard a rather unusual noise – a moan. I pulled my cap up over my ears and stood still until it repeated itself again.

My mother faked a bewildered look. "What could that be?" she asked, seemingly confused.

I shrugged and ran to the back of the driveway and onto Denver's back porch that overlooked the entire world – a run of fields that layered like a quilt stitched together with red and yellow trees. It was just shy of 150 acres. The closest yard was the size of a football field and housed a dozen or so of the fattest cows I had ever seen. A baby I would later come to learn was named Mighty called out again, and my eleven-year-old intellect kicked into overdrive with an all-too-exciting realization.

"Cows, momma. Cows!" I repeated the phrase over and over, as if she were deaf. "I want one! Can I have one, please? Please, can I have one?"

"I don't know. We're gonna have to ask Denver."

My mind was racing. *You mean there's a chance?* my exuberant eyes asked. *I can have my own cow?*

When Denver walked out of his house, my mother ran over to him and gave him an enormous kiss. The two of them tongued each other as if I were invisible. And I didn't care. She was helping my cause – putting in a good word with his tonsils apparently.

Denver was a different type of man, weathered and

soft compared to my dad. My dad was the COO of a major watch company. Like his timepieces, he coordinated all his movements and acted with great precision; he worked the gears. Denver set everything on cruise control.

Denver was six-two and two hundred and thirty-five pounds. He had played guard for the Georgia Bulldogs and hadn't lost the pounds the offensive coaches had pushed down his throat in the form of Salisbury steak and fried catfish. Hugging him, though, was like embracing a giant pillow – fresh and cool with the scent of country living. I would later nickname him "Judgie."

That morning, I ran across the pasture toward the cows and marveled at how the cool air pulled tears out of the corner of my eyes. My breath billowed like steam, and I was thankful for my cashmere Saks Fifth Avenue hat and sweater, as well as my boots and leather gloves. As I sped across the pasture, I held little Mighty in my sights – my first pet. With each leap, I could barely believe my luck. My own four-hundred-pound cow! At that moment, life was immeasurable, perfect – that is, until my boots flew out from underneath me without warning. So sudden, so unexpected. Somehow the ratio of my body weight in comparison to the force of moving forward kept my head positioned directly over the moon pie that accelerated my right foot, so that when I began to fall, my head landed directly into the warmest patch of grass I'd ever experienced. Using my Saks Fifth Avenue leather gloves to pick feces and mucus out of my cashmere hat became one of my fonder memories of Judgie's farm.

Judgie exploded with laughter. His happiness was contagious. He was like candy for my soul, which had become soured by my mother's foul temper. He had a deep bellow like I imagined Santa Claus had, and a loving set of wrinkles around his eyes that kept his face in a permanent smile. Having Judgie in our lives meant I had a witness and an ally – someone to stick up for me when Carter berated me or spoke down to me. Someone to tell me she was wrong for talking to me like that. A hand to hold. A hug to be given later. A hero.

Judgie gave me a total and complete pass, and for the first time since my parents' divorce, I got to be a kid again. The oppressive grime, once dried on my back and shoulders, washed away, leaving only a clean feeling of joy in my heart. I didn't have to think about supporting my mother, consoling her, or using my shoulder to support her breakdowns. I no longer had to worry about the spotlight. Judgie was man enough to take on that role himself. He brought a sense of knowing security into my life. When he wasn't around, I counted the minutes until he'd arrive. So did my mother. She was totally in love.

My dad was there for me too, but Judgie was on the front line. With my dad, when it came to my mother's tirades, I either had to call him or wait until he saw me on the days I spent at his house. By that time, the emotion had come and gone, and I was numb again, shifting gears and leaving the dust of my emotional breakdown to settle as I pretended to drive toward sunnier horizons. With Judgie there, though, I didn't have to explain my mother to him or the way she made me feel. He saw it firsthand.

"You can't talk to a boy like that," he'd tell her.

"Oh, he's fine."

"He's a child. You're crushing his little spirit."

I loved him like a father.

Later that first day, I sat elevated fifteen feet off the ground in the mouth of a giant bulldozer and picked apples. At the top of the apple tree, there was nothing between the sky and me. Pure blue enveloped me, and I breathed absolute joy. It was a fantasy world based on the reality of Judgie's oversize life – a reality that kept on coming.

Upon entering Judgie's house for the first time, I dropped my armful of apples in exchange for what I thought was the better trade – a loaded twelve-gauge shotgun that leaned against the refrigerator. My mother freaked, in part, because after I picked it up, I spun around to show it to her with the barrel pointed at her torso.

"Look, momma. A gun!"

She held her breath and walked calmly over to me, maintaining the all-too-fake smile of a weathered flight attendant. She gently removed the weapon of death from my hands.

"I thought you were going to put these away," mom told Judgie as she thrust the handle into his chest.

"That's just what I'm going to do right now."

"But mom..." I said.

"No," she insisted.

Judgie loved guns. He was an enthusiast. A rifleman. That morning, I followed him around the house as he attempted to make the place childproof. I felt bad for my new best friend. My mother could be a real buzz kill. Judgie thought the environment was perfectly normal for a child. He had grown up that way. He winked at me as if to say, "I'll put these away to quiet her down, but one day soon I'll teach you what it's like to be a man like me."

There had to be at least two or three dozen handguns, shotguns, and rifles, all lying around as if the Wild West had sneezed its violent past over everything. They were everywhere. Some broken down. Others in cases. Some just leaning up against the walls. For a moment, all the laughter we had experienced that day disappeared. Judgie frantically pulled steel from tables and countertops and carried armfuls of weapons like firewood to the closest hall closet. I picked up the apples as my mother chewed Judgie a new asshole.

"I told you I didn't want my son to see any of this."

"Calm down, darlin'. I'm getting 'em up."

"Don't you *darlin'* me, and don't tell me to calm down! He could have blown his fuckin' head off with that thing!"

They disappeared into a back room where the yelling got louder despite the growing distance. I balanced a handful of apples in my arms and set them on the counter right next to a loaded pearl-handled Smith & Wesson .44 Magnum. I heard Judgie trying to be insistent that she not raise hell like that against him in his own home.

"Wow," I whispered, looking at the gun.

With my mom gone, I reached out for it and pushed the handle with my finger. The metal scratched the countertop as the weighty firearm turned on its side. I pushed it harder, and the barrel spun around until it stopped and pointed just above my left eyebrow. Better not pick it up. Quietly and cautiously, I looked deep into the black hole.

On the refrigerator hung a target with holes in the center of it. It must have been something Judgie was proud of because we always hung important stuff on our refrigerator, too.

I picked up the gun and aimed it at the target. I pulled the trigger, which was very hard for me to do. Then there was a deafening boom. My mother and Judgie came running in to find the smoking gun on the ground and a giant hole in the refrigerator a few feet away from the target.

"I found another one," I said.

My mother nearly passed out.

For years after, Judgie loved to tell that story. As I got older and accustomed to his sense of humor and the way it royally pissed off my mother, we both howled with laughter until our stomachs ached and eyes watered. My mother would get up from the table and leave, which of course made us laugh even harder. It was the first time in my life I was able to laugh *at* my mother, to judge her without recourse and find humor in her personality shortcomings and not just fear. It was all because Judgie was there.

Two years later, grandmother died. Due to the speed of progress of her illness and death, my mother drowned in sadness despite her fight to survive it. She felt like a little girl, robbed of her mommy. I told her that I would take care of her, that I would protect her and "be a man." I was thirteen. When she saw me crying while I was trying to console her, she scolded me for being a liar to say that I could be strong for her.

"Some man you turned out to be," she said.

"She doesn't know what she's saying," Judgie told me. "Your grandmother was very important to her."

Looking into Judgie's face was the easiest thing I had ever done. To me, his eyes revealed a chest full of gold; his red cheeks balanced perfectly on either side of his nose and bore the gifts of sunrise and sunset. He took care of everything. He protected my mother from any hassles and never asked anything of her. Grandfather now acted like even more of a child than I did – demanding attention and that my mother forget about her own grief and attend to his. Judgie embraced his role as peacemaker. He stood up for me and did his best to create harmony between them all. With my mother so depressed over her mother's death, Judgie became my closest friend. I told him that I loved him.

It was after they returned from the funeral that I secretly asked Judgie if he could live with us together as a family. I told Judgie I wanted him to be a dad and there all the time. That we could have fun all the time. Judgie's heart melted. He cherished his relationship with both of us. He felt he could be good for us both.

My mother was totally resistant to the idea. While Judgie was a good man, whom she loved, she had been a "kept woman" twice already, first by her father and then by my dad. She had spent a decade trying to make her voice be heard, then understood, then respected. She was not looking to become bound to another man.

It wasn't until one night near midnight several weeks later that my mom, Denver and I were sitting at the counter at an all night Dunkin' Donuts when she saw the love between her two boys. I lifted my head up from my jelly donut to find my mother suddenly kissing Judgie softly.

"What are ya'll doing!" I cried.

"We're moving in together," Judgie said.

I screamed for joy with a mouthful of donut.

As time brought my mother further away from her mother's funeral, she found solitude and silence in her work. Judgie was right by her side and a good influence on her regarding how to focus her attention away from her grief. His trial calendar was light – nothing but pleas and arraignments for defendants who wanted to plead guilty and get it over with. With this extra time, he chose to focus his attention on the less fortunate and encouraged my mother to help him. My mother thought of nothing but making money and feeling powerful again, but as always, Judgie was able to imbue a sense of righteousness within her and persuade her to focus part of her time and energy on some charity cases he was focused on. Judgie was hard to refuse; my mother signed on wholeheartedly.

They couldn't work on cases in his courtroom. A judge and a defense attorney working *ex parte* to resolve cases would clearly violate the rules of ethics. They could work after hours on cases that were of interest to them both, just not matters pending him. Together, as judge and lawyer, they were able to do good work with criminal defendants who suffered from mental health issues - misdiagnosed convicts or wards of the state who needed a place where they could get better and become productive members of society, not just rot in jail. On medication, these individuals could wash cars and bag groceries or work on a farm or do construction. Danny Curtis, a skittish Vietnam War vet, was one such case that needed extra attention.

In the winter of 1986, Veterans Memorial Hospital released Danny after a twelve-year stint in the mental rehabilitation unit. Having been exposed to just about every known plant killer the US government could manufacture, Danny had swallowed more than his share. That, combined with the usual tragedies of war, made him one very seriously charred cookie crumb sunk into the deep recesses of the Department of Veterans Affairs' conventional oven.

Prior to being released, in the fall of 1974, he had escaped. The police got a "suspicious person" call from a pawnshop owner. The owner, a Japanese immigrant, whispered hysterically into the butt of the phone as he ducked behind his oak and Formica countertop. Danny whistled curt positional calls and signaled for his platoon to forge ahead to the mouth of the river; the "enemy" was close by. The local police department had a field day with the 911 tapes; in fact, they became a regular feature at the annual Christmas party.

Danny's ward was crowded, but the closeness was nice. He and the other vets had bonded; they formed support groups and shared their nightmares. He was actually happy when the ambulance took him back to the hospital. For one thing, he hadn't realized he had even escaped. Similarly, the stimulation of planning an offensive left his head spinning and craving the drone of the overhead lights in his ward.

When Danny learned about his impending release, he became terrified. He didn't have much family, and he assumed that the family he had was sure to reject him. They were the ones who had let him go to war and who had asked that he be placed in the nuthouse in the first place. Plus, the last he heard, his mother had moved two thousand miles away, and his brother was a gambler and would surely see Danny as a handicap – a fucked-up younger brother no man about town would want as a wingman. As a side note, Danny had watched *Rain Man* several times and loved it. It often gave him hope that one day he and his brother might team up again. Aside from Danny being crazy, he couldn't count cards like Dustin Hoffman, which was something his brother surely wouldn't forgive. As for his father, Danny felt like his dad didn't want him before and that he certainly wouldn't now. He would be alone and in the dark once again.

His nightmares and tremors returned, but with the number of patients rising exponentially and the government's plan to opt out of domestic social reform and focus on international capitalism, Veterans Memorial Hospital didn't have funding or enough bed space to care. They opened the cage and turned Danny loose on society. Danny, however, wasn't ready and neither was society.

A few days before Danny's release, Judgie stopped by our house to speak to my mother. Judgie knew all about Danny and his complicated mental situation. He explained his concern over the hospital's decision to release him when he clearly needed to stay in the hospital for the rest of his life. With his release inevitable, Judgie wanted to help make sure Danny wouldn't get off track or jump off an overpass before he could find him a proper place for further treatment. One night over dinner, he pushed my mother hard to represent him in a hearing that would enable Danny to stay in the mental hospital via a court order for involuntary commitment.

"Reagan has totally fucked-" Judgie paused and looked at me. He continued: "*Screwed* this kid with these anti-funding initiatives," he told her. "He's got a hearing coming up, and I need you to make an entry and represent the kid."

"I mean, I can, I guess, but you seem to know all about him. Plus, you and Judge Cooper are good friends. Maybe you should do it. You'll probably get further faster."

"His case is complicated. I'm not the best person to handle it," he said.

"You're the perfect person. Who better than Denver Forrester?"

"It's gotta be you, babe. I'm just... too busy."

"Too busy – what are you talking about? You're wide open."

"Look, the kid's got real problems. I need you to do it." Judgie looked uncomfortable.

"What's the matter with you?"

"He cannot be released, Carter. He's a danger to himself and society. He's a perfect case for commitment, and I..." Judgie searched for words. The combination of his demeanor and speechlessness confused my mother.

"Who is this kid?" she asked him.

"I need you to handle this one. I can't."

"Denver, who is this kid to you?" she asked him. He let out a deep sigh. "Denver?" she insisted.

"He's my son."

Actually, Judgie had two sons: Danny, the schizophrenic, and Marty, the sociopath. My mother put her hand to her chest to make sure her heart was still beating; it was... and faster than usual.

Although Judgie loved his two boys dearly, he didn't have a relationship with either of them and disowned them to the extent that he had denied their existence. Marty wanted Judgie's farmland and wouldn't talk to him or introduce him to his grandchildren until Judgie gave him a certified copy of his will showing Marty the portions of his estate he planned to leave him. Danny took his mother's maiden name and went to war. Afterward, all he wanted was a dark room with no loud sounds and a soft pillow. Judgie couldn't manage either of them. He was determined, however, to step back in and help Danny through this brief yet necessary period. And there was more bad news.

"Where is he now?" my mother asked.

"With the ward being shut down, he'll be staying with me."

"At your home?" she asked. He grimaced. "Jesus Christ!" she said.

"It's only temporary," he said. "Until I can get him into another facility somewhere. Or maybe he'll do all right living with me. I don't know."

My mother nearly fell over. "Living with *you*? What about Benjamin and me living with you like we talked about? What about us? How are we gonna have an *us*?"

"That'll have to wait, darlin'."

"And our engagement?"

He didn't want to say it, but her look was filled with impatience. "That'll have to wait, too." Her disappointment draped down her brow and into her shoulders. Judgie clearly felt stuck. "Danny's my son. What do you want me to do? I can't just abandon him like the hospital did."

My mother was devastated at the idea of delaying her progression with Judgie and the plans they had made to become a family. More than anything, she wanted to see their union through and have what she wanted. She thought about it for a full day. When she woke up the next morning, her mind was made.

She forgave Judgie and took Danny's case with abandon. Not since her days dealing with crooked cops had she fought against something so hard. More focused on preserving her relationship with Judgie than truly helping Danny, my mother unloaded on the court system. In order to have the life she wanted with Judgie, Danny could never leave that mental hospital.

Danny was crazy. Period. He needed to be locked up or he would either kill himself or someone else. The exceptions to involuntary commitment necessitated that Danny be a danger to himself or others. The problem was that she really didn't know if it was true. Was he really a danger on that level? She did what all lawyers do and took a position. She would not split that baby.

"He escaped before and practically called in reinforcements to destroy the Asian pawn shop owner," my mother told the judge.

"That may be, but in a shop full of guns, he didn't go after a single one," Judge Cooper said.

"They were locked up."

"But don't you think that if he were a true danger, he would have exercised his options on the owner of the shop? I've got to have something, Ms. Scales, to sink my teeth into, and we just don't have it."

"Well, maybe the police should have given him a few

more minutes to see if he actually would have shot the guy and given us a dead body. Then maybe you could've *sunk your teeth* into that!"

Judge Cooper didn't appreciate her tone, but my mother knew she had the weight of Denver Forrester behind her. So she took extra liberties.

"You're making this personal, Ms. Scales. I have to consider the law."

She deflected his truthful observation. "Your Honor," she continued, "it is a fact that this man is a train wreck. And his case is very much like one of those train wrecks on a small back country road where there's not a warning system in place and everybody just ignores the dangers, and before you know it, somebody is dead, and all it would have taken is for somebody to just put in a stop sign. We need you to put in a stop sign, Your Honor. He needs this."

"Ms. Scales, these restrictions are tight. Believe me, I understand the position you're in – trust me – but my hands are tied. Even if I wanted to put him in, I've got nothing to base it on. I'm sorry."

She felt her relationship slipping away. "But, Your Honor, this is going to be devastating for everyone. He needs to remain committed. Please reconsider. If it pleases the court, I can put additional material together – a supplemental packet – which will further demonstrate that he needs to be committed. He can't be released."

"You've already done that, Counselor. And you've done an excellent job. But I'm sorry. My ruling is that I deny your motion."

My mother's eyes fell with her heart.

"Release him," the judge said.

On the day of Danny's release, Judgie left a key for Danny under his pineapple-shaped welcome mat. Danny hadn't wanted any outsiders to see him at the hospital, including his father. The hospital was evidence of his disease, and he'd much rather pretend it had all been a dream. He refused to be fussed over; his homecoming wasn't going to be a big deal. He insisted he travel by taxi. Judgie stayed away, as Danny had instructed, and left fifty bucks under the mat to pay for the cab.

That night, Judgie ate dinner with my mother and me. She cooked her famous Worcestershire sautéed filet mignon. As the candles burned down and the bottle of wine emptied out, the mood settled nicely for Judgie to confess his sins of omission and of his indiscretions.

"I wasn't good to Danny or Marty... as a father."

"That's impossible," I interrupted. My mother cut her eyes at me.

"Thank you, son, but... I was hard on my kids. I treated them like men, made them grow up too quickly. They were only boys. Marty left to go be with his mother when he was fifteen, and I didn't fight it. Danny enlisted to prove something to me. Neither of 'em could stand me."

I watched Judgie carefully. He was humiliated about his failures. So open about it. I grabbed his hand then hugged his oversize neck. It was the first time I had ever seen an adult apologize.

After dinner, Judgie put together a new bed for me. I had finally gotten rid of my childhood bunk bed and had traded up for a big boy queen. I was thirteen years old and studying for my Bar Mitzvah. I certainly couldn't head into manhood on the top bunk. By the time I was ready to sleep in my new bed it had gotten late. My mother asked Judgie to stay. He said he couldn't. He had to make sure Danny had gotten in okay.

"It's almost midnight," she told him.

"I know, darlin'. I'll be fine."

"It's forty-five minutes from here."

I climbed out of bed half asleep and peeked down the stairwell. "Judgie?" I interrupted.

"Yes, son," he answered.

"If you stay here tonight, we can all sleep together. Like a slumber party."

Judgie thought about it for a minute. "I tell you what – next weekend you got a deal."

I waved goodbye as my mother and Judgie headed out to the driveway. I went into my bathroom, which overlooked the driveway, and watched through the wooden blinds.

My mother made a few more pleas, and he politely said no. The cold air fell quietly between them, and there was nothing left to do but embrace goodbye.

As she stood next to his car, holding his hand and cuddling his neck, she noticed a nail on the driveway positioned underneath his front tire. It was large and poised perfectly to puncture. How the nail didn't flatten the tire on the way up was a mystery to her. He would surely not be so lucky on the way down. My mother bent over and picked up the nail. He noticed it in her hand.

"My goodness," he said. "That would have put a damper on things."

"You're lucky I'm so observant," she said, bragging.

"I'm lucky for many more reasons than that, my dear," he corrected.

They kissed gently and he left on four good tires.

When Judgie got home, Danny wasn't there. Denver opened the kitchen door from the garage and flipped on the light. A pan sat on the stove with eggs burnt to the bottom. A stick of butter melted on the countertop. Judgie smiled and returned the butter. He picked up the pan and soaked it in the sink. At least Danny was hungry. That had to be good.

Judgie looked around the kitchen. The place was a disaster. My mother cleaned it every time they went up there, but he was just messy. Judgie and some of his buddies had gone hunting the week before, and the place was a wreck. Piles of newspapers and cashed cigars. Camouflage vests, duck whistles, rifles, and handguns. He wanted to straighten up the place before Danny came back, but the long task list led to procrastination and stagnation. So much to do. Too much to do. *Oh, well*, he thought, *I'll clean it up tomorrow*. With so many guns lying around, he failed to notice that one was missing.

Right around one a.m., Judgie decided to shave. He often found it difficult to sleep with an itchy beard. As he turned on the hot water, the first story window overlooking his back porch steamed over, preventing him from seeing outside or the pair of eyes that watched him from three feet away. He gently pulled the razor down his left cheek. He didn't see the shadow. He rinsed the blade beneath the whistling tap. He didn't hear the whimpering. He dragged the razor across his Adam's apple and then to the side of his neck. He didn't see the gun tip touch the glass. The razor jerked and nicked his throat as the window crashed and a bullet exploded through the side of his neck, rupturing his carotid artery.

STATE JUDGE MURDERED BY MENTALLY ILL SON, the headlines read.

When Carter got the call from Judgie's neighbor, she collapsed in the kitchen. Her love. Her man.

Her eyes scanned the room, searching for answers. Panic struck her and she started suffocating. Shrinking into a child, she heaved for breath and couldn't find it. She cried herself to sleep at the base of the refrigerator.

Although no one was there to see Denver's last moments, my mother was able to put them together. Danny must have seen Judgie as a Viet-Cong, or maybe he just wanted to kill his father after so many years of neglect. Either way, on the second go-round, there was no hesitation about Danny's involuntary commitment. Judge Cooper attended the funeral and cried like a little boy over his dead pet dog. He helped make sure that this prophetic train wreck would never happen again.

Danny turned himself in three months later after living in the woods in the dead of winter. The state brought murder charges against him. Judgie's ex-wife called my mother and asked her to help Danny. "Maybe you can be his lawyer," she said. "Denver would have wanted it."

"Denver's dead," she told her and hung up the phone. This chapter too was now closed.

For years afterward, Carter would open her jewelry

box every now and then - one small drawer in particular. The drawer was lined with velvet and held two objects – an old used-up cigarette and the nail she found that night. She would take out the nail and clutch it in her hand. She would roll it between her fingers and feel the weight of the metal. Its coolness. The sharpness of the tip. She would fold it in her fingers and return it to the drawer and close her eyes to her one inescapable thought: *If only I hadn't noticed that fucking nail.*

Judgie was a bridge between my mother and me. He softened so many of the hard edges between us and bandaged so many of our wounds. With Judgie gone, I began to lie to myself about my mother and made excuses for her behavior. I continued to tell myself, *she doesn't know what she's saying*, just as Judgie had told me when grandmother died.

My mother hid her pain in anger again and shut herself down from feeling anything. She cursed herself for having opened up to someone, knowing that her luck wasn't that rich. With Judgie gone, she would be an outsider once more. Within a month, she flew back to New York to gear up her Mafia business again. It was time to bust some balls.

There was one last task of sorts, which she did undertake. Marty the sociopath instituted suit for his father's land. He wanted to flip the acreage into condos and single-family homes. My mother fought against him, trying everything she could to demonstrate that Marty was a looting bastard and that Judgie's intent was to leave the land to her and me. Marty, of course, won. Bulldozers came in the next day. The apple trees became firewood. The cows were sold.

Eighteen:

Hold The Pepperoni

I was back at Lynn's for Round Two. This time, I was ready to punch back.

With all the time that I had spent thinking about my mother, I convinced myself that I could get over my past by using this opportunity with Lynn to convince my mother that she was wrong for so many things and obtain my long awaited apology. Lynn would be our "marriage" therapist of sorts. He would surely take my side.

Knowing my mother like I did, I could guarantee that she hadn't begun to tell Lynn the first thing about our past. If she had, he never would have joined in on her imposition on me.

I checked the nicks on my face in my rear-view mirror and walked up to the front door of Lynn's office. When I opened the door, they met me in the lobby like a team of real estate agents meet a potential buyer during an open house.

"Come on in!" Lynn exclaimed. "Let me take your coat. Can I get you a cup of coffee, perhaps, or tea?"

"Oh, I'll do that!" cried Bobby-Charles. "Cream or sugar or both or none – we can do it any ol' way!"

As I was being disrobed by Lynn, my mother approached. She was blowing on a cup of tea and then put her hand on my shoulder. "It's so good of you to come," she said, earnestly "Really. We just need to get through this and everything will be just fine."

It was like we were at the funeral of someone we liked but didn't love or just got into a car accident – something inconvenient but not traumatic.

We all sat back in Lynn's office as he gathered some papers. Lynn had a collection of art around his office that, while curious, immediately said what he liked. And what he liked was a lot of it! Hawks. Lots and lots of hawks.

Brass ones, wood ones, ones made of pinecones and others painted on canvases. They all either had a fish or a rabbit clutched in the claws or the beak. My favorite take on the representation, was a small-framed cartoon that had a mouse flipping the "bird" to a pouncing hawk. His demise was eminent but he would have the last word. It read: Last Great Act Of Defiance.

"I'm glad you agreed to come back, Ben. I – well we – can't thank you enough," Lynn said.

I sipped my coffee and nodded slightly.

"I thought it might be good if I explained ourselves a little bit more. The last time you were here, it got a bit emotional and it's always good to take some time and just breathe in and breathe out and gain a little perspective."

I nodded some more.

"So," Lynn said, "how about we start by-"

"What did you tell him about us?" I asked my mother, interrupting Lynn.

She thought about my question. "I told him we had an argument – that you got angry with me and left. And we haven't really talked ever since."

I nodded again, but this time my face gave away my obvious disagreement with my mother's characterization of the facts.

"That it?" I asked her.

"I mean, I'm happy to start with your birth if you'd like and move through girlfriends, high school football, and drinking parties, but I thought what I told him was appropriate." Her sarcasm was perfect.

Still painting over the blood on the walls, I thought. I didn't respond.

"What do you want from me, Benjamin?" she asked me with irritation.

"We covered that over ten years ago," I said.

She let out a sigh and shook her head.

I turned my attention to Lynn. It was time to get him on my side. "We did speak once, a couple of years ago," I corrected myself to Lynn.

My mother looked confused.

"Yes, it was somewhat out of the blue. You called. We hadn't had any semblance of a relationship. A lot was still unsaid. I thought perhaps it was going to be a conversation about the past but, in fact, it was just more of your total and complete unappreciation for reality," I said. I felt my heart start pounding with heavier strokes.

"What are you talking about?" she asked.

"When you had the whole..." I stopped speaking and made a circle motion with my finger while pointing to my face.

Now Lynn looked confused. So did my mother.

"You don't remember the last time you called me for help?" I asked her.

"What, the thing with my surgery?"

"Yes, the 'thing' with your surgery."

Lynn clasped his hands and looked back between the

two of us. "What are we talking about here, folks?"

It was about ten thirty at night when Ayla and I stood in our kitchen, peering through the oven window at a bubbling pepperoni pizza. Our naked bodies glowed from the blue electric clock on the oven. If this were a scene in a movie, the director would gladly feature Ayla. But even as much of an over-the-shoulder of me would reveal enough body hair to scare the most avid moviegoer.

Sex obviously had been our appetizer and now, like a dog crazy for a squirrel, I couldn't let go of my desire not only to devour the crispy pepperoni, melting cheese, and steaming sauce but also to practically cover my body in it and spend the night licking it off. I would later be told by other similar-minded food psychopaths like me that I wasn't crazy, just a "foodie", which meant my odd desires for bathing in food were "normal."

Ayla and I ate ourselves into cured-meat bliss, moaning with each bite, until we nearly fell asleep at the kitchen table. The march back to bed was concise, as was our getting under the covers. Like two cows in the field, we settled in to chew the cud and dozed off into dreams of yesterday, today and tomorrow.

At six thirty a.m., the phone rang. "Hello. It's six thirty a.m.," I said to the caller.

"It's your mother," the voice said.

I sat up. "Mom – it's early," I rasped. That was the best greeting I could muster. Ayla's eyes opened on the word she'd never heard me use to address anyone and mouthed it back to me. I eeked my face.

"I assumed you'd be up," my mother said.

"No," I said. "It's Saturday."

On the other end of the phone, I heard my mother busy with something. "I know it's early," she told me, "but I just had a *feeling* you'd be up," she emphasized.

"No."

Ayla started mouthing entire sentences in silence, which I, of course, responded to even though I couldn't decipher what the hell she was saying.

"Oh. Anyway, now that you're awake," she said, "I need to see you." Her voice was tense, pained, and she was somewhat breathless. Something was wrong. The thought of seeing her stirred a hibernating anxiety in me.

"Mom, it's six thirty. I'm not dressed. I'm not even awake. I haven't had my coffee or anything."

She pushed and pushed. I turned to Ayla like I was a contestant on *The Price Is Right*. "What do I do? What do I do?" I mouthed.

"Go," she urged.

"Lunch," I said. "At a restaurant!" I added.

I didn't want the complications of privacy. A loud public restaurant with a lunchtime crowd would ensure that our voices would be raised and that personal conversation between us would be inappropriate for the venue.

She asked me to meet her at her home instead. I immediately feared that she would attempt an awkward and lengthy hug followed by ten minutes of tears. I felt my shoulders tighten and my teeth clench.

"Why can't we just eat at a restaurant?" I whined.

"Because we can't, okay?" she said. Her voice was annoyed. "I really need you to come by the house."

As I drove to her house, I thought about my life and how it had developed around her – the missing piece. Eight springs. Eight winter holidays. Eight years of dating and broken hearts. My life had been a field of ivy, running in all directions, and then, with one giant scoop, I had removed my mother. Although the remaining ivy had grown over the hole, the earth still dipped.

I had convinced myself that she had finally opened her eyes about our fight so many years before and was going to ask for forgiveness. The scene would be something out of *Better Homes and Gardens*. She'd set up a nice little lunchtime table. She'd cook, put out my grandmother's special plates. She'd look nice – something soft and motherly. She'd talk remorsefully, apologetically and probably cry a lot. It would be therapeutic for me to hear her out, though. My impending maturity urged me to forgive her and just get it over with. We'd had some tough times, but let's just move on with it. I sped up a bit.

Her new neighborhood was "totally exclusive," she'd said, as she gave me directions. I turned into the entrance and stopped at towering gates that blocked my passage. No call button. No security guards. Just black iron and steel. A man drove down in a golf cart from a booth I hadn't seen and pushed a remote. He waved me through.

Half-million-dollar homes stacked side by side like dominoes. Large plots but small enough that you could see which section of the newspaper your neighbor read on Sunday morning.

I knocked on the front door, but she didn't come. I looked through the glass for signs of life. I felt a bit awkward just walking in, so I cracked the door and peeked in. "Hello?" I entered and listened for house noise. Nothing. I sniffed for cooking food. Perhaps she was in the kitchen and didn't hear me. I didn't smell food, though. I peeked around a corner and saw the kitchen. The lights were out. The stove was off.

My mother heard the front door close and hurried down the back hallway and into the living room, where we met eyes for the first time in years. I expected her initial words would be conversational. I'd prepared myself to talk briefly about my additional twenty pounds and the fact that my hair had thinned. I expected she would pick at the thinned areas or bunch her fingers in it and comment about how nice it still looked or, at a minimum, cry at my maturity.

There were no tears. "I'm so glad you're here," she said.

She wore a robe, and her face was swollen the size of the moon and wrapped a dozen times in white gauze that rolled over her chin, cheeks, and forehead. The skin around her eyes was black and yellow and held together with stitches in the corners. Her upper lip was fire engine red and coated with what appeared to be Vaseline.

"What the hell happened to you?" I asked.

"What are you talking about?" she asked, as if she were modeling a new line of cosmetics.

"Oh, I don't know... your face."

She checked her reflection in a framed picture. "What? I had a facelift. I felt I *deserved* it," she said, eyeing me sharply at the word "deserved."

"I'm sure you did," I told her.

"Yes... well..." She paused.

"Well, what about lunch?" I asked her.

"I can still eat."

"No, I mean, when you first called, you said you wanted to meet *out* for lunch." She let out a sigh. "You had no intention of ever meeting me out, did you?"

She was antsy but paused to level with me. "I really just needed to get on your schedule," she said.

"My schedule?" I realized I wasn't there to get an apology. I was pissed. Tricked and now pissed.

"Look," she said, "can you just come back here for a minute and then we can... *discuss*... whatever issues you're having with me?" She turned down the back hallway. "Okay? Now, come on, please." When I hesitated, she called out again. "Are you coming?"

Her tone was oddly indifferent and all too familiar. My ruined expectations were much like those of a two-year-child who had just been denied a cookie and was now draped across the floor kicking and screaming a garbled mouthful of incomprehensible toddler curse words. Instead, I stood there and chewed on my bottom lip. I wanted an apology, damn it. Just a simple "I'm sorry," filled with real remorse and some goddamn tears. *Be cool,* I thought. *Be cool. Just go along, and slowly but surely you'll get your apology.*

"I'm coming," I mumbled.

I followed the darkened hallway to a light that spilled into the back part of the house. It led into a bathroom vanity area. I stopped suddenly at the sight of medical paraphernalia on the countertop: creams and pills, sterile gauze pads, clear tubing, tape, and scissors. It looked like someone was about to perform surgery in the supply closet at the ER.

"You haven't started medical school yet, have you?" my mother asked as she grabbed some fresh gauze.

"Uh... no," I said.

"Really?"

"I didn't get in the first time. Or the second time."

"You're reapplying, aren't you?"

"Of course I'm reapplying," I said, irritated. But the fact that I lied so easily to her taught me something about the boy I used to be. I was no longer that boy and no longer needed to lie anymore. But here I was doing it again. On the flip side, I had obviously out-foxed her because she seemed totally unaware of what I was actually doing.

"But aren't you doing a rotation at an emergency room?"

"How do you know about the emergency room?" I asked.

"I keep up," she said.

"I'm not doing a rotation. I work as an EMT on an ambulance."

She returned her focus to cutting pieces of medical tape. "This tape is so sticky. I prefer the paper tape to this silk stuff." I watched her keenly. "But you're in the emergency room, right?" she emphasized.

"On ambulances that go to the emergency room, yes," I said carefully.

"And you're a nurse, did you say?"

I looked at her bruised face again. "No, I would have had to go to *nursing* school for that."

"Please, Benjamin," she urged. "I wasn't really around for your college years, if you recall."

"By your choice," I told her, trying to steer her toward an apology, even if it was brief and uncomplicated.

She stopped all movement. "I can't go there right now, okay? I just can't."

I didn't want to show my disappointment. "Then where are we going with this?"

She laid short pieces of tape side by side and let them dangle off the edge of the counter. "So what are you then?" she asked, distracted.

"I told you, I was an – I mean, *am* – an EMT."

"That's not like a junior doctor, is it?"

"I do emergency procedures and *assist* the doctors and nurses. What's this all about?"

She paused and took a deep breath. "I've had some surgery."

"Really," I said. "I hadn't noticed."

"Less than seventy-two hours ago," she said, ignoring me and uncapping a tube of antibiotic cream.

"You didn't do it yourself, did you?"

She ignored me and ripped off another piece of tape. "I need you... to check something for me."

I took a small step backward. "Like what?"

"I need your medical opinion."

I'd seen some things that fell into the category of "outside the box" in my day. Some real wild and gruesome stuff – blood, guts, giant pus-filled pimples, rat-chewed feet, shredded bones – but if she expected me to watch her peel tape and gauze off her stitched-up face, she was out of her mind. Strangers are one thing; your mother's bruised and bloody face sewn on with plastic wire is entirely different. *I'll pass out*, I thought. "No, thanks," I said.

"You work in the medical field!" she exclaimed.

"I don't want to see the borders of your face stapled to the side of your head, mother. Thanks, but no thanks."

"Look, it's really just a circulation issue. Nothing complicated. I just need you to check my coloration." She reached for the edges of her robe. "I need you to look at my nipple."

"I'm sorry?"

"My nipple."

"Your '*nipple*.'"

"Yes."

"By '*nipple*,' I assume you mean your face."

"No, I mean my breast."

"By '*breast*,' I assume you mean your face."

"Stop it! I mean my breast, okay?"

"Oh, I'm sorry." I paused. "I'm just a little confused because it seems you just asked your *son* to take a look at your fucking *nipple*!"

"I also had breast reduction surgery and it hurts," she pleaded.

"And?" I insisted.

"I'm worried about it." She was panicked.

"So call your doctor," I said.

"The office is closed!"

"Get the on-call guy," I said.

"What's the big deal?" she said, her eyes callous. "You wanna be a doctor, don't you?" Her logic was staggering.

"Well... yes, but..." I paused, waiting for her to say,

"Oh, never mind," which she didn't say.

"C'mon, Benjamin."

"Of course you're right. Forgive me. Why don't I just take a little peeksy at your nipple there and then how about I, uh, lay you up on the dining room table and give you a gynecological exam while I'm at it? Would that make you happy – just get all your yearly visits over with right now?"

She began to think this wasn't going to happen.

As breasts go, I was always very interested. Whatever their shape or size, I didn't care. But I never meant it to include the ones hanging off my mother's torso.

"It's just skin," she insisted.

"There are rules, mother!"

"You used to breastfeed off them."

"Yes, when I was two days old and blind." I grabbed my forehead. A gigantic headache started to splinter into each of my eye sockets. "Dollar signs are flying past me right now. Thinking of the years of therapy I'll need."

As I turned away from her, she opened her robe and whipped out her left breast. "Just look at it," she said. The sight of the flesh slapped me in the face, and I spun around, stumbling. "What? Are you crazy!" I screamed. I reached for the wall and felt my way into the hallway. "I thought I was here for an apology!" I ran back into the living room.

She tucked her breast back in her robe and ran after me.

"Call your doctor's office, mother!" I told her as she followed me into the living room.

"I can't!" she pleaded. "He's in Switzerland skiing. I

don't have anyone else to call." Now she was visibly upset. "I'm scared, and I don't wanna lose my nipple," she said.

"Do you realize how ridiculous that sounds?"

"You know that's not true. It's been cut off and reattached."

Truth be told – and I was still partially big on the truth – she was right. Any skin that's been cut off and reattached could fail to regain circulation and die. If indeed there was a problem, she could wind up deformed.

I braced myself at the edge of the couch. It was the only shoulder I had. I felt so alone – in a strange home with a strange-ass woman. Her face was hidden beneath bandages. Puffy. Unrecognizable. My heart drooled in anticipation of its own repair. My mother was now further away than ever.

I didn't want to be repulsed by my mother. On the way over, I had begun to appreciate the chance to meet with her and possibly resolve our issues. But this? This was our new beginning? A nipple exam on my mom?

Inside I battled between trying to understand her predicament and the inescapable realization that this was totally fucking crazy. I wondered whether any of my friends' mothers had ever asked them to look at their nipples. How would I know? It's not like they'd ever share it with anyone. My own sick need to have her in my life became obvious by the fact that I hadn't walked out of the house.

I let out a deep sigh. "Fine," I heard myself whisper. "I'll do it."

"You will?"

"Jesus Christ, I'll do it!"

She pulled out her breast again. "Son-of-a-bitch!" I yelled. "Can you wait a goddamn minute? Cover it up! Christ, I'm not ready."

"Hurry," she said. "It's turning purple."

I held my finger up to silence her just as she had done to me. I wagged it in her face.

"Oh, please, hurry," she begged.

I shook my head as if arguing against my decision. *All right*, I thought. *If she wants me to examine her nipple, that's exactly what I'll do.* If I was going to be permanently scarred from this, I sure as hell wanted a clear picture of the object I was going to pay a therapist thousands of dollars to help me forget. I took a deep breath and waved her forward. She pulled open her top, and I leaned in close.

"And?" she asked.

"Well," I said as I furrowed my professorial brow and crossed my doctorate arms. "For starters, it's lopsided."

"What?"

"*To*-tally lopsided."

"It is not."

"Like it fell asleep taking a bow."

"What?" she demanded.

"Old gal needs an espresso." She looked down inside her robe. "And your areola is *massive*," I said.

She snapped her head down again. "What?"

"It's the size of a sombrero."

"It is not the size of a sombrero!"

"Sure is."

"No, it is not!"

"*Muy grande!*" My high school Spanish was coming in handy.

My mother was getting annoyed. "All right. That's enough!" She tucked it away. "I just had one simple request. I just wanted you to look! But if you can't handle it, then fine, be a smart ass!"

"Hey, I got an idea for you," I barked. "Why don't you look at my erect penis? How 'bout that? See if the *circulation* is flowing." I scoffed at myself. "Your fuckin' nipple is fine!"

As I left her with her tits hanging out, I wondered if I even still cared about her at all and whether I still possessed any of the forgiving, unconditional love I'd once felt for her as a child.

Lynn's mouth gaped open like a wall-mounted bass. He actually had one of those in his office too. His eyes were stretched open so wide I thought he was having an aneurysm.

"I left her home feeling like I'd just had sex with a sibling or... my mother for that matter," I explained to Lynn.

My mother crossed her arms, cocked her head and chewed on her bottom lip.

"Is this true?" Lynn asked her. His voice was incredulous.

Her faced opened, innocently. "It's not as bad as it sounds – I mean, he's making it sound worse that it really was," my mother said.

I cackled. Lynn looked confused by his client's

impudence. He checked his watch. We had already gone an hour and it looked like he didn't set much time aside.

"Ben, I'm sorry, I didn't realize there was this kind of water under the bridge. Can you give us a minute?" Lynn asked, regaining his composure.

"With pleasure," I said.

Fuck yeah, I thought. *Bull's-eye.*

I stood and reached to open the door. It was heavy and opening on me quickly. It knocked me backward as Bobby-Charles fell through the opening once more. He screamed again and it startled Lynn, who jumped from his seat.

"Christ, Bobby-Charles!" he yelled.

Lynn walked me outside and thanked me. He said he would call me and we'd work out another time, if I would agree to come back. I said I would and told him I had more where that came from.

My mother began to realize it would take more than a skilled "surgeon" like Lynn to rejuvenate our relationship and make it fresh again. It would need a will and a way. And at this point, she saw that my will to reconnect with her was running as dead and dry as the skin that had been removed from her face.

Nineteen:
Legal Unease

Later that night I met Ayla for dinner at an obnoxious Greek restaurant. The giant neon sign over the door that read OPA! was a promise by the owner that you'd better have fun or else. Inside, the owner's fat wife, Ambrosia, draped herself in silk shrouds and, with finger chimes on, paraded around the room as if she were the Lost Princess of Virility and Virginity. Their seven sons who worked as cooks and waiters simultaneously confirmed and denied these pretensions.

Ayla bobbed in her chair and snapped her hoisted fingers as if she were Zorba himself. I looked at her judgmentally.

"What?" she asked.

"Your boobs are bouncing," I heard myself say, sounding like a stuffy diplomat.

"I thought it was your 'fav,'" She jested, as in "favorite."

"Not here," I said.

"If not here, then where?" she said. The music was intoxicating and she kept it up.

Ambrosia made her way to our table. Every inch of exposed skin poured out of her silk wrappings as if she was the *Titanic* and her breasts were trying to jump ship. She chinged and changed the finger cymbals in my face then traced her pointer under my chin to turn my eyes toward her ample breasts. Somewhere behind a counter, I could see her husband saying to himself, *Yes. Yes! Get the stupid American to spend the money. Slide the dollar bill into her blouse and lose yourself in her unending beauty.*

Unending, yes. Beauty – not a chance.

Ayla sensed my irritation and mouthed for me to "be nice." I faked a smile to Ambrosia's makeup-covered face and found myself wondering why she chose to wear so much eyeliner. Ayla reached out and put a five in the woman's bra strap, and like a swamp gator, she spun off to wreak havoc elsewhere. Fortunately, the music had crescendoed and Ambrosia made her bow and took her sweaty ass to the back.

"I know," Ayla said. "You're not in any mood for this, are you?"

"It's fine," I said, lying.

"Look, babe," she said, as she straightened herself. "It's out there now. You're talking about it."

"What's so crazy is after all this time, I still don't understand what made me think I could get away with it. Why not just tell her? 'Hey, mom, just to let you know, I'm not gonna be a doctor anymore' or 'Hey, mom, just to let you know, I'm going to law school. Thought I'd give it a shot. Stay out of my life. Kiss my ass,' et cetera. That would have been so easy."

"Oh, I know exactly why you didn't tell her."

"No, it's not because of that!"

"Because of what?" she cried, suddenly feeling accused.

"Some subversive psychological unspoken Freudian babble that you think is suddenly percolating up to the surface," I said.

"Then you *do* know," she said convinced.

"Whatever," I said, shoving a bit of food into my

mouth.

"You wanted this," she said.

"'Wanted' is a strong word."

"I'm a strong woman."

"Okay, so wow me and tell me how you figure that?"

"What's the legal standard of responsibility that always irritates the hell out of me?"

"*Should* have known."

"That's it," Ayla said. "But you didn't just have an idea that this would happen – you *knew* it would. Eventually. You go to law school in the city where she earned her reputation. You practice here in the same discipline. You're in front of the same judges she knows, the same prosecutors. How many times a day are you asked if you're Carter Scales' son?"

"A few."

"You knew, you little shit. Or you *'should have known.'* Any time when you should have known, you're just as guilty and you go to prison for just as long as the bastards who knew it."

Ayla was right. "Fuck," I said. "And here I thought it was because I was afraid of her."

"Does it feel as good as you'd hoped?" she asked. I didn't answer, which was an answer.

I must have been insane to think I could do this without my mother finding out that I must have done it on purpose. I had been walking the halls of the same buildings within which she had made her name, driving the same state highways, traveling the same country roads to the same jails, feeling the same pain. It was only a matter of time before our paths would cross again.

Twenty:
My First Pair Of High Heels

I went to work immediately after passing the bar. It was the Monday after the Friday I'd found out. I'd spent the last eighteen hours at an 80's-themed party wearing Ray-Ban Wayfarers and my graduation gown, pretending to be a judge who presided solely over the question of which female class members looked the best in their combination of ripped sweatshirts, exposed single bare shoulder, Lycra miniskirts, and leg warmers. The weekend was a "radical" success. Even the smart girls threw up. Ayla was a real trouper and aptly played the role of my courtroom deputy, faithfully announcing my presence everywhere I went.

"Da mo-fuckin' judge has entered up in this mo-fucker!" she shouted.

With gentleman's C's and no six-figure offers from the much-desired skyscraper law firms, I had to rely on my silver tongue to get myself a ground-level job. I'd received my only A's and top honors in my trial classes. I even won the coveted Cunning Linguist Award that was secretly awarded by a mysterious faculty member – although it was rumored to be the dean herself. I had talked my way into just about every internship or clerk position I'd ever been given. As tiring as it was, I got used to the hustle.

My first boss after law school was Patrick Ruler, who saw within me a set of street skills he admired immediately and didn't care what my papers said. He wasted no time having me sworn in by a friend of his who was also a judge. While the state organized a mass swearing-in that was attended by hundreds of other graduates, Patrick convinced me it was for litigators and other "paper pushers." Real lawyers – in particular, criminal defense trial attorneys – got sworn in and argued in front of the Supreme Court, on the same day if they had to. According to Patrick, who was also my first mentor, I was going to be a real trial lawyer like him.

Patrick and I weren't the typical mentor-mentee pairing. He was a slick-minded, sharp-witted, flamboyantly dressed black man who practiced criminal defense and divorce law. He also specialized in dance moves, with purple suits and alligator shoes to match. I was a white Jew from the Northern Atlanta suburbs, specializing in heavy-wool navy pinstripe suits. Our backgrounds and styles were as different as sushi and fried neck bone.

But Patrick saw something in me, despite my immature judgment at times. And since I was Patrick's first white mentee, he was determined to make my experience worthwhile for me... and for him. The benefits I'd accrue by practicing with Patrick were clear: knowledgeable mentor; busy practice; immediate courtroom experience; a well-rounded education through a varied caseload. The benefits to him of being able to parade me – one of "God's chosen people" – into client meetings as an asset to the firm was equally clear. Black clients said things like "oh, wow" and "I see" like I was a new interest-only loan that had a competitive variable rate.

As a kid growing up in the 'hood, Patrick didn't have a legal mentor. He came up slowly and forged relationships, crossed racial lines, and maintained a legendary practice for more than thirty years. Not much for heights, he shied away from penthouses offices and kept his hustle to the streets, where he and his career were born. As one of the most well-known attorneys in town, he walked the halls of the courthouse like a rock star. He was also a mentor to countless other young attorneys like me, but not like me. Dozens had come up through Patrick's office during their initial years in the practice, including those who are now prosecutors, judges, and state legislators, yet, because he was black and his office was well ensconced in the black neighborhoods, the only mentees were also black – that is, until I came along.

"I don't wipe noses, and I don't do Pampers," Patrick told me. His euphemisms were uncharacteristically direct, and I understood his meanings without much interpretation.

Patrick didn't just *expose* his attorneys to the nitty-gritty side of client management and trial practice; he grabbed them by the ankle and elbow and threw them in the water. Feet first, head first; it didn't matter – they would be submerged.

"You just might be the first Jewish kid ever to be baptized!" Patrick said, howling with laughter.

His entire body shook when he laughed. Depending on where he sat or stood at the time, he'd knock pictures off the wall, topple floor lamps, or dump a potted plant.

When Patrick called me over the weekend amid my Sunday-morning hangover, I thought he had momentarily lost his mind. Using his deep and commanding preacher-like voice, he informed me that the party was over. It was time to work, starting with a 'go 'n' see' for a new client, a criminal defendant named Slyrickus Lester, III.

"It's time to shake the trees, young brother!" Patrick

told me.

"You mean, like, *yard work?*" I asked through a hoarse voice.

"No, I mean it's time to turn things loose - see what's what and get to the bottom of things," Patrick clarified. My instructions were simple: impress the client; sell the firm; bring home the money.

"How much money?" I asked him.

"It should be right at a hundred."

"A hundred thousand?" I said, incredulous.

"Yeah, and it's gonna be cash, so be sure to count it," he said nonchalantly.

"Who in the hell has a hundred thousand dollars in cash?" I asked him.

"Hopefully, our client."

Our client, Slyrickus, was a "businessman" who had been on his way home from a two-day overnight trip to Birmingham with no luggage, change of clothes, or toothbrush to speak of. Call it unprepared or forgetful for some, but the county officer who had stopped him for wearing no seatbelt called his lack of luggage "suspicious". This prompted a long series of questions about Slyrickus and his background. After a genius move by Slyrickus to consent to the officer's request to search his vehicle, the officer *surprisingly* discovered five duffle bags filled with approximately 150 pounds of marijuana. The officer called "10-13" for help just as Slyrickus ran into the adjacent field and tried to outrun the radio. But then came Tinker Bell – the cop's dog. Of all things loved and adored by cops, nothing gave an officer more pride and pleasure than to release his canine like a bolt of lightning from his fingertips. Tinker Bell did as lightning does and struck its object to the ground with the ease of a hot knife through room temperature butter.

Patrick got the court to agree to give Slyrickus a bond on Patrick's word that he would be the lawyer and that he would personally ensure Slyrickus's presence in court. The bond was "cash only" – meaning that Slyrickus paid for it himself and not with the assistance of a licensed state bonding company. No lawyer ever should put themselves on the line like that for their client – making personal assurances and all – but Patrick did it for several.

For additional insurance, the judge, a man in his mid-forties with only a few years on the bench, added that Slyrickus would be under "house arrest" and required to wear a state-of-the-art GPS ankle monitor system that linked him to several satellites roaming overhead. If Slyrickus so much as stepped off his sprawling country estate, it would beep incessantly and allow the local sheriff to pinpoint his location even if he were swimming underwater, flying in the air, or running away again through some field of his choosing.

After Patrick's personal assurance to the court, I was insulted by the idea of house arrest and the GPS monitor. Patrick later explained that the judge was a little hyper and often added the GPS anklet as a precondition before release on bond.

What Patrick didn't tell me but I later learned is that Patrick and the judge were motorcycle buddies and the "personal guarantee" by Patrick was a "code" that served as a request to the judge to, in fact, place his client on house arrest with the added GPS lockdown. Apparently, Patrick also wanted to ensure the whereabouts of his client. Using code, though, Patrick would avoid blame for the conditions and still look like a champ for his client. Like I said, *many* attorneys came up through Patrick's office.

As a new lawyer, I truly felt like a real man, employed and empowered. People wanted to talk to *me*. To see *me*. To hear *my* opinion more than anyone. As I was a criminal defense attorney, they practically begged me to make it all go away. The entire experience was nerve racking and intoxicating.

As this was my first assignment, I desperately wanted it to go well. A stellar first impression was essential, and Slyrickus's stamp of approval on me to Patrick was imperative.

Unfortunately, for me, I was running behind, after getting lost on back roads, trying to make my way to Slyrickus's country estate. Patrick wanted me to use the "company car," a '95 Mercury Cougar XR7 coupe with a supercharged engine that delivered 210 horsepower. It was white with red interior and had seven-spoke chrome-finished wheels. He called it the "Cool-ger." It rocked like a boat around corners but had decent pickup when you needed to get away from anyone who saw you in it.

I had been pedal heavy through the country until I hit a bridge reconstruction job in a small town and got directed to fall in behind a chicken rig. We rolled over gravel and boards and metal plates until we got around the mile-long detour. I got a few nods from some of the men of color working the job. They liked my ride.

Finally, me and the chicken rig picked up another two-lane country road and I spent about ten minutes at twenty miles an hour before I could find the right straight section of road to nail the gas. Away from the dust and debris of the construction crew, I rolled down my windows to take advantage of the country breeze and mashed the gas.

The Cool-ger was ready, too, as it surged forward to thirty-five mph, then forty, then forty-five. As I pulled up alongside the chicken rig, I could see all of the chickens trapped in their cages. *Poor bastards*, I thought, as I depressed the pedal further.

I nodded at the birds as I leaped my way past, until BOOM! My front tire exploded. The sound was supersonic and sent the entire fleet of birds into a dizzying panic to the point they started flapping wildly in their crates. Even with the wind in my window, I could hear their frantic clucking.

Because the cages were exposed to the wind, the rig blew out feathers like a snow blower. The draft around my windows sucked them in by the dozens.

The Cool-ger immediately dipped down to the left and I heard the sound of grinding metal. It shot off the road and down an embankment into grass and mud. I tried to clear feathers while I tried to steer clear of roadside hazards. I hit a tree and halted to the sound of steam coming from my engine and the sight of soft white feathers drifting slowly around me. The Cool-gar, it appeared, had made her last prowl. And me? I wasn't sure.

Prior to leaving to see Slyrickus, Patrick informed me of the ways of the world, in that officers were not the nice, helpful, and smartly dressed fellows we citizens had come to know and love; rather, they were corrupt and power hungry. He predicted that the officer in our case didn't really have any reason to stop Slyrickus; instead, the officer saw free labor in a black man who could wash his patrol cars and run to the store and back.

This confirmed my own suspicions and mirrored my own experience. "Bunch of racists," I told him.

"Why do you think I'm sending you?" he said, roaring with laughter.

There was another reason Patrick hired me to work as his associate, and it too was as superficial as the first. This reason wasn't externally obvious, like the color of my skin, though. It was internal. The reason, as Patrick explained to me, was because being a lawyer was "in my blood."

Patrick knew I wasn't the first criminal defense attorney in my family; he knew my mother by reputation. This fact, Patrick believed, meant that my ability to "fight the good fight" – to fight to uphold the constitutional rights inherent to every US citizen – was as ingrained in me as the blood in my body.

The reason this was true, Patrick told me, was that criminal defense attorneys like him and my mother didn't merely practice law on the "nine-to-five." They lived and breathed their practice to the detriment of everyone in their lives, except their clients. This was a point I knew well growing up with my mother. Practicing law lived and breathed inside of them like the weather lives and breathes over the earth's landscape. With their minds and their words, they became the winds and the storms that carried their clients to brighter horizons. Their knowledge was power, and their brand of knowledge didn't happen in a forty-hour workweek. It was a way of life.

It meant reading the paper at four thirty a.m. when it

hit the driveway. It meant a full pot of coffee twice a day. It meant a hundred phone calls every twenty-four hours. It meant people lining up to see you. It meant praise and anger and emotional outbursts and fights and terrible nights of restless sleep and sometimes even victory and changing the law and the way other lawyers practiced after you. For me, it also meant growing up with Dragon Lady Scales, as they called her.

Patrick was adamant that every son *must* love his mother.

"What about loving his *father?*" I asked him, knowing how he felt about his own father after overhearing several long speeches to his clients that his relationship with his father was less than affectionate.

"Not that son-of-a-bitch," he told me.

I offered up a smile to his reverberating anger, and he got my point. Mentors hate it when their mentees teach them a thing or two. Patrick was no different. And as he was a middle-aged black man who had survived the frontal assaults and the subterfuge of racism, I learned quickly that you couldn't tell him shit. But despite loving his own mother dearly and knowing and admiring my mother, Patrick agreed to keep our relationship a secret. He warned me, though, that Atlanta was a small city. And he was right. My mother and I both lived in Atlanta and worked in the various jurisdictions around the state. Over the course of my early childhood years, I met most of the lawyers she practiced with, including other criminal defense attorneys, prosecutors, and judges.

It was a lie that I knew would catch up with me sooner rather than later. But just as a three-year-old will tip over the vase he's not supposed to touch, I wasn't afraid to break a few things myself.

Sitting in the Cool-ger, I began to think about my real survival. Work. I cursed my misfortune and that I would be late to my first assignment. Patrick surely would muse about fate and how changing earlier behavior would have totally removed me from this accident at this precise moment, despite my argument against it.

I exited the Cool-ger to inspect the damage. The hood of the vehicle was folded around a large oak, which stood erect between the headlights like a middle finger. The front left tire was blown due to a nail I had most likely picked up near the construction site. The engine hissed as if exhaling air in total exhaustion and disbelief. While some things in life that don't kill you make you stronger, this event only made me feel stupid.

The only good news, if any were to be had, was that I was still looking good. Despite, mud and grass and chicken feathers in the thousands, my suit was still in pristine condition. I could still make a good impression.

Five hours later, I carried my briefcase to the lamp-lit front portico of Slyrickus's 8,000-square-foot home. Even in the darkness of the country, the place looked enormous. The portico vaulted two stories into darkness and seemed unending. It was like stepping into a giant's gaping mouth. I flattened the lapel of my jacket, straightened my tie and put on a confident face: a piercing look with a slight all-knowing grin. I wiped my feet on the doormat, knowing I would be invited in. It was peppered with black and white specks. I made sure I didn't get my shoes any dirtier.

I reached the knocker on the door, opting against the doorbell in case there were young children, and hit the ring hanging from a brass lion's mouth to the brass plate behind it.

The sound was loud and immediately echoed in the portico. And then came the sound that led to my demise: a half dozen birds flapping wildly that, in their panic, began dropping shit all over my suit. They fled the scene, leaving me speckled and understanding the mystery of the black and white dots on the mat.

The door suddenly opened. Slyrickus stood there looking me up and down. He was large and toned and had a partially picked-out Afro with the remaining hair combed neatly in braided rows. He looked at me with anger and then like I was an idiot.

"Didn't chew see the bird shit on the mat?!" he cried.

"Well... I wasn't sure," I said, trying to find the words.

"Well, you're goddamn sure now, aren't ya?!" Slyrickus burst out laughing.

I tried to take it in stride, wiping some droppings from my forehead. "Yes, well, good evening, Mr. Lester," I said, clearing my throat. "I'm here from Patrick Ruler's office. I'm his associate, Benjamin Scales." He laughed harder and harder still and slowly closed the door in my face.

Great, I thought.

Fortunately, he returned with a large clear, suitcase-size, air-suctioned plastic pack that contained stacks of bills, thousands of them in different denominations. I hesitantly took the pack into my hands and looked at Slyrickus, who took a step closer to me.

"Tell Patrick I didn't hire no white boy. I wanted a black attorney. That's why I hired him."

"Okay," I said.

He looked me up and down, rolled his eyes, and closed the door in my face for the second and final time.

I looked down at my hand and the fifteen-pound bag of money, until the porch light turned off, and then it was just dark. Me and the crickets.

"Thank you, Mr. Lester," I said to the darkened front door. "We'll be in touch."

I sat in a Ford Focus rental car in a Burger King parking lot under the cover of darkness and a dimly lit kiosk that read, JESUS IS LORD AT BURGER KING, counting fives, tens, twenties, fifties, and hundred-dollar bills. The sound of the rhythmic thumbing of bills nearly put me to sleep, except for the fact that I was actually in possession of just under $100,000.

I thought about my exact location in space and time – being in a car in the middle of nowhere, an off-ramp at a fast food restaurant, sitting in the only rusted-out car the rental agency manager trusted me with, nursing a broken ego and a suit covered in bird shit, counting money in the dark like a felon. For a minute, I thought about my estranged mother and that she was about my age when she had started her trial practice. A woman with an eight-year-old son and everything to prove. I knew it had been difficult for her; those years of torment were not lost on her alone. I remember her "being on assignment" like I was right now. It was an insight I'd never had before now.

I turned on the radio and Pearl Jam's *Elderly Woman Behind the Counter in a Small Town* filled the speakers. I raised the volume and listened to the tormented rock star, Eddie Vedder, recall a painful reunion.

I cranked the clunker and exchanged the dough for bread; I was starving and my Whopper was cold. It had taken me nearly two hours to count the cash. Aside from occasionally hiding the money as someone walked past, I counted it twice to make sure it was all there, knowing that no matter how badly I messed up my first impression, bringing home the money would cleanse all sins.

I saw myself introducing myself to Slyrickus, remembering the look on his face and the words that didn't hide his disapproval. I imagined my mother had it just like that.

"You must be fucking kidding me. A woman lawyer?"

I thought about those nights when she had brought home her insecurities or rage. Those nights where I'd sat dutifully on the sideline of her fledgling career and tried not to be in the way when she got home and spat the shit out. Although hers was a gender war and mine somewhat of a race thing, we shared some common themes, including our inexperience at our beginning moments. It made us equals, although I didn't like the idea of that.

I mashed the gas and closed my eyes to the jolt of the factory horsepower and tried to pull the recurring thoughts of my mother and the past from my mind as the wind swept through my hair. Suddenly, I was back on the law school commuter train, the film of the past lying over the present, two reels rolling at once.

I needed to focus on Patrick and the job at hand. This moment, like many others to come, was part of my initiation into the practice of law. Necessary, but painful. Sharing in a similar initiation, though, driving these Georgia backcountry roads, I knew I wasn't riding alone.

My mother and I were together again.

Twenty-One:
Trial And Error

Aside from coining phrases such as "Dat's just some mystique-ass bullshit," Patrick was also a masterful legal writer and orator – a true and clear legal scholar of the Constitution and the rights inherent to us all: black, white, Hispanic, and the affectionately known "other" group. But he never lost touch with his roots or failed to come through on his street cred. He kept it all very real and frank. He once told a client who had been giving him lip, "Son, I will climb Mount Everest for you, but I won't walk across the *goddamn* street for bullshit!"

I had gotten his name through one of my professors, who said my mother always spoke mixed feelings about Patrick, which meant he probably didn't take any shit from her. We were already a good fit.

In the months following "Nipplegate," my mother had called a few times. I returned the calls, and we even met briefly at a deli. She wore a wrap shirt, and I couldn't help think about the edges of her robe. Every time I was around her, I searched my soul, looking for a foothold to climb out of our cavernous past. My being a lawyer was an obvious one, but I didn't know how to start the conversation. I felt like I was standing at a closed door, wanting to talk to her on the other side, but not knowing how to knock.

So, mom, a funny thing happened over the last three years. I got a law degree.

We ate our latkes and lox and bagels and said goodbye with an awkward half hug.

My work became an easy distraction. Within my first

year as a lawyer, in addition to handling about thirty-something divorce petitions, Patrick assigned me my first criminal trial to handle all on my own – a murder trial. "There's not enough money in this case for me to leave my practice for a three-week trial," he said. "I have faith in you."

"Excuse me?" I asked, somewhat shocked out of my fucking mind.

"It's not like I'm asking you to *drive* anywhere," he jested.

"We're talking about defending a man's life!"

He responded to my shock and indignation with his own. "You know what my momma used to say when the water got deep?" My blank look was an assurance that I did not. "Thank God I taught you to swim." Somehow, Patrick believed that after a year with him I was perfectly capable of defending an eighteen-year-old kid from a life sentence.

The murder allegedly had taken place in a neighborhood known for drugs and violence. One night, two rival groups of high school kids went to a girl's birthday party. The birthday girl, of course, was the common factor as she had attended both schools. At some point during the evening, a boy from one school grabbed the butt of a girl whose brother went to the other school. Guns were drawn and waved as tempers flared. The client and his three classmates decided to go home but not before passing a gun between them and shooting it into the air – or, rather, into the crowd of the other kids a few hundred feet away. One kid got shot in the ankle and then in the chest. He died on the front lawn of the girl's home. My client, Tyler Sims, was the alleged shooter. The other three boys, all co-defendants, supposedly had aided and abetted his efforts to shoot. They were all charged with murder and faced life in prison if convicted.

Even for my first trial, I knew the prosecuting attorney was going to have a field day with those facts. He was a short, chubby black man who dressed like a goofball with his mismatched slacks and sports coat and bow tie combination. Sweating profusely, he patted his forehead with a stained hankie and said, "Let me you ask you a question" before asking each question. It was unnerving. He was also quite the thespian.

I could just hear his opening.

"An innocent boy!" he'd say. "A young man filled with the promise of a bright future! Gunned down by a gang of murderers! All because a girl got her butt grabbed!" he'd yell. Then, with tears in his eyes, he'd point to my client and the other defendants and say, "And there they are!"

The jury would undoubtedly look at the lawyers, including me, and think, *How can you represent that piece of shit, you piece of shit?*

"Patrick, I'm handling dozens of divorce petitions right now. I'm in court almost every day," I told him. "And you're never around! You can't just disappear."

"This is a man's business, and it demands you act like one! Let me tell you somethin'. When I first started practicing law, I took everything that walked in the door. I didn't care if I was up all night, all weekend, whatever. I was makin' money, and I was going to get and *keep* business. You ain't no different. And I expect no less."

"I understand that Pat, but maybe it's not the best time right now for me to do this. I'm not just here to get business. I'm here to successfully run the majority of your practice so you can focus on the bigger cases," I said.

"Benjamin, I've been doin' this for thirty years – practicing law in every situation imaginable. This ain't no big deal, man. I know you can handle it." He handed me a book and a folder. "Start with statutes the state has alleged he violated and look at the corresponding jury charges. You should be thinking of your closing argument at all times."

Panicking, I asked, "What about pretrial motions?"

"Yeah. There are quite a few of those. Photo lineups, severance issues, Bruton issues, Brady issues, Jackson-Denno, suppression issues, conspiracies, kids being taken out of their homes in the middle of the night and questioned by police, threats of violence against neighbors, prejudicial autopsy photos, people changing stories and impeachment, bias, motives, "similar transactions," recidivist punishment, and the fact that it was darker than Dikembe Mutumbo that night." He suddenly nodded. "Yeah, just about every damn thing you learned in law school's gonna come up in this one case."

"Everything I learned in law school?" I asked. "I don't know three-quarters of the shit you're talkin' about."

"You've got some time. It's as much about how you prepare for a trial as it is about how you try it."

I went back into my office and closed the door. I sat at my desk and melted down. Sweat dripped down my chest and side, down my back. Beads formed on my scalp. Suddenly, the papers on my desks twisted upward in a mini tornado and flew all around me in a violent storm of tasks, discovery, and paperwork.

The photos from the murder case were on top. Photos of the victim's chest sawed open. The bloody chest tissue shot open by the tracks of bullets passing through his body. His anklebone blown to shreds. A blood-soaked t-shirt. His gaping mouth and pale tongue. His body draped across the lawn, his arms spread open to heaven.

My thoughts barreled out of control – *my client. Jesus Christ, my client.* An eighteen-year-old kid, looking to me to save his ass. In a courtroom. With a judge who was probably going to eat my lunch every second of every day. And a prosecutor who was going to relish sticking it to a virgin like me. And then there was the jury. Twelve strangers whose trust I had to gain so I could convince them not to convict my "innocent" client. How the hell was I going to do all that?

I fell to my couch. Like a child lost in a sea of strangers, I thought of my mother. The immaturity associated with my wanting my mommy didn't cross my mind. And it wasn't as if I was curled in a ball, sucking my thumb. But figuratively I was.

How had she done this? Handle a profession so wrought with peril, chaos, and disharmony? And done it with a kid? Before I found the answer, sleep found me and I happily allowed it to suffocate my thoughts into darkness. When I woke up, I was hot, sweaty, and still facing the obvious problem of putting out fires all around me.

I wanted to call her, to confess my goings-on then skip to asking her for all the answers. I felt pathetic. *Grow some balls, Benjamin,* I demanded of myself.

Over the next few months, I memorized my case. I memorized what every witness wrote in their personal handwritten statements – all thirty-three of them – all high school students. I made tables and charts and cross-referenced everything for inconsistencies. My case would be about inconsistencies and how they related to reasonable doubt. Some people wrote things like: I ain't seen nothing or *that gun just unloaded bap, bap, bap and I just turn and duck under somebody car. Don't know who shot.* Regarding these people, I had two thoughts: *Yay for me,* as they didn't see anything. And - *holy shit. What's happening to our education system?*

There were two witnesses, however – two girls – who had written detailed statements about having seen the shooting. With four defendants, that wouldn't have been too terrible, if they hadn't concluded that my client was the one who had pulled the trigger. Out of all of the problems I anticipated having with my case at trial, I feared those two witnesses the most.

When the trial was a week away, I met the other three defense attorneys who represented the other three defendants. We were getting together to discuss how to parcel up the witnesses and jury selection, so as not to overlap one another. At Pat's suggestion, we could work together as much as our defenses would allow, which they should since the state was lumping us all together. We met at an office that was an old warehouse, which had been converted into a glass-and-concrete modern marvel.

I arrived a few minutes late and found all three attorneys huddled tightly together in the conference room. There were two men, Thomas Sanders and Dwight Smith, and one woman, Sherry Billings.

"Good morning, everyone. I'm sorry I'm running behind," I told them, interrupting their conversation.

"I'm Ben Scales."

"You must be representing the guilty one," Sherry said. They all laughed.

"Yeah, right," I said, forcing a chuckle. "Let's get started, shall we?" said Dwight, as he pulled his three banker's boxes onto the table. The others followed suit. I only had a small, thin expandable file and a legal pad. Sherry noticed and moved toward me.

"You look like a really nice kid," she said, "so I'm just telling you this for what it's worth. I looked you up on the bar website, and I know you've only been out for a year. Honestly, I can't believe Patrick put you on this case. But like I said, for what it's worth, I just thought you should know."

"Know what?"

"We're all coming after your client."

I was stunned. "Why would you do that? We should stick together."

"Aside from two of the witnesses who ID'd your client, Sims, specifically, most of the other witnesses' general descriptions of the shooter match your guy. He had the dreads at the time."

Dwight's ears must have pricked up enough to hear. "Did you tell him our theory?"

"Yeah," she said. "And he's not taking it very well."

"All of you feel this way?" I asked.

In unison: "Yeah."

"Well..." I exhaled. "Sherry, there's one witness who swears your client was the shooter."

"Yeah, but that guy also said the shooter shot the victim at point-blank range in the forehead. Assuming you read the autopsy report and the other thirty-something statements, you know that the victim was shot in the chest... from about two hundred feet away. No stippling. No powder burns. Nothing to support that."

"Right," I said.

"I ain't worried about that witness," she said, smiling.

"Well, I'm not worried," I said. "All the defendants had dreads at the time."

"But not as long as your client's," Dwight said, "which brings me to my next point. Bad move to have your client shave off his dreads. With all the testimony about the shooter having shoulder-length dreads and the photos of your client having shoulder-length dreads, the state is going to eat you alive for trying to change his appearance now."

I panicked, which became visible to all. Sherry suddenly seemed to care.

"All right, everybody, let's not pick on the new kid," Sherry said. "And I'm sorry. I didn't even offer you some coffee. Would you like a cup?"

"I think some lube might work better," I told her.

They laughed. "It's not personal kiddo," she said. "It's where the chips have fallen. This round, you lose. Next one, you might fare differently."

"Look, is this really necessary to team up against me? I mean, we all have reasonable doubt here with these facts. With the distance, the darkness, the number of kids at the party being over a hundred, all the inconsistent statements, and all the other kids at the party having dreads too, it could be any-damn-body."

"Sorry, kiddo," she said. "The state's trying to fuck us all with this 'party-to-a-crime' bullshit, which means, as far we're concerned, we're gonna fuck the culpable-looking guy – which is you... or, rather, your client."

I felt very alone.

The first thing I did that night was look up the other three lawyers on the bar website. Combined, they had sixty-four years of trial experience. I had one, and it was divorce trial experience at that.

For the three weeks of trial, I didn't sleep. Every day I arrived at the courthouse, my heart was racing. Sitting through the trial, I could barely breathe at all times, waiting for the next hammer to come crashing down. As the state directed their witnesses to implicate all four defendants, the defense attorneys crossed the witnesses to implicate my client and exclude theirs. But I didn't play that game. Instead, I cornered every witness regarding the inconsistencies of their statements.

Some witnesses swore they knew my client but then couldn't ID him in open court. One older lady who said she saw the whole thing from two hundred feet away on a poorly lit street at midnight couldn't even see her own daughter sitting in the front row of the brightly lit courtroom.

When the prosecutor asked that old lady to look around the courtroom to see if she could spot the young man she saw shoot the gun, she looked everywhere, including the defense table, but said something about one of the boys looking familiar. She clarified that she couldn't be sure because it appeared my client had cut his hair or "concealed his identity" as she put it.

Sherry gave me a look that said, *I told you that would bite you in the ass.*

The prosecutor jumped in, too. "Oh!" he exclaimed.

"Right! You can't ID the person you know as Tyler Sims for sure because you say he's changed his appearance! Mr. Sims don't look the same, so you say!"

"No, he doesn't," the lady said.

"Well, let me show you a picture," the prosecutor continued as he approached the overhead projector. He placed a picture of Tyler taken at the time of his arrest – a picture of Tyler *with long dreadlocks*. The prosecutor stood proudly next to the picture and smiled at the witness. Without saying who was in the picture, he asked the witness, "Do you recognize *this* young man?" He stood there anticipating her obvious answer, knowing his witness would see my client with dreadlocks and immediately say, "Now *that's* the Tyler Sims I know. That's the guy who shot the kid." But she didn't.

She looked confidently at the picture and said, "Nope."

The jury laughed.

"I'm sorry," I said. "What did the witness say?"

"Ma'am, please repeat your answer," the judge instructed.

"No," she said. "I don't know who that boy is."

The prosecutor pointed at the picture again.

"No," he demanded. "This one here." He pointed again to the five-foot by seven-foot screen. "Do you know who this is?"

"No." One lady on the jury covered her mouth to hide her chuckles.

The prosecutor grabbed the photo off the projector and sat down. Then I got up. I was so excited I was drooling.

"Ma'am, you've stated today that you know the person who shot that young man that night was Tyler Sims. Correct?" I looked at the jury, waiting for her answer.

"Yes."

"And you said you know this because you saw Tyler do it."

"Yes."

"And looking around the courtroom today," I said, "you told the prosecutor you didn't see Tyler in the courtroom – meaning you don't see him over at the defense table."

"Right."

"You clarified that a bit by saying you thought one of the young men sitting at the table might be him but that the young man's appearance was altered."

"Right."

"So, if the prosecutor had put a picture of Tyler Sims with dreadlocks up there on the overhead projector, you feel you would be able to identify him by the picture?"

"Oh, yes."

"For sure?"

"No doubt."

"Well, I guess it's too bad we don't have a picture of Tyler Sims with dreadlocks."

The jury laughed again.

In my closing argument to the jury, I told them the state hadn't met its burden, and I told them I wasn't going to play games with them and point fingers. That's exactly what the state wanted us to do. As they had seen over the last three weeks, the state didn't have a clue who shot the victim in this case. They probably didn't care if the jury ever knew as long as the silly defense attorneys pointed fingers at one another and, in their ultimate confusion, the jury took down every one of those boys.

"But you see," I told them. "I know you're smarter than that. You know, as I do, that I don't have the burden here. The state has the burden to show you what happened."

Thus, while all the other attorneys went to war against one another, I went to war against the state. By the end of my closing remarks, I had made the jury smile, laugh, think, and feel. It was my proudest moment to date. Standing at the podium, as I made my final closing remarks at my first jury trial, I again thought of my mother. And like before, I gained insight into the roller coaster that caused her to have highs higher than the moon and lows that barreled straight down to hell. The life of a trial attorney was a thrill ride.

I thanked the jury and gave my sympathies to the victim's family for losing a son. As I sat down in my chair, having finished my first opus, I had the irresistible urge to call my mom. I didn't know what I'd say. I didn't care anymore. I had to end the silence, confess my sins of omission, and use these feelings – these very real feelings – to bridge our broken town with the City of Tomorrow.

I needed to get some space to think about what I'd say. The judge excused the jury to return first thing in the morning and gave some instructions. "Don't discuss the case with anyone, including your husband, wife, boyfriend, girlfriend, bunk mate, bed buddy, or best friend. Don't even tell your dog about it."

As they exited the courtroom through a back door, I

gathered my things. Just then, Sherry came up to me. "Your closing was amazing. Smart choices. Nicely done, Counselor."

"Thanks," I said, shifting my attention to my papers, as I packed them up to leave. I had to get out of there. My mind was racing about the call.

More lawyers approached – lawyers who had come to watch the closing.

"This couldn't have been your first trial," one said.

"This is his first trial?" another questioned.

I nodded.

"Wow," they said.

Even though the jury surely would convict, the scouts were impressed. I felt like the quarterback on a losing football team that had managed to run for a hundred and fifty yards and throw five touchdowns.

"Thanks," I said. "Thank you so much." I shook my client's hand.

Sims reached out and hugged me. "Thanks, man. Your words meant a lot."

"Okay. No problem. Thank you, man. Okay, I've gotta go."

Then his mother approached. "You have been so kind to my son. We really appreciate everything you and Patrick have done for us and for him. Whatever happens, we're pleased with you."

"Thank you. I really appreciate that. Look, we're not out of the woods by any stretch. And I've got to go make a call, right now. I'll see ya'll in the morning when the jury starts to deliberate."

Breaking free from the chaos, I turned to cross the

bar of the court and walked into the public seating area. I stood a bit more erect and began to open up my stride when, amid the movement of the court, I saw my mother standing at the back wall. It was the combination of her bunned hair, icy-blue eyes, and tightly bound gray double-breasted suit that made her statuesque. Our eyes locked like hand and glove. Her scowl grabbed my face. My heart collided with my sternum, and I thumped to a halt. I recognized her expression immediately. Equal parts: Quandary, shock, betrayal.

I knew the countless miles of roads and turns behind me that had brought me to this point. Seeing her face, I saw her realizing each and every one of them at that moment. Graduation. Acceptance to law school. All the courses. Studying for the bar. Passing. The celebrations. The honor of the achievement.

Before that moment, I didn't really appreciate how far I'd come or how hurt my mother would be that I'd done all this without her. In a way, though, that was the point – doing this without her. Feeling my new desire to share my legal war story with her illuminated just how dark and obvious the cloud was that hung just inches from the ground.

Within the bustle of the courtroom, I stood powerless until my mother let go and walked out the door. The air went with her and returned like a deep wave that hit me almost minutes later. I imagined her next thoughts and the ones that were sure to follow hours, days, and weeks later. I purposefully had deprived her of so much joy.

I felt cruel, heartless, self-centered – qualities I had only assigned to her in the past. I lifted my head out of the sand and sat in the pews of the courtroom until so much time had passed that I was the only person remaining. The sheriff deputy walked up to me. "All right, big dog," he said. "We lockin' up. Gotta take your show on the road."

I nodded, still in a daze, and grabbed my papers.

Twenty-Two:
It's About Time

It was a beautiful day with a clear blue fall sky. A slight breeze spoke through a set of wind chimes and it settled my nerves a bit as I watched a few red and orange leaves tumble to the ground. I looked upward and marveled at the size of the sky until a voice pulled me back down to earth.

"Ben, if I may," Lynn said, drawing my attention to his face. "I've got some thoughts I want to share with you."

We were sitting together on the bench outside his office.

"After doing a bit of my own research on you, I've learned a thing or two about you. You've got quite the reputation. You're a rising star."

I laughed at myself, remembering that my mother was his client and that he was here to convince me to do something I didn't want to do.

"Complimenting me, Lynn won't – wait, did you really hear that?"

"I did."

"Well, that's very nice. Thank you. But... but, so what."

"You're mother is a complicated woman, Ben."

I huffed.

"I've worked a long time in this business and there is no one like your mother. Now, her ways are radical and inappropriate. But that's her. It's not you, you understand, it's her."

"What do you mean 'it's not me?'" I asked.

"You ARE NOT your mother. She is who she is and you are who you are. Just because she raised you, doesn't mean that you are like her. You are your own man. You just happened to grow up in her home, you understand?"

"In the same way, that I AM NOT my clients," I said.

"Similar, but not the same. As children, we feel very attached to our parents. We feel their pain, we feel their experiences, and, because we are so connected to them, their pain is our pain. Their experiences are our experiences. So, when they are hurt, we are hurt. When they act the fool, we feel embarrassed or ashamed."

"I get that," I said.

"You need to disconnect from those feelings, son," Lynn said, putting his hand on my shoulder. "Understand that all that craziness is her. It's not you."

I thought about his words and decided something. I really liked Lynn.

I slapped my hands on my thighs. "Should we go back in?" I asked.

Moments later, we all settled back in Lynn's office. Lynn held the door open for Bobby-Charles, who was now invited in by me and my mother. He flitted through the door in a hurry.

"Sorry, I had to pee," he said in a tither.

Lynn sat behind his desk again and took over as lawyer.

"After talking with your mother, it has become very clear that it's in her best interest to have someone handle this case who knows her unlike anyone else in the entire world." My mother looked at me and nodded in agreement.

"I don't understand, though, how that's even relevant? Either she did it or she didn't. What's it matter who says what? I mean... do they have it on videotape?"

"As a matter of fact they do," he said.

"Well, then, you're fucked," I told her. "You're fucked."

"Not necessarily," Lynn corrected. "The act is done. It happened. No one can undo it. The question now is what is the best remedy? What should they do? It's called mitigating evidence; you deal with it every day as a criminal defense attorney."

He was right. I did deal with it every day. When a client pleaded guilty, he always admitted the facts. But the judge was always willing to hear about the good side of the client – the family man, the churchgoing man, the volunteer, the community supporter, the hard worker, the man who had fallen on hard times and needed food and money. It all factored in. Still, I didn't like the idea of being the one to do it – be damned how much I was starting to like my mother's attorney.

"Lynn, you don't want the Ethics Committee to know what I know about my mother. Trust me, it won't help her. I mean, the state bar's ethical division is not the criminal court. It's not about the act and whether the other side can prove you guilty beyond a reasonable doubt or where you can argue the evidence doesn't add up and do sleight of hand for dumb jurors. This is the place where the rest of the truth about the person comes out and in my mother's case, it will convict her. You are guilty of being a bad mother. I'm sorry, but that's the truth. I've promised myself I'm going to tell the truth."

My mother wiped her eyes, but the tears kept coming. I did not want to see it. I had worked hard to get away from these moments. I felt myself breaking. Feeling like I should temper my emotions. Not get so frustrated. Try to communicate better. "Look, I'm not in the right state of mind to deal with this on the level she needs, okay."

"Benjamin, look," my mother began, but now Lynn interrupted.

"Why didn't you tell your mother you became a lawyer?" he asked.

I clammed up and raised the corner of my upper lip to show my incisor, wondering what the hell they had really been talking about. I started to feel a little betrayed by my new friend. "What's it any of your goddamn business?" I barked.

"Benjamin!" my mother exclaimed.

"Oh, please, mother." I held up my hand and looked back to Lynn. "It may have been stupid or immature to not tell her, but I had a reason, and I made a decision and it was a stupid decision and immature and I should have fucking called her." I looked at my mother. "I should've called you, okay? It was stupid, but I live with that decision because I made the choice. And I stressed about it. Lost sleep about it. Cried about it. And I'm done feeling shitty for it, okay?"

"Fine," Lynn said. "But–"

My mother interrupted him. "I've made choices too, Benjamin. Just like you. And I live with my decisions. I had reasons. I've done things that may have been stupid or immature," she said, "but nonetheless I did them, just like you."

"And you have to live with those choices just like me."

I sat down defeated. "*Shit.* I'm making your points for you." I put my head in my hands. "I'm not ready for this. I'm not good enough to fix this problem for you."

"The point is nobody's perfect," Lynn said.

"I get your point," I said, irritated.

I hadn't planned on arguing with anyone today, but there I was. All pissed off and kicking resentment around the room like an explosive soccer ball. And my mother and Lynn were sticking to their game plan. I could see why she had hired him and why he'd had such a long career as a negotiator and ethics defense attorney.

"Will you at least hear us out?" my mother asked. I felt like I was back in her home about to take a look at her nipple all over again.

I sat back down in the Thinking Man's position. "Can I at least have a cup of coffee?"

Within a minute, Bobby-Charles reentered with a sterling tray and a lofty assortment of sweeteners, cream, and a glorious cup of coffee.

"All right," I said.

I took a deep breath. I was not going to run. I was not going to close the door. If my mother wanted to tell me her story of how she got into this mess in the first place, I guess the least I could do was listen, although I felt I had a pretty good grip on our past. How I felt about what she had to say and whether I thought it was worth a damn was still up for debate.

Twenty-Three:
A Dilemma To Dye For

An alarm went off. Carter watched the cardiac monitor throw her EKG lines across the glowing green screen in a haphazard pattern as she paced the room while speaking on her cell phone. The siren that went off caused her to speak louder into the phone. The machine flashed NO HEARTBEAT DETECTED over and over again.

"Oh, shut up," she told the machine. She scooted off the gurney and pulled the opening at the back of her hospital gown closed. "No, not you," she said into the phone. "We're having a fire alarm at the office, and I'm in the middle of trying to lock myself in my office so I don't have to go outside." She bent down to the machine to figure out a way to silence it.

Her doctor and a nurse came in the room. "Salli, I gotta go. No, these assholes are gonna make me go outside. No, it's fine. Stop it! I need to go! Look, Salvadore, call me back after court. I'll be here," she reassured. She hung up the phone.

"Hello, Gwen. It's nothing personal. It's just business."

"Carter, I've known you long enough. I understand. But today I really need your attention." Gwen flashed a smile, trying to recover from her serious tone. She looked to the nurse to follow suit, but she wasn't so capable of faking a smile and instead chose to look away. Gwen let out a sigh. Suddenly, Carter knew she was about to die.

As cancers go, pancreatic cancer was the equivalent of a passenger jet ripping in half at thirty thousand feet;

you didn't survive it. To reach a pancreatic tumor, a surgeon would have to do a very complicated procedure that included completely removing one's gallbladder and part of one's stomach and small intestine just to get to the point where he could view the pancreas. Then he would laterally cut portions off the pancreas until he completely sliced the tumor out. It was much like trimming a brisket – against the grain of the meat diagonally in very thin slices, which Carter did very well and topped with the most delicious sweet and savory sauce.

"About fourteen hours of surgery," the doctor told her. "Fourteen hours, that is, if it all goes off without a hitch." She had just been hit with the Big C. Instead of slowly sinking in, it hit her like a brass knuckle. She stumbled left and right and tried to stay on her feet.

"And if there's a hitch?" she asked.

"Uh... well. Carter, you could die from either the disease or the surgery. You shouldn't deal with this alone. You need to call your family."

"Well, that's not gonna happen."

To her irritation, the pancreatic tumor totally conflicted with her schedule, which included a long-awaited hair appointment with Armando – a cut and color she had to reserve five months in advance. Her gastroenterologist, a nail-biting chain smoker herself, insisted she have the operation if one more blood test came back positive. She would have to remain in the hospital until the result surfaced. Then, if the result was bad, it was imperative that she leave for MD Anderson in Houston for surgery immediately.

"Texas?" she exclaimed. "This time of year?" She would wait until the results came back before she canceled her color appointment.

That night, Carter lay alone in her hospital bed listening to the sound of her heart monitor and blood pressure cuff inflate every fifteen minutes, as the nurse took her vitals.

"Are you comfortable, Ms. Scales?" the nurse asked.

"Just fine."

"Do you have any family here? To be with you?"

"I have a son in Miami."

"Oh. So far away."

"He's studying to be a doctor."

"You can't go wrong with a doctor in the family," she said.

"I expect he'll be in any time now. It's what he always wanted to do – since he was a little boy. My father was a doctor."

"Wonderful. We could always use some good doctors." Carter smiled. "Is he gonna come home to be with you?" Gwen asked.

Carter sat motionless until she realized she had been doing it for too long. "No," she said.

Just as Carter had surmounted the gender wars of her early professional beginnings, she was determined to survive pancreatic cancer without her Benjamin. In truth, taking on the world alone required great bravery.

When her test results came back as predicted, her doctor began making her arrangements for Texas. "I'm not going," she told her gastroenterologist as she packed up her things at the hospital.

"Carter, only nineteen percent of women your age survive pancreatic cancer one year after diagnosis. That means eighty-one percent die. A mere three percent survive after five years." Her gastroenterologist pleaded with her. "With the size of this tumor, though, your prognosis more resembles four to six months."

"I'm not interested," she told her. "Besides, I have a hair appointment."

With a fabulous new shade of red, Carter went shopping... for a second opinion. This time she saw a tumor specialist. The specialist viewed her films, did more x-rays, and confirmed her gastroenterologist's predictions and recommendations. "You've wasted another two weeks," he began. "You wanna live to meet your grandchildren? Then you get your ass to Texas." That was another heartstring she didn't need pulled. The thought of losing Benjamin was hard enough. The thought of never being a part of his childrens' lives was double homicide.

"I can't go there," she said.

"Where?" he pleaded. "To Texas?"

With two strikes and no pinch hitter available, Carter was forced to make the most important decision of her life without the person she cared about most. The specialist did his best to give her support by assuring her that a life-saving operation was waiting for her in Houston. Her flight was set to depart in two days; she would be in surgery the night she arrived. She just couldn't swallow it. It was all happening too fast. There was too much to look after – work, clients, and what if the doctors were wrong? And then another crisis arose. Carter's new secretary – a twenty-three-year-old weekend warrior named Rhonda – said too much to clients about her condition.

Throughout her life, Carter told countless lies to her clients when she felt under the weather. Just after vomiting and stuffing a tissue up her nose to stop the bleeding from the force of throwing up, she took a collect call from a new potential client and began the conversation with a giant guffaw, which faded into a fabulous "So nice to meet you" followed by a heroic "Let's get down to business, shall we?" She was the greatest illusionist who never took to the stage. Ben learned his lesson once when he filled in at her office by answering the phones for her then secretary who was out with migraines. Carter had the flu and was at home with the chills and a high fever.

"Mr. Saluditorre, she's at home with the flu," Ben told him. "I'm not sure when she'll be back."

"You what?" she yelled and coughed. "Never, never tell a client I'm sick! Oh, God, this is terrible," she said from under a mound of comforters. "He's gonna go somewhere else. I'm gonna lose my fee!"

When the news of her cancer spread, she fielded two-dozen calls. Clients called her collect from prison on her dime to let her know that it would be better if Richie in New York handled the appeal or Marvin out of Chicago. Bob in DC would cover the oral argument. They'd bring her back on the next one, though – once she got better, they insisted. Maybe she could *consult* on the case, but she needed to take care of herself first and foremost. Suddenly, she was no longer a powerhouse lawyer in their eyes; she was a sick little girl.

"Really, I'm fine," she told them. "You know these fucking doctors and how they cover their asses. I seriously doubt it's actually cancer. It's just a minor thing. I'm not even in the hospital. It's nothing." There were only so many fire alarms she could fake.

In the end, they insisted. And because ninety percent of her clients were organized crime bosses and goodfellas, their insisting was a closed door to her downplaying.

She cornered her secretary, a new hire in a string of new hires that had only just begun to appreciate the 180s Carter was capable of swinging. "What have you done, you stupid cunt?" she said.

"Mrs. Scales, I thought you needed some time away."

"You've ruined me!"

When the dust cleared from her secretary's A-bomb, Carter didn't have one active client remaining. Zero stream of income. She lived to work and worked to live. If Benjamin was her lungs, her work was oxygen. Together they had kept her alive. For the first time since her doctor's consultation, she felt herself dying.

Now truly frightened, she turned to the one person she felt could unequivocally advise her on her current state of affairs. When she pushed open her old psychic friend's office door, she was glad to see that Mary Rivers' office hadn't changed.

Countless magazines and books filled her bookshelves and spilled onto the floor in piles against the wall. She had a 24 by 36-inch picture of Jesus and several needlepoint tapestries of prayers hung at various heights, along with dozens of photographs of friends, family, christenings, and weddings; holiday cards; and birth announcements - all of which were haphazardly taped to the walls. Mary surrounded herself with all the love she felt in her life as a way to bring peace and harmony to an uncertain and unsettled world.

After a brief, "Hey, darlin'. How ya doin'?" Mary led Carter to her sitting area and sat her down in front of her. The two women sat knee-to-knee, barefoot toes to shoe, as Mary had done with thousands of clients over the years, and took Carter's hands and said a prayer. Mary closed her eyes and shifted her focus deep into the back of her mind, where her thoughts became clear and clairvoyant. A minute later she opened her eyes and told her that she would be fine.

Mary opened up her monthly planner and read a note to herself, then said, "I want you to see a friend of someone I know."

"Who's the friend?"

"Don't worry about who it is. Just go and see him!" she demanded.

Fueled by Mary's prediction and introduction, Carter drop-kicked caution and spun the wheel of fortune. She returned to the tumor specialist's office the next day and informed him that she wouldn't be traveling to the land of the Longhorns; there was entirely too much bull to begin with. Mary's friend's friend was a British oncologist – a blood cancer specialist – and while he saw the tumor sitting in her pancreas, the blood counts just didn't add up.

"There's something about this that just makes me want to pause," he said in a heavy British accent. "Time is everything here, but I don't think it's cancer. I think it's a cyst."

"A what?"

"A pus pocket, a localized infection. Give me one week. Let me confer with my colleagues," he told her. "If it's a cyst, the antibiotics I'll give you will shrink it."

"So if it shrinks with the antibiotics..."

"Tumors don't shrink with antibiotics."

One week later, when the doctor held Carter's x-rays up to the viewing light, he crinkled his nose and sucked on his teeth: "Poof," he said. And just like that, it was gone.

Days prior, Carter's future had been written in the sand; etched with the pointy end of a stick was the word *doom*. But just as her cyst came and went, so did the word, erased from the sands of time by the smoothing sea. It was so like her not to die.

Amid the health crisis of her life, she realized she was able to stand on her own, to view the fight while standing on her own two feet. She felt invigorated, convinced she was stronger than ever. But the feeling of not being able to choose her state of solitude left her with a realization more painful than the cyst.

She tried to remember what led to their break. And why it became so final. It had been eight years since Benjamin graduated college. What could he have been so mad about? She closed her eyes and remembered the moment it all ended.

Twenty-Four:
Rising Tide

I was senior in high school when I finally decided to confront my mother, the attacker. Sure, the woman had experienced plenty of heartache in her life, which gave her some psychological exposition for her head case, but I refused to let that be an excuse.

I needed to deal with my heartache too, to fight back for once. But not as a reactionary measure to her scolding me for doing something wrong. My mistakes could not muddy the waters. Instead, I would wait for my mother to bite my head off without cause, and then, exactly like her lie-in-wait games, I'd masterfully and systematically force her to her knees, using a psychological chokehold. She would see that she was out of line and a tyrant and that her bullshit had to end. I wasn't asking much.

Just as it always seems to be, though, when a person is ready for something to happen, it never does. The old watched pot. Weeks went by. Nights of laying in bed, replaying rehearsed lines, with no action. Nothing. My mother seemed perfectly nice. Despite turning up the heat and throwing in a tablespoon of salt, I couldn't get that old pot to boil.

Then, one afternoon around five, my mother came home early. She usually was home at six. She'd had a day from hell and needed the inner sanctity of her four-hundred-square-foot master bathroom and closet. Me and my girlfriend, Sarah, were blaring my new Milli Vanilli CD and memorizing the same lyrics Morvan and Pilatus were apparently too tone deaf to sing themselves. We couldn't hear the incessant honking in the driveway that had been going on for approximately seven-and-a-half minutes.

Outside, my mother sat in her car. Her whitened knuckles gripped the steering wheel, while she stared at my truck, which sat diagonally inside the garage.

"Like he's paying the goddamn mortgage," she said. She lay on the horn again until she got out of the car and announced her intention to kill me to the driveway and front door.

"Benjamin!" she yelled from downstairs. "Move your fucking truck!"

Upstairs, Sarah drained the volume and made a "whoa" face. I leaped from my room and into the hallway. "Mom?" I yelled. "Mom, is that you?"

"I've been sitting out here for ten minutes. Jesus Christ, your truck is blocking the entire garage!"

"You're home early. I didn't hear you."

She didn't say anything else, other than some words to herself, as she walked back out to her car and got into the driver's seat, impatiently waiting for me. Sarah, concerned about the rest of the assault Carter would commit on me, gave me a look that promised her assistance in the confrontation – maybe if she stayed, my mother would be nice to me. My heart raced. "No, it's okay," I told her. I had it all under control. Despite the sick feeling in my stomach, I was beyond ready.

I reacted quickly and raced downstairs. Her foul moods always gave me greater speed. I backed my truck out and pulled it to one side in the garage so she could pull in. In my rearview mirror, I watched Sarah go out the front door and walk down to her car on the street. She waved to me and blew me a kiss. I stayed in my truck and acted like I was doing something while my mother got out of her Jaguar. I didn't want to start my attack until she was inside.

My mother closed her door on her suit skirt and fumbled for her keys to reopen the door. "Oh, goddamn it!" she said as she opened and slammed the door again. Then she dropped a legal file folder. "Goddamn it. God damn this very minute!"

I took a deep breath. Maybe this wasn't the best day.

Inside the house, I heard her high heels walking around on the hardwood floors. Even her shoes sounded pissed off. I felt my resolve weaken. My heart raced. I was nervous, scared even. I figured I'd wait a bit. Maybe give her a second to come in and get her shoes off.

The event of her coming home early and getting pissed off was a small occurrence on the scale of those past, but it had teeth. Typical mother. She certainly could've come inside and said, "Hi, honey. Surprise, I'm home early. Can you move your car?" She didn't have to scream and yell like that in front of Sarah. I was angry and embarrassed. I would use those emotions, however, to my advantage. About thirty minutes later, I entered the kitchen and stood behind my mother as she read the mail. She felt me watching her, staring at her.

"Order a pizza, okay? I'm not up for cooking," she said.

"Bad day?" I said, alluding to the obvious.

"Please, Benjamin. Just order a pizza. I need you to leave me be."

She sat down at the kitchen table and turned on our little television. *Wheel of Fortune* was on - one of our favorite shows. A contestant had spun the wheel in an attempt to solve a puzzle titled *Before and After*. We loved *Before and After* puzzles, because they were clever, and we considered ourselves *very* clever – more clever than any contestant. But at this moment, inside me, my thoughts were screaming. And the sound of the excited audience felt more taunting and caused me anxiety.

My mother turned up the volume and slouched in her chair. It was typical for her to turn her back to me like this, as she felt her anger gave her the right to totally ignore anyone at anytime. In actuality, she just wanted me to go away. Instead, I steadied my emotions. They wanted to rattle and boil, but that wasn't part of my plan. I certainly could have just walked off and disappeared. That would have been typical for me and easier. As in the past, she would cool off later and things would be harmonious, and then it wouldn't make sense to rock the boat and more weeks would pass and then I'd have to create another opportunity.

"Two hundred!" Pat Sajak exclaimed as the wheel rested on the number.

"I'd like to buy a vowel. 'I'," the contestant said. The board lit up, and the audience applauded again. "I'd like to solve the puzzle. Rising... Tide... Detergent." A bell dinged. "You got it!" Pat said. The audience applauded. "Rising tide," Pat said, "and Tide Detergent!"

I had to do it now, I thought. *I'm embarrassed now. I'm angry now*. I had to confront her. I was entitled to be mad. And mad people who are brave people stand up for themselves in the moment. And with the puzzle solved, it just made sense.

I tried to say, "Mom," but in my nervousness only said, "Ma..." I cleared my throat. "Mom?"

"What?" she said, exasperated. I paused at her

aggressive tone. My silence annoyed her. "What is it? What is it? Talk!"

I knew she'd go with volume and anger. Separately they were usually enough to get me to back down. Together they were overpowering. I stayed strong. After all, I had expected this. *Jesus, come on*, I thought. *Say something.*

"Why couldn't you..." I paused again, swallowing my dry throat. "Why couldn't you have just come inside the house and asked me to move the truck? Why did you have to yell and curse like that in front of Sarah?" My question caused her face to bend. I was even irritated with it.

She let out an elephant-sized sigh. "I don't have time for this, okay? I've had a hell of a day, and I am not in the mood."

"Well, I had a really great day and now... I just don't understand why you couldn't have come inside and just been nice about it." And there it was. A set of words so normal for any other person but me – like pulling a rhino out of my mouth.

She twisted at her waist, without getting up, and deadpanned at me.

I readied my throat by swallowing again.

"You were blocking the entire garage," she explained.

"You were home an hour early."

"I'd been honking for ten minutes."

"Well, didn't that clue you in to the fact that maybe I didn't hear you?"

Her eyelids jerked, and her pupils narrowed. "Don't get smart with me," she said.

"I'm just saying..." My heart raced, but I felt more comfortable with the nausea now that I was actually doing it.

"Benjamin, look... It started to rain, okay?"

I thought about that. "No, it didn't. Your windshield is totally dry."

"You weren't out there, Benjamin. It started to rain."

"I was just out there. It wasn't raining at all. And even if it was lightly raining, you would rather come inside and curse and yell at me and call me names in front of my girlfriend than get a little water on you?" My anger returned.

"I told you, it—"

"I'm your son. The one you say you love so much and-"

"And I'm your *mother,* and I don't need your shit right now." She slowed me down by cursing and raising her volume even more, but I forged ahead.

"It's not shit. I'm just telling you..." I paused.

"Telling me what?"

"How I feel."

"You wanna know how I feel? I've had a very long day, something you will probably *never* fully understand and..." She started to cry. "And you are *totally* disrespecting me right now."

I wanted to retort, but her tears made me pause. I took a deep breath. The tears didn't let up.

"No, I'm not," I began. "I'm just trying to understand why keeping a few drops of rain off your clothes was more important than speaking nicely to your son or taking a moment to think about all this love you say you have for me before you came in here and spoke to me like that."

She scoffed, wiped her eyes, and turned back to the television. She didn't turn back around.

The room fell silent but for *Wheel of Fortune*. Apparently, we had arrived at the moment in the fight where both parties began to reassess their opponent, the point after a few punches had been thrown where the two fighters watched each other as they circled the ring. I watched my mother watch the television. She watched me out of the corner of her eyes. Minutes passed as the show went on and the next puzzle went up on the board. The audience applauded, and the contestants spun the wheel and smiled and clapped. Pat clapped. Vanna clapped. They all clapped at all the right moments. It was the only sound in the room.

As the show broke to a commercial, my mother spoke. "What do you want from me?"

"Just... for you to be nice, for you to be calm. You get so angry so fast, and you shout and scream."

"Be *calm*? I suppose I'm some kind of maniac and you're just perfect and I'm the crazy one?"

"What are you talking about?" I asked.

"I have had a very upsetting day, okay?"

I considered that something had, in fact, happened to her, but really I didn't care. I wasn't going to relent – come hell, high water, or even a bad day.

"You have never once in your life ever stopped to actually listen to yourself speak," I said. "To hear the words that come out of your mouth." She didn't recognize my persistence or the confidence in my glare. She was so prepared to see everyone as an enemy, every comment as an attack, but an assault from her dutiful, well-meaning son? Never. They were words I said aloud to myself in the privacy of my room, lying awake at night.

"I know everything I say and do," she countered.

"Then it's purposefully hurtful, which is much, much worse."

The *Wheel of Fortune* audience applauded again. She turned off the television. "Why don't you just leave and go to your girlfriend's house."

She didn't mean it. I knew she didn't. She never would want me to choose Sarah over her, but she said it as a new tactic – an approach at dismissing me much like the times she tried to just ignore me.

"I'm not going to Sarah's," I said.

"No, go over there, and tell her all about this... and how your mother is fucking insane."

"I wouldn't do that."

"Oh, sure you would." Her tears returned. "She'll know all about it, and you two will have a great laugh."

"What makes you think I want to laugh about this?"

"I know you, Benjamin. You'll just sit there and disparage me and tell your precious girlfriend all about it, and then you'll accuse me of ruining your life, just like all the times you and your father ganged up on me."

"What are you talking about?"

"Especially after that bastard stole ten thousand dollars from my father and never paid it back!"

"You *both* borrowed that money!" I screamed. "And you've been taking money from grandfather your entire life and never paid it back."

"That money is mine!"

"That money is *his*. Who are you kidding? He earned

it. He saved it. And you call for a chunk of it every year to pay your taxes. Pay your own fucking taxes!" I didn't know where we were going with all this, but fuck it – I'd wanted to say it for years.

"All right, that's enough," she said.

I pushed further. "No. What about that money could possibly be yours?"

"Shut your mouth." She started to yell again. "I want you out of this house. Right now!"

She was livid and hyperventilating. I didn't want that. "Just calm down," I told her.

"No! After all, I've been through, I don't deserve this. I deserve nice things, to have people in my life who actually give a shit."

"You know I care, mother. But that's not the point."

"How can you have so little respect for me after all I've given you?"

"For you? Where's my respect?" I demanded.

"I don't have to respect you," she said. Her face hardened with each word, and her resolve strengthened. She took a step closer to me. "You haven't earned it."

"Stop trying to bully me. You know you do this thing where you wave your finger in my face. It's enough. I'm tired of you yelling at me then acting like everything is fine. I don't understand how you can't see how that hurts my feelings."

"Your feelings? Your feelings are hurt?"

"You have no insight into the way you talk to me."

"I don't know what you're talking about," she said.

"Or the way you talk about my father."

"What do you want me to do?"

"I want you to think before you speak," I said.

"Oh, I see. Well, how about I just never say another word for the rest of your life? That would make you so happy, wouldn't it?"

"Why do you have to go to extremes like that?"

"No, you'd like that, wouldn't you? Just keep my mouth closed, as long as I keep writing you checks and giving you money..."

"I am not here for your money."

"All you care about is your girlfriend. *Sa-rah* this or *Sa-rah* that. Dime-store hooker for a mother. I mean, really, Benjamin, she's gonna grow up just like that tramp."

I had been dating Sarah for nearly two years. My mother struck a nerve with me every time she spoke about Sarah – one I couldn't suppress. She saw it immediately. "Truth hurts, doesn't it?" she asked.

I scowled at her. "Why can't you just be somewhere remotely in the middle instead of just going off on some irrational tangent?"

"I'm just being honest," she said.

"No, you're being cruel." My throat closed slightly, and my eyes welled. It came out of nowhere. My emotions were overwhelming.

Seeing a sign of weakness, she went in for the kill. "You are so pussy whipped."

"What?" I asked, my eyes were incredulous. *Did I hear her correctly?* "What did you say?"

"That girl has got you so far up her ass, you can see the back of her teeth." She smiled, loving every second of her creativity.

"What did you just say?"

"I said, you're pussy whipped!" my mother repeated.

I turned away from her and walked out of the room, my thoughts evaporated like steam, leaving me caked in a gloomy yet obvious reality. I moved slowly up the stairs from the kitchen and into my bedroom where I tried to breathe. I stood there looking around the room. All my posters, my television, my king-size bed. My life. My existence in her home. I felt empty. Willing to give it all up. But I never did. I always returned. I always came back, letting her buy me more things to clutter up my fake, lie-filled life.

I jumped on top of my bed and grabbed my Apollonia Kotero poster by the left corner and ripped it from the misty blue-and-green rain across her bosoms and through the leopard-print one-piece. Then my Quiet Riot Poster – the one with Kevin DuBrow in the red leather straitjacket and metal face guard. A fitting image of my life with my mother. I ripped it down like the Berlin Wall. Everything came down until the yellow walls were bare except for thumbtacks and tape.

I saw the past very clearly. Our fight had recapped it all quite nicely. The years of toleration. The years of abuse. And I stuck it out through it all. I suddenly realized my mother was right. *Goddamn, she was right.* I turned back and walked down the stairs and back into the kitchen.

"You know what?" I said to her, poster shreds in hand. "You're right."

She looked at me, suddenly interested, not expecting my acknowledgment.

"I *am* pussy whipped," I said, smiling.

"Yeah, you are."

"By you," I corrected her. Her eyes widened. I just looked at her, proud at my revelation and delivery.

"Don't you dare talk to me like that," she said. "I am your mother."

"You know what then? You're a bad mother."

"Fuck you. You hurt me, Benjamin!" She started to wail.

"Did you hear yourself?"

"I heard myself fine. I'm the rational one. You just walked all over my heart."

"Oh, please," I told her. "Save it. You're full of shit. You don't even realize how hysterical you are." Suddenly, there was something different about me. As if a switch had been flipped. I was done, through with her. "You're irrational," I said, somewhat distant. "It's... it's really pathetic."

My mother feverishly wiped her nose and eyes. "I am not irrational," she promised. "Wait, Benjamin. Wait. I am not irrational." I sat there and watched her struggle to regain her composure, as if a panel of judges were timing her.

It was the first time I could remember actually witnessing the cover-up in action. She watched me stare at her. She saw my cold expression, the lack of love on my face. "Have a nice life, mom," I said. "I'm outta here."

"What?"

"You can go fuck yourself," I said.

"What?" She was fumbling. "Leaving? Wait. Why?"

"Because you're fucking insane!" Now, I was pissed. My voice suddenly raged.

"Wait. Come here," she said, as she patted the chair next to her. "Just come here for a second." I just looked at her. "I know we've both said some things we didn't mean. I know you're mad at me for whatever reason. But let bygones be bygones." She sounded convinced of her own words. I stood there, incredulous. I couldn't believe she was trying to mend the situation. "Come here," she said. "Let momma rock you. Come on, momma's big boy."

"You're not listening to me." My voice was hoarse from yelling. "I'm six feet tall. I'm seventeen years old. I've got chest hair for God's sake! I don't want you to rock me or talk baby talk to me. I'm not gonna sit on your fucking lap." She cried more. "I'm not a kid anymore. If anything," I said, "I think we should try to be friends."

"I'm your mother," she said. "I'll never be your friend."

I thought about her words and turned to leave. "In that case," I said, "I don't want a mother anymore."

Twenty-Five:
Riddle Me This

My mother remembered it all. While she lay in bed, receiving antibiotics, she culled through every detail. That I moved in with my grandmother for the last few months before I went to college was disemboweling torture. My father's mother was a self-righteous woman who spoke volumes of truth from her four-foot, five-inch frame. The first time she met my mother, she criticized her skirt for being "too slutty." Talk about your stage-setters.

My mother's eyes darted around, fixing on a multitude of questions. Was she a bad mother? Hadn't she tried her best? She was nothing like her father, was she? She had the soft touches of her mother, didn't she? The hospital bed sheets pooled around her. She gripped them with her hands. *Why shouldn't she ask for forgiveness? Shouldn't he?* she thought. *Could it be better? His face was so cold,* she thought.

As she twisted the sheets, she considered her specialist's words about living to see her grandchildren. Something she wanted very much. To hold baby toes again and snuggle her nose to soft pink skin. The idea of not fulfilling her dream of becoming a grandmother drew tears from her eyes. She dropped her head backward and held the tears there. She didn't want them to fall – to know that they were connected to real, tangible, deep pain.

What was wrong with her? How was she so broken? How had she come to this place? Standing before a door that had no place for a key. No knob to turn. More clearly than ever, she realized something stood in her way of accomplishing her truest desire. Something more powerful than death: me.

My mother felt her love for me viscerally, deep within her from the moment I was born. I was all hers. Just by looking into my deep-brown newborn eyes, she knew I would bring her great joy. The fact that I was a boy also gave her great excitement and jubilation. She couldn't believe her luck. *A boy,* she thought. *And one day I'll turn him into a man.* She cherished the hard-copy paper birth certificate and the box checked for *boy.* She even kissed it.

My mother constantly felt unappreciated by men, like somehow they all conspired against her. She was the last great cornfield, and they were a cloud of locusts. When she was a girl in the 1940's and 50's, men defined her world. When she was a lawyer in the 70's and 80's, men still tried to confine and dominate her. Her biggest hurts came from men. And those injustices men had exacted upon her had turned her into a person who created enemies among men. Those men, in turn, attempted further wrongs against her, which kept the cycle intact. As a boy – a male – I offered her a fresh start. Outside their house, men thought she was a joke. Inside, she demanded respect from the only man in her life she could control – her little boy.

Like a cat raising a puppy, she was determined to educate me against the instinctual chauvinism she assumed was hardwired into me like all men. My fight with her so many years ago was treason, plain and simple, and proof positive that I would bite her like all the other dogs before me had. I deserved to be treated like the rest of them, didn't I? Cut off. When I didn't call and beg for her forgiveness, she decided to play it out. A test of wills. An experiment. She, the experienced trial attorney, knew how to play out a situation like this. She would keep the pressure on by not calling and push me further into a corner, until I begged to give her what she wanted. My mother believed I would die without her, like a fish on wet sand. But she underestimated me. I was finally becoming a man.

Twenty-Six:
Every Thorn Has Its Rose

At the point of her cancer scare, she had been working hard but only for a few select clients. She was clearly at the top of her game again, but she was lonely.

As more time filled the space between us, it began to hurt. She felt as if I had completely crushed every positive thing she'd ever done for me. She couldn't untangle the anger and betrayal she felt. Her clients became her source of company.

Actually, it was great for them because they too needed company. When I was younger, they never liked it when she said she had to go to bed or be at home to cook for me or care for me because, when the phone call ended, they had to go back into their cell. With me out of the picture, they got all of her. It was her one flotation device.

Of all the client's my mother represented, none truly gained entrance into my mother's inner circle. While she shared with them and babied them, she didn't reveal her true self to anyone. That is until one man, in particular, got pinched and ultimately received a life sentence in federal prison: Antonio De Silva.

The time I first met Antonio, it was obvious to me that he wanted to be with my mother and that she wanted to be with him. But they never did. They kept it professional, aside from an occasional brush of the hand and hug goodbye that lingered a bit too long.

In the twenty years of her legal career, my mother met many clients who flirted, some who asked, and others who even tried to take. All were shunned with the shooing of her wrist and hand. But Antonio was different. Over the years, they had spoken on the phone for hours, laughed together. They acted as client and attorney and as friends and confidantes. But something changed when it came to Antonio.

When my father died, I was fifteen years old. It was a year after my Bar Mitzvah – the Jewish ceremony of a boy's transition to Jewish adulthood – which was apropos for him, if that's even possible, in that he refused to allow his cancer to return and take him until he was sure I was "man" in the eyes of God.

Antonio and other "family" came down for the funeral to comfort my mother. I buried my father under a winter sky while a collection of linebacker-sized goodfellas in stark black suits sniffled and teared behind tinted sunglasses at the sight of me shoveling dirt onto my father's simplistic white, pine box casket.

At a Jewish funeral, the family used the *back* of the shovel to drop dirt on the casket. It was not meant to be "work" and was done to pay respect but show a reluctance to part with your loved one. For those who were unaware of the custom, it was also shocking to see and very sad. Who actually buries their parents anymore?

I remember seeing Antonio holding my mother and kissing the side of her head. After all the things she said about my father, I couldn't imagine she really cared that he died. I imagined on that day that when my mother died – if she ever did – I would use the full scooping power of the shovel to fill her grave to the tippy top.

After the burial, all of the attendees were meant to line up on either side of a path that my mother and I would walk. It was a chance for the attendees to pay respect to us.

As we walked in between the attendees, the boys from the "family" reached out their hands to me, one by one, and gave me a "little something" to help me through tough times: a wad of cash, rolled in a rubber band.

There they were, these giant, grown men, sobbing like little babies, handing off cash to me, grabbing my shoulders, heaving tears in a blabbering mess. "Ya – ya – you're gonna be okay, Benny boy. It – it – it's gonna be okay, buddy."

Are you sure? I thought. I felt a smirk growing.

In fact, it was fucking *hilarious*. After a few of them, I started to smile – so big, in fact, that the giggles I was concealing in my ribs overtook me to the point that I had to run to my mother's car so I finally could release the surging cackle that would sustain me for years. Inside the car, I laughed so hard I started to cramp and scream "*Oh, God!*"

Outside the car, hearing my screams, my mother told the concerned goodfellas that I would be okay.

It was no surprise to me that my mother fell for Antonio. I had an inside line on him from the very beginning. After Judgie's death, there was a time that the fun returned in my mother's practice. The big band was back and it was playing Sinatra's *That's Life*. With Judgie gone, my mother was working several cases for a new family in New York – not that the family was "new" to the scene, rather she had not yet been called up until now. She was happy once more.

It was mid-summer and things in the federal court

system were heating up. My mother had several briefs due in the 2nd Circuit – the federal court of appeals that served New York, Connecticut, and Vermont. She was appealing her clients' convictions to the higher court and had to do so by filing her argument in writing, aka by "brief," but it took a lot more work and a lot more time than the name suggested.

My mother needed an extra set of hands to organize documents, make copies, binders, type letters, do mailings and such, everything a fifteen-year-old boy loves to do. Truthfully, I already knew how to answer the phones and most of the clients knew me. It was part social, part work but more than anything it was the first time in my life that I really got to see behind the scenes of what my mother did and who she worked for.

Also working for my mother was Janice, a large-breasted, plump, short and very horny twenty-three-year-old college dropout and legal secretary. Janice had full red cheeks and a button nose and wore short red skirts that stopped mid-ass much like her black bangs stopped mid-forehead. In her defense, she wore red tights underneath, which she thought made up for the skirt's absence of total taste. She also loved red v-neck sweaters, which were similarly tight, and her nipples were always "on." If Santa Clause ever had a slutty estranged daughter, Janice was her.

I constantly caught her looking at me, especially if I was working in the back storage room moving boxes and getting sweaty. I'd wear cut off jean shorts and a sleeveless half-shirt and she would bring me water regularly. We were an '80s porno waiting to happen. I often wondered what it would be like to lose my virginity to a woman like Janice. A hotdog bouncing down a hallway came to mind.

It was *the* time to be working for my mother because she was constantly in a good mood. The latest and greatest family she was doing work for was the Salucci Crime Family, which was currently being run by Antonio De Silva. All of the five major Crime Families had namesakes. The Boss, however, wasn't necessarily a member of that original family. The De Silvas owned several businesses, including a limousine company, and were multi-millionaires. I was surprised to learn that Antonio was married and had children and grandchildren. He was, by my mother's promise, a family man, which seemed odd to me because "family men" didn't cut peoples' throats or distribute heroin – at least that's what the documents in the case file said about his associates. I thought her assessment was misinformed at a minimum, forgiving at a medium, and outright bullshit at a maximum.

Ultimately, Antonio decided that he needed my mother to come up to Brooklyn for a meeting with him and his brother, Terry, who ran the limousine business. She decided to turn it into a family trip and invited me to go along.

"He's got a fourteen-year-old granddaughter named Italia," she told me.

"Not really trying to be clever with that one," I told her.

"Be nice," she said. "She's very beautiful."

"She probably 'twalks' with a 'nor-thun ack-sent,'" I said doing my best Jersey.

My mother laughed. I couldn't wait to get to New York and meet these people for myself.

They sent a limo for our ride into Brooklyn and we went straight to their garage where we met Antonio and Terry. Antonio was six feet and handsome with thinning hair, a broad nose and full lips. He had on a camel blazer that caused my mother to exclaim, "My god, that's gorgeous!" He had olive skin and looked like he took afternoon naps on the deck of a yacht anchored off some Mediterranean shore.

Terry was shorter and had a healthy mid-section. He had spaghetti sauce on his clothes, which not only telegraphed his most recent meal but also explained why he wasn't boss.

Both guys were over the moon about meeting me and I immediately felt welcome. The worry I had about meeting the people accused of such heinous crimes left me at that moment. They pinched my cheeks, hugged my shoulders and told me how "beautiful" I was. I felt like I was with my grandmother.

"Would you look at this heartbreaker," Antonio told Terry. "A million dollar face, for Christ's sake!"

"Thank you, thank you," my mother said. She nodded and smiled at me and nodded some more, which meant I was also to say thank you, which I did through bright red cheeks.

When Antonio told my mother they needed to "get down to it," the small talk vaporized and I received my next set of instructions.

"Benjamin's gonna go with my nephew, Richie, and his friend, Vinny, to get some lunch and we'll head over to my office," he told her.

"Sounds good," my mother responded. She looked at me: "You go with Richie and Vinny and get some food...

maybe some pizza or something. Pizza's your favorite, right?"

I had a blank look.

"Oh, Christ, you like pizza?" Terry asked. "My kid'll take you to the best pizza place in the world – right here in Brooklyn. Best pizza in the world!"

"Okay," I said. "Sure."

My mother sensed my hesitance. "Don't worry, honey, it's fine," she told me.

"Worry?" Terry asked. "No way – no problem. Richie and Vin got it covered. They're outside in the shop just waitin' on you."

Antonio put his hand on my shoulder and guided me through a door and into the garage. He whistled and yelled "Rich-chie!" and Richie waved back.

"Right over there. There they are. Go have fun," he told me. Richie waved me over. "Wait," Antonio yelled after me. "Benny boy, wait up," he said. I turned back and he extended me a hundred dollar bill. "Get a couple of pies," he said. "You pay for the boys, they'll think you're a big shot." He smiled at me.

I took the hundred and raised my eyebrows.

"Yeah, go ahead," he said. "It's fun. They'll get a laugh."

"Okay," I said. "Thanks."

Richie was a wiry twenty-eight-year-old with a blonde Q-Tip 'fro and a brown mustache. Vin was thirty-two and obese. He had red sauce on his fucking shirt too and drove a 1977 burnt orange Cadillac Coupe DeVille. We drove through Brooklyn, me sitting in the back, leaning over the ridge of the front seat bench and acting like I'd been riding as co-conspirator for years. There weren't two minutes of driving that didn't include Richie and Vin honking the horn and shouting out the window to another driver or pedestrian they knew, which was nearly everybody.

Watching Vin drive had its own entertainment value. He was so heavy he barely had room to steer the wheel. He rested his left arm on the open windowsill and propped his right arm up across his belly. He reached the wheel with only his pointer and middle finger and, with just these two fingers, was able to adeptly swing his 18-foot-long Caddy from lane to lane and around any corner.

They talked about eating pussy and getting laid or eating pizza and getting paid – I don't remember which. It was all a blur and funny as hell and unfolded in an afternoon of flickering moments. At one point they parked the car and left the keys in the ignition. I made a comment about their car getting stolen, at which they howled incredulously.

By the time the bill came, I dug in my pocket and pulled out the hundred. It was compressed and wadded from being stuffed. I unfolded it and subtly announced, "I got it." Richie and Vin erupted with cheers and laughter, as if they were sitting in the stands when the '86 Mets won the World Series.

Suddenly, it was "this-fucking-guy" *this* and "this-fucking-guy" *that*. Balls were being busted – "badda's" were being "binged" and "banged." I was an instant hero.

Later that night, Antonio took my mother and me to dinner. He parked his Cadillac in an alley behind the restaurant and left his keys in the ignition, too. I thought about Richie and Vin, but Antonio was older. I chalked his actions up to a mistake.

"Mr. De Silva, you left your keys in the car," I told him.

He paused and put his hand on my shoulder. "Don't worry, son. No one's going to touch my Caddy." He shook his head at me and smiled.

It hit me hard at that moment: my mother was actually doing work for The Mob. Antonio's Caddy wasn't anything special. It didn't have a vanity plate or dice in the mirror. No special rims or trim or paint job to distinguish it from any other Cadillac. Just a plain black Caddy. But I took the clue from Antonio that everybody knew *his* Caddy and nobody – from the bum in the street to the man in the know – was gonna fuck with it, not even with the invitation sitting in the ignition.

At the candlelit dinner table that night, I noticed the playful glances between my mother and Antonio "the family man" De Silva as he regaled her with tails of how the younger members of his crew were fucking up the business.

"You know, I want for nothing," he told her, "but I don't throw money around. If it were just me, I wouldn't be worried, but it's the cousins and nephews who make it a living hell. It's about the booze, the women, the cars, the cash. These kids – they got no head for it, you know?"

She looked at him intensely and expressed total understanding. He kept his arm on the back of her chair and, as often as he could, touched the nape of her neck.

The restaurant was crowded and everyone knew Antonio. The hostess knew him, the waiter knew him, the customers. I wondered if they were wondering the same thing I was wondering. If I had a dollar for every time my mother had mentioned that my father was a cheating son of a bitch, I'd have *my* own Caddy. Yet here she was – we were – participating in what felt like adultery.

"Do you bring your wife and kids to this restaurant a lot?" I asked him. My mother kicked me under the table and looked at me in disbelief.

"All the time," he said without hesitation. "They love it here." The tone of his voice said he was telling the truth and that he didn't perceive the vexed tone in mine. It confused me because the moments unfolding between him and my mother felt very much like a secret.

Twenty-Seven:

Prison Makes The Heart Grow Fonder

Years later, after he was convicted, Antonio called from the prison, asking meaningless questions. Carter could tell he didn't have anything to talk about, but then, as in the past, when he didn't have anything to discuss, they still talked about something. This conversation, though, was like an awkward first date chat. After they hung up, she was confused and somewhat excited. She was very intuitive and knew something was up. Then the phone rang again.

"Hello?" she said.

"Carter..." Antonio's sandy voice whispered. "I love you. I just want you to know that. I really love you." She immediately told him she loved him too... desperately.

Antonio was worlds apart from her last great love, Judgie. On the surface, Judgie was a law-abiding jurist, Antonio a criminal. Judgie was from the Deep South; Antonio was from Avenue L in Brooklyn. Both were passionate men, though, and nothing exceeded the passion they felt for her. With so much life experience, Antonio was also highly intelligent. He was a scholar like Judgie, albeit via the streets of Brooklyn or the prison library. He crafted his intelligence with deliberate strokes – each lesson self-taught.

Before he hired her to do work for the family, he had studied her career. He had her "rookie card" and watched as she came up through the federal court system – following appeals she handled and reading the opinions handed down from the court. They always listed her name in the appeal, and Antonio could tell the judges appreciated her skill. They either included many adjectives to describe her arguments or wrote a sixty-page opinion to cover their own ass. Either way, both served as a form of respect regarding her initiative and skill.

Carter immediately saw past Antonio's criminal ways. She considered his past acts as part of his inescapable culture – not an excuse, just an explanation. His neighborhood was all about the block; everyone was on the block. You couldn't escape it. The corner was the checkpoint. The pressure was always on to become a part of the whispers. Antonio had grown up poor, just like his friends. Success stood out on the avenues and streets of Brooklyn as much as it did in the Hollywood gossip rags. Their alligator shoes and cashmere overcoats were declarations of success. So, when some of Antonio's friends donned silk suits, drove nice cars and got the girls, he wanted in.

His cleverness created in him a good business sense. And his grasp of the law for a jailhouse lawyer was unbelievable. He was rarely off point – only because the jail didn't have access to the up-to-the-minute decisions like she did. He and Carter fought like siblings over the finer legal issues. He insisted she was dead wrong – she was reading the text out of context; he was a legal scholar, too. She callously criticized him, cursed him, and mocked him. In the end, they educated each other and became stronger as a pair.

When it came to her loving Antonio, Carter knew it was wrong. She didn't understand why her words came so easily with him. She should have been able to walk away from her feelings just like she had been able to walk away from me. Maybe it was that she was alone, without judgment from others. Maybe it was because he was in jail – for life. But she also knew she couldn't lie to him. She knew he would know because the subtleties of her emotions would give her away. For her to say she loved him, she must have meant it.

For several months, they continued their weekly calls – hours of conversation. Thousands of dollars in collect call phone bills. She always accepted the calls as his attorney, which clued the operators that the communications were private. Her number was on file with the prison as the number associated with his legal counsel. Despite this, the prison recorded the calls anyway. They couldn't use them, but they kept all recordings on file just in case.

Carter knew it, too. She didn't care. She knew they didn't listen. The fact that they could listen, though, seemed to give her an extra thrill. She was resigned to the fact that their phone calls would be the extent of their relationship, until the one day he called with a request.

"Hey, babe," he said greeting her.

"Hi, Tonio." She smiled. "How ya doin'?"

"I been thinkin' about you."

Her heart skipped as it always did when she talked to Antonio. "I been thinkin' about you, too."

They sat in silence for a second, both thinking the same thought – wishing they could be together.

"How's everything?" he asked.

"It's all right, you know. Up and down."

"I want you to come see me. I'm thinkin', you know, about... another appeal." When she heard the word "appeal," her jaw dropped. Another appeal was not an option.

"Okay," she told him, holding her breath. "When?"

"As soon as possible."

The idea of an appeal was a cover, which meant this visit was personal, which meant she would have to tell the prison that she was coming as his lawyer on business, and not a social call, in order to get privacy. She would have to lie.

She packed her bags faster than ever and put the risk out of her mind. She would have her secretary call and make the arrangements.

One month later, Carter did her best to hide her joy as she walked into Antonio's jail. She attempted to look lawyerly. She moved through a metal door after being buzzed through and toward a scanner and two guards. "Attorney Carter Scales here to see Antonio De Silva." She extended her bar card and driver's license. They ignored her.

One guard pointed at the conveyor belt that ran through a scanner. "Purse, wallet, keys, belt, watch, glasses, etc.," he said, not looking at her. "And the cell phone stays here with me." She complied and moved through the iron scanner doorway. After gathering her things, she waited by another door near a double-sided mirror. She checked her reflection but tried not to primp too much. Lawyers visiting clients on business wouldn't primp at all.

A speaker box near the mirror clicked loudly, then a metallic voice echoed over itself. "Ms. Scales, your visit has been approved. Just give us a minute to have him brought over to attorney visitation. You did request a contact visit, right?"

"That's correct," she said with calculated indifference. Inside, though, the thought of a contact visit made her heart flip, flop, and skip.

The speaker box clicked again. "Ms. Scales, you can go back now. Just around the corner. Number seven."

She opened the door to a sterile white room. Antonio was already inside, sitting in a chair at a table, wearing khaki pants and a khaki short-sleeve, button-up shirt.

"I brought the papers," she said, more for the guard than Antonio.

"Good."

She sat down across from him, and they squeezed each other's hands as tightly as possible in the form of an awkward handshake. Their only embrace. Antonio examined her intensely. He'd been waiting for this moment for years, to finally look at her as his lover, knowing she loved him back. He studied her every move, focused on her mouth and lips. The corners of her eyes. The smooth skin on her arms.

"How much time do we have?" she asked. Her voice was wanting and soft.

"An hour or so before the count," he said. She watched him, too. His nice shoulders. Weathered hands. Hairy arms and chest. His overall warmth and sexiness. The temperature in the room seemed to rise. The air moist from racing hearts and flushed skin. They breathed as if climbing a hill, not able to touch.

Antonio moved his hand to his lap. He shifted uncomfortably then looked back to her. She locked onto his eyes. When he looked away, she looked down to his lap to his hand. It was covering his erection.

He looked at her, embarrassed. He was not the man he wanted to be in there. She looked at him. It would take two seconds to crawl across the table and be on top of him, running her fingers through his thick Italian hair, finding his lips with hers and sinking into unabashed lovemaking.

The thought of him hard for her stirred a frenzy of fantasy and delusion. Carter wanted Antonio more than anyone in her life. She didn't care that he was in prison or that he needed permission to take a piss. He was still powerful, and he ached for her; he moaned for her. She had to have him, too. There was no question, though, that he would remain in federal prison for the rest of his life; that there were no conjugal visits of any nature; and that she only would be able to see him in the attorney-client room.

"I can't," she said, her eyes begging him to understand. "I just can't."

That night, back at her hotel, she imagined him as she saw him in the room that day. Wanting her. Trying to hide something his body could not. She felt a new resolve inside herself. She was determined to change the fact that the world and the law and the powers that be would not let her have him.

Leaving him there in that state, under those circumstances, was like cutting off her own arm. She had to get back to him. She had to reclaim what was rightfully hers.

Someday. Somehow. She would have him.

Twenty-Eight:
A Job Well Done

The catalyst for my mother's predicament occurred on the day she saw me in court. Even though she was desperate for Antonio, she had not crystallized a plan to bring them together. When she found me in court, though, following my first closing argument at my first trial as a criminal defense trial attorney, she felt totally betrayed, misunderstood and alone. She didn't find any excitement in the fact that I had entered her field or that rumors were circulating that I was outperforming my level of experience.

Her emotions took over and rightly so. There was only one conclusion she could draw from my actions – I did not love her at all. She needed to feel wanted again – to feel love again.

She made immediate plans to see Antonio. She paid extraordinary fees to book a last minute flight, but she didn't care. Antonio was her only safe haven now. She was so happy she had him. Because he was in prison, she knew just where to find him. She knew his every move. Every second of his day. And that he always would be there. For her. Whenever she needed him. And he loved her.

She wanted to show Antonio how much she loved him, to make him understand in his own language, and on terms that were unique to him. Because his world was so regulated, so confined, Antonio no longer felt like a man. Handcuffs. Chains. Shakedowns. Male guards watching him piss and shower. She wanted to help him feel like a man again.

She hadn't seen him in over a year. She had no legal reason to be there. Without a legal reason, she wouldn't get a legal visit. Legal visits were private because they were conditioned on attorney-client business, which meant attorney-client privilege. Regular visits were held in a large room with other inmates and guards. Legal visits had closed doors, no audio equipment. They offered a place where they could be alone, free from interruption. She called her friend, Catherine Connor-Robins, at the Bureau of Prisons – a colleague and director of inmate services – and asked her to set up an attorney-client visit.

"You guys got something going on?" the director asked.

"Uh... yeah. We might," Carter said. Suddenly, she felt awkward and regretted that she had ever befriended Catherine to the point where the lady felt comfortable asking such questions. She lied. "We may have some new evidence."

"Oh, great," the director said. "What time would you like?"

"Ten a.m. is fine. And the Quad C conference area, if you have it."

"Sure," Catherine said.

Carter found some relief in the absence of any suspicion in the director's voice.

Her flight was intolerable. A red-eye flight to California and then a two-hour drive to a dumpy roadside hotel ten minutes away from the penitentiary. She checked in around three a.m. California time, which was six a.m. her regular time. She wanted to look nice for Antonio. She found her room and dropped her overnight bag on the bed. The room featured brown décor with large green banana-leaf patterns on the curtains and comforter. She had a television with bunny ears and a white washcloth with tattered edges and a burn mark on it. Normally, her clients and their families put her up in the city's finest and booked her a car to the prison. But her client didn't tell his family that Carter was coming to see him. Nobody knew except Antonio and the jail personnel. Despite wanting to sleep, she couldn't. She used the only true perk the room provided – a coffee machine – to keep herself going and to calm her nerves. Caffeine did that, surprisingly. She closed her eyes and sipped her coffee and imagined herself at the prison. As the sun rose through the banana brown curtains, she focused on Antonio's smile and thought, *Today is going to be a great day.*

Antonio knew exactly what was wrong with him. He was a dying ember, discarded and dull, covered by ash. Carter, though, brought him great joy and fire. With her, he found his ability to visualize a good life again. After being in prison for so many years, he had given up on thinking about the good things he'd once had. He only saw walls and bars. With Carter at his side or on the other side of a phone line, he had a balcony seat to the show below – not close enough to participate, but close enough for the thrill. He saw the world again in the sound of her joyous voice, in the words of her adoring praise.

He sat waiting in the private attorney-client visitation room – on this particular day a kitchen the size of a modest walk-in closet with a coffeepot and microwave, a table, and two chairs. The door would remain open until Carter arrived. A guard sat outside the room at a booth, which was in the center of two large converging hallways.

"De Silva," the guard said to Antonio. "Fix me up a cup of Java, would ya?"

"Sure, Sergeant," Antonio said. "How'd you like it?"

"Like I like my women, blonde and sweet."

"Extra cream and lots of sugar – comin' up." The sergeant nodded with approval as Antonio poured and stirred. The jail staff loved to task the big boys like Antonio. They got to brag about it at work functions and parties with their friends that the Boss fixed their coffee or shined their shoes.

Carter walked down the hallway to the desk just as Antonio handed the cup of coffee to the sergeant.

"What, you can't get your own coffee, Sergeant?" she said, somewhat joking but partially annoyed. The sergeant focused on the annoyed part of her tone.

"He was just doin' me a favor. That's all. Right, Mr. De Silva?"

"Exactly," Antonio said. Carter didn't look at Antonio. She didn't want to exhibit joy in front of the guard.

"Where are we today?" she asked the sergeant.

"In the kitchenette there."

"The kitchenette?" she asked, now only annoyed. She peered through the doorway. The room was disgusting. She saw a coffee-stained countertop with coffee grounds strewn about. The microwave smelled like burned hotdogs and rotting cheese, which filled the tiny space. The floors had a sticky buildup of spilled drinks and shoe dirt, leaving it pocked with black smudges. "What about the attorney-client conference rooms?" she asked.

"All booked up. It's this or nothing."

Carter hated being told she only had one option.

"I can't be expected to have confidential conversations with my client with our voices echoing in here and you sitting five feet away," she said.

"Ms. Scales, I don't know what to tell you. We're understaffed. We have no additional space. We could only make this room available to you because I'm stationed here already overseeing intake. So, unless you want to wait 'til tomorrow, you may just have to whisper. At least you have free hot coffee, which is decent, I might add."

Antonio led the way in, and she closed the door behind them. She didn't want to wait to see him tomorrow. She may not have the nerve then. It had to be today. She promised herself she would do it today. Of course, the kitchenette wasn't what she had imagined. The other conference rooms were soundproof and more private, in that the guards had to walk down a short hallway to enter, which placed them twenty or thirty feet away instead of five.

Carter grabbed Antonio's hand.

"What's up?" he asked her.

"I had to see you. I know they probably told you I had somethin' going on," she said.

"Hell, yes, they did. I didn't know what to say," he whispered. "I just said, 'New evidence.'"

"Good, that's what I thought..." She smiled. "I knew you'd know what to say."

"Well, that's all we got left as an option, but I know

you don't have any new evidence, do you?" He suddenly looked hopeful.

"No. I don't." He nodded and dropped his eyes. "But I do have something." She smiled at him. He looked at her curiously.

What then took place in that tiny kitchenette just five feet from the sergeant, Carter couldn't come to grips with. At best she knew that she loved Antonio very much; that she felt alone; and that she wanted to show Antonio how much he meant to her – damn Benjamin, damn her career, damn everything. She also may have felt a bit impervious to scrutiny or reproach. And she liked that feeling and the danger associated with it. She didn't know how she lost her senses, only why she did – which was that she wanted to connect with the one person in the world she knew without a doubt she loved and who loved her back.

She got up from her chair and moved closer to Antonio. She looked past the scum on the floor of the kitchen when she knelt down next to Antonio's side and planted her high heel to keep it from sliding on the grease. She kissed him at first on his lips. He responded without question. Madly. They had both dreamed of that moment for years. And then she moved down his chest.

"Wait," he whispered, but she ignored him.

She then grabbed his leg, undid his pants, trying to quiet his metal belt buckle, and pulled his underwear to the side. He, of course, was shocked but "ready." She took him into her hand and began to rub him. He bit his fist to keep himself from moaning when she put his penis in her mouth. The moment was thrilling for them both.

There was a loud knock on the kitchenette door. "Just tryin' to get a refill," the sergeant announced.

Startled, Carter jumped up, forcefully bumping her head on the table, causing it to topple with a loud crash. The sergeant pulled the door open and found Carter rising awkwardly from the floor, holding her head and wiping her mouth. Antonio was ineptly yet quickly trying to tuck his penis into his pants and zip his fly and buckle his belt – all of which was impossible in the course of the one second it took for the sergeant to figure out what was going on.

"Madam, stand aside!" he instructed, which she did by falling into a chair and nursing her head injury. "Inmate, stand up!" he demanded of Antonio. Antonio complied, still holding his pants, and the sergeant grabbed him, cuffed him, and put him up against the wall outside the room. He radioed for an additional officer to assist.

Carter, totally humiliated and hyperventilating, walked out of the kitchenette and moved down the hallway, despite the sergeant's orders for her to halt. Another officer, hearing the radio call, entered the hallway and followed the sergeant's orders to stop Carter.

"Cuff her," the sergeant told the officer, while keeping his hands on Antonio.

"Cuff *her?*" the other officer asked, nodding toward her.

"Just do it!"

"What's going on?" he asked.

"Caught her givin' him a blow job," the sergeant said.

"Holy shit!"

Carter's head was pounding with emergent thoughts.

She couldn't believe they were talking about her. She closed her eyes tight and squeezed her fists. All rational thought returned, which was quickly followed by more panic.

"What do I do with her?" she heard the officer ask.

"We'll have to call Admin to figure it out," the other responded.

Suddenly, she cried out. "No! Please... just wait." She started formulating what she wanted to say but then stopped, knowing that saying nothing was better than admitting anything by way of trying to reason with the officers. She knew with silence she could maybe spin this somehow despite the obvious incriminating evidence. A good criminal defense attorney could always spin facts.

On her way to the administrator's office, she started to formulate theories. Maybe she was kneeling down to pick up something, then suddenly her insane client whipped out his penis and that's when she jumped back right at the moment the officer entered, thank God for that, and he just misunderstood the situation. *Oh, Christ*, she thought. At least it was something.

The officer walked her down the hallway. The bowel of the jail was a labyrinth of hallways she'd never seen before, including the inside of her own personal cell.

"No hard feelings," the officer told her inside an all Plexiglas booth. "Just wait here, and I'll get the administrator on the radio and figure out what's next." The officer was polite but all business.

Carter sat alone for about ten minutes until another officer came by and placed another woman in the booth with her. That lady wore an orange jumpsuit. Carter had on a pantsuit. That lady had white socks and brown flip-flops. Carter's feet were adorned with Stuart Weitzman. That lady was a criminal. And Carter? Surely not.

She thought about the administrator, her friend, who was about to realize that she had lied to her about the status of Antonio's case. Carter was terrified at her own deception. What would her friend do? Surely she would defer to Carter's explanation. Maybe she'd go back and listen to her and Antonio's phone conversations, where they confessed their love for each other. That wouldn't be good.

Carter sat in the administrator's office alone. She'd been there for thirty minutes. When one of the staff members entered and told her the administrator wouldn't be coming due to a conflict of interest, she knew she was screwed; someone else would be addressing this particular problem, another person on the inside of the jail who wouldn't be biased by a friendship with her.

Well, she'd just explain that Antonio had acted inappropriately and that it was no big deal and everyone had overreacted. She decided she would play hardball with them and chastise them for handcuffing her and locking her down for all that time. It was no way to treat a decorated attorney such as her; in fact, it was completely inhumane. Despite the jail being a part of the Federal Bureau of Prisons, it was still located in a small West Coast cowboy town outside of another somewhat bigger but small cowboy town. She could handle these people.

After an hour-and-a-half, a man walked in.

"Ms. Scales?" he asked.

"Who are you?" she replied.

"I'm Buddy Griff, the District Attorney out here. I

understand we have somewhat of an issue that's cropped up." Although they were in California, Carter couldn't tell. He spoke like all the other hicks she'd ever met.

"Excuse me, sir. Are you here to bring some sort of prosecution on me?"

"That's right."

"Did they tell you that I'm a criminal defense attorney?"

"That don't matter none to me." She was surprised when he didn't just spit tobacco on the floor.

"I have nothing to say to you. I'd like to be able to leave now. May I leave?"

"Naw. Naw, you can't."

"Am I under arrest? Because if I'm not, I'm leaving."

"Well, apparently you sucked a man's dick just about a hundred yards down that hallway." The country twang in the man's voice disgusted and unnerved her to the point of almost crying. The fact that he enjoyed confronting her in such a fashion made her nauseous. She couldn't believe she was back in this position, being judged once again by a slimy bumpkin the likes of the men in her past – this time of her own doing.

"I did no such thing," she said, mustering confidence. "Now," she directed, "I want to call an attorney. And there will be no further questions."

"Stand up and take off your shoes, and put your hands against the wall," he ordered.

"What are you doing?"

"I'm placing you under arrest. Now stand up, and do as you're told."

"I'd like another individual in the room please,

preferably a female."

"Either you stand up and put your hands on the goddamn wall, or I'm gonna grab you by your fucking wrists and put you there. *Now stand up!*" His voice shook the cinder block walls. She did as ordered, slipping off her high heels and putting her hands on the wall. District Attorneys did not do these tasks. It was an officer's job. But there she was in the middle of nowhere. She knew how these types operated anyhow. She was no rookie. All bets were off.

"Spread your legs," he commanded.

"Are you going to frisk me? I've already been through security."

"Ma'am, you've had intimate physical contact with an inmate at this facility. There's no tellin' what you have on you." He ran his hands down her thighs and over her buttocks. He hiked her skirt and moved up her legs, just shy of her groin, and then down her shoulders and back.

"Turn around and face me," he said.

Being that close to him made her step back, but the wall was there.

He ran his hands up her sides into her armpits and then across her breasts and into her cleavage. "Turn around and face the wall," he commanded. "Hands, please."

"Is that really necessary?"

"I don't think you understand your predicament. We have rules out here just like anywhere else. The state might have dumped a prison out here, but we're a good town and a good people. It's people like you and your client who dirty up this world and make it harder on God-fearing Christians like us to keep the peace."

Griff marched Carter out of the prison like a common street whore and put her in the back of his state-issued Mercury Marquis. The next forty-eight hours were intolerable. She was housed at the county jail in a general population cell with a dozen or so drug users, all jonesing for their next hit, and women who had beaten their children or husbands, depending on their size and proclivity. Guards snickered at her and laughed with each other at the idea of her performing oral sex on one of the inmates at the prison. They didn't know Antonio had been one of the most powerful family leaders on the East Coast. They were county employees making eleven bucks an hour who had to work in a shit-hole jail babysitting society's rejects for three twelve-hour shifts a week. Whether at the prison or the county jail, inmates were cockroaches. In their minds, she had given a blowjob to a cockroach. This hoity-toity city lawyer bitch all dressed in her fancy suit. They mimed the act to each other, acting as if they were gagging on an imaginary dick.

She fought off her tears as long as she could. Only when the guard shut down the lights and some of the other girls cried did she allow herself to cry. The criminal system was built for resolution and negotiation, but they seemed to have their prize pig in Carter Scales.

While most busy city DAs would let their assistant attorneys dismiss the smaller nonviolent felonies or allow pretrial/pre-indictment resolutions for the ones against first-time offenders, Carter knew Buddy Griff would make an entire show out of her one act. He was determined to stuff her as if she were a big bad bear that had wandered into his small innocent town. Her only saving thought was that at least this was a local case in a small town miles away from Atlanta. No one ever would know about it – or so she hoped.

Twenty-Nine:
Midnight Crisis In The Garden Of Good And Evil

Three weeks later, Carter sat in her office chair with one pen behind her ear and one in her mouth. She didn't realize she had been writing on her tongue due to her immense concentration. She easily buried herself in her work, with one book on her lap and three on the desk, all opened to various pages, as she cited multiple principles of law for an upcoming brief, which was due in three days.

The document itself was a train wreck. She had nothing. An adjective count revealed over-usage, which was a sign of a thin legal argument. All good facts had been used up on the direct appeal to the state court of appeals. She needed some new evidence or extraordinary evidence, but like the Illinois winters of her childhood, all was cold.

She had countless hooks in the water with her private investigator, hoping he'd call with great news about some witness who had fabricated his testimony or enhanced his testimony – something that would demonstrate that the eyewitness was actually locked up in prison at the time he allegedly had seen her client shoot another man at the titty bar. Then the phone rang. It was the back line and after six, which meant it had to be her investigator.

"Tell me you have something," she said.

"Ms. Scales?"

It wasn't her investigator. "This is she," she said, rolling her eyes, which were filled with contempt for clients and families who somehow got the number to her back line. "Who's calling?"

"Ms. Scales, this is Bob Shruter from the *Journal*. Do you care to comment on allegations that you performed an act of oral sex on Antonio De Silva?"

She felt pain in her toes. In her wrists. Jolts from her heart.

"Well, Bob," she said, with staged authority and clarity. "I don't have a clue what you're talking about, and if this is some kind of joke and you print lies about me, I'll have you prosecuted for stalking and/or sue your ass for fucking libel. Do not call me again!" She hung up the phone and gasped for air. Tears followed but were immediately pushed out by waves of panic. She gathered as much composure as she could and shoved her books off the desk and pulled the phone book off a shelf. She scrounged through the pages until she found the listing for the *Journal*. She dialed.

"*Journal*," a female voice said.

"Yes. Hi. Do you have a Bob Shruter who works there?"

"Shruter?"

"Yes." She waited while the woman paused in silence. Every second that ticked by gave her hope that the woman couldn't find the name because no one by that name worked there. Maybe it was just a prank call.

"*Bob* Shruter, you said?"

"Yes, Robert Shruter," she said, annoyed.

More silence, until... "Oh, here we go. Robert Shruter. He sure does. You want his extension?"

"Uh... no," she said. "Thank you." She hung up the phone. "Fuck." She rubbed her temples. "Fuck, fuck,

fuck," she said until her words choked on the lump in her throat.

She sat forward in her chair and stared at the wall. Her eyes scanned the wallpaper blankly as she zeroed in on her next move. She needed a rational, unemotional mind to help her. No, she thought. She couldn't tell anybody. No one could know about this. She'd be a laughing stock. She knew every powerhouse attorney in the country. They were all men, of course, and they'd all eventually, after hanging up with her, shake their head and call her a stupid woman. And even though she had acted like a stupid woman, she couldn't do that to herself.

Able to find an ounce of self-control, she reasoned herself into a state of calm by promising herself that she was strong enough to make one phone call that might just make a difference – a call to her friend who was the administrator at the prison. The administrator had been too conflicted to speak to her on that day. Maybe she had some compassion for the situation now and would be willing to talk about it off the record.

It was a dangerous move because the woman was a witness against her, but she was also a woman, and the two of them had shared many conversations about working as women in a man's world. She over-thought it for about an hour then decided to call. Maybe she'd give her the courtesy of rejecting her without also reporting her.

"Ugh, please," she groaned, dialing.

"Administration," a woman said.

"Catherine Connor-Robins, please," Carter said.

"Sure. Who's calling?"

"Carter Scales."

"Oh," the lady said with exaggeration. "Um. Okay, Ms. Scales, let me see if... she's in." Carter knew damn well she was in based on the lady saying "Sure" before she knew it was her calling. If Catherine let her secretary screen her out, that wouldn't be good. A sure sign she was doomed.

"Carter," Catherine said, "hold on." Catherine muffled the phone and told the secretary to close her door. "You shouldn't be calling me," she told her.

Carter broke into tears again. "I know, but..."

"Look, here's the deal – and I'm only telling you this because I like you very much. You're the only woman I know who's probably been called a bitch more than me. But what you need to know is that what you did – whether you did or not – isn't a crime in California. That's the good news. It was consensual sex for all legal purposes, and there's no crime against doing it in a prison. It's not like it's contraband, which would be a felony, okay? I mean, it breaks all the rules, of course, but it's not a crime."

"I'm sure Mr. Griff isn't happy about that."

"No, he's not. He's trying to fit it into some kind of federal deceptive act, but it's not gonna stick. So, I'm pretty sure, with some pushing by a top lawyer out here, you'll get a dismissal. Make sense?"

Carter wanted to be very careful about how she replied. She didn't want to appear guilty, but she also didn't want to appear to be ungrateful. Catherine was taking a huge risk. "I understand," she said.

"Your biggest problem is the ethical issue. On that one, there's nothing I can do. Knowing he can't get you on the criminal charge, Buddy has vowed to report you to your state bar ethical division, which means your license to practice is at stake. If he hasn't done it already, he will soon."

"I understand," Carter said again, now fearing public disbarment and ruin.

"So get a good attorney, and do what you can."

"Is that the worst of it?"

"No." Catherine paused. "Carter, we have you on video. All of it. And the BOP's Internal Affairs department has backlogged your phone recordings with Mr. De Silva, and we have you on audiotape – the two of you discussing your relationship and feelings – so the tapes arguably show premeditation rather than any coercion or act of desperation, which could mitigate it a bit. But by the way our beloved DA is talking, he wants your license."

"Okay," Carter said, bracing her hurried breathing.

"On our end, Carter, I expect you won't be allowed back in this facility. Could be *all* federal penitentiaries for a while. That's all I can give you. I hope you understand. I really need to hang up."

"Okay," Carter said. "And Cathy?"

"Yeah?"

"Thank you."

"All right. And... take care of yourself." Catherine hung up the phone.

Carter contemplated it all. The tip on the act not being a crime and Buddy knowing that it wasn't a crime would arm a local lawyer with the ability to slam a dismissal through the system. The ethical issue was truly the issue for her career, because Catherine was right – she could be disbarred. What seemed like premeditation wasn't, but Buddy could argue it that way easily. She certainly would be barred from federal prisons for a while, if not for the rest of her career. She could live with that, but not disbarment. A disbarment meant she was through. Forever. Publicly humiliated and foreclosed from ever earning a living in the career to which she had given her heart and soul, her whole life.

To make matters even more enjoyable, there was a videotape. Buddy Griff obviously had called the *Journal* and reported the story. She wondered whether he had given the reporter the tape, too. Surely, Catherine would try to maintain the property and keep it under wraps. No criminal case meant no subpoena power to get the tapes. But those things always got out and circulated. It didn't matter that the people holding it were sworn to serve and protect in the interests of justice; they were beer-drinking voyeurs like everybody else and loved to have a good laugh or jerk-off session. It would be out there on the same shelf as the pawn shop owner's 911 call to police, circulating on law enforcement closed-circuit television.

If it existed, which apparently it did, everyone in the business would see it eventually – prisoners, too. Antonio would be a laughing stock... or a hero. Either way, he was a very private person and would be embarrassed nonetheless.

Carter picked up the phone and jockeyed a referral from a lawyer she knew out in California for a ball-busting female criminal defense attorney who wanted an opportunity to stick it to Buddy Griff. It was for a "friend" of hers, of course. The lawyer gave her the name of Grace Kilpatrick. Carter smiled upon hearing the name. A woman having both Grace and "Kill" in her name had potential.

Grace called Carter from a courthouse in California. "Well," she began, "I don't think it's a crime either. It's foolish, but I've done some foolish things in my life, including riding cross-country on the back of a Harley with my father's business partner so we could watch the sun rise over the desert and have sex on acid." Carter laughed. "I understand the delicacy of your situation, but with your permission, I'll ram Buddy Griff so far up the ass with his bullshit that he'll be wiping the brown out his Aryan eyes for weeks, that SOB." Carter loved her. "I'm no flower, Carter."

"I don't want a flower."

"Then we're in agreement."

Within a month, the charges were dismissed, leaving one very pissed-off Buddy Griff. And the story was squashed as well. With no charges filed, she was just another woman trying to *satisfy* her imprisoned man. It was no surprise, however, when she received a letter from the State Bar of Georgia shortly after that. It was delivered by server, and she had to sign, saying that she had officially been served. She opened the letter and read it.

Dear Ms. Scales

This letter is your official notice that a bar complaint has been initiated against you by Attorney Buddy Griff, wherein he has alleged that you committed certain unethical acts, to wit: committed sexual acts upon an inmate at a federal correctional institute, specifically that

*you performed oral sexual acts on Antonio De Silva, your
client.*

The letter went on about procedure and her time to
respond and that she was facing permanent disbarment
and that this was no joke. Her palms began to sweat.
She read the letter several times. The edges crumpled
under her nervous grip. She had never dealt with a bar
complaint before. Usually, bar complaints were initiated
by clients, and her clients loved her. They would never
do such a thing.

She did what most people do when they had acted like
a moron and began to consider herself as a person. Like
waking up from a hangover and finding a naked stranger
next to her, she questioned the moment she had cast this
unfortunate boomerang into the cosmos, which was now
barreling down on her like the dive-bombing cropduster
in *North by Northwest.*

She considered it a quid pro quo – a measured
reaction to something she must have done over the
course of her life. Like most karma, you get back what
you give. Bad attorneys deserved retribution from their
clients; kill a man, his son kills you – eye-for-an-eye kind
of stuff. But this? A blowjob fiasco that could cost her her
lifeblood? What form of cosmic turnabout was this? The
answer wasn't simple, if there was an answer at all.

She picked up the phone and called an old friend who
specialized in malpractice defense. Lynn Turner
represented many lawyers who were sued by their
clients for failing to adhere to the standards of practice,
which the law required. Many lawsuits were
accompanied by a bar complaint, which wasn't a lawsuit
but was a way to make the attorney under civil scrutiny

even more nervous and upset. Often, attorneys would be encouraged to settle civil actions against them and pay up in exchange for the client dropping the unethical investigation. Lynn Turner was well versed in that area.

Despite the name, Lynn was a man. He was also gay. It was the reason Carter chose to call him, aside from his expertise. With no marriages to speak of and no children and with a name like Lynn, he hadn't had an easy road himself. He had come out six years ago on his sixtieth birthday and revealed that his paralegal of twenty-two years, Bobby-Charles, was also his lover. Like my father, Lynn was fucking his secretary.

Lynn Turner was the perfect person to keep this secret and advise her regarding what to do. If he thought she could handle it herself, she trusted his opinion. If not, she'd hire him and he'd do a great job.

"Bobby-Charles?" Carter said into the phone, upon hearing a man's voice.

"It i-sssss," he said, drawing out his "s."

"It's Carter Scales."

"Hi, there, Ms. Thang! How you-eeeew, sugar?" he squealed with exaggeration.

"I take it Lynn isn't there."

"No, he'd kill me if he heard me actin' all sweet on you." Bobby-Charles had a heavy Southern drawl, which he drew out with his dramatic use of vowels and consonants. "The office is the office, and the home is the home," he said, imitating Lynn's deep voice. "What he means is, '*Steer* the *queer* straight outta *here!*'" Carter laughed. It felt good.

They caught up for about thirty seconds, until she couldn't take the small talk anymore. "I need a favor," she said. "And it's a real big one, if that's okay."

"Sure, pun-kin. You know Lynn loves you. What's up? Oh! Hold on," he told her. "That's my back line. It's probably Lynn now. Here, you stay on the line but don't say anything," Bobby-Charles said snickering. "We'll give him a little wake me up."

He joined their call with the back line and produced his most effeminate welcome greeting. "It'ssss a fabuloussss day at Lynn Turnerssssss' office!" he said, stereotyping gayness and dripping it from his vocal chords. Carter covered her mouth. Anticipating Lynn's irritation made her giggle.

"Goddamn it, Bobby-Charles! What'd I tell you about answering the phone like that?" Lynn yelled.

"I knew it was you, baby cakes!"

"Well, it could have been a goddamn client, and some people just aren't–"

Bobby-Charles cut him off. "Relax, Lynn!" he said in all seriousness. "I need you to focus! I've got Carter Scales on the line. She needs a favor. A big one. And it sounds serious."

"Well, have her come in."

"You hear that, Carter? He said come on in."

"I heard him. Thanks, Lynn."

Lynn sighed deeply. "What are you two up to?"

"We're getting ready for an important meeting. Now, will you bring me a grande-non-fat-white-mocha-i-love-you-a-latte?" Bobby-Charles asked.

Lynn sighed. "You know, I'm the boss in the relationship. You oughta be bringin' me the damn coffee."

"Baby, I bring you the *cream*," Bobby-Charles corrected, and laughed.

"Carter, if it were anyone else listening in on this little slice of heaven, I'd seriously consider suicide at this moment."

"Oh, please," she retorted. "After you hear why I'm coming in this afternoon, you'll feel like you two have been living in a G-rated movie.

That afternoon, Carter pulled into the driveway of Lynn Turner's detached office building, made of yellow brick with white Victorian accents. Two concrete lions flanked the driveway and were large enough for multiple drunks to straddle, usually at Lynn's annual Christmas party. She walked in the front door and was greeted by a King Charles Spaniel named Deirdre, which means "raging woman" in Irish. Deirdre certainly was upholding her namesake as she barked incessantly at Carter for daring to step onto the expansive red and gold Persian rug.

"Hey, there!" Bobby-Charles said upon seeing her. He got up and kissed her cheek. "He's waitin' on ya." Bobby-Charles tried to quiet Deirdre by squirting her with a water bottle as Carter headed to Lynn's office. Deirdre responded by yelping.

"Don't you make her tinkle on the carpet," Lynn yelled out to Bobby-Charles just as Carter walked in his office. "Carter Scales' got that weak bladder," he said, winking at Carter. "You never know when she'll just piss on something."

"Stop it!" Bobby-Charles yelled from the other room.

Lynn smiled warmly at her and gave her a comforting

hug. He was tall and soft with large shoulders and a tummy. He reminded her of Denver.

"What's going on?"

"If you don't mind, I need to get right to it. This is just killing me," she said.

"Go right ahead."

She took her seat on an expensive couch. "This is gorgeous."

"Oh thanks, I just had it recovered."

"Wow. Where'd you get this fabric?"

"At Rhonda's."

"They always have such amazing stuff."

"I know."

"Well," she said, rubbing her hand over the fabric, "to the reason I'm here."

"Just come out with it, Carter. It's easier that way." Lynn tried to comfort her by taking a sip of tea and not staring right at her.

"I got caught giving one of my clients a blowjob."

A gag, a snort and a spray of hot fluid from his nose sent Lynn hacking away. After he resolved his personal conflict, he spoke through flushed cheeks: "That's not quite what I was expecting you to say."

Carter hung her head and welled up. It was more real when she said it out loud. "I assume you have a bar complaint," he said. She nodded. "And I assume it's *not* from the client."

"Oh, hell no. He loved every second of it." They both smiled. Her eyes dropped, though, as she went on to explain Antonio to him and how they had fallen in love.

Carter didn't have any male friends. Most had grown to despise her. At a minimum, they dismissed her. Lynn understood her immediately. For him, it was like hearing his own story being told; only his prison was self-created by his fears of public rejection and ridicule.

"It's a pickle," he started. "And your friend is right. The phone calls to the prison beforehand and using the legal visit to cover it is what elevates it to a more serious ethical violation. I have to tell you, you could be disbarred."

"What do I do?"

"Why don't you just start from the beginning?"

"About Antonio and me?"

"About you and how you got to that point, because you're what's important here. 'You,' as a person, is what's gonna make or break this thing."

Carter wondered at that moment if she and Lynn could actually be good friends. *An honest to goodness male friend*, she thought. *That would be something*. She could tell he was trying to be kind to her. Sitting quietly while she thought. She liked the feeling his thoughtfulness gave her – like he was already caring for her. His eyes were warm and open, like two arms wanting to heal her pain with a hug.

Lynn is a good man, Carter. You can trust him.

Thirty:
Get Over Yourself

The fall sky had turned dark. Our shoes were off and we had gotten up and sat down in various positions around the room several times over the course of the afternoon. My mother's confessions to me about Antonio and their love had caused me mixed feelings. I knew she was crazy. I just didn't think she was crazy in love.

Lynn stood behind his desk and placed his fists onto the leather mat that sat in the center. He gently rapped his knuckles on the soft pad as he spoke in a deliberate rhythm.

"Benjamin, it's our opinion that we don't run from these facts," Lynn said. "We embrace the facts. 'Embrace the bad facts' – isn't that what they say?" The saying panged my memory back to moot court.

"Yes, that is what they say," I agreed.

"Now, she can hire me, and I can lay on the honey and beg and plead and tell them this elaborate story of your mother and try and turn these sour grapes into wine, but it's different if it comes from you."

My mother added, "Not just because you're my son – and believe me, we've discussed the obvious benefits that accompany that choice, but because – especially after today – I'm convinced there's no one who can bring in the real Carter Scales like you. No one."

"But I'm arguably a victim in your story," I said. This time my voice was sympathetic to her.

"Exactly!" Lynn cried.

I thought about his excitement. "I've got to stop

making your arguments for you," I told him.

He smiled. "I've been in the business a long time."

I let their words sink in, not knowing why.

In any defense case, no matter how strong, when the victim comes forward and begs for mercy, the judge always listens. I wasn't the victim in my mother's blowjob story; the public was. But I was a victim in her life story, which was the story they would focus on.

My mother and I looked at each other for a very long time. My mother dotted her wet eyes with a tissue. When mine started to tear, I did the same. Lynn sensed she and I weren't going to speak and took the moment to tie it all up with a nice little bow.

"That... silly *woman* sittin' right there is my man," Lynn said, gesturing toward Bobby-Charles. "There's no one else. Never was. Never will be." We both looked up. "My father and I lived in silence for decades over that man until the day he died," he continued. "I stood over his grave until I was the last person there. As the sun went down, I grabbed a shovel and started to bury his ass myself. With every mound of dirt, I cursed him and raged against him. For almost an hour, every word I never said to him when he was alive came out of my mouth and fell into that hole and lay right on top of his dead body until I filled that hole with eight feet of dirt. Eight feet of things never said – eight feet of feelings unspoken – a lifetime of being too afraid to speak what was right in my heart."

"I got blisters, and my skin cracked. The poison was coming out of me. But you know, it wasn't good enough. I got to say all the things I wanted to say, but I didn't get to see it on his face. I'll never see the realization on his face that his son, even though he was gay, was still a man."

We were all watching him. Bobby-Charles was doing everything he could not to run to Lynn and hug him or kiss him softly.

"I wanted him to feel the pain in his realization that he had been cruel, maybe even understand me or feel proud of me. He had been so angry, but maybe, just maybe, we could have laughed about it or... hugged. I don't know." Lynn snapped out of his reverie and looked at us. "This silence between you is going to kill you... both of you. It doesn't matter who's right – even though one of you is surely right and one of you is surely wrong. It just doesn't matter. It's being understood that matters. It's setting the boundaries that you need to be comfortable with each other, then respecting those boundaries. You get to be you," he said, looking at me. "And you get to be you," he said, looking at my mother. "Just accept it, goddamn it, and get over it. Use this opportunity to fix what's been broken between you. It's just life! It's just emotion. It doesn't have to be any way you don't want it to be. Just turn it around."

I knew he was right. Although my mind tried to push it away, I'd been feeling it for years. I looked away from Lynn and at my mother, who looked truly ashamed. I looked back at Lynn. "I have to warn you," I said, suddenly feeling very self-conscious. "What I do well with juries I lack with judges. The last hearing I had in front of a panel of judges..." I paused and shook my head. "It was not my best work."

My mother's face showed concern. Lynn tried to think of something positive to say but my slouched shoulders were doing all the talking.

"Do you care to explain," my mother asked.

"You wanna order some food?" I said.

Bobby-Charles sat straight up: "Chinese – already ordered – on the way!"

"So..." I began.

Thirty-One:
Flighty Casey

Three years earlier, the College of Law had held the annual Moot Court Competition for first-year law students before three members of the Supreme Court of Georgia.

The first unlucky bastard who had to appear before the three-judge panel was Tanner Harbin. His blood drained from his face as he gripped the sides of the oak podium in the large auditorium at the College of Law in Atlanta. He cleared his throat, straining to free the phlegm. Tanner's shoulders slumped forward and he rested on his elbows. He looked worn out.

Sweat beads collected in the grove above his quivering upper lip. He lowered his mouth to a small microphone and put his lips right up against the black sponge. "I'm sorry," Tanner said, his voice at an awkwardly full volume. "Could you repeat the question?"

A panel of three Georgia Supreme Court justices glowered down at him, straining to understand how Tanner didn't understand the question. They looked sideways at one another, confused.

To the left and right of the podium sat two tables. On the left, two male law students snickered at one another and fist bumped each other under the table. On the right, Tanner's partner, a young woman sitting in a skirt suit, tried to maintain an air of confidence and gave Tanner an encouraging look.

The auditorium behind him seated an audience of 300 who shifted nervously in their seats, as Tanner's meltdown unfolded. In the front two rows, ten additional law school first-year students and their advisors watched, all dressed immaculately in suits and dresses, watched as their chances of success increased every second Tanner couldn't get his shit together.

There was an eleventh student, a young woman with red hair, poised perfectly in her typical shell-shaped bun. Her name was Paige and she was the girl from my first class. She sat next to an empty chair.

Justice Dickerson, the one woman on the panel, nodded at her fellow justices and then looked back to Tanner. She smiled warmly and lowered her reading glasses.

"Take a deep breath, Mr. Harbin. It's always hardest to be the one that goes first."

Justice Dickerson then looked out into the auditorium and addressed the audience.

"Right, folks? Shall we encourage Mr. Harbin?"

She began to clap her hands, looking for similar camaraderie from the rest of the room. They joined in, as did the other Justices.

Tanner nodded and wiped the sweat from his brow and lip. He felt himself trying to stand a little taller. His partner stood up and patted him on the shoulder. *Poor bastard.*

"Everyone, just take a deep breath. It's going to be a long day. Myself and the other Justices are not here to trick you or bait you." She paused. "No, that's not true. We are." The room laughed. "*But*, you've had a year of it already and you've risen to the top. Isn't that what law school is supposed to be all about? The grind, we used to call it. But we sincerely want you to have the greatest chance at success today. Okay, everyone?"

Tanner nodded at the Justices. The audience clapped again.

"Now, Mr. Harbin, I will repeat the question: please state *YOUR NAME* for the record and your *PARTNER'S NAME*, the law school you are from, and tell us what side you are taking."

Tanner nodded. Take two.

"I am, um, Tanner Harbin the 3rd. And my partner is Shelly Atkins-"

Shelly nodded excitedly that Tanner had actually remembered her name.

"We are from Tennessee College of Law and, um, I – um, I mean, we, um, represent the state – the, uh, the District Attorney's office."

"Very good, Mr. Harbin. Ms. Atkins. Thank you both for being here. You may begin, Mr. Harbin."

Paige looked around nervously and over her shoulder at the entrance to the auditorium. Where, oh, where was her partner? She pulled out her cell phone and moved from her seat and out of a side door.

The paralyzing winter of my first semester of law school had thankfully come to a crashing conclusion. Spring was upon me and I felt the warmth of second chances. It was easy to feel this way, standing at home plate of the softball field at Piedmont Park in Midtown Atlanta.

It was a cloudless day in April – 72 degrees – with a slight breeze that skipped across the green grass. I twisted my hands around the grip of a wooden baseball bat and eyed the cute blonde girl on the other team who was about to underhand pitch me the ball. *God, what a great day.*

My first year was nearly at an end. My biggest achievement was not the home run I was about to crush past the outfield, although nothing felt quite as good; it was my ascension onto the Law Review. Law Review remained the most highly sought after extra-curricular activity in law school. For the top firms seeking the brightest students from across the country, Law Review was mandatory.

I didn't have the grades for automatic acceptance. Only the top ten students out of our class of 240 had such a dubious honor. The other ten spaces on Law Review were reserved for students who could demonstrate excellent writing abilities. This was called "writing on" to Law Review and could be accomplished simply by demonstrating one's worthiness without the whole ruthless grade battle.

My teammates that day were the other members of the Law Review. Surprisingly, they were mostly a group of shameless partiers who acted as if law school was a second chance at college, but with better loans. We all joined a city-based social softball organization that hyped itself as a "drinking club with a softball problem."

"Here-now, here-now, Koh-tex! Let's get it, Koh-tex!" one of my teammates shouted with an undulating voice, as if he were an auctioneer.

We spent some of the law review budget money on uniforms. Shhh, don't tell. Matching white pants with blue pinstripes and a navy jersey. My jersey, of course, featured the word "Kotex" between my shoulder blades.

I had actually embraced my nickname, especially at times like this. I would never wear it out "in the real world," but the jersey was a conversation starter with women. It required no effort on my part and always involved the subject of a woman's vagina. It really couldn't get any better. Most guys I knew had to endure at least a few dates before broaching that particular issue. My mother would have abhorred the name. Anything that delineated women from men irritated her – especially anything that she had to "cope" with as a woman.

I tipped my hat down low over my eyebrows and wagged my bat across the plate. The pitcher put down her beer and lofted the ball. I rotated the bat around until it connected squarely with the larger softball. I think I heard the sound barrier break.

My team rose up and cheered. I ran the bases, but not before winking at the pitcher. I couldn't tell if she almost threw up or if she just belched a little.

Home runs were greeted with great fanfare. You got a beer poured on your head when you arrived at home plate. The cold Budweiser drained down my head and the back of my neck. I married that with chugging a beer of my own.

My law review buddies loved that I was able to retain my drinking ability, even after being out of college for so long – the joke being that I, Kotex, was *super* absorbent.

I also had managed, in my second semester of the first year, to outperform every other student in the first year law student's school-wide Moot Court Competition. Moot was the practice of making oral argument to a judge who would ask questions about your position and try to unnerve you with questions and facts that tested your theory and argument. By being the winner of the school-wide moot competition, I was automatically invited to participate in the intercollegiate moot court competition team, which was comprised of two members, Paige and me. Professor Peters, our former criminal procedure teacher, was our advisor.

The competition was scheduled to happen on this very day... next week. Or so I thought. I hit two more home runs that day – and had two more beers poured on my head - before I got the "memo."

Inside the auditorium, in the wings of the stage's side curtain, Professor "Ichabod Crane" Peters was standing next to Paige. She was wearing another skirt suit – one that fit her a little better and showed off her curves. I often teased her that she should do something, anything to accentuate her hips. I reminded her daily that I didn't have any sexual attraction to her whatsoever but I hoped that someone would.

It was now 1 p.m. The competition had been going since 9:00 a.m. Four of the six teams from colleges around the southeast had performed their argument. The fifth was about to conclude and then we would be up.

Ichabod looked Paige in the eyes and demanded to know my whereabouts. "I mean, did you call him?"

"Yes, Professor, I called him," Paige said.

"What about texting? Did you text him?"

"Several times."

"Email?"

"This morning and just a minute ago."

"What about that... that other thing?"

"What are you referring to?" Paige asked.

"Like, post on Myspace?"

"Myspace? No, not exactly."

"I don't know! Jesus! Smoke signals? Bird calls. Get in your car and go by his house?" Ichabod paced. "How does an entire adult go missing this day and age?"

I burst through the solid oak front doors of the law school and drove my cleats into the white marble tile floor. Clumps of mud sloughed off with each heel strike and slipped and scuffed the floor as I made my way. I lifted my knees like I was running through a field of tires, trying to high step my way into a faster speed and greater control. My baseball bat stuck out of the top of my backpack.

"Make a hole!" I yelled. "Make a hole!"

The clicking sound of the hard plastic echoed with my words as I ran past two-dozen students browsing at their lockers, pulling books for their next classes.

I rounded a corner and hooked my hand on a staircase railing, pulling myself up to the first step and then the next. The stairs were filled with students ascending and descending. I passed a few male students in suits. A few girls wore skirt suits and carried briefcases.

"Make a hole – make a hole!" I said as I ran up and past them.

"Kotex!" I heard one guy say.

"No time!" I yelled back.

"Koh-tex!" the guy yelled after me again. "Give 'em hell!"

I stuck my fist in the air as a sign of solidarity and thanks. Hell was the appropriate word, as it clearly defined my current predicament.

Paige and I had developed a nice platonic relationship. She was a cat person and a mother, which meant she had great patience. I seemed to be the one person who could get under her skin. I loved to irritate her. We often took opposite sides on an issue. Although she was a pacifist at heart, I imagined she was going to advocate for violence against me for being so late. And the uniform. She would be mortified.

I crested the top of the stairs and met Marvin, the law school's head janitor, who was busy mopping a portion of the floor. I knew Marvin from the law school's library entrance, as I met him there most days. I was usually the first to enter and last to leave.

I leaped to avoid the wet floor but when I landed, the black plastic cleats drew black lines amidst dried mud crumbles.

Marvin threw his arms in the air. "Kotex!" he yelled.

"Sorry, Marv!" I yelled back to him. "I'll – I'll come back and clean it up later!"

Marvin waved me off and sighed at the additional work.

"Juris Doctor, hell," Marvin grumbled under his breath. "Just damn dumb, if you ask me."

I was now in the back halls of the professors' office suites, making haste towards a back exit and stairwell. Many of the professors were turning off their lights and closing their doors. This was a good sign, as they were coming to watch Paige and me, which meant that I wasn't totally screwed. A few men swung their suit jackets on.

One teacher was donning pearl earrings. She was the

First Year Legal Writing course instructor, Sheila Gaines. Professor Gaines was in her late 50's but had the flowing blonde hair of a twenty-four-year-old swimsuit model.

"Don't you let me down today," she admonished.

"I won't!" I yelled.

"Where's your *suit*?" she called after me. But I was already into the stairwell, descending to a back courtyard exit. I looked decent in my white baseball pants but not next to other lawyers dressed in suits with Versace ties.

I hopped a bench, cut across a small grass garden, hopped another bench and punched through the entrance to our illustrious auditorium.

Two finely tuned first-year law students from the University of Florida sat at a table, at attention. They were perfectly groomed as Ken and Barbie might be and had the tans of the Malibu collection. They nodded professionally at the panel of three justices who then looked from them to Paige and me.

Paige sat upright and tried her best news anchor smile. The oldest justice of the three, a man named Winterthur Adams who was eighty-one years old, nodded at Paige politely but then scowled at my attire.

"What were you thinking?" Paige whispered sharply. "Clearly nothing," she said, answering her own question.

"Don't worry," I said.

"You smell like a bar," she said.

"I wasn't at a bar, I was-"

"Dicking around – I can see that. Do you know that I

have 4-inch high heels and eye shadow on for God's sake? And you show up-"

"Team Georgia State," the Justice said. "You may proceed with your opening presentation."

"Hey, I'm here," I told her. "You need to chill out. I got this."

"You have no appreciation for this moment, do you?"

"Lighten up, Paige." Her eyes widened at the suggestion.

"This is just about you, isn't it? And you've 'got it covered,' yeah?"

"I'm here, aren't I?"

"Are you? Are you *really*?"

"My god you're uptight."

"This is not just about you turning your 'I don't give a shit' button on and off as you see fit. I'm actually trying to impress these people."

"Fine. Jesus! I just remembered it wrong, okay, it's no big deal-"

"No big deal? Are you nuts?"

Justice Adams raised his gavel and rapped his desk. *BOOM, BOOM, BOOM!* We stopped suddenly.

"Are we all done, counselors?" The question was condescending. I felt like a three-year-old.

"So sorry, Your Honors," Paige said.

"Yes, sorry. We're ready," I said. *Classic me.* Never wanting any public attention. This was choking on a nut for sure, or just a nut choking. "Please proceed," Justice Adams said with great effort.

I rose from my chair as professionally as possible and slid the chair back into the desk. "Yes, Your Honor." I started walking but the sound of my hard plastic cleats *clicked* as I made my way up to the podium. The audience giggled and then audibly gasped as I turned my back to them and faced the panel.

I could hear Professor Gaines chortle. The starch-white letters of the word Kotex glowed under the bright yellow spotlights. My head wanted to drop but I held it up with all my might. The team across from us snickered to each other. I thought I heard the sound of Professor Peters throwing up somewhere backstage.

Of course, I was already nervous, even though I had prepared with Paige for weeks. There wasn't a question I didn't already know the answer to.

I always dressed the part, meaning up, not down, because I truly believed in the adage, the better you look, the better you feel. A waft of dried beer rose to my nose. At that moment, I saw myself through the eyes of the entire room. They didn't disagree. I looked like a goddamn fool. *Fuck*, I thought, suddenly conscience-stricken.

I took a deep breath. *Why am I such a fuck-up?*

I drank with the law review gang and flirted with as many women as I could, but Paige was my only true friend in law school. She and I spent a considerable amount of time studying together, which often led to eating together and talking about our futures. She had me figured out within an hour of our first study session.

"You are just like my son," she once told me.

"And by just like, you mean just like your five-year-old?" She replied with an emphatic yes.

I tried to turn that into a positive. "Is he, like, *really* smart for his age?"

Her eyes deadpanned at me. "No," she said.

Truthfully, the reason I couldn't feel Paige's anger was because I smothered it like every other uncomfortable moment I've ever experienced in my life.

I took the podium in my hands, after spreading out my cheat sheets, and looked over at Paige. She was conveying a smile of encouragement, albeit plastic, and hidden rage. I was here to try to show off. Paige was doing this for her son.

"May it please the Court," I began. I looked at Paige and tried to reassure her with a smile. She exhaled and closed her eyes. My heart hurt for a minute. I guess I kind of cared about her.

All said and done, my presentation was good. Solid. I was able to answer all their questions and after a few minutes forgot about the disappointment Paige and Professor Peters must have felt. My words were strong. I just pretended like our competition was being held on Halloween. Everyone wore costumes. Most people just weren't as creative as me.

The panel of three Justices allowed me to conclude my opening. Paige would be up and doing her rebuttal and closing on our team's behalf after Ken and Barbie got to make their presentation. The spotlight was about to be off me.

I thanked them for their time, gathered my papers and tried to quiet my cleats as I started back to my chair. Then old man Adams spoke up. His voice was salty and grave.

"Mr. Scales, off so soon?" he said. I froze mid-step like

a thief suddenly spotted while carrying off the goods. The audience giggled.

"No, sir," I said, taking my position back at the podium.

"There's a saying we have in the English language. Actually, I believe it's called a *metaphorical idiom*. You've probably heard it before – the saying, I mean. It's about an *elephant* and its unacknowledged existence *in the room*." He exaggerated the word room like only old men with old vocal cords could do.

The audience laughed louder. I chuckled too.

I acknowledged his acknowledgment. "Might you be referring to the fact that I wore the *wrong* pinstripe suit this afternoon?" I asked.

The audience laughed harder.

"Mmm," he said. "Interesting choice."

"I apologize to Your Honors and my co-counsel." Paige suddenly sat up, ready to receive the apology about the injurious conduct so insultingly put upon her. "I was-"

Justice Adams held up his finger and waggled it back and forth – "Uh, uh, uh," he said. "Don't go there," he said and then looked at the other Justices. "Isn't that what they say these days? 'Don't go there, dude,' or something or other?" The other Justices nodded. Justice Dickerson giggled a little.

The audience felt giddy at the exchange and laughed again.

Justice Adams was having a little fun at my expense.

"As I see it, Mr. Scales, you have an opportunity. It's no time for a confession."

"Never let a mistake go to waste, I always say,"

Justice Dickerson added. The judges all seemed to be in agreement, although, I wasn't sure about what.

"Have you heard the saying about the 'bad fact'?" Justice Adams asked.

I thought about the question. "I believe I have, Your Honor," I said.

"And?" he asked.

I could actually hear the audience get nervous for me. We were totally off script, something any moot performer abhorred. This was about preparation and sticking to one of half a dozen scripts just in case the Justices wanted to address any of the possible issues. I began to perspire. I looked at Paige. Her eyes looked giddy. Payback time.

"Well, uh – hmmm," I said. "Bad facts are, um, bad, of course." I felt myself slipping. "What I mean is that, in a legal case, bad facts exist. They are a part of the facts of every case and, as such, are totally unavoidable so you have to just accept it and deal with it and make it a part of your presentation because if you ignore it and fail to address it altogether, the other side will exploit it, use it against you and ultimately win." I took my first breath since beginning the long answer.

"Good," Justice Adams said. The other two judges nodded, in seeming approval of my answer.

"Would you agree that your attire today is a bad fact for you?"

"I would, Your Honor. I had prepared to wear a very nice suit and tie."

"Oh, but what fun would that be?" he asked, rhetorically. The audience hung on his every word and thought him undeniably charming. He was Johnny

Carson or Jay Leno for the first time in his life. This whole exercise may have even taken a year or two off his life.

He smiled at me. "Why don't you let us see how you embrace the *bad fact* in this situation, shall we, and make it relevant to your case and our exercise this afternoon? What do you say?"

I looked at Paige. She shrugged. I spotted Ichabod over in the wings of the side-stage curtain, breathing into a paper bag.

"You, uh, want me to, um, make it relevant to our case – meaning the issue of ineffective assistance of trial counsel?"

"Yes. Do your best – do we all agree? Is this okay with everyone? Audience members?" They all applauded, of course. "It is, after all, what distinguishes great attorneys from the rest, Mr. Scales," he said. "As the only elephant in the room, will you stand alone or will you simply join the rest of the *herrrd?*" He emphasized the word herd.

Someone shouted, suddenly. "Get 'em, Koh-tex!" My face paled. *You cannot be serious*, I thought.

Justice Adams wrapped his gavel gently on the wooden gavel plate. "Please, now, no outbursts," Justice Adams said. "We are thinking on the fly here."

The murmurs quieted. I felt my heart beating in my throat. I deserved this.

"Of course," I said and tried to stand more erect. I thought hard amidst the deafening silence of the auditorium and then began. "Your Honors, as I said earlier, the issue, in this case, is "ineffective assistance of counsel" which is about the *absence* of zealous advocacy at the trial by the trial lawyer." It was a fine opener and I meant to restate the issue, but it didn't address the added element of my attire. I continued anyway to build to the point I was furiously trying to figure out.

"Our client has been convicted and is serving a life sentence. The question for Your Honors is: did the trial lawyer do enough? Did he *think* of everything he could and *do* everything he could to help the client at trial?"

I looked at Paige for her approval thus far. She looked as if she had just emerged from a carnivorous jungle, ready to die. I wondered whether or not what I was saying made any difference. I needed to get to the point.

"In order for an attorney to be effective in their representation of their client, they must not only understand the facts of the case but also their client's *role* in the case. Because criminal cases are about life mistakes. Zealousness is not just about being vociferous. It's about understanding what the fight is about."

What is the fight about? I asked myself. *Did I even know anymore? Forget her,* I thought some more. Instead, I paused to consider this screwed up, yet awesome moment – a moment where I was totally fucked, yet actively thinking on my feet with three of the justices of the Supreme Court. That was pretty cool. I continued.

"The fight can be about innocence and sometimes it's about convincing a jury that the state did not meet their burden. And to do that, a lawyer must-"

I stopped on the thought. *That's it. They must understand. And what better way to understand anyone than to-*

I interrupted my own thought and said, "-put

themselves in the shoes of their client."

My mother's face flashed again before my eyes. This was her specialty – making arguments to a panel of judges, thinking on her feet. What a rush! And here I was, doing it too, just as she had done for so many years.

I said it again. "You have to put yourself in the shoes of the person you need to understand. I looked at each Justice. Their faces remained stone. Not quite the response I had hoped for. I continued.

"But it's not just that. The attorney must *adorn the colors* of the cause. They must understand the nuances of the *game*." That got a murmur from the audience. I felt somewhat bolstered. I suddenly had an idea.

I left the podium and retrieved my backpack that held my glove, hat, and bat from beneath the table and brought it back to the podium. I removed the bat and adorned the hat. The audience commented and chuckled a bit. *He's doubling down*, they thought.

I looked at Paige and said, "Fear has no place on the courtroom *playing field*." I was trying to gain some momentum. "A trial attorney must stand at the *plate*, out in front of our clients who watch us meet the controversy from the stands..." I paused and gripped the bat and placed it over my shoulder, as if I was going to drill the microphone with it. "With *bat in hand*, we defend our clients against those bad facts and pound everyone that breaks across the plate, right out of the *park*!" The audience cat-called and hooted. Ichabod appeared to be a bit hopeful.

"In order to satisfy the Constitution's guarantee of zealous and effective representation, an attorney must be the cleated foot placed firmly on the courtroom's *slippery field*... no matter who is throwing the curve ball, witness, prosecutor or judge." And with the word "judge," I pointed the bat right at Justice Adams. Professor Peters nearly fainted.

Justice Adams gave me a favorable touché nod in return. The audience shouted and hooted. This was no longer a hoity law school Moot Court Competition. It was a raucous rap battle between the jester and the Court.

I saw my conclusion and took it. "We do it for the benefit of our clients, at the risk of looking like total fools," I said, sincerely. "Because, if it helps to make your point and to save your client, including wearing an outfit like this, then, Your Honors, Justice *requires* it." I lowered my bat and bowed my head.

The audience erupted into cheers and applause. The Justices all nodded at one another and clapped along with the audience.

"Mr. Scales, you may take your seat."

"Thank *God*," I said, and promptly sat down next to Paige.

"You are such a dildo," she said to me.

"Well aware," I said. "Well aware." I put my hand on hers. "Paige?" I asked. "I'm really sorry."

For a moment, I thought she blushed.

Despite the fact that I was able to turn things around somewhat, I was still bruised from the experience. I vowed to never put myself in the position again of having to face a panel of judges.

Thirty-Two:
Boom, Bang, Blip

At Lynn's office, the air had somewhat gone out of the room. The idea that I would appear in front of three Justices of the Georgia Supreme Court wearing a baseball uniform was staggering to my mother and Lynn. The point was not moot.

"I don't know," Bobby-Charles said. "It sounds like you did really well." He shrugged and looked to the group for approval.

My mother was speechless. I looked to Lynn.

"Any thoughts?" I asked him.

"Do you have a nice suit?" he said, suggesting I might at least *look* like I know what I'm doing.

"Navy pinstripe," I said.

My mother smiled. "There's nothing more attractive than a Jewish man in a navy pinstripe suit."

"I remembered you said that once, so..." I told her. She touched her heart for a second.

"Actually," she said, "I was only quoting-"

"Playboy magazine, I know."

"That's right," she said.

We looked at each other for a minute and then chuckled. Lynn and Bobby-Charles watched us and smiled too.

I stood up and brushed my slacks straight and centered my belt buckle. "OK," I said. "I'll do it."

I lay in bed with Ayla that night and watched reruns

of *The Andy Griffith Show*. Old Sheriff Taylor and his dopey deputy solving the oft times simple problems of the town that some felt were just too complicated. Of course, they weren't. I loved the whistling in the theme song at the beginning. I wished my life was that way sometimes.

I turned my attention to Ayla and watched her sleep. I found that when stress hit, I looked to those things in my life I could truly connect with – that I could truly count on. Making the decision to represent my mother was beyond stressful. I needed Ayla more than ever.

The fact that Ayla and I nearly didn't happen was something I held as a reminder of how truly lucky I was to share my life with her. For a while, I felt like baggage to her. She was a bright star and I was an imploding one – a black hole that could suck the life out of her and send her reeling to some other dimension, at least that's how I felt.

The day we met started as a day that had only one purpose: survival.

It was a day for coffee. I had been up since five a.m., as I had been for nearly a month, studying for the bar exam. With the smoking ashes of the past three years of law school behind me, not to mention a few relationships as well, I had one last set of hot coals to cross. I walked into the neighborhood Starbucks and threw my backpack onto a purple velvet chair. It still had one of my note cards from the night before stuck in the seat cushion. *The privileges of being the last out and the first in*, I thought. I held it up and read the question to myself.

"Tortious interference with business practices," I answered. I flipped the card over and smiled.

Just then the barista came out. "Back for another round?"

"Make it a double!" I said.

"Grande-double-espresso-three-Splenda-latte!" he shouted to his assistant.

The hot beverage was literally eye opening. The first five minutes were always the same in that I needed a few minutes to sift through the nightmarish dreams I had had over the course of the night. Most were of faceless people from the future trying to stab me with Aboriginal spears or of masked home-invaders shooting me with assault rifles. I could actually feel the hot lead go into my skin. I frequently woke with sweat-soaked shirts. The few remaining minutes were spent on my mother.

I was officially off the radar with her. I was a low flying aircraft. And she really didn't seem to care. There were some calls, but they were brief. She touted how busy she was and I did the same. Each call ended with my promise to eventually get into medical school and her promise that she knew a different senator in each state who could write a letter for me. It was a ridiculous charade.

"I got it covered," I told her. My voice squeaked out a whisper when I spoke of going to medical school. The lies were choking me.

There was another side to the story of my emotions, though. Because of law school, I had gained tremendous insight into my mother and her past. I found myself truly understanding her for the first time in my life. My thoughts of her came and went, returning every day – a constant tide, eroding away at my decision to break away from her, pulling at the strands of my decision, unraveling the faith I had in the choice I had made to free myself from her tyranny. I began to acknowledge that my newfound understanding of her could lead to forgiveness. I couldn't imagine what that would mean or how it would come to fruition. At present, I found myself pleased at withholding it from her.

After a few hours at Starbucks, I had gone through hundreds of note cards on every legal subject imaginable – torts, contracts, wills and estates, tax law, criminal, property, family law, evidence, constitutional law, civil procedure – all amid Bar test preparation books, empty coffee cups and a crumb-filled plate. I had made great progress and was nearly through my thousandth card, when I was overwhelmed by the sound of muffled giggling from several seats away.

Two twenty-something girls sat with their heads pressed together like conjoined twins, staring at me out of the corners of their eyes. Despite their very different styles, they looked like two desserts. Both had glowing skin – one porcelain, the other tanned. Both were dressed in tight-fitting designer jeans, shoes with large gold designer emblems on the toes, and a multitude of accessories – glasses, handbags, etc. The one with bleach-blonde hair was more of a strawberry shortcake, and the other with jet-black hair looked like a double chocolate cheesecake with caramel accents and two double-D cookies on top.

Other than having the same immediate thoughts that most cavemen have about women – "yeah, I could do her" – I didn't think much of them, until the blonde girl pulled a tampon from her purse. How embarrassing for her, I thought, but then I realized I should be thinking how embarrassing for *me*. The brunette, who seemed to show some signs of maturity, grabbed the girl's hand and shoved it and the tampon back into her purse. The laughter grew into a squeal, at which time the brunette, sensing my embarrassment, rose from her chair and sat down next to me.

I gave her my official patronizing smile, as I had by that point endured three years of the same, and said, "Yes. It's me. Would you like me to autograph it?"

The girl looked shocked that I had picked up on what they were doing. With no answer, I looked over at the instigator. "Would you like me to sign your tampon?" I said, as I motioned my signature. "It'd be my pleasure."

The instigator got up to bring the tampon over, but her friend held her hand out to stop her. "No. Please," she told me. "Just ignore her." She turned back to her friend. "Stop," she said, as if she were using the Jedi mind trick on an approaching drunk, her eyes now a serious shade of green.

Her friend turned away and sat back down. "She's a moron," the brunette said.

"Agreed," I told her.

The beautiful stranger sat there, confident enough to just stare at me. Being around seven years her senior, I had the confidence to stare back. It was immediately thrilling. Our gazes were like public fornication.

I closed my book and set my cards aside. "And here I thought it was her who was the instigator." The girl spread a beautiful smile and shifted in her seat, suddenly a bit shy. I loved that I was finally confident with women.

"I'm Ben," I said.

"Ayla," she said in her soft British accent.

Later that week, I remember waiting outside her midtown townhouse for her to appear from the second-floor balcony. She poked her head out and gave me the finger – the one to tell me that she'd be right down. Ayla was from London. She immigrated in 1985 with her parents who were doctors. She was very bold and friends with a girl who went to law school with me.

Ayla was many things. She was extremely friendly and opened up to me about every little thing she wanted out of life. I could tell instantly that she was creative and had a zest for simply existing. She also got easily excited about things, which made her very cute. And she was very direct, which didn't scare me off. I had my wit and a wry approach to life, which made her laugh loudly. I liked the way she made me feel like a comedy star. Our attraction was intermolecular.

We sat in a garden area of a local restaurant that was named after the matriarch of the family, who had a knack for blending flavors. Her spirit was alive in Ayla and me, as our dish began to simmer.

"I've been told I'm a very shrewd businesswoman." She said this as if it were her very favorite fact about herself.

I grinned. "I don't doubt it."

"I'm serious."

"I'm prepared to buy whatever you're selling."

She didn't believe I was convinced. "I'm a ball buster," she said, her British accent accentuating the word "ball," as she flexed her dainty bicep and smiled cutely.

"Oh, obviously."

"I do kickboxing."

"Like, in a ring?"

"In a room," she said.

"Oh, an aerobics class," I corrected her.

"Well, it's with gloves and kicking and what not."

"Like fan kicks and jazz hands?"

"No, smartass. I kick a bag with my foot, and we grab it like it was a thug and knee it in the bloody balls."

"Ow."

"Absolutely." She gave me a cheeky smile. I felt myself stare a bit too deeply and smile a bit too broadly. When I didn't look away, it made my heart pound. Ayla was mesmerizing. We started inspecting each other in a very thrilling way. Quietly looking at each other's features. We didn't look away even when the waiter approached. He didn't seem to notice.

"Good evening, folks. I'll just launch right into Chef's late-summer menu, which features a variety of..." Finally, he stopped, realizing our attention wasn't on the specials and thus not on him. He tried to start again, but Ayla and I were too captivated by each other. "So, as I was saying, Chef has prepared a delicious menu of... chili-rubbed Ding Dongs, fatback, and pickled pork knuckle." One of his coworkers overheard his resuscitation of the menu and shot him a look of horror. The waiter shrugged him off and nodded back to us. "We've paired that with a pine-nut fart cake and a prune based–"

I interrupted. "I'm sorry, did you just say, 'pine-nut fart cake?'"

He smiled. "How about I get the lovebirds some water, and we'll try this again?"

Lovebirds? I thought. *Is that what's going on here?* The thought gave me a bit of indigestion.

After dinner and half a dozen frozen margaritas, Ayla and I walked along the oak-lined sidewalks of the college's historic district, our fingers locked like yin and yang. We were buzzing from the alcohol and the connection we felt before it took hold. It was like we had been doing it for our entire lives, without ever wanting to let go. The word future kept popping into my head.

"I probably should tell you a little more about me, since you were kind enough to share with me your love of havoc."

"Figurative havoc," she corrected.

"Right, well, I'm not a freak or anything – and I don't want this to undermine the awe that you're currently feeling about me, but..." I paused and couldn't find the right words.

"What?" she begged.

"It's pretty hard to say."

"It must be. Better come out with it then. We don't want to waste any more time."

"I love..." I began to say, as I looked her in her eyes and watched carefully. She raised a brow, and I continued, "...astrology."

"Oh, my," she said.

"Yes, which means I'm well aware that I'm a Leo, which means I'm very proud and I like to... win?"

"Was that a question?" she asked.

"Maybe."

"Continue," she said.

"Being a Leo also means I like to get back scratches,

and I will pout if you don't give it to me and I'll be annoyingly sad and morose until I get my way, because I need to be the center of attention." I let out a big sigh. "There. I said it."

Ayla contemplated all of this while crossing her arms. "Well," she said, "I'm very smart."

"You mentioned that already.

"No, I didn't. I said I was shrewd, which brings me to my next point, which is that I'm usually right about everything, and even if I know you're right, I'll tell you you're wrong, because I too love to win."

"Hmm," I said. I thought for a moment. *Just go for it.*

"I'm a total narcissist," I said.

"I don't believe it. I think you're probably quite thoughtful but also a bit vain, which makes you feel like a narcissist, but in fact, you are too kindhearted to be one."

I contemplated this. "I think you might be right."

"Of course, I am," she said.

"Yes, right."

"I also love astrology," she said, "which means I know that I'm a Virgo and that I like my things just so and I like to plan everything so that it'll be perfect, which can be quite annoying to a person who likes to fly totally by the seat of their pants and eat salsa out of the jar and not from a dish specified for salsa."

"Oh, you *are* a tricky one," I said. "Well, if this is a negotiation, which I believe it is, then I will eat your salsa out of a bowl, although it is better out of the refrigerated jar – you should just note that for future samplings – but I will continue to reach into the bag of chips and lay the chips across my chest and on my shirt and eat them in a very messy fashion."

"I will wash your messy shirt and try to remove said chip crumbs but explain to you that you will extend the life of your fabric if you don't place greasy items directly on it. And I will *consider* your offer of cold salsa in the refrigerated jar."

I thought about that for a minute. "I have a bit of a tummy," I said.

"My ass is a bit full."

"I have very strong pectorals."

"And my breasts are quite lovely."

I tried not to stare. "Um, I like Pixar movies," I said.

"Well, you're a man-child, now, aren't you?"

"You're very observant."

"I have an American Girl doll named Samantha that I just can't give up."

"Which makes you a woman-child."

"I believe it does."

"I used to wear Spider-Man underwear, but now I wear tighty whities."

"I wear thongs."

My heart thudded with excitement. "Now you're just being cruel."

"But I also wear granny panties when I don't feel well."

"Well, we're all entitled to a little comfort."

Ayla nodded. "Consider the following," she continued. "I will take you shopping and totally change your entire wardrobe. Slowly at first, so you won't quite notice, but then it will be obvious that you no longer have any polos, plaids, or flannels."

I thought about it. "I don't have any of those now."

"I think I love you," she blurted.

I smiled but then it faded quickly. Ayla noticed it and corrected herself. "I don't really love you. I hardly know you."

"Of course. That would be ridiculous."

We both thought about it and then smiled at each other again. "While you're feeling a bit prematurely amorous-" Ayla's eyes lit up, horrified that I was calling her out on her premature Freudian ejaculation. "I'm just sayin'," I defended with a smile. I continued to tease her. "You might want to consider that I..." I paused and thought carefully about this admission. "What the hell... I have hair on my back." She cocked her head and raised her eyebrows, ready to play again. I reached for the buttons on my shirt. "I'll show you right now if you don't believe me."

She held out her hand. "Not necessary. I'll take you at your word." She thought carefully. "I don't care. My father has hair on his back, and I quite like it."

"Impossible!"

"It's true!"

"You like it, really?"

"Yes, but you should know that I also have hair on my back."

I smiled, and so did she. "Well, perhaps we can electrolocize together," I suggested.

"Yes, perhaps we can," she said. "Anything else you'd like me to know about you?"

I thought about it for a second and wondered if I should release my next thought and, if so, how I should put it.

"I'd like to... hang out... with you again," I said carefully. I knew the words hang out wouldn't play as well as she might have hoped but I was applying the brakes purposefully.

"I'll think about it," she said, coyly. It was the perfect answer.

We held each other in a stare, her greens around me and my browns around her. Slowly, we moved closer into a real embrace and kissed each other deeply. From high above the earth, as viewed through a satellite infrared lens, our kiss caused a downtown Atlanta city block to explode red.

While our first date was better than any I had ever experienced, I wasn't ready. Following that magical kiss goodnight, I chose not to call Ayla again. I went radio silence. In fact, now that I think about it, I may have put her in that black hole after all.

At the same time, I met Ayla, I ran into the girl I had met two years earlier at the softball game – the game that I was playing right before my presentation for Moot Court with Paige. She was the cute pitcher who attended another law school.

She had a lovely string of rose tattoos that corkscrewed their way down from her left breast, around the small of her back and to the crest of her right hip. Delicious really. It was the only thing currently that kept my mind off my mother and me away from the one girl I thought I might actually fall in love with and try to have a future with. I think her name was Bethany. She went by B.J.

B.J. was a daddy's girl and talked incessantly about her father who was a wealthy tort lawyer from Savannah, Georgia. He did trucking cases. His website showed him standing next to an eighteen-wheeler that had been hoisted up on a rope like a giant great white after being caught. His catch phrase was "Go Big or Go Home."

B.J. had wispy bleach blonde hair and a small frame. She was the furthest thing from Ayla. She drove a pickup truck and wore a baseball cap. I laughed at her a lot over the course of the three weeks we had been screwing each other. She was very entertaining.

I still thought about Ayla every day. The longer I didn't call, the worse I felt. She called me a few days after our date and left me a message about going to the Comic Con show in Atlanta, something about us not wearing shirts and going as werewolves. I just couldn't bring myself to call her back. I thought it was for the best. I mean, was I really commitment material?

Laying in bed with a hot blonde should have been fun, plain and simple. I felt more like a stalled sailboat on a windless ocean. I refused to accept that my mother had anything to do with it.

Most importantly, I was about to take the bar. I had graduated law school on my fucking own. Was becoming my own attorney. Doing it my way. Getting laid when and how I wanted and with whom I wanted was a bonus. I was finally going places, wasn't I?

B.J. was not the only one. Paige, my law school best friend, was a similar cautionary tale. Following our victory at the Moot Competition, we had gone back to her apartment.

She peeked through the front door first and saw her mother asleep on the couch. The lights were low but not low enough to see that her décor was similar to the way Paige dressed. Basic, simple, no frills. There were a few buckets of kid's toys and a small kids table by the dining room table.

We walked through the front door and closed it quietly due to the fact that Paige's son was also sleeping on the couch. Paige carried her high heels in one hand and held my hand with the other and led me around the couch and toward the darker part of the room that led to her bedroom. I noticed a few sheets of coloring paper on the kid's table, along with markers and half a glass of chocolate milk.

Well, this is different, I thought.

Paige was a bit tipsy. She swaggered a bit more than normal as she walked. It caused me to watch her backside and see that I had underestimated it. She had let her long red hair down and the tips of her hair tickled the small of her back like wispy fingers. It was hypnotizing.

We stopped at her bedroom door. She kept her back to me as she lowered her shoes quietly to the floor and let go of my fingers. I looked behind me to make sure the kid and her mother were still asleep. I felt like an intruder.

Paige reached behind her and unzipped the back of her gray skirt. The sound turned me back towards her. I saw the top of her red lace panties and felt myself get more aroused. She shimmied out of the skirt and turned around to face me. Her confidence vanished as soon as she looked me in the eyes. I recognized the sign of weakness and knew how to bring her back around. For a second I considered stopping but then realized that this is what she wanted, too. I was not there to disappoint.

I lifted her face in my hand. My fingers touched her fallen hair. It all felt somewhat assuming and I was sure I was not meant to know the side of her face or to touch the pink underbelly of the hair she normally kept hidden away in her formidable bun. But there I was pulling her porcelain jaw to my mouth.

We welcomed the moment, our eyes closed and we found each other's tongues. Her confidence returned, as did mine. I leaned into her body and reached my hand down to her ass. We moved backward into her room. I closed the door behind me and let the security of the darkness lead us deeper into temptation.

The next day and all the days after that were awkward because I assumed that Paige wanted more than a fun night of uncomplicated sex and that I had to make a decision to be all in or not. Even if she were to tell me that she just wanted to keep fucking, I knew me and I knew I would have a hard time accepting it. Paige became another complication of my relationship with my mother.

I had real feelings for Ayla. When I thought about her, my heart began to beat faster. But like any singularly functioning object, once it got started, it became hard to tell whether the pangs I felt in my heart were for Ayla or from my guilt and separation from my mother. My being somewhat fucked-up about it all was very confusing, to say the least.

I wondered if my future had a career and a great love as part of it, which could include the role of a husband and father. I daydreamed about Ayla and began to feel excitement, even an understanding of and a longing for the love that I would one day have for my children. I even felt the hope I would have as a parent about their loving me in return. But there was always the family I already had – the one I was trying to leave back in the woods. There was also the belief that I was too screwed up to have a normal anything.

After two months of daily studying and worrying and throwing up and using B.J., I took the bar exam twenty pounds lighter. It was a miserable experience. I invested in a bit of witchcraft and lit a candle to help me pass. I packed cold anger chicken for lunch. My one piece of comfort was the piece of paper Ayla had given me at Starbucks with her name and number on it.

The exam took place in June, just as the summer was heating up in Atlanta. It was given in a series of airplane hangars that had been converted into a conference center. The conference center was filled with about three thousand people. Only 1,500 of them were recent graduates from the four law schools in the state. This meant half of the test takers had failed the exam previously. The guy next to me had failed the exam twice. The girl behind me, three times. I couldn't help but think I would fail too.

The results wouldn't be out for four months. October. I found work at a divorce firm, which confirmed my decision never to practice divorce law. My parents' divorce was painful enough. Having to make money off of the hate-filled dissolution of marriage was no dream. It was going to be criminal defense and only criminal defense.

My birthday hit right on time, as usual. Thirty-two

this year. B.J.'s birthday was also in August. She was set to come over and trade birthday presents.

B.J. knew our relationship was just about "hanging out." It was something we promised each other. Essentially it meant we were not going to fall in love. We were just going to have fun. I couldn't help but feeling like I loved Ayla, though. After one date. *Jesus, was that even possible?*

B.J. came over with a giant bag filled with presents. Like something straight off Santa Claus's sleigh, she hoisted the bag over her shoulder and dropped it into the center of the room. She looked at my face, said "Happy Birthday, Baby," and kissed my lips. Then, she pulled back. "What's wrong?" she asked. She was right to inquire. My face was stoic.

"We need to talk," I told her. Her smile vanished. "Oh," she said. "Let's sit down," I said. She did, slowly, like she was about to be told her father was dead.

I knew what I had to do. I realized one morning that screwing a lot of women didn't make you a man. Truthfully, inside, I still felt like a child. I didn't want to hurt B.J. I loathed emotional confrontation. I felt my voice slip away and I was right back to that moment in my childhood kitchen where I could barely whisper to my mother that I wanted her to leave me alone.

Jesus, I am supposed to be a fucking lawyer. How can I be a criminal defense trial attorney and save people from wrongfully being convicted if I can't even talk to a girl and tell her-

"I met someone," I began. I cleared my throat and tried to speak up. "I didn't mean to – actually, it was before we met, and I didn't think it was anything, but now I do."

"What?" she asked. Her mouth hung open, her eyes squinted. "What do you mean?"

"I'm sorry, B.J., I don't know how else to tell you other than to tell you. I met another girl a while back before I met you. We went on a date and... it's something I'd like to pursue."

"A date? Like one date?"

"Yes."

"And you want to *pursue* it?" The tone of her question underscored my stupid choice of wording.

"I'm sorry. I'm just trying to be honest with you."

"I mean, we're supposed to exchange birthday presents. I'm here with all these presents."

"I know. And I'm sorry. I just felt like I had to tell you now. You're a great-"

"Don't. Just fucking don't," she said. She had her own Just Don't degree.

B.J. stood up and walked toward the door. She paused and picked up the bag and fell back to the wall. Her eyes started to tear. "I love you, Benjamin," she said.

Her words punched me in the gut. All I could do was take a deep breath and exhale. She shook her head at me and slowly walked out. It was a funeral march.

I stood there paralyzed for a full minute until I heard pounding steps. It was B.J. and she was coming back up the stairs to my apartment. Suddenly, the door kicked open and she entered, holding a gift-wrapped box on her shoulder.

"Well, I'm certainly not going to drink this shit!" she said and threw the box at me. It thudded to the floor with great weight. As it turned out, one of my presents was a twelve-pack of Milwaukee's Best Light Beer – a classic and cheap favorite of mine. A twelve-pack cost about four dollars and it tasted just a bit outside of delicious. It always packed a good punch. We called it The Beast.

She slammed the door on her way out. I picked up the beer, grabbed one to drink and refrigerated the rest. No use in wasting it.

I vowed to return the Starbucks travel mug I bought her and sat down in contemplation of my next move. I didn't know if Ayla would even remember me or would want to talk to me but I had to do something for the first time that I had never done. I had to open a door I had all but nailed shut.

I waited for Ayla outside her three-story townhouse with a bouquet of flowers and a box of chocolates. I also had several other items: a horoscope book: Leo man – Virgo woman; a jar of salsa; a nice big plastic bowl to keep chips neat; a hair trimmer and a pack of Fruit of the Loom "granny panties" - comfortable ladies underwear. I sat on a bench next to all my items. I felt a bit like Forrest Gump.

Around 6:30 p.m., she pulled into her garage and came out to the bench at the bottom of her ascending front door staircase. She looked from me to the items.

"What, no Snuggie?" she quipped. I was expecting her first words to be filled with anger. Maybe she just didn't care. "I'm not interested, if that's what you're selling." *There's the anger*, I thought.

"Actually, I just came here hoping to tell you the truth," I said.

"Haven't made up your mind yet?" she responded.

"No, I have. I mean, I came here hoping that you would talk to me, if that's okay. If you have a minute."

She turned back toward her garage and stood there for a minute. She then turned to me with her arms crossed. I tried to settle on the right words. I couldn't. "I've got about seven things I want to say all at the same time."

She shifted in her stance and looked a bit irritated. "I'm not looking for anything, Ben," she said – her voice devoid of emotion. "I mean, it was one date that was, like, over a month ago, okay? I mean, certainly, I thought you would call and I called you and you didn't even respond, so, whatever, okay? I mean, an apology would be nice-"

"I'm sorry," I said. "I'm very, very sorry."

"Okay," she said.

"Ayla, I tried really hard to close this door, 'cause it's just easier for me to do that – that's my thing. It's not an excuse, it's just me, apparently."

She didn't say anything.

"And we laughed a lot and you're very funny and smart and that really goes with me – and beautiful, by the way, so beautiful. But I think I'm also kind of a more serious person, I guess. I don't know, I'm trying to figure it out."

I felt defeated and undesirable by my own words. I sat down. I had to. I was starting to get light-headed.

"Going through something, perhaps?" she asked.

"Yeah, kind of a... quarter life crisis kind-of-a-thing," I agreed. She nodded. "I don't know," I said, trying to think of the right words again. "I really want-"

"To see me again – yes, that's obvious," she said.

Ayla looked at me sitting there like a damn fool. The risk I took. The things I brought with me that told her I had never forgotten our conversation months ago. She didn't turn to leave but shifted her stance, which suggested she wasn't going anywhere just yet. I felt my heart finally beat again.

"Is it weird to tell you I... missed you?" I asked.

As my words mixed with my obvious attempt to win her back, she honestly considered my question. Then she shook her head, no. "You really hurt my feelings," she said.

I stood up. "I am very sorry. You didn't deserve that." The fact that she didn't tell me to fuck off or the fact that she didn't give me one of her karate fan kicks was a good sign. I found my strength and stepped closer to her. We inspected each other's eyes. She smiled at me. As soon as she did, I stepped in to hug her. She reached out to me and we held each other's bodies in a deep embrace. We put our noses against one another's necks and found memory and warmth.

She pulled away. "So I guess you're hoping that I'm still single," she said. "Because certainly, you must have *assumed* I'd be taken."

"Oh, was I not clear about that?"

"Well, I assumed by the collection of gifts that you-"

I interrupted. "Oh, yeah. Those," I said, chuckling. "No, unfortunately, I *am* actually seeing someone *else*." She gave me a wry look. "Oh, how embarrassing for you!" I told her. "You thought these items were for you! Oh, god, no, I'm just on my way home from the grocery store!"

She smiled at me. "You are a such a *sonofabitch*," she said.

I accepted her comment wholly. "I know."

We moved in together two months later. Ayla was the best thing that ever happened to me. I nearly lost her. I would try to be that best thing for her, too.

Thirty-Three:
A Time To Cry

With Ayla back in my life, I was prepared to endure my anxiety about passing the bar exam. I had been laying in bed with knotted bed sheets in my hands and between my knees and having impossible dreams for several weeks as the bar results were approaching.

On the morning the results posted online, I woke up at four a.m. I rolled out of bed and went to the kitchen.

I heard a thud at the front door. I got up from the kitchen table and opened it to find *The Wall Street Journal*. I unfolded the paper and poured through the opinion page. Before I knew it, the coffee machine chimed, and the pump gurgled water up and into the grinds. It was five a.m.

Moccasin slippers scuffed the floor, and Ayla and her shapeless nightgown entered like a spirit. She rubbed the back of my neck and kissed my ear.

"Oh, baby, you shouldn't have," she said, as she moved to the coffee pot, taking the pot out mid fill.

"I think the timer was set," I said, not taking credit for it.

"I was teasing you."

"Oh. You're always on, huh?"

Ayla flashed a goofy smile through her knotted hair and pillow face and held up her mug. It read, "Morning People Suck."

"What's wrong?" she asked, as she filled her cup.

"Aside from the bar results coming out this morning?"

"Ah, yes, the *other woman* in our relationship."

"Don't joke. I've almost thrown up three times this morning."

Ayla sat down at the table Indian-style in her seat like a little girl ready for a story.

"There's also the issue of starting a job and the whole shitty-son thing. Just another day, I guess."

Ayla rubbed her eyes and stretched. "Excuse me. You said she was a bad mother. What can she expect?" Ayla always got right to the heart of it, even when she was half asleep.

"I also said starting a job and waiting on bar results."

"Baby, you were born to be a litigator."

"Trial attorney," I corrected her.

"Whatever."

"There's a difference," I cranked.

"I know, litigators *push paper*. Trial attorneys enter the ring and *do battle!*" she mocked.

"Damn right!" I said.

"Whatever, Jet Li Van Damme. It's not the issue." Ayla drank deeply, which opened her eyes fully. She was now officially engaged. "You feel guilty. You're a guilt collector. You don't think I hear you and those deep sighs?" She demonstrated by exaggerating long exhales followed by "ohs" and "my mother this" and "my mother that." I hooked on the other thing she said.

"Guilt collector?" I asked.

"Precisely – like the bone collector, but you collect guilt."

Now I had to have a cup. "I don't collect guilt like the bones of dead people. That's totally creepy."

"Well, in this case," she said, "it's not creepy. It's sad."

I crossed my eyes. "Some people just collect guilt and you are one of those people. It's okay, you just need to stop."

I got defensive. "You know, if she were actually in my life, she would never have allowed this relationship to take place."

"How so? I'm perfect."

"True, but so was Lindsey McIntyre."

"*Unforgivable*," she cried.

"I'm serious. When I was in the third grade, she accused Lindsey McIntyre of being a whore."

"To her face?" Ayla cried.

"Well, no, but to me. Lindsey had these cute blonde pigtails and big halo-sized ears." Ayla giggled. "It's not funny. She was my broad-eared little angel," I told her.

"No, it's just I'm glad to see your taste in women has improved," she said laughing.

"She was nine and I was in love with her!" I cried.

"Yes, of course, my darling. I understand completely."

"I mean *whore* is something you yell before slapping a prostitute or something!" I said.

"Like when you're golfing?" she asked, sincerely. "Whoooore!" she yelled, lengthening the vowel.

I blinked at her, dryly. "That's fore."

She thought about it. "Oh, my. All these years," she said.

"Been there done that," I told her.

"I'll need to make a few apology phone calls today," she noted.

"Um, excuse me. Crisis here," I said.

"Yes, of course, continue on," Ayla said.

"I remember one time when I was about thirteen, after Judgie and my grandmother died. She came to me in the middle of the night like some princess that had been cast away in a dark tower, and fell to my bedside in a heap of tears, which woke me up from a dead sleep. She cradled me in her hands and stroked my neck and ears as if I were a little mouse she'd found in her dungeon corner. 'Don't ever leave me, okay?' she told me."

I visualized the moment as if it was happening again. "She made me promise."

"She was insecure, babe. It sounds like you were all she had."

"I was – you're right. I was everything to her." I suddenly remembered something else she said. "'You're the man in my life, now,' she told me," I said to Ayla. "Can you imagine that? Me – the *man* in her life."

Ayla saw the realization crystallize on my face. "That must have been an overwhelming amount of pressure for you," she said. She could see she was right. "My god, babe, you still feel it."

I stopped. I couldn't talk.

Ayla put her fingers through my hair and held the back of my head. My throat thickened. Ayla recognized it immediately, although she had never seen me cry.

"You were so little then," she said.

The lines on my forehead pushed down, dipping my brow and pinching the corners of my eyes, which caused the tears to fall.

"Oh, baby," she said. "I didn't mean to tease you."

I shook my head to pull the tears back in. "I never even told her I was accepted to law school. It's going to kill her to find out."

Ayla thought about this for a minute. "How is that even possible?"

"I don't know. We've spoken on the phone a few times. I kept it short. I just kept saying, 'I'm fine. Things are fine. I'm so busy.' She went along with it."

"Didn't she think you were going to med school?"

I nodded.

"You never told her you changed your mind?"

I shook my head.

"For... let's see..." She started to count. "For four years of undergraduate and five years after undergraduate and three years of..." She stopped and had her number. "For twelve years?" she exclaimed. "You kept this a secret for twelve years?" Ayla smiled, so much that she began to laugh.

"Well, for ten – no, nine years, because I changed my mind my senior year. So, not for twelve years – for nine years."

"Well, la-dee-dah!"

I sighed. "I know."

"How is that even possible?" she repeated, but with added perplexity and volume.

"I don't know," I said, and then chuckled. "When you put it like that it seems pretty fucking retarded!"

"If I had known this about you on our first date, I'd have shagged you for sure." I raised my brows. She grabbed my face and kissed it. "You're a mess, and I love it!"

I fell into a blathering sob. "I'm a *total* mess!"

We sat at the kitchen table for a while and hugged. I

placed my head in her lap, under the edge of the table, and she stroked me like a child. Time dissolved into simple touches that carried my thoughts into feelings of deep romantic love. All was washed away.

At seven a.m. my watch beeped. The alarm clock in our bedroom played music, and an old-fashioned egg timer on the kitchen counter dinged with metallic rhythm. I jumped up and slammed my head against the kitchen table, as I had forgotten where I was sleeping.

"It's time!" I said. I tried running out of the kitchen but slipped on my socks and fell to the floor. Ayla let out a scream and a cackle and tried to pick me up.

"Jesus, Benjamin. Calm down!"

"It's time. It's time. Oh, God! Oh, God!" It was all I could say, as I slowed my feet and shuffled out of the kitchen and into the living room.

Ayla went around to silence the egg timer and the alarm clock. My watch alarm beeped incessantly, but I didn't have enough wherewithal to think to push the damn button to shut it off.

Ayla found me on the couch with my laptop. She calmly sat next to me and put her arm around my shoulder and looked at the screen. I tried to type but was having problems.

"I can't type the fucking website name!"

Ayla looked at my watch. *Beep. Beep. Beep.* "Are you gonna turn that thing off?" I ignored her and kept trying to type the website name.

"Double-u, double-u, double-u, dot, Georgia bar, dot com." I messed it up again. "Fuck, I can't do it! I'm too nervous!"

"Here, let me."

"No, I got it!" I took a deep breath and chicken-pecked the keyboard with one finger.

Beep. Beep. Beep. The watch alarmed on like an emergency room monitor.

"Okay, I got it." I scanned the page for the link to the list of names. "Results, results, results."

"There!" Ayla said, pointing to the screen. I clicked it. The list populated. "Scroll down."

"I am scrolling down."

"No, it's farther down. Keep going to the S's."

"I know how to spell my last name!"

"Just click on the 'S' right here!"

"I will!" I clicked the "S." We both started saying it: "Scales, Scales, Scales."

The watch kept beeping.

"Sable, Sadler, Sales," she read out loud.

Beep. Beep. Beep.

"Just give me the damn watch," she said, as she grabbed my arm and pulled it off. She hurled it into the other room and closed the door. Finally, silence. "Sbaro," I said, reading as fast as I could. She rejoined me.

"The pizza guy?" she asked.

"Scales!" she said.

"Where?!"

"Right, *fucking* here, baby!" Her eyes were unbridled. I found the word on the screen and read the full name: Benjamin Scales.

"Scales," I said, almost in a whisper. Then I turned to

her, my eyes as wide as hers. "Mo-fuckin' Scales!" I said. New tears started to form, but these were better. "I passed!" I screamed.

"You passed!" she screamed back.

I started to dance – a ridiculous African-type dance that made me look like a damn fool. I chanted with each fist thrust and hip bump. "I passed the bar! I passed the bar!"

Ayla joined me. The two fools.

We stopped our foolishness just long enough to sincerely respect the awesomeness of the moment.

"Congratulations, counselor," she told me. "You are now a prestigious member of the bar."

It was certain. With Ayla, I could do anything - including representing my mother as it turned out.

Thirty-Four:
Blood Is Thicker

There was something daring about a middle-aged woman who didn't wear pantyhose with her suit skirt – the kind of woman who still had fabulous legs and could let her bare skin glisten and stretch across the bones without the muting effect of a flesh-toned screen. It spoke volumes about her self-confidence and lack of insecurity. It also said the woman was uncouth and a whore and just the type to suck a prisoner's dick.

"Ugh," my mother groaned as she kicked off her skirt and slid on a pair of black pants and black socks. That day's ethics hearing was a funeral and nothing less. Black was more appropriate anyway.

Two months prior, my mother had prepared a five-page outline, which she handed to me the day after I made the decision to help her. It wasn't relatable at all. It was written like a resume, highlighting her scholastic and professional achievements.

I thought about Lynn's words and the unique strategy, which seemingly fell into his lap – the great son lawyer – and ripped it up without further consideration. I didn't like being told what to do or even being the recipient of a suggestion when it came to me being the designer of my fate. If I was the architect – whom they assured me I was – I worked by the settings of my own instruments, and I created because of my own need to create. I had the final say.

My mother had asked me to help her, and I was willing to do that. I devised a plan and schedule to get to the heart of the matter. I was going to treat my mother like any other client.

"I need you to understand something very important," I told her. "I am your lawyer. And what that means is that you and I have a very special relationship." My mother pretended that I was talking about our personal relationship.

"I know we do," she said. "I'm your mother."

"I meant, as your lawyer," I corrected.

"Oh."

"You need to tell me everything. And I am instructing you to tell me everything. Every juicy, salacious, illegal, unethical detail of your life with the mob, Judgie, me. Everything." Her eyebrows raised.

She sat back in her chair. "We're going to be here for awhile."

"I expect so. I also expect that I will have many questions. And I expect that you will answer every single one of them, honestly, without anger, without judgment or tirade toward me."

"I promise," she said.

We met several days a week for four weeks. By the end, I knew everything, including that she knew I had been in law school and that she used the nipple incident as a way to pressure me to tell her the truth. Every time I got mad at her about that I saw my own lies staring back at me.

"We are quite the pair of aces," she said.

"Or ace *holes*," I said smiling.

After our sessions together, I tried to type up an argument – a palatable defense in mitigation of my mother's absurd behavior. I sat in my office and stared back and forth between my computer screen and my numerous degrees and certifications into the various state and federal courts around Northern and Middle Georgia, which promised that I was an excellent lawyer. They all seemed as worthless as the fake gold seals that stuck to the ten-cent paper.

Late one night, a few days before the hearing, my secretary, Pat's secretary, Rosie, entered my office. She was an older, heavy-set black woman with large curls in her hair and a raspy smoker's voice that dragged like a wire brush on a snare drum. She loved to pamper me.

"Baby, Pat said you might need some help. You want me to proof your latest draft before I go?" she asked.

"No." I rubbed my eyes. Stretching, I said, "I give up. I give up. I can't even believe I'm doing this."

"She needs your help," she responded.

"My help," I snorted, somewhat in disbelief. "I'm blank."

"You'll get it right. You've had tougher clients than this."

"They weren't my mother, though." Rosie put her hands on her hips and shifted her weight onto her heels.

"Is she a good person?"

"Depends."

"Oh, no, sir," she said. "It's either a yes or a no."

"Yes, she is, but she's also a real bitch and a pain in the ass," I said.

Rosie smiled. "You say it like that's a bad thing."

"What, being a bitch?"

"Yeah. What's wrong with that?" Rosie's question

irritated me. I didn't feel like having a philosophical discussion.

"Try being raised by one, and then you'll know," I told her.

"Not only was I raised by one, I am one."

"Trust me, Rosie. You're not a bitch."

"Trust me. I am."

"What's your excuse?" I asked her.

"I don't feel like it needs an excuse. I'm a survivor. Always have been – always will be. If a man or anyone else thinks that makes me a bitch, then fine. Put it in the dictionary and slap my picture right next to it." I laughed. "I have no doubt your mother had it tough as a woman in this business," she continued.

"I agree," I said.

"Had to have been tough."

"Yeah."

"She came up, did she not?" she asked.

"Yes, she did."

"She rose up."

"Yeah."

"Fought and survived," she said.

"Yeah," I said.

"Well, then?"

"I'm just having some difficulty swallowing it all."

"It's not your pill to swallow, baby. Think about it this way. My husband's in the army. The army isn't the real world. It's different, okay? My husband, after all these years, came up through the ranks – got beat up, hazed, talked down to, twenty pushups here and there, get me my coffee, make my bed, carry my pack. Finally made it as a major, okay? Now it's respect. 'Yes, sir' – the whole thing. Now, do you know what they call a *woman* who comes up and makes it the same way?"

"What?"

"A major."

"You mean they don't have a rank for bitch?" I asked.

"Honey, if they did, I'd have on a uniform." I laughed. "My point is: in the real world, there is no orderly decoration of achievement. It's only survival."

I nodded understanding. We fell silent for a minute.

"You might also appreciate that you're finally getting to know your mother. And maybe even a little bit about yourself."

Hers was a good point. *More than a little bit, actually*, I thought. I trailed off into thought again. It wasn't fair that my mother had come so far and hadn't gotten the stripes for it. I knew it all along too but chose to get bogged down in my emotion and personal experience.

I flipped a switch and made a new choice and decided to embrace another very real side of my personality – a side of me that had been with me from the beginning of time – the robot side of my personality that cared without rhyme or reason.

When it came to following the path of right, I realized that – even though I was an ever-changing, asymmetrical being without a blueprint, roadmap, or even a guiding star – I always followed a similar path of right versus wrong. The way I tried to be a man for my mom when grandma died, the way I stayed with her for all those years, the way I stepped in for my friends, the way I tried to save lives at the hospital. I was flawed but

I was...

"Did you hear what I said," Rosie asked, interrupting my thoughts. My blank face said no. "You're a good person, Benjamin Scales," she said.

I took the compliment, partially, at least. "I'm trying, Rosie. I'm really trying."

Patrick once told me a story about a guy in high school who had ridiculed him because he was black; he had beaten him up, called him a "nigger" – modern-day hate crime kind of stuff. Patrick was the first and only black kid to desegregate his high school the first year they opened the door in the 1960's. His mother was an activist who had lobbied for the rights of blacks and eventually succeeded.

"I need you to go to that high school," she told Patrick.

"I don't want to go, momma," he said.

"But I need you to," she urged him.

Decades later, after Patrick became an attorney, the kid's father called Patrick and told him that his old classmate had been arrested on serious aggravated assault charges. The father told Patrick that his son had read about Patrick in the newspaper and wanted Patrick to represent him; he didn't want anyone else. Patrick looked at the man who had raised the racist who used to beat him – and who was most likely a racist himself – and told him it would be an honor to try to save his son from prison.

"Everyone deserves a defense," Patrick told me. My mother fit that mold, too. I was going to be the one to try to save her.

I compartmentalized her in my mind and treated her

like every other client – the stalker, the drunk driver, the con artist, the murderer – and thought of her as a story. In the world of criminal defense, everyone has a story – a part of his or her life that starts with some duration of innocence, no matter how short-lived, and then some learned behavior, which usually adds nitrous oxide to the next critical phases in the person's underworld life, which is action and then consequence. "Action and consequence" were where prosecutors and punishers focused their attention. Action and consequence were usually where I came into the picture. As a defense attorney, I had to combat against my client's *actions* to try to lessen the *consequences*.

To do so, I focused on their stories – the innocence, the good, the mitigating evidence that filled their lives just before they leaped into action and ruined them. My mother had such a story which, for the first time in my life, I was able to remove myself from. *I don't always have to be my mother's son*, I told myself. I can be Benjamin Scales, Carter Scales' attorney.

As her attorney, I would tell it the best way I knew how. When I really thought about it, my mother had quite a story. I'd tell the committee about all the nuances in her life that had molded her and made her into a single mother and then an attorney and the type of person who had risked everything to become the best she could possibly be – the best in her career, in her reputation, as a mother – and then how had she risked it all for one moment of connection with a man she loved with all her heart and soul. That was her story.

The night before the hearing, my mother sat awake in her bed, leaving messages on my cell phone and on my home voicemail. Thirty missed calls. Seven messages –

from sincere pleas ("Please call me so we can catch up" and "I really need to talk to you"), to faux excitement over our pending adventure together ("Let's discuss where we'll meet, or should we ride together?"), to being outright pissed ("You're not returning my calls is very unprofessional!").

She had thoughts and wanted to strategize – really just to tell me what she thought was best. Her last message was twofold, in that first she gave up on trying to get me to call her and simply said, "I hope you're ready." Second, she apparently also noticed the word choice in my home voicemail message, where I said, "*We* can't come to the phone right now. But *we'll* call you back."

"And Benjamin, who is 'we'?"

I didn't return the calls. My mother was facing disbarment, which meant everything fell on my shoulders in the form of my presentation to the committee. I was Atlas, holding her up, and this was no time to shrug. I needed alone time. I wasn't thinking about what her stress was doing to her; I was thinking about what losing her license would do to her. It would kill her. And even though I wouldn't be pulling the trigger, I didn't want to be the one holding the gun over her bloody body. I also didn't want to get into my relationship with Ayla at that moment.

I went to bed at one thirty a.m. but didn't fall sleep until about four thirty and then got up at six.

Thirty-Five:
A Prick, A Bandaid, And Time To Heal

The morning of the hearing, my mother entered the building in her all black outfit and found me standing outside the hearing room, already with a cup of coffee in my hand.

"I called you all night," she said, clearly pained. "I have no idea what's going on. And who's that woman? Please tell me you're not married and I missed that, too."

"I'm not married. You didn't miss anything. There is more, but one thing at a time. Today is about your license, okay?"

"I want to know what's going on. You can't just keep me in the—"

"First of all," I interrupted her, "calm down and focus, all right?" She didn't like my patronizing tone but took a deep breath anyway. "Now," I instructed her, "I'm the lawyer today, okay?"

"And I'm the client," she said.

"A nonpaying client, I might add, which means I *really* don't want to hear what you have to say." She stood there surprised. "Second, I know you. I know all about you – so stop trying to tell me all about you. I don't need you to tell me about you, okay? Third, I know you haven't forgotten the little meeting we had in Lynn's office where you both blindsided me with this task. You recall how I handled that? With poise and charm, if I recall correctly, so stop worrying and just sit down and be quiet, and let me just do my job."

"Your job?" she asked.

"Well, what would you call it?"

"This requires sensitivity, Benjamin," she insisted.

"Would you please sit down?" I said, now totally irritated. She finally sat down, annoyed at the insistence on my face that she do it and shut up at the same time. I turned back to my thoughts and walked deliberately down the hall. My heels clacked on the floor, echoing in the empty hallway. I liked the sound of my heavy, purposeful steps. The rhythm relaxed me.

My mother fidgeted on the bench and crossed and uncrossed her legs a thousand times until she got a shock. Buddy Griff strode around the corner. He was dressed for action – leather suit with matching bolo tie – and had combed out his handlebar mustache for added bad-ass-ness. In the light of the courthouse, you could see the pockmarks on his cheeks and forehead, which made his rather lovely blonde George Michael-esque quaff of hair *rather* pointless. She froze and felt no escape. He walked right up to her without changing his pace and stopped with his crotch biscuit just a foot from her face, which made her nervous and nauseous.

"You might have been able to buy your way outta my jail, little lady, but I'm gonna mount your fucking license to practice law over my fireplace like a goddamn boar's head." My mother couldn't speak. She was afraid to see him there and even more so at his *ballsy* confrontation. I overheard it from down the hall and quickly positioned myself between Griff's groin and my client's face.

"You must be Mr. Griff," I said.

"Yeah, and who are you?" he said with total disdain. *Prosecutors can be such pricks.*

"I'm her lawyer. We spoke on the phone."

"Her son, you mean. You're her *son*," Griff said, a grimace growing beneath his evil eyes. "Well, this is just too perfect," he added, looking down at my mother.

"Why don't you take about four steps back, partner, and stop standing over my client like a goddamn pervert."

My mother snorted a surprised chuckle.

"I don't appreciate the way you're talking to–"

"I don't give a flying fuck what you appreciate, asshole – especially from a guy who wraps himself in a leather sofa and cowboy boots." Griff looked down at his outfit and pulled on the leather straps of his tie. "Did you fly your steed out here too, you country prick?"

My mother laughed again.

"Wait just a goddamn minute," he said, stepping closer.

"I said, step back." My voice lunged forward like a two-hundred-and-fifty-pound bouncer. "You're lucky I don't fly out to California and report a bar complaint against you as the shithole prosecutor who arrested another lawyer for *not* breaking the goddamn law in the first place and sue your ass for false arrest, false imprisonment, and malicious prosecution, not to mention assault and battery for rubbing your stubby little fat fingers all over her tits and ass, you Western throwback. Now back away from my client!" I put my finger on his chest.

"If I ever see you trying to as much as talk to her again, I'll get one of my deputy friends to search your asshole for contraband and have you barred from the State of Georgia. You got me, you piece of shit?"

My mother was speechless. So was Buddy Griff,

although he tried. "You two are... Ya'll are just... so deserving of... Just a real piece of work ya'll are," he said.

"Get an education, moron," I told him.

Trying to pick up his nuts, Buddy Griff walked somberly down the hallway. I looked down at my mother, whose mouth was gaping. "You just sit back and enjoy the ride," I told her. Her eyes batted.

When the door opened and the deputy asked us to enter, I grabbed my mother's hand. "Let's do it," I told her.

She followed me in like a lost little lamb and sat at the table and chair where I indicated. Typical client. No matter how confident before a matter begins, clients always feel the pressure of the courtroom and judgment day. Feeling totally vulnerable, she placed her hands in her lap and slouched in her chair. When the bar committee members entered, she nearly passed out.

"All rise!" the bailiff announced. "Honorable Jimmy Braxton, Honorable Shep Darling, and Honorable Miles Lawson are now presiding."

One by one, the three members took their seats at the judges' bench, a large oak desk that elevated them about four feet off the floor. Like three vultures on a dead branch, each one perched, facing my mother, ready to dive down for carnage. I felt a thousand tacks up and down my spine, a bolt of lightning in my toes, and a dense heat that burned my neck and shoulders. It was the panel from hell. My mother grabbed my hand and nearly pierced it with her nails. I looked at her sharply and saw the thoughts racing across her face like the NASDAQ ticker. They were all men, all prosecutors – people who traditionally couldn't stand defense attorneys, and all around the same age as my mother.

"Be seated, and let's get started," Darling said. He sat in the middle and was the presiding member.

"Your Honors, if we could have just a minute."

"Make it brief."

"Yes, sir," I said. I turned to my mother. "Do you know these people?"

"Yes."

"Did you work cases against them?"

"Probably. We all started around the same time."

Although I lacked specifics, I imagined that all three "neutral-minded" members of the committee had – at one point or another – probably tried to touch my mother's ass or had their ass kicked by my mother. Her panicked look was confirmation enough.

I grabbed her hand. "Remember when you used to bring me along when I was a kid and how it made it all better?"

"Yeah," she said.

I held my arms open as if to say, *Ta-dah*. "Well, here we are again," I told her. "Team Scales." She looked at me and smiled. "Let's just hope they have daughters. You ready?" She nodded.

I stood and addressed the court. "Thank you, Your Honors."

"Let's proceed. Bailiff, sound for Mr. Griff," Darling said.

The bailiff exited the courtroom and called out Buddy's name. Within seconds, Buddy Griff entered and sat at a table next to ours. I smiled at him and said, "Good morning, Mr. Griff." He grumbled something under his breath.

The three committee members took out their paperwork, and my mother and I noticed they were looking at the charge. Buddy Griff got out his paperwork and made some notes on a tattered legal pad he'd pulled out of an old shoulder bag. He couldn't wait to make his charge against my mom in the open proceedings and talk about all the explicit behavior. He looked around the room, hoping members of the public would be there to listen. They were not, as this part of the proceedings was closed, unless the panel decided to publicize it.

I stood up. "If it pleases the panel, we do not contest the charges. We are prepared to admit the allegations and argue sentencing."

Buddy Griff looked up sharply. If we admitted the charges, his testimony wouldn't be necessary. He wouldn't get to talk about my mother kneeling on a dirty prison floor in her skirt and high heels and hitting her head on the table or trying to run. His trip had been a waste. It wasn't my idea to admit the charges. My mother and Lynn already agreed that's what she'd do. It was my idea, however, to save the announcement until the day of the hearing, after Mr. Griff had spent his county's money on a flight, hotel, and car and actually flew out here.

"Oh," said Darling. "Well, then, Mr. Griff, that means we won't need to hear from you today."

"But I've come all this way to be here, and I really think... this committee needs to... uh, hear, uh, what I've... uh, got to say about all this. Because this just... isn't something we as lawyers can tolerate... uh." He was struggling to make himself relevant. My bombshell had blown him straight out of his strategy and into unexpected waters. I just let the panel push him out to sea.

"We appreciate that Mr. Griff, but I'm sure as the district attorney out there you have more important things to handle than this – especially if Ms. Scales is prepared to admit the charge. Is that correct, Mr. Scales?" Darling asked me.

"That's correct, sir."

Griff stood there for a full minute, staring at the panel and then at me. Finally, he slammed his pad. "Well, goddamn it!" he said. "At least you could've had the common courtesy to call me and let me know 'fore I bought my ticket out here," he barked at me.

"You have my sincerest apologies, sir," I told him – my smiling lips meant as a middle finger. He smirked at me, dipping his chin and staring hard. "Well, to hell with all of ya!" he hollered. And with a forceful about-face, Buddy Griff left my mother's life.

Thirty-Six:
Mitigating Circumstances

The panel refocused. "Let's get to sentencing, unless you'd like to be heard first, Mr. Scales."

My nerves panged at Darling's suggestion that we would go silently without taking a stance.

"Uh, no, Your Honor. I'd like to be heard, please."

He continued, "All right, well, let's make a record. As you know, we're here to listen to the matter of the State Bar of Georgia file number 000979, wherein Carter Scales, licensed as of June 1977, has been reported for unethical client relations. Although you've been in the practice as long as you have, Ms. Scales, I must advise you that you face one of several disciplinary measures. It's my understanding that you wish to admit the allegation and thereby waive a formal hearing on the matter as to your guilt or innocence of the charge and just plead guilty. Is that correct, Ms. Scales?"

"That's correct," she said.

"Okay. The punishment is very broad and ranges from a verbal warning at these closed proceedings, to a sealed written warning, to a public reprimand by a Superior Court judge in open court, to temporary suspension of your license, to a permanent suspension of your license. Based on the nature, extent, and aggravating circumstance of the infraction, one of the particular punishments will become the ruling of this panel. At this time, the matter is closed and shall not become public unless it is the ruling of this panel that this matter be made public as part of your punishment. Do you understand?"

"I do," she said.

"Mr. Scales, whenever you're ready." Darling smiled, but it was short-lived and without any flair – a courtesy really. I knew they'd play hardball with me. I certainly didn't expect an audience seated for entertainment, but I also didn't expect these three curmudgeons. Either way, as a criminal defense attorney, I was used to finding ways out of very dark spaces. Sometimes, though, just because I found a way didn't mean others would follow me.

The real payoff would come in their decision. That's how we'd know what they thought about my presentation and my mother. I could tell my mother was still terrified. She had been wringing her hands since she sat down. Her knuckles were white. Pulling the curtain back to reveal this embarrassing event in front of a panel of men was a humiliation cherry on top of a very cold and runny sundae.

I walked to the podium without any paperwork and began. "What does it take for a woman who has successfully practiced law for nearly thirty years – a woman who built her career on grit and tenacity at a time when women were still expected to be housewives, a woman who overcame decades of sexual harassment and deriding misconduct from our most beloved and decorated state officials... present company excluded, I'm sure – to risk all her accomplishments and go barreling headfirst into a career-ending suicide?" I looked to each panel member for the answer, and when they didn't give it, I gave it to them myself. "Love," I said. "Simply, love."

"My client and I are not here to contest this matter. She did it. She planned to meet Antonio De Silva at his home, the prison – the place where he lived, bathed, ate, and slept – and planned to use her status as an attorney to get a private room where they could be alone. She planned to perform oral sex – to his surprise, which she did until she was caught. She had never done this before, never had planned to do it before. She never talked about it with him, never asked him to do anything to make it happen – to pay off the guard or guarantee added privacy. She just did it. And she admits it freely. And now she's embarrassed. Devastated. Humiliated. And she's also ashamed and disgusted with her deceit – as a person, as a mother, and most importantly as a lawyer.

"I've put those three things in that order for a reason – although I'm sure she'd argue with me that my words 'most importantly' should precede the word 'mother,' but I beg to differ, and I'm the one acting as the lawyer today, so I get to be right." I smiled, trying to infect them with my personality. It hit them flat, like a pie in the face. "As you all know, Ms. Scales is my mother. But I'm not here today as her son. Although I support her as her son, I'm here as her lawyer. I do have to be honest, though, and tell you that much of what I have to say to you today I say because I learned it as her son. So, while you may have thought this charge to be very *personal*, I can assure you that things are about to get much, much more personal.

"You see, love caused her to do what she did, and that's all nice and fine, and you all as the panel members can write that down on your pad and say, 'Okay, then, she did it for love,' and make your ruling, but you're missing the juice, the pulp, the heart of the matter that's wrapped tightly beneath the exterior. Because the heart of the matter is what she was willing to give up to do that act – because if you understand what she was willing to give up, then you'll understand how profound it was for her to do it in the first place." I put my hand on her shoulder. "I ask for your indulgence," I said to the three panel members.

"Please," Darling said.

"The first thing I remember about my mother, as a lawyer, was that I was her very first secretary. I was six or seven and was quickly taught how to answer the phones at home when the collect calls from prison came in. You know, business was business, and she was trying to get off the ground and needed as much help as she could get. It didn't matter that I was her kid or that I sounded like a kid on the phone. She never wanted to hide from the fact that she was a single mom and an attorney. We sort of learned it together – mother and son.

As her secretary and confidant, I learned the system with her, including the business of greeting other professionals. And for the longest time, I was confused about the greeting system in the professional world. I went to court with her often and sat in prosecutors' offices and judges' chambers and picked up rather quickly the difference between how men greeted each other and how men greeted my mother. Men shook each other's hands. My mother tried, but they seemed to prefer patting her ass."

The panel looked up from their notes, and I continued with my planned attention-grabber. "I don't know if any of you have daughters, but how would you like it if I walked up to your daughter and smacked her on the butt?" I let the question hang with no answer from the panel. "I'm sure you'd want her to steer clear of me, but my mother couldn't steer clear of men in the professional world. She had to deal with those prosecutors and judges on that level. Had to. No choice. So that's what she did – she dealt with it. Her child depended on it. Her career depended on it."

"It's an intense thing we do, the practice of law. As prosecutors – as you all have experienced – you have the support of the state and dozens of other similarly minded comrades. Carter Scales didn't have the support of anyone, including the legal community. She had to fight, to commit herself to a level of passion that kept her going, because every fight became a personal one – with everyone."

I continued on from there and built my story of sexual harassment as I'd imagined I'd say it from the moment I took the case. My line about a judge who mistook her as a hooker raised a few eyebrows.

I moved on to my mom's successes and how she had gotten into the federal system. The Mafia and complicated conspiracy and racketeering cases where dozens of men all acted in concert together to break the law. Kicking the government's ass. And I told them about her commitment to her clients. Forget Antonio De Silva – she had thirty years' worth of clients for whom she would lay down across the tracks and take on a steaming locomotive. I spoke about how she cherished being the one who could step in during the most trying times of these people's lives and solve the problem. She wasn't just a sledgehammer; she was a surgeon, skillfully removing cancers so these individuals could function again and have a second chance at life. And she did it twenty-four hours a day.

"She was always on," I told the panel. "Which meant

that other things in her life came in second place, including her relationships outside of her profession, which... included me. Clients came first; they always came first. But that's how it had to be, not just because they were paying the bills but because their problems were bigger than mine, really. Their families were always on the phone, calling... stopping by the office, waiting for her. Pleading with her. Begging with her. Stealing her attention. It made her life's work seem worthwhile, because she saw the effect her work had on their lives. It was proof that she was the lawyer she wanted to be. It was also proof that she wasn't much of a mother anymore. She was a provider, sure; a safety net, yes; but when her clients called, she went and sacrificed arguably the most important relationship in her life – for her profession. With so much scrutiny from the men in her profession weighing her down in an attempt to drown her out, she had to push herself harder and harder just to keep her head above water. She became a lawyer at all times, at all costs, which drove a wedge between us – a small one at first, but then as time went on and I realized her emotional abandonment, I began to feel differently about her."

"It wasn't just that she was busy. Rather, she became a product of her oppressive environment, which made her – quite frankly – a bitch." The panel members sat up straight and looked to my mother for confirmation that she had heard it, too. Her one raised eyebrow indicated that she had. I continued, unaffected by my choice of words. "Her promise and commitment to her career – like a blood oath with her clients – to become the best lawyer, the most studied lawyer, the most perfect lawyer, made her just that. And I hated her for it."

I looked down at my mother and saw that for a moment she had forgotten all about the panel. Her face was open and receiving like the sea after a storm and still under dark clouds. The panel saw the searching look on her face, too. They noticed her emotion.

"That's when her life really changed, because that's when I left. I said goodbye to her and went off to college. I didn't call. I didn't look back – even when her doctor told her she had pancreatic cancer and that she had four months to live."

Out of the corner of my eye, I saw her watching me with a look of surprise that I knew so much about her condition.

I looked down at her and revealed a secret of my own. "Mary called me," I told her. "I knew all about your cancer scare."

My mother's mouth gaped open and she couldn't speak.

I turned back to the panel. "Even after hearing about the seriousness of her diagnosis," I said, "I didn't call her."

My mother felt again the loneliness of that time.

"But I did go see her."

"What?" she asked, totally stunned.

It was late one night when I entered the hospital. I could barely bring myself there for fear I would find her dead. I wandered onto the oncology floor, my hands concealed in my pockets, my eyes not wanting to see anything bad. I had daydreamed a thousand times about the day my mother would die and what a relief it would be to my life, but it was another thing entirely to believe it was actually going to happen.

Mary told me she didn't think my mother was going to die but I wasn't so optimistic. It fit within our destiny that she would die before I had a chance to tell her all I felt about her.

When I found her room, she was asleep and hooked up to a lot of equipment. The nurse told me she was sedated on painkillers, by her request, and she would mostly likely not be roused from sleep. At a time that I thought I would be hardened about her leaving this world, I found myself so desperately sad that all I could do was cry. In the still of the room and her corpselike state, I cried into my hands over my very sick mommy.

I swore the nurse to secrecy and lied that if my mother knew I was there it would kill her.

I turned back from the panel and looked at my mother. She was crying, uncontrollably. To learn that I cared about her at a time when she believed I did not, was too much. The moment sucked the air out of the hearing room. The panel was taken aback by the revelation. They saw how it impacted my mother and caused her real tears. I felt my own sadness, too.

I tried to gain my own resolve and continue without becoming emotional again. I cleared my throat and got back on subject. "Fortunately, the right specialist found that the 'tumor' wasn't a tumor. It was a cyst, and he treated her with antibiotics and she was done. Saved her life."

"I gave Mary the specialist's name," I said. My words were yet another explosion at the foundation of my mother's reality. At this moment, when I was committed to her, I felt great joy at the look of disbelief on her face.

"I don't understand," she said.

I looked back at the panel. "I happened to be sleeping with a girl whose father is a world-renowned cancer specialist – like *the* guy. Serendipity, I guess. Believe me, the guy didn't like the fact that I was sleeping with his daughter with no promise of marriage in the future, but, hey – gotta do what you gotta do, right?"

The panel members looked at each other like, *A son screws some girl so his mother who's dying of cancer can get an appointment with her father? Who the hell are these people?*

My mother spoke to me like we were the only two in the room. "But I thought you just didn't–"

"I know what you thought. I wanted you to think it." I reached down for her hand. "I'm very sorry."

She squeezed my hand hard and her liquid-blue eyes filled with contentment. The panel watched us reconnect.

I took my cue and continued.

"The most amazing thing about what I'm telling you," I told the panel, "is that my mother continued to be a lawyer. Despite wanting me back in her life, despite her feelings of remorse and betrayal and sadness and devastation, she picked herself up and continued the fight, upholding the laws and the oath that gave her the power to help people in need. Still, after losing her son, she could not, *would not* abandon her career. As you can imagine, that wasn't a good time for her. It was a time of emptiness. Sadness. Loneliness. Fear. And that's when she and Antonio De Silva became closer."

I told them a little about Judgie, just to make the point about her love lost and being welcomed into a community, only to be ostracized upon his death. "And that loneliness is as powerful as a gun when it comes to motivating a person to do something they wouldn't do without it staring them in the face. We could listen to the phone conversations between them to hear the love they had for each other. We also could apparently watch the video, which I understand is being circulated within the prison system." The panel tried to hide their faces as they publicly imagined the tape. "With Denver dead, her mother dead, a son who abandoned her, a community who turned their backs, and a very real fear of dying alone, she did the one thing anyone would do in that situation and allowed herself to reach out for the only rope anyone would extend to her – and it was a rope that came with excitement and caring and, most important, a chance at real love again – even if it was with a man in prison.

"She was a criminal defense attorney. She was used to that world. The bars meant nothing to her." The panel members clearly didn't want to show anything on their faces, but their bodies gave me a clue. No arms were crossed. One guy leaned forward with his elbows and wrists on the table. Another member rested his head in his hand and gazed at my mother. The other sat with his arms and hands in his lap, as he leaned forward slightly. All seemed totally enthralled.

"Today we're here to represent the truth... to you... and ask you as you sit in judgment to consider the *whole* truth. Because, truthfully speaking, the whole truth begins and ends in our inability to be anything other than human. We all act and do things we regret." I looked at my mother. "We abandon our promises. We exercise faulty logic. We hide our true identities even.

And oftentimes we publicly turn our backs to our mistakes and reject much-needed explanations and apologies, when we should just say, 'I messed up. I'm sorry.'" My mother closed her eyes upon hearing my words. "But that's not what Ms. Scales has done. She took an oath – like we all did – a promise that bound her to a set of ethical rules and regulations, which she holds so dear to her that she was willing to come here today and admit without a hearing on the facts that she violated that promise.

"Ms. Scales understands the purpose of the rules, that they were created to ensure that our lawyers are good people who follow through on their promises – not to their families, not to their friends or political connections, but to their clients in need – always doing what's in the best interest of their clients. I ask you, after hearing what you've heard today – despite her fleeting, total lapse in professional judgment – can you honestly say that this woman who has endured a lifetime of struggle and sacrifice for her profession does not deserve to keep the license that enabled her to give so much for so long? She did something so in contrast with everything she'd ever stood for – and stood for in the face of losing everything she ever loved. Do you think she deserves to walk away finished? Cast away from her truest love? Her career? I think she deserves a medal." A *goddamn medal*, I wanted to say. Truthfully, I really believed it.

"*We've all crossed the line*," I emphasized to each member, looking at them individually as if I were accusing them of a specific secret act I knew about. "We've all acted in a manner – at one time or another in the course of our careers – that we look back on and hope no one will remember." I looked at them all so intensely that each member diverted their eyes. "And when we act in this manner, the right thing to do – the ethical thing to do – is to admit our wrongdoing, accept the consequences, and move on to a greater state of being. As her son, I've forgiven her," I told them. "As lawyers, I hope you will too."

I thanked the panel and sat down. They asked my mother if she wanted to say anything. She spoke briefly.

"It's very hard to sit by and let another lawyer do the talking for you when you're so used to doing it yourself." The panel members smiled a bit. She thought about her next words. She wanted to beg them. She wanted to promise them a million things she would never do. She wouldn't do that, though. "As a mother, I've always tried to instill the same legal principles I believe in so much into my daily family life. When my son was a child, I taught him the principles of the Golden Rule, to 'Do unto others as you would have others do unto you.' I made him recite it to me every day when I dropped him off at school." My mother paused, not wanting to reveal the sudden influx of emotion. "I didn't mean to bring any disgrace upon the profession I love so dearly. I'm so very sorry." She looked at them individually and thanked them for their time. The panel adjourned from the bench and retired to their meeting room.

My mother and I gathered our belongings and went back into the hallway and found a coffee machine. We walked silently together and read the vending choices. I reached into my pocket for the change.

"I got it," my mother said.

"Thanks."

"Consider it your fee," she quipped. I smiled at her

attempt to change the mood.

"A fifty-cent fee? That's not too steep for ya?"

She smiled but traded it for something a bit more serious. "Did you mean what you said, or were you just doing your job?"

"Every word of it, mom," I told her. "Every word." She smiled and grabbed my hand.

"Well, you also called me a total bitch," she quipped.

"Like I said... every word of it." We shared another smile, then sat and drank our coffee. When she finished hers, she turned to me again.

"So... I've held my tongue as long as I could," she said. I turned to her, expecting her question.

"We're engaged," I told her.

"Engaged?" She said, forcing her words through a tightening throat.

"Don't worry. It just happened. Her parents don't even know yet. They've been out of the country for two weeks on a cruise."

"Who is she?"

"Her name is Ayla, and she's Jewish. You know her dad, and her mother is a biologist researcher at the CDC. Ayla is a consultant who specializes in business affairs."

"Wow."

"She is, in fact, a 'wow,'" I told her. "And I'm lucky to have her."

"Trust me," she said. "She's the lucky one." I nodded in thanks.

"We were waiting for her parents to get back before we broke the news to anyone."

"So I'm the *first to know*?" she asked, excited.

"As a matter of fact, you are."

She smiled. She liked it that way.

Within ten minutes, the panel returned with their ruling. The verdict was in. We stood together, side by side at the podium, and held hands as Mr. Darling announced their decision. "It's the decision of this committee that this matter will remain closed with a verbal warning only at these closed proceedings," he said. He explained that if my mother's love for Antonio was as deep and true as I had described it, the panel felt a ban from Antonio's prison while he was incarcerated there and the potential ramifications from the circulating tape were punishment enough.

"And Ms. Scales?" Mr. Darling asked of her. "I speak for all us when I say that your legacy over the last thirty years has not gone unnoticed. If my daughter – who's now in law school – practices with the same grit and determination that you've displayed over the course of your career, I, as her father and as a lawyer, will be exceptionally proud."

"Thank you," my mother said.

"You may be excused, Ms. Scales."

Back in the hallway, my mother grabbed me for a hug, and I squeezed back, both excited at the win and appreciative for the unique opportunity to blend back into each other's life on a different level than before. She realized at that moment that it wasn't bad karma that had surfaced this moment in her life. It was simply an opportunity to create a second chance.

As the good news settled in and she was able to

breathe again, she grabbed my elbow as we collected our things to leave. I stopped and found her eyes.

"She deserves a *medal*?" she asked with a wry look on her face. "For sucking a client's dick? 'She deserves a medal?'" she said, now a full smile on her face.

"What, I really feel that way," I said.

She shook her head and sighed. "You were so close," she said.

"To what?" I demanded.

"To perfection," she said. "And then you had to go and ruin it with that line!"

"Oh, come on," I chided her. "You've got to be kidding me. I thought it was great! I'd have played the goddamn national anthem and raised an American flag if I had one."

"Well, there you go already – forgetting your exhibits. A lawyer always must be prepared before coming to court," she said, trying to maintain a resolved expression.

I picked up my briefcase, "Oh, now, you're just being ungrateful," I said, turning down the hallway.

"A client is always right," she said.

"And a client can be fired too," I added.

"You're gonna fire *me*? In that case, *you're* fired!"

"Well, who the hell are you? I've already finished the job."

"I'm your mother!" she said, suggesting the fabulous.

I stopped at her words. "Oh, God. Here we go again!" I said. She broke into a healing laughter that rose from her gut to her shoulders and beamed from her eyes. "You obviously didn't get the memo," I told her.

My mom laced her arm through mine, smiling. "No, I didn't get it," she said, as we exited into the bright daylight where the street noise outside smothered our laughter.

Thirty-Seven:
Clarity

My mother and I walked to a small bistro to order some dinner. I hadn't eaten anything that morning except for a thick cup of coffee, and my head was ringing from all the thinking I'd done over the last few days. I needed a soothing bottle of merlot and a hero's pat on the back for kicking total ass.

I called Ayla and told her I'd be home late. She was happy about the opportunity and recognized that a dinner with my mother was a good idea. I had explained to Ayla about my mother on a few occasions and did what I'd never done with any other woman and laid it out straight and to the point. I wanted her to know the potential pitfalls she should expect. "They will happen," I told her. "Without fail. But you have my word that you're the most important woman in my life, and when it comes down to her or you, I choose you." Ayla didn't expect that type of law, although she appreciated the sentiment. She understood the predicament in a very mature and balanced way. "I'm sure your mother and I will get along just fine. Don't get me wrong, though. I know if I were to upset you, she'd want me dead – no matter how nice she was to me up to that point – but I'm a big girl. I can handle myself." I loved her even more after she said that.

At the restaurant, the waiter came by and laid down a fresh white linen tablecloth. He pulled a candle from his back pocket and stuck it into a glass vase and then gave us some light. We started with small talk about the menu. Both of us urged the waiter to bring the wine and make it snappy. Slowly, as we consumed bread, butter, and alcohol, we began to open the closet doors to the past eight years. By the time we finished our salads, our lives came tumbling out. We watched each other as we laid out the past and quickly saw in the other that no one was trying to win points. Instead, we wrote off our anger as settling dust from the fallout. It was easier for us to share some blame and call it gray instead of black-and-white.

"Everything I've done – every lie I've told, every secret I've kept – is all because I was so afraid to be honest with you because... truthfully, I knew you'd have an opinion about it, because you're my mother, but I didn't want to hear it. I just wanted to be my own person without your opinion." Perhaps, it was that I'd just saved her ass, but for some reason, it was easier at that moment to express my feelings.

"You've wanted to be a man since you were a little boy. Believe me, I get it. I can't tell you anything."

"It shouldn't be that way, though."

"But it is and I will just have to respect that." She was looking at me differently. I could see the respect already. It was pride and awe. Even the angle had changed. Now she was looking up. "I'm so sorry, Benjamin," she said. I felt her words as they drifted slowly down and rested on the table in front of me.

"Me too, mom." I really was sorry. I played with my napkin then arranged my silverware. We both thought about what to say next and sipped our drinks to pad the silence.

"You look good," she said. "The weight looks nice on you."

"You've always liked chubby men."

"You look strong," she said.

"Hair's thinning."

"Looks good, though. You've got a good square face – good jaw."

"Grandfather's ears," I added.

"Nobody's perfect," she said with a smile.

"I should have been there for you when you were sick," I told her. She looked at me. Her face softened, and her eyes sighed, reflecting hurt still buried deep within.

"When you started talking about that at the hearing, I was shocked. I had no idea that actually came to the hospital or that you called Mary. You knew everything about it."

"I did, yes. I had to make sure you were okay." She closed her eyes tight for a minute and had a thought. Although she didn't say anything, I imagined that she was thanking God that I still cared for her at a time when she'd thought I didn't care at all.

After a brief silence, she said, "I really messed things up on so many levels."

"You had it tough, mom. What you did wasn't easy. It's hard doing what we do."

"Yeah, it is. But I would have liked to have tried harder to forget all the negative stuff so I could've been less... me, I guess."

"Yeah, but I get it now. One trial under my belt, and I get it. I never agreed with it, but I get it. I understand it. I see it in myself, how the job affects me, and I don't have half the problems or stress you had – not even a third."

"I appreciate that," she said.

I asked her about her work, her plans. She told me how things had slowed with her health scare, how her sickness had run her dry. She had lost a lot of her business because her clients had lost their confidence in her. She held on to one $10,000 case she had taken as a favor – reflected in the fact that it was a quarter of her usual fee. She had tried to ignite some referrals and reached out to a bunch of new lawyers by speaking at a conference. She had some interest – some state-level appeals in various Georgia counties – but nothing exciting. There were no callers in the middle of the night needing her to step in to rescue them. There was no edge to her work. No thrill. No interesting clientele or issues to grapple with. After the incident with Antonio, she got a bunch of prank calls, which toughened her up, but they also frustrated her. She assumed her days of keeping her finger on the pulse of cutting-edge legal issues were over and that she'd be resigned to just making a living.

"It's fine, though," she said. "I don't know why I'm telling you all this. It's my problem. I'll survive. I always do." She put on a cheery face.

I knew better. For as long I could remember, my mother used her fangs to suck adrenalin from the neck of criminal defense. As the Mafia's lawyer, she had stayed in a drunken state of euphoria. Even when she had first started practicing and did trial work on a regular basis, she thrived on the fight. She loved being needed at all hours – especially the calls she received at one a.m. when the person on the other end of the phone cryptically said, "I need you now. Get on the next plane to New York." I could see she was dying inside – duct taped and chained to her new fate. Like a mare left to wander in a sun dried pasture, she sensed her own fate and that I felt sorry for her. She changed the subject.

"So what did the jury do in the Sims case?" she asked

me.

"They convicted him," I said, nodding to her sympathetic eyes. "I guess I can expect someone like you to come along and point out all of the mistakes I made, huh?"

"Comes with the territory."

"The waiting to find out was the hardest part. After the trial, for those three or four days, my client sat in his cell, and I sat in my office and actually thought he had a chance of going home. I totally bought into all my arguments. I honestly believed I had found a way out of the darkness for that kid."

"The fact that you even had an argument is impressive. Most lawyers just say 'the state didn't prove it.'"

"His fate was sealed."

"It wasn't!" she urged. "You never know what a jury will do," she said. Her face lit up, and she smiled at me. "And that's the *best* part. With a jury, there's always a second chance – a real get-out-of-jail-free card."

Yeah, right, I thought. My mother didn't miss working up a case like a greyhound didn't miss chasing that ever-elusive rabbit. They lived to run the track, and so did she. The Mob had wined and dined her for years, and even though she had moved into post-conviction appellate work and out of jury trial work, it spoiled her, because even the federal appellate work was fast paced and filled with opportunity and reward. She sat as the ultimate Monday morning quarterback to massive conspiracy and racketeering cases and did what she did best: judged others. And if she couldn't get the trial attorneys to fall on their swords and admit their shortcomings, she'd masterfully lull them into a false sense of security, close off all escape routes, and lead them to the dining room where they would be the main course.

The state-level appellate work she was doing now, though, was simply boring. It's why I wouldn't touch it. But trial work? Trial work on any level is exciting – state or federal. Trial work is fighting the good fight with prosecutors who are paid to think about every way possible to send your client to prison. They invest in their cases, rain or shine, and refuse to back down unless your client is ready to accept responsibility and admit the crime – whether or not he or she is guilty. Good defense trial attorneys don't play that game, though. They work their cases up for victory from the moment they get them. It's the only way to get respect from a prosecutor; it's the only way to make them fear their own case and to bend them in your direction to get what you need for your client. If they don't break, then fuck 'em – you're gonna take that shit to trial. It's a 90-mile an hour fastball and full of chest bumping and dirt kicking, like the best arguments between umpire and manager. And although my mother hadn't done trial work in more than twenty-five years, I began to realize it was exactly what she needed.

As my mother turned her attention away, my mind began to race. She was dying out in the pasture, wasting away. I could see it in her posture, in her shoulders. Something had to be done. It would officially be my next great Grand Plan since my high school party. I motioned the waiter for the check.

As my mother and I said goodbye to each other, standing at the curb outside the restaurant, she let out a huge purposeful sigh.

"I know, I'm stuffed," I said.

"I don't know how to thank you, Benjamin," she said. "I don't know what to say."

"No," I said, shaking my head. "It's good. I'm glad I could help." The night had been enjoyable, and we took it as far as we could for one night. We were both exhausted and found ourselves trying to figure out how to end it before it went on too long or got off track.

"So, I guess I'll just talk to you soon, huh?" she asked. "Just let me know how you're doing, okay?"

"I will."

"Good. Okay... well..." She started to say something, but an internal kill switch told her to just let it be. We stood in the still night air and looked for other signs of life in the world around us. It was a true hands-in-the-pockets kind of moment.

"Mom," I said, "I really want you to be in my life,"

"I want to be," she said, her eyes earnest and sincere.

"Then you will," I promised her.

Thirty-Eight:
My Trick, My Treat

A year later, Ayla was pregnant with our son, and as nature would have it, he was born right on time, February 14th – Valentine's Day, the *exact same day* as Judgie's birthday.

The hospital was a peaceful place and had managed to drown out the sounds of hyperventilating mothers cursing their husbands with tranquility fountains and soundproof birthing suites. Grayson Jacob Scales weighed a light six pounds, but his thick jet-black hair gave him the look of a toddler. He had Ayla's full nose and my heavy eyebrows and made small grunting noises as he buried his fists under his chin and snuggled into the crook of Ayla's armpit and chest.

My mother stood patiently to the side, waiting for the moment when Ayla would allow her a second to steal him away. Due to fifteen hours of labor and an epidural only at the last minute, Ayla and I both needed a few days of sleep to recuperate. My mother scooped up Grayson and wrapped him in a warm blanket and slid a cap over his head and the tops of his ears. He pursed his lips and mini-stretched his chest and let out a deep exhale as he sank into my mother's arms.

My mother hadn't felt this kind of pride since the day she had walked me down the aisle at my wedding the year before, knowing that I was about to marry a *Jewish* woman of all things. It lasted only long enough for Ayla and I to rip the microphones from the band and perform a horrendous and slightly tipsy version of *Endless Love*. Oh, man, we were in love.

My mother looked at Grayson deeply – a stare without judgment or thought. She opened the iris in the camera of her mind and absorbed the radiant light that was Grayson Jacob Scales. She took him to a quiet nook where she found a large, welcoming ottoman touched with sunlight and slid into the soft corner of the chair where the sunlight would warm the shoulders and arms that held her grandson. She probably thought nothing about the moment itself or that it would surely become a favorite memory in time, only the perfection of being alive and experiencing a new joy never before felt. For a fleeting second, Grayson opened his eyes and looked directly into her face just inches away. He blinked twice and looked again. My mother felt her nose tingle as her eyes filled with tears and her lips spread into a grin not meant for any other audience. It was simply a reaction to joy as raw as love itself.

"Grandma's big boy," she said, her words a whisper. She kissed his head, and her warm breath closed his eyes. The weight of the sunlight pushed down on her eyelids too, and the warmth relaxed her body. Grayson found stillness again in the simple bliss of her firm embrace and the shared space. Together they fell asleep as one.

Grayson was a second chance for my mother. I knew all the promises she was making to herself and to Grayson in her own mind to be the best grandmother possible. I knew she was thinking of her mother as a grandmother and how special she was to me and that, if she tried hard enough, she would be equally as wonderful to Grayson. I hoped that her Act Two would be more successful than her Act One. Even my mother was entitled to at least one standing ovation in her life.

As time went on, my mother experienced another major change in her life – she took on a partner. Well, actually, I did. Originally, my mother resisted the idea, but I talked her into it. As I explained it to her, it was a new spin on an old idea, in that she could work with her son – an idea beyond reproach by cynics and critics and respected colleagues alike – and, since I was still kicking ass and making a good name for myself in the eyes of my contemporaries, it was a win-win situation. It was also a no-brainer in that it didn't involve mother and son; rather, it was partner and partner. Equals. And it was another way for us to continue to reconnect and strengthen our bond, something important to me as a person building a family.

We both loved the law. We both loved talking about the law and practicing it. It was a constant point of connection for us where we both felt much joy and excitement. Practicing together, then, would not only add those two experiences to our lives but also make them the experiences of our new relationship. It was a double-win-win-no-brainer. We even got creative with our logo – Scales and Scales, Attorneys at Law, with each "Scales" centered over one of the two scales held by Lady Justice. It was clever and corny enough to be memorable to our clients.

The agreement itself was fairly straightforward. I'd do the client contact and courtroom stuff, and my mother would work behind the scenes as the legal scholar and expert, writing motions, drafting briefs, and crafting oral arguments for me to make in court. She loved this idea and was excited to show me all that she had learned over thirty years of practice. And while I wanted her to do all that behind-the-scenes work I didn't want to do, I also knew she was far too good on her feet to play it safe in the office. She needed to be re-released on the public and the trial court system. Appeals were for pussies and snobs. She was neither. She was a warrior. Thus, despite the promise of her remaining behind the scenes, I had other plans.

"You've been cross-examining me for thirty-something years," I told her. "You run your mouth all the time. You say the most asinine stuff I've ever heard. If you're not a trial attorney, then you need to be fucking committed. Besides," I continued, "it's time I made some money off you." It would only be a matter of time before I had her back in the field and working up cases for trial – i.e., sitting back in a prison cell where she belonged, strategizing with clients, even if I had to trick her to get her there.

Thirty-Nine:
Back In The Saddle

One afternoon, while my mother was sitting in the office, I called her in a panic.

"I need you to go see a potential client. Patrick referred a case to me. Apparently, the guy's family has some money, and they want him to see an attorney right away. Patrick has a conflict. He represented the guy's wife in a previous case, and she's the alleged victim in this case."

"I'm not dressed for it," she insisted. "I can't do it. I look like hell."

"Isn't that why you paid two hundred dollars for that new makeup? Go home, slap some of that on, get dressed, and go to the jail, please. This is a juicy one, and I need it!" What I told her wasn't a lie, but I could've gone myself.

"I'm working on a million things right now," she said.

"It's not a done deal, and I really want to pick this case up."

"I'm busy!" she exclaimed.

"Get off your ass, and go get us some money," I said.

"Ugh."

Our new relationship was awesome, I thought. Open. Honest. Unafraid. And filled with mutual respect and the dual ability to tell each other to go to hell at a moment's notice without any dire consequences. Of course, we never told each other to go to hell due to said mutual respect, but the unexercised option added a bit of roller in our professional coaster. Plus, we finally had reached a point in our lives where I knew enough about her to know she got emotional when she was stressed. Whatever the tune – irrational, angry, petty or maniacal – stress was the rhythm section that plugged away throughout the song. The other change was that she respected me and actually wanted my opinion – professionally and personally. Now, that was something.

An hour and a clothes change later, my mother stood outside the jail and straightened her blouse. She turned her attention to her Louis Vuitton briefcase and meticulously straightened the pens – all ten of them – and counted the five notepads she had to ensure she had enough.

"I think you have office supplies," I said.

She spun around and saw me standing there in my navy blue pinstripe Versace suit.

"What are you doing here?" she said with a brilliant smile.

"I sensed your hesitation and didn't want you to go alone."

"You look very handsome," she said.

"Why thank you."

"Seriously, what are you doing here?" she asked. "I got this."

"This guy is a real badass – he isn't going to be like the gentlemen you've been representing. Did you read the police report?"

"Yeah – whoa!" she said. "Held his wife at gunpoint after he polished the bullet with his son's underwear and put the gun to her head."

"Also, says he set the couch on fire and tried to throw

her on it," I added.

"A real charmer, this guy. You really know how to show a girl a good time," she said.

"We're partners, after all," I said with the Cheshire cat's smile.

I moved over to her and squeezed her shoulder. "It'll be fun."

"No," she said. "I got this. I wanna do it. You can come in, but this is *my* show."

My mother sat on a metal stool that jutted out from a cement wall in a jail cell visitation booth while I stood outside the room in the hallway pressing an intercom button.

"Attorneys Scales and Scales to see Mr. Grady." The woman on the other end told me to wait, and so I did.

Back inside the lawyer's booth with my mother, we were restricted to four feet of width and six feet in length. There was a bullet-proof window at one end. My mother perused the stack of discovery that had just been turned over by the state and that we retrieved from Patrick's office. Discovery was the collection of police and crime lab reports, witness statements, and photographs (mostly), which the state compiled for each case to assist them in the prosecution of the case. It was the reflection of the testimony and other evidence the prosecutors would have at trial and was therefore "discoverable" by defense attorneys prior to trial if the defense attorney agreed to share his or her paperwork with the state. Defense attorneys would also use the discovery to size up the state's strategy and create their own.

This was the first time in two decades that my

mother had handled a fresh stack of discovery. If we got the case, it would also be the first time in decades that she would be able to use the discovery to make the strategic decisions herself and not sit in judgment of the trial attorney after the fact regarding how he or she had utilized it or not.

She had organized the discovery neatly in multiple folders and rested her arms and wrists on top of it, as she waited for the individual who would be sitting on the other side of the bulletproof glass. She wore a wool skirt suit and stockings, which was smart because the jail was cold. She spotted the only decoration in the space – a set of words that encouraged imagination but left nothing to chance: "Suck my cock." I saw her find the words on the wall and chuckled to myself.

She looked at the file folder in front of her, pulled an ink pen from her purse, and fingered through the pages again. She clicked the top of the pen and wrote the date on a notepad. *Stop fidgeting*, she told herself. Despite her verbal cursing of me, she was somewhat excited to be there. After a lifetime of dealing with the Mafia, she was dying to see what my idea of a badass was. The deputy at the front desk had warned us that the man we were there to see was on "Admin," a term used by the jail to denote problem inmates.

"Where in the hell is he?" she asked me.

"The lady on speaker told me it was gonna take a minute to get him up 'cause they have to 'clear the floor when he walks,' she said. It's all the time. 'When he walks from his cell to the bathroom, they clear the floor. When he walks from his cell to the chow hall, they clear the floor. When he walks from his cell to see his lawyer, they clear the floor,' she told me. Apparently, the jail thinks this guy might rip out another inmate's esophagus and fashion it into a belt or a whip," I joked.

Allegedly, over the course of a morning, Clifford Grady had also held his four children – ages four, six, nine, and eleven at gunpoint. As for his wife, when he placed the gun to the back of her head, she pissed herself from fear. My mother had been writing appellate briefs from the comfort and safety of her office for twenty years. That morning's jail visit was reminiscent of times long past when she was braver. When they finally brought Clifford up into the visitation room, the cell-door buzzer sounded. We both jumped in the tiny space.

Clifford Grady was big – short but big. A dark-skinned black man, he had shoulders like cantaloupes and arms the circumference of his head. He had multiple burns on his chest, which were visible behind his prison-issue V-neck jumper, and he had a tattoo under each eye, an upside-down triangle centered perfectly. Per Clifford's brother, they stood for the face of a joker, "always changing, never the same"

"Well, as long as those tattoos don't mean he's taking credit for murdering somebody, we'll be all right," I'd said.

Clifford was a five-time convicted felon who had just finished up a 120-month sentence in the federal system. None of his prior convictions were similar – i.e. there was no pattern of criminal behavior. Lazy prosecutors never had dropped the hammer on Clifford like his current judge had threatened. This particular judge – a mid-forties mother of five with a penchant for maximum punishment – had promised Clifford that if he were found guilty, she'd put him away for 157 years, based on his current twenty-two-count indictment. The fact that he was eligible for recidivist punishment meant that this one-hundred-and-fifty-seven-year sentence would be "door to door," or without probation or parole. He had looked at the judge during his first appearance and told her, "I don't give a fuck about that shit, bitch." He wound up wrestling with the guard a bit after that. The stage was set for a juicy trial.

Clifford's indictment also accused him of arson and aggravated assault, as he had thrown his wife onto a burning couch – just trying to rekindle the relationship, I guess. The house burned to the ground. Like I said, he was a real badass.

I explained to Clifford's brother that my partner and I would go see Clifford to get the skinny on the case. Then we'd quote a fee and, if he accepted, Clifford would get two lawyers for the price of one.

"Two lawyer?" Clifford's brother said, dropping the "s." "Who the fuck you think he is? O.J.?"

Clifford lumbered up a set of stairs to the inmate visiting area then through a door into the small space on the other side of the booth, where we were waiting. Leg irons were shackled around his ankles, and he wore handcuffs around his wrists. The handcuffs were cinched to another chain around his waist. He couldn't scratch his chin without a key from the guard. Immediately upon seeing my mother, he barked at me, "Who the fuck is this chick?" Clifford's deep voice made the small space vibrate.

I started to respond but my mother held up her hand to silence me.

My mother looked him up and down and got up from her seat. She exited the small booth, leaving Clifford staring through the bulletproof glass at me. I crossed my arms, knowing that he needed us a lot more than we needed him.

In the hallway, my mother moved expeditiously to the wall-mounted speaker box. She pressed the button.

"I need the guard," she said.

"Yes, ma'am," the woman said.

My mother came back into the room and sat back down on the stool. Clifford heard the guard coming up the stairs.

"What the fuck is this?" Clifford demanded.

The guard entered the room, nightstick in his hand.

"Guard," my mother said, "I specifically requested through Captain Pitts that my client have his hands free to sign documentation and to be able to handle paperwork. Un-cuff him now, please."

"He's on Admin," the guard began.

"I don't care if he is. I've arranged through Captain Pitts that he is to have his hands free." Now her voice boomed in the small space. Clifford looked at my mother, his eyes squinting with confusion. The guard radioed into the captain's office, and after a brief ten-four, he unlocked Clifford's handcuffs. He touched his nightstick to the convict's shoulder and said, "I'll be right outside, Mr. Grady."

"Thank you, Deputy. That will be all," my mother told him.

The guard exited, and Clifford rubbed his wrists.

"I appreciate that–" he started to say, but was interrupted.

"If we reach the point where we decide that we'll take

your case, Mr. Grady, I suggest that the next time we meet you address me with respect. I am Ms. Carter Scales. I'm not some chick or bitch or ho. Don't talk to me like I'm some kind of asshole. If you do, I walk, and you can have your handcuffs and Admin all to yourself, Mr. Badass. You understand?"

Clifford looked at me and raised his eyebrows. I raised mine back at him. I knew it better than he'd ever know it when it came to Carter Scales.

"Yes, ma'am," he said. It seemed he respected her tone. It was most likely the only tone he understood.

"All right. Then let's get started." My mother looked back at me. I nodded at her.

"Mr. Grady, I'm Benjamin Scales. Carter here is my partner. I wanted to come by and meet you briefly. I'm going to head over to the courthouse and see about getting you a bond."

"That judge ain't gonna give me no bond," he said.

"Well, it certainly makes it more challenging when you tell her to fuck herself, but we're still going to try."

I looked at my mother. "I'll leave you two to talk."

Forty:
One Badass To Another

Upon my departure, Carter unpacked her papers again and started to read. Per her earlier discussion with me, it was decided that she was to set the fee for the case. It had been a long time since she'd gone to the jail to meet a client who wanted to hire her for a trial and not an appeal. It also had been a long time since she had worked a case from the ground up and not done so by following after another attorney who already had botched things up. In her appellate practice, the normal routine was that the family called first, and then the client called collect from prison. Because all her appellate clients were in prison, she was restricted to quoting over the phone, unless she wanted to spend money on a flight or a four-hour drive to a rural prison without first getting paid. Nobody did that.

That morning's face-to-face consultation with Clifford was the first she'd had with a client in fifteen or twenty years, which meant she had to perform to get the fee. It was also the first time she'd been back in a prison since her last meeting with Antonio. She was nervous about that too and was happy to find that they didn't have her picture plastered on the wall with all the wives, girlfriends, and whores who had been banned from the jail, as she had been banned from federal prisons.

She paged through the file and looked at the police report and charges. Clifford watched her every move. She knew he was watching. It was all part of her act. She sighed at the nature of the charges and rubbed her temple in staged agony. Truthfully, she had already reviewed it eight times, but that was another rule –

always let the client see you looking at their papers. Let them see how it affects you. Then they know you've actually read it. The highlighted text and notes in the margins gave her added comfort that when she spoke about the case she knew what she was talking about. Clifford watched the top of her head for a minute, then interrupted her reading.

"Do I know you?" he asked her. "I mean, have I seen you around before?"

"No," she said, not looking up.

"It's just... you look really familiar. Maybe I saw you on TV or something. You on TV a lot?"

"Not recently, no. Anyway, why don't we focus on your charges, okay?" She was trying to get back to the act of building drama. She pointed to a particular paragraph. "You gave a statement to the police?"

"What?" he said. "No way."

"Says here you admitted to being in the house."

"So?"

"So, it's not quite *not making a statement*," she said. "Puts you at the scene." She read some more. "Jesus," she said.

"What? What?" Clifford asked, as she turned the pages.

She held her hand up to silence him, and he obeyed. She was back in control now. Enough of his bullshit and questions – he was interrupting her performance. "My God," she said while reading. She wrote down six names on her legal pad then counted them out loud. Clifford tried to read them upside down.

"Who dem people?" he said.

She was building to the moment. Truthfully, the allegations against him were horrific, but she'd seen these types of allegations before. Aggravated assault, false imprisonment, cruelty to children, arson – she'd handled it all. Clifford's case was a simple case of "He said, she said." His ex-wife was the one telling police everything, the one who allegedly had suffered the most trauma. His ex-wife was the star witness. His ex-wife was also a two-time felon with multiple tattoos on her breasts, arms, and neck, and who had changed her story as many times as she had told it. Carter would have a field day with her on the stand, grilling her about her contradicting stories. She'd destroy her. Then, once the wife felt like a total asshole for lying, Carter would lay out her felony convictions for the jury to see, and the woman would be reduced to a pile of dog shit – a worthless witness for the state.

Clifford deciphered the upside-down name of his wife. "Oh, she ain't gonna show up," he said.

"Who? Your ex-wife?"

"Ex?" he said. "She ain't my ex. She still my wife!"

"Not according to the petition she filed for divorce in the superior court. I take it you didn't know?"

"How you know?"

"I know everything, Mr. Grady. It's my job to know everything."

"Awe, man. That bitch!" Carter gave him a cross look. "Excuse me," he said. "What I meant is, I ain't worried, 'cause she ain't gonna show anyhow. And they ain't got no case without her. I know that much."

All defendants seem to think that the person they allegedly committed crimes against won't show up at court to point them out, like they're just going to forget about everything. Clifford's confidence annoyed my mother.

"Mr. Grady, I can assure you she will be at court to testify against you either by her own free will or by the sheriff's escort. Either way, we don't sit back and assume that the state's star witness will be a no-show."

"What-chew mean, sheriff's escort?"

"If they subpoena her to court as a witness, and she doesn't show, the judge can attach the subpoena and have her arrested, which means she'll be at court, albeit entering from the back door in an orange jumpsuit like you, but present nonetheless."

He nodded his head, understanding. "I feel ya," he said. "So I got a chance to win on a jury?"

Now she knew he wasn't as confident as he let on. If he were so confident that his wife wasn't going to show, he never would have asked how the case against him looked. Truthfully, his question had come a little sooner than she wanted. She was still paging through documents and furrowing her brow for effect, but it was time to move on with the process and quote the fee. She missed doing it live – face-to-face. She missed the thrill of dashing the client's expectations with a fee three times what he'd expected and seeing the look of sheer panic on his face when he wouldn't be able to have the lawyer whom he now so desperately wanted more than oxygen itself.

From the moment the facts of the case had been relayed to her, she had known how much the fee would be. After thirty years, it came naturally to her. With a smile, she looked up at Clifford but then struck her folders with her hand, which knocked them to the cold concrete floor. "Shit," she said, frustrated that she kept getting off track. *Nervous like a child*, she thought.

She got off the stool and knelt on the floor in her high heels to pick them up. From the other side of the glass, Clifford watched her until he realized something. "Oh, snap!" he said, looking at her in the kneeling position. "That's how I know you! You that lawyer that got with her client!"

Carter paused and looked up at Clifford. "You've got to be kidding me," she said.

Carter picked up the papers and sat back on the stool. While contemplating whether he really recognized her, she remembered that Clifford had just been released from federal prison. What were the chances? She took a moment and thought about her next move in light of the obvious unfortunate truth that the video had reached whichever penitentiary had housed Clifford. "You're goddamn famous!" Clifford said, smiling from ear to ear. "I mean, I'm right, right?" he asked again. "It's you!"

She let out a sigh. She was suddenly *very* glad that she was alone with Clifford. She persevered. "Let me be very clear with you, Mr. Grady. Whatever you saw – whatever you think you saw – I can assure you that that woman you saw on that video was not me. I don't know who that woman was... but she is not the same woman who's sitting here with you today. Okay?"

He dropped his smile.

"Oh... okay," Clifford said, as he seemed to grasp the deeper meaning behind Carter's indirect admission.

"Now, can we get back to business?"

"Yes, ma'am," he said still staring at her in total

shock. "If I'm lyin', I'm dyin'," he said.

Of all the defendants in all of the jails, she thought, *this asshole is wise to my past.* And she was a grandmother now! Was it really possible that her one big mistake could follow her into a county jail some two thousand miles away from the federal prison where it had happened in the first place? Like a model who spreads her legs for *Playboy,* then becomes a mother to a boy who is one day confronted by his own friends with a copy of the spread, she tried to shake it off and the heavy reality that her past might be a large liability for me and quite possibly Grayson, too.

Grayson, she thought. *He's just magical.* She had just taken him to tea at the Ritz Carlton where he helped her devour the yummy biscuits and breads that came with the beverage. The servers adored him, which helped temper their irritation at the strawberry jelly he had smeared on the oriental rug. Carter let Grayson do whatever he wanted even if it meant sucking on her diamond necklace after a plate of corn and peas, she didn't care. It was the ultimate privilege and sign of the times. The additional colored "gemstones" were more valuable than the diamonds.

She shook herself out of an inner smile and focused back on Mr. Badass. She glanced at him briefly. He didn't seem discouraged at all by the possibility that she was the lawyer he'd seen on a government-issued black-and-white television as guards huddled around and laughed and pointed. He considered her a maverick. Like him, she apparently didn't give a shit and wasn't afraid to flip a middle finger to the Institution. He was hoping she would be his lawyer. "Ms. Scales?" he asked, while sitting on the edge of his seat more attentive than ever, wanting to hear her opinion. "I mean, just tell me, Ms. Scales," he said. "How you think the charges look against me?"

Enough of my insecurities, she thought. She was a goddamn lawyer and needed to act like one. Plus, Clifford was all but disemboweling himself to relieve the growing pressure he felt inside his belly to get an answer from the lawyer he was so desperate to employ. His obvious anxiety filled her with a growing satisfaction that she still had him hooked. She inhaled the smell of his fear and mentally photographed the pain on his face. It was a nice moment for her. The way it used to be. And she was grateful that I'd suggested the union and for having faith in her despite her terrible choice with Antonio. I had been with her as she had gotten back on her feet. It was a satisfying turn of events.

She thought about step number one and purposefully put down her pen, careful not to knock over her papers again, and looked Clifford dead in the eyes. She shook her head. "Mr. Grady," she said, the weight of his fate on her face, "you're in a lot of *fucking* trouble." It was an old line for her but a new one for him.

He swallowed and nodded. She was gritty. And she was right. He knew it, too. On whatever level, he knew he was in for some serious reality. Even if he hadn't done everything the state was accusing him of doing, he was still a career criminal with an "I don't give a shit" attitude and a wife who would clean up nicely for trial and put on a devil of a lie. He kind of figured his luck had run out and his day had come. He started to shake his head. Plenty of guys had gone to prison on a lie. He knew it well. And this time around, his sixth felony, he'd never see the light of day again.

"What's it gonna take?" he asked.

"With these facts, the chief assistant district attorney isn't going to negotiate. It would be a losing play to even ask for a deal. While all the other assistant DAs wear suits, this asshole practically wears a SWAT flak jacket to work with his DA badge on it, which means trial. And to work this up – with these facts, even if they are a lie – it's going to take a lot. A hell of a lot."

"But like you said, she's lyin'," he said.

"Come on, now. You're smarter than that. You know good and well that people go to jail on a lie every day."

"I was just thinkin' the same thang."

"And if she comes to court and says it – that you put a gun to the back of her head and she pissed herself – then it becomes evidence, and the jury can consider it. Now, we can call her a liar, but if the jury believes her, then they can find you committed the crimes she testifies about and the judge will–"

Clifford interrupted, "Throw away the key. I know."

"No," Carter corrected. "She'll keep the goddamn key in her front pocket and make sure nobody will ever find it or take it away."

"So what do I do?"

"We've got to discredit your wife – protect your interests and keep your past out of the picture. The state will want to drag out your past convictions and tell the jury, 'Once a felon, always a felon.' It's called similar transaction evidence, which we'll have to fight. And then we'll have to dress you up for a jury of twelve uppity housewives and bankers so they aren't afraid of those tattoos you've got under your eyes."

"A bunch of white folks?"

"Mostly, yes. Not all, but mostly."

"Damn."

"We'll find the good ones and get rid of the bad ones, but these facts are a hard sell if we can't discredit your wife."

"Okay," he said.

"I think we can do it. Based on what I've seen, though, I've got a lot of work to do when it comes to your ex-wife. Now, you married her, but that doesn't stop me from having an opinion about her – and I think she's a real piece of shit. From these inconsistent statements, she's a liar, and she's out to ruin your life. Period. We've got to crush her – plain and simple. But you've gotta pay for it." Clifford nodded. "So," Carter continued, "for that and all the other investigative work we'll have to do to punch holes in the state's theory, it'll be forty thousand dollars – paid in full before we even touch this case."

She watched him with stone eyes, her confidence as old and strong as the bulletproof glass that divided them. My mother held her stare and felt like a million dollars. Now she just waited.

Clifford stared back at her – a hustler himself, a street thug, unafraid of anything or anyone. He didn't give a shit. He was hard from life and was equally as strong.

"Forty thousand?" he asked.

"That's right," she said confidently, her arms crossed.

"Hmmm," he said. "That come with a blowjob?"

His words snapped through the air like a whip and cracked her across her head. He straight-faced it for a few seconds then broke into a broad smile.

If it were anyone else but a guy with a past like Clifford's and a lifetime of mistakes under his own belt, she might have been somewhat affected by his question. But this guy? Not a chance. As a matter of fact, he was starting to grow on her. She returned a fixed stare to his pointed jibe, knowing this was the reason she was a goddamn criminal defense attorney in the first place – her irreproachable, dogged survival of the unexpected, the highs and lows, the ups and downs, the mistakes and the victories, the game, the rub, the thrill, and even the ridiculous.

"Well?" he said.

She played a subtle smile that cradled her diamond eyes. "Sixty thousand," she said.

Forty-One:
And Then There Were Two

Back at my house, my mother, Ayla and I sat at our dining room table and watched Grayson "eat" his dinner. It was a blended collection of hotdogs, mac and cheese, and peas. He shoved fistfuls of food into his mouth and offered up the same to Ayla and me.

"Momma!" he said, squeezing his fists full of macaroni and cheese – the mushy bits pushed out between his fingers like worms reaching for sunlight. "Momma!" he said again.

My mother hooted with laughter.

"He wants you to eat it," I told Ayla.

"I know exactly what he wants me to do, and I'm not touching that," she said, smiling.

"Momma!" he said again.

"Mommy doesn't want your nasty little fistful of cheesy mac, but Daddy will eat it!" I leaned forward and wrapped my lips around his fingers and sucked the cheese worms right off. Grayson squealed with delight. I saw my mother watching us and felt her joy.

"Oh, my God," Ayla said, as I licked my lips and looked at Grayson for more.

My mother stroked Grayson behind the ear and pulled a cheesy pea off his cheek. Then she pulled one from my face too. Her hand stayed there for a second and cradled my cheek. She held me with her stare.

The three of us watched Grayson do basic functions of life as if we were watching a fireworks display – with eyes wide open, mouths open, and a low, murmuring "wow" in our voices. Seeing him eat food brought joy. I'd laugh, but often it was interrupted by a tear-like surge that came from my throat and nose – an uncontrollable jolt of happiness that changed the pitch in my laughter and choked the joyful sounds that came from my mouth.

I studied his entire body. I loved the fat rolls on his legs and elbows and wanted to gnaw them with my teeth. His tushy, too. My baby. My boy. My one truest, most immediate love.

I imagined that everyone felt this way about their child – a total and complete inability to control the feeling of overwhelming love. And it was a feeling I knew would never go away. I didn't know what to do about it, how to deal with it.

It was how my mother felt about me – *feels* about me. This is how much my mother loves me. All the times she told me she loved me – constantly, incessantly. All the times she wanted to hold me, hug me, touch me, and be near me. And then, in the past, when she realized she hurt me and wanted to do everything in her power to make it right. "Come sit next to momma. Let momma rock you. Let momma hug you." And I wouldn't let her. I felt the same love for Grayson. I wanted to have him next to me, to squeeze him, to rock him, to kiss him until he pushed me away – to hug him all the time, nonstop, forever.

My past irritation with my mother when she tried to do the same thing gave me a new perspective regarding her love and my withdrawal from it. I'd be devastated if Grayson pulled away from me like I had from my mother. Crushed. A broken man. For the first time in my life, I finally understood my mother's love.

My mother was busy cleaning Grayson's face with a

wet cloth that Ayla brought to the table. Ayla was clearing the dishes to the kitchen, which gave me a moment alone with her.

"You handled yourself really well today," I told her. "You never know what to expect when you meet a guy like Clifford."

"I don't know," she said. "Maybe I should've accepted his counter offer for a blowjob. That extra twenty grand would be nice."

I raised my eyebrow at her. She quickly winked at me and laughed.

"Oh!" she said, leaning in and touching my shoulder. Her eyes were alight with sudden enthusiasm. "I got a call from New York. The acting boss's nephew got arrested coming out of Florida. The detention hearing is next Friday and they want me to go see him. I told them I work with my son now and they liked the idea: a seasoned appellate lawyer and her brilliant trial lawyer son."

Dread splashed across my face like red paint on a white canvas. She saw it. I tried not to panic. "I don't know, mom," I said. "Is that really the best place for you."

She shook her head. "Do not worry, Benjamin. That horse is dead and buried." She looked down at Grayson for a moment who was sucking on his fingers. "There is nothing more important to me than this," she said, her look unwavering. "Nothing," she repeated, as her eyes began to melt with tears. She wiped them away and laughed at herself.

I knew she meant it.

She picked Grayson up from the high chair and

knocked clinging macaroni from his shirt and legs.

"Looks like someone needs a bath!"

Grayson shrieked.

"Here, you missed some," I said, as I grabbed a wet towel.

"Nonsense," she said. She lifted Grayson into her chest, smudging macaroni on her blouse and suit. She kissed him hard on his food face. "Grandma's big boy!"

"Mom, your suit is... Oh, no... You've got cheese on your shoulder."

"Honey, it's only food. It'll dry clean." She looked at Grayson. "Grandma doesn't care what you do. Right, big boy?"

As she walked away with Grayson, she paused and looked back at me. "So, you'll call them?" she asked.

I paused on her question and looked at her raised eyebrows. My mother's seasoned resolve had returned.

"Yeah, I'll see what they want."

"Great," she said.

"But they'll deal with me," I told her.

She gave Grayson another smooch on the cheek. "Whatever you decide is fine with me."

My mother placed Grayson in our master Jacuzzi tub where he sat upright in a tub support chair so he could play without slipping all over himself like a walrus on ice. Grayson sucked in his breath to the feel of the water but then, with as much force as the air went in, howled it out into a summit squeal of pure joy. The pounding of his chubby macaroni fists was proof that he was ready to entertain.

My mother leaned over the side of the tub and watched him with all the joy in the world. Her eyes glistened; she was totally in love. Her blouse was soaked within seconds.

I watched the two of them from the doorway into the bathroom. I saw in her eyes a new beginning – a second chance that unfolded with every new Grayson experience, an opportunity to be the kind of mother or grandmother she couldn't be before she had reached this kinder, gentler time in her life. Now she could just stay loving. Now Grayson would know only of her love and nothing else. It was much better this way.

I entered and handed my mother a washcloth and gave her a kiss and squeezed her shoulder.

"He's all yours," I promised. She held my hand for a second, drawing my attention to her eyes.

"Thank you, Benjamin," she said.

"No, mom," I smiled. "Thank you."

Acknowledgements

This book does not exist without the 100s of people who have encouraged me or given me criticism and feedback. It does not exist without the countless shoulders and coattails that carried me incrementally out of the vast darkness of the publishing world. Actually, it also does not exist without me getting rejected from medical school or me struggling to find success as an actor or going back to law school at 29 years old where I finally found my true calling. My path to this moment has forked many times over.

This book and its debut is the stuff that dreams are made of and I could not have accomplished it alone. For that, I thank my loving and supportive wife and children, my exceptional parents and stepparents, my wonderful in-laws and extended family, my lifelong friends, and my friends in the Jewish community and the legal community. Without your love, support and friendship, I would be lost.

Finally, finally, I give my sincerest thanks to my friend and creative mentor, Eddy Von Mueller, to my friend and brilliant entertainment attorney, Lisa Moore, and to Michael Terence Publishing...

Jason B. Sheffield lives in Atlanta, Georgia where he is a practicing criminal defense trial attorney. His passion for performance and storytelling is second only to his love of his family.

Available worldwide from

Amazon and all good bookstores

————————

www.jasonbsheffield.com

www.facebook.com/authorjasonbsheffield

@authorsheffield

9 781999 836610